Sidney Sheldon's

The Tides *of* Memory

Tilly Bagshawe

HARPER

Harper
An imprint of HarperCollins*Publishers*
77–85 Fulham Palace Road,
Hammersmith, London W6 8JB

www.harpercollins.co.uk

A Paperback Original 2013
1

A catalogue record for this book
is available from the British Library

ISBN: 9780007442867

Set in Caslon by FMG

Printed and bound in Great Britain by
Clays Ltd, St Ives plc

MIX
Paper from
responsible sources
FSC **FSC® C007454**
www.fsc.org

FSC is a non-profit international organisation established to promote
the responsible management of the world's forests. Products carrying the
FSC label are independently certified to assure consumers that they come
from forests that are managed to meet the social, economic and
ecological needs of present and future generations.

Find out more about HarperCollins and the environment at
www.harpercollins.co.uk/green

*For Heather Hartz
With Love.*

PROLOGUE

"Was there anything else, Home Secretary?"

Alexia De Vere smiled. *Home secretary*. Surely the most beautiful two words in the English language. Except for *prime minister*, of course. The Tory Party's newest superstar laughed at herself. *One step at a time, Alexia.*

"No, thank you, Edward. I'll call if I need you."

Sir Edward Manning nodded briefly and left the room. A senior civil servant in his early sixties and a bastion of the Westminster political establishment, Manning was tall and gray and as rigid as a matchstick. In the coming months, Sir Edward would be Alexia De Vere's constant companion: advising, cautioning, expertly guiding her through the maze of Home Office politics. But right now, in these first few hours in the job, Alexia De Vere wanted to be alone. She wanted to savor the sweet taste of victory without an audience. To sit back and revel in the profound thrill of power.

After all, she'd earned it.

Getting up from her desk, she paced around her new office, a vast aerie of a room perched high in one of the Gothic towers of the Palace of Westminster. The interior design was more functional than fabulous. A matching pair of ugly brown sofas at one end (*those must go*), a simple desk and chair at the other, and a bookcase stuffed with dusty, unread tomes of political history. But none of that mattered once you saw the view. Spectacular didn't begin to cover it. Floor-to-ceiling windows provided a panoramic vista of London, from the towers of Canary Wharf in the east to the mansions of Chelsea in the west. It was a view that said one thing and one thing only.

Power.

And it was all hers.

I am the home secretary of Great Britain. The second-most-important member of Her Majesty's government.

How had it happened? How had a junior prisons minister, and a deeply unpopular one at that, leapfrogged so many other senior candidates to land the big job? Poor Kevin Lomax over at Trade and Industry must be spitting yellow, coffee-stained teeth. The thought made Alexia De Vere feel warm inside. *Patronizing old fossil. He wrote me off years ago, but who's laughing now?*

Pilloried in the press for being wealthy, aristocratic, and out of touch with ordinary voters, and dubbed the new Iron Lady by the tabloids, Alexia De Vere's sentencing reform bill had been savaged by MPs on both sides of the house for being "compassionless" and "brutal." No-parole sentences might work in America, a country so barbaric they still had the death penalty. But they weren't going to fly here, in civilized Great Britain.

That's what they *said*. But when push came to shove, they'd all voted the bill through.

Cowards. Cowards and hypocrites the lot of them.

Alexia De Vere knew how unpopular the bill had made her, with colleagues, with the media, with lower-income voters. So she was as shocked as everyone else when the

2

prime minister, Henry Whitman, chose to appoint her as his home secretary. But she didn't dwell on it. The fact was, Henry Whitman *had* appointed her. At the end of the day, that was all that mattered.

Reaching into a box, Alexia pulled out some family photographs. She preferred to keep her work and home lives separate, but these days everyone was so touchy-feely, having pictures of one's children on one's desk had become *de rigueur*.

There was her daughter, Roxie, at eighteen, her blond head thrown back, laughing. How Alexia missed that laugh. Of course, the picture had been taken before the accident.

The accident. Alexia De Vere hated the euphemism for her daughter's suicide attempt, a three-story leap that had left Roxie wheelchair-bound for the rest of her life. In Alexia's view, one should call a spade a spade. But Alexia's husband, Teddy, insisted on it. *Dear Teddy. He always was a soft touch.*

Placing her husband's photograph next to their daughter's, Alexia smiled. An unprepossessing, paunchy middle-aged man, with thinning hair and permanently ruddy cheeks, Teddy De Vere beamed at the camera like a lovable bear.

How different my life would have been without him. How much, how very much, I owe him.

Of course, Teddy De Vere was not the only man to whom Alexia owed her good fortune. There was Henry Whitman, the new Tory prime minister and Alexia's self-appointed political mentor. And somewhere, far, far away from here, there was another man. A good man. A man who had helped her.

But she mustn't think about that man. Not now. Not today.

Today was a day of triumph and celebration. It was no time for regrets.

3

The third picture was of Alexia's son, Michael. What an insanely beautiful boy he was, with his dark curls and slate-gray eyes and that mischievous smile that melted female hearts from a thousand paces. Sometimes Alexia thought that Michael was the only person on earth she had ever loved unconditionally. Roxie ought to fall into that category too, but after everything that had happened between them, the bad blood had poisoned the relationship beyond repair.

After the photographs it was time for the congratulations cards, which had been arriving in a steady stream since Alexia's shock appointment was announced two days earlier. Most of them were dull, corporate affairs sent by lobbyists or constituency hangers-on. They had pictures of popping champagne bottles or dreary floral still-lifes. But one card in particular immediately caught Alexia's eye. Against a Stars-and-Stripes background, the words *YOU ROCK!* were emblazoned in garish gold. The message inside read:

Congratulations, darling Alexia! SO excited and SO proud of you. All my love, Lucy!!!! xxx

Alexia De Vere grinned. She had very few female friends—very few friends of any kind, in fact—but Lucy Meyer was the exception that proved the rule. A neighbor from Martha's Vineyard, where the De Veres owned a summer home—Teddy had fallen in love with the island whilst at Harvard Business School—Lucy Meyer had become almost like a sister. She was a traditional homemaker, albeit of the *über*-wealthy variety, and as American as apple pie. Alternately motherly and childlike, she was the sort of woman who used a lot of exclamation points in e-mails and wrote her *i*'s with full circles instead of dots on the top. To say that Lucy Meyer and Alexia De Vere had little in common would be like saying that Israel and Palestine didn't always see exactly eye to eye. And yet the two women's friendship, forged over so many blissful summers on Martha's Vineyard, had survived all the ups and downs of Alexia's crazy political life.

Standing by the window, Alexia gazed down at the Thames. From up here the river looked benign and stately, a softly flowing ribbon of silver snaking its silent way through the city. But down below, Alexia knew, its currents could be deadly. Even now, at fifty-nine years of age and at the pinnacle of her career, Alexia De Vere couldn't look at water without feeling a shudder of foreboding. She twisted her wedding ring nervously.

How easily it can all be washed away! Power, happiness, even life itself. It only takes an instant, a single unguarded instant. And it's gone.

Her phone buzzed loudly.

"Sorry to disturb you, Home Secretary. But I have Ten Downing Street on line one. I assume you'll take the prime minister's call?"

Alexia De Vere shook her head, willing the ghosts of the past away.

"Of course, Edward. Put him through."

SOUTH OF THE RIVER, LESS THAN a mile from Alexia De Vere's opulent Westminster office but a world apart, Gilbert Drake sat in Maggie's Café, hunched over his egg and beans. A classic British greasy spoon, complete with grime-encrusted windows and a peeling linoleum floor, Maggie's was a popular haunt for cabbies and construction workers on their way to work on the more affluent north side of the river. Gilbert Drake was a regular. Most mornings he was chatty and full of smiles. But not today. Staring at the picture in his newspaper as if he'd seen a ghost, he pressed his hands to his temples.

This can't be happening.

How is this happening?

There she was, that bitch Alexia De Vere, smiling for the camera as she shook hands with the prime minister. Gilbert Drake would never forget that face as long as he lived. The proud, jutting jaw, the disdainful curl of the lips, the cold, steely glint of those blue eyes, as pretty and empty and heartless as a doll's. The caption beneath the picture read *Britain's new home secretary starts work*.

Reading the article was painful, like picking at a newly healed scab, but Gilbert Drake forced himself to go on.

In an appointment that surprised many at Westminster and wrong-footed both the media and the bookies, junior prisons minister Alexia De Vere was named as the new home secretary yesterday. The prime minister, Henry Whitman, has described Mrs. De Vere as "a star" and "a pivotal figure" in his new-look cabinet. Kevin Lomax, the secretary of state for trade and industry, who had been widely tipped to replace Humphrey Crewe at the home office after his resignation, told reporters he was "delighted" to hear of Mrs. De Vere's appointment and that he "hugely looked forward" to working with her.

Gilbert Drake closed his newspaper in disgust.

Gilbert's best friend, Sanjay Patel, was dead because of that bitch. Sanjay, who had protected Gilbert from the bullies at school and in their Peckham public housing project. Sanjay, who'd worked hard all his life to put food on his family's table and faced all life's disappointments with a smile. Sanjay, who'd been imprisoned, wrongly imprisoned, set up by the police, simply for trying to help a cousin escape persecution. Sanjay was dead. While that whore, that she-wolf, Alexia De Vere, was riding high, the toast of London.

It was not to be borne. Gilbert Drake would not bear it.

The righteous will be glad when they are avenged, when they bathe their feet in the blood of the wicked.

Maggie, the café's eponymous proprietress, refilled Gilbert's mug of tea. "Eat up, Gil. Your egg's going cold."

Gilbert Drake didn't hear her.

All he heard was his friend Sanjay Patel's voice begging for vengeance.

CHARLOTTE WHITMAN, THE PRIME MINISTER'S WIFE, rolled over in bed and stroked her husband's chest. It was four in the morning and Henry was awake, again, staring at the ceiling like a prisoner waiting to face the firing squad.

"What is it, Henry? What's the matter?"

Henry Whitman covered his wife's hand with his.

"Nothing. I'm not sleeping too well, that's all. Sorry if I woke you."

"You would tell me if there were a problem, wouldn't you?"

"Darling Charlotte." He pulled her close. "I'm the prime minister. My life is nothing but problems as far as the eye can see."

"You know what I mean. I mean a real problem. Something you can't handle."

"I'm fine, darling, honestly. Try and go back to sleep."

Soon Charlotte Whitman was slumbering soundly. Henry watched her, her words ringing in his ears. *Something you can't handle . . .*

Thanks to him, Alexia De Vere's face was on the front page of every newspaper. Speculation about her appointment was rife, but no one knew anything. No one except Henry Whitman. And he intended to take the secret to his grave.

7

Was Alexia De Vere a problem that he couldn't handle? Henry Whitman sincerely hoped not. Either way it was too late now. The appointment was made. The deed was done.

Britain's new prime minister lay awake until dawn, just as he knew he would.

No rest for the wicked.

PART I

CHAPTER ONE

BILLY HAMLIN WATCHED SEVEN LITTLE BOYS in swimming trunks run squealing toward the water, and felt a surge of happiness. The kids weren't the only ones who loved summer at Camp Williams.

Billy had been lucky to get this job. Most of the camp counselors were Ivy League kids. Tuckers and Mortimers and Sandford-Riley-the-Thirds on a "break" between Harvard College and Harvard Business School. Or the female equivalent, Buffys and Virginias passing the time between graduation and marriage by teaching swim class to the cute sons of the New York elite. Billy Hamlin didn't fit the mold. His dad was a carpenter who'd built some new cabins at Camp Williams last fall, earning enough goodwill to land his boy a summer job.

"You'll meet some interesting people up there," Jeff Hamlin told Billy. "Rich people. People who can help you. You gotta network."

11

Billy's dad was a great believer in networking. Exactly why, or how, he thought a summer spent rubbing shoulders with spoiled bankers' sons was going to help his charming, unqualified, and utterly unambitious boy get ahead in life remained a mystery. Not that Billy was complaining. By day, he got to hang around on the beach playing the fool with a bunch of sweet little kids. And by night, Camp Williams had more freely available drugs, booze, and what his grandma would have called "fast" women than a New Orleans whore-house. At nineteen years old, Billy Hamlin didn't have many skills. But he did know how to party.

"Billy! Billy! Come play pothum in the middle with uth!"

Graydon Hammond, a knock-kneed seven-year-old with a lisp brought on by at least five missing upper teeth, waved for Billy to come into the water. Graydon would grow up to inherit a majority of shares in Hammond Black, a boutique investment bank worth more than most small African countries. Waving people over to do his bidding would be a big part of Graydon's future. But right now he was so sweet-natured and lovable, he was tough to resist.

"Graydon, leave Billy alone. It's his afternoon off. I'll play possum with you."

Toni Gilletti, unquestionably the sexiest of all the Camp Williams counselors, was supervising Graydon's group. Watching Toni run into the surf, her Playboy Bunny body barely contained by her white string bikini, Billy was morti-fied to feel the beginnings of an erection start to stir in his Fred Perry swimming trunks. He had no choice but to dive in himself and use the ocean as a fig leaf.

Like all the other boys at camp, Billy lusted wildly after Toni Gilletti. Unlike the other boys, he also liked her. They'd slept together once, on the very first night at camp, and although Billy had been unable to persuade Toni to repeat the experience, he knew she'd enjoyed it and that she liked him too. Like him, Toni was something of an outsider. She was no workingman's daughter. Toni's old man owned a string of thriving electronics outlets along the Eastern Seaboard. But neither was she a prissy freshman from Wellesley or Vassar. Toni Gilletti was a wild child, a thrill-seeking troublemaker with a taste for cocaine and unsuitable lovers that had gotten her in deep shit back home in Connecticut. Rumor had it she'd only avoided a prison sentence for credit-card fraud because her father, Walter Gilletti, paid off the judge and donated a seven-figure sum to pay for a new bar and wet-room at the local country club. Apparently Toni had stolen the gold AmEx from a neighbor to keep her latest dealer boyfriend in the style he'd become accustomed to. The Gillettis had packed their daughter off to Camp Williams as a last resort, no doubt hoping, like Billy's dad, that Toni might "network" her way to a better future; in her case, marriage to a decent, well-bred white boy—ideally one with a Harvard degree.

Toni had kept half of the bargain, dutifully sleeping with every Harvard grad at camp who wasn't completely physically repulsive, before settling on Charles Braemar Murphy, the richest, handsomest, and (in Billy's view) most obnoxious of them all. Charles was out on his parents' yacht today. The Braemar Murphys had "stopped by" on their way to East Hampton, and Mrs. Kramer, who ran Camp Williams, had given Charles the day off. It was irritating, the way Old Lady Kramer favored the rich kids. But every cloud had a silver lining. Charles's absence gave Billy his best chance yet to flirt with Toni Gilletti uninterrupted and try to persuade her that a second night of passion with him would be a lot more satisfying than sticking with her stuck-up stiff of a boyfriend.

He already knew he had a chance. Toni was a free spirit with a libido like a wildcat. Only a few days ago she'd come on to Billy outrageously in front of Charles. It was a crass attempt to make her boyfriend jealous, but it worked. Later, Billy had heard Charles Braemar Murphy grilling Cassandra Drayton, another of the girls Billy was known to have slept with, about his appeal.

"What is it about Hamlin that women like so much?" Charles demanded angrily.

Cassandra smiled sweetly. "Do you want the answer in inches or feet?"

"He's a fucking carpenter, for God's sake!" spluttered Charles.

"So was Jesus, darling. Don't be bitter. Anyway, it's his father who's the carpenter. Billy just sticks to fucking. And boy, does he know what he's doing."

As gratifying as it was to hear Cassandra Drayton sing his praises, the truth was that for all her flirting, Toni Gilletti had yet to allow Billy to seduce her a second time. The longer she held out, the more Billy wanted her.

Toni was like no other girl Billy had ever met. Not only was she a wildcat in bed, she was funny and smart, not to mention a brilliant mimic and natural performer. Her impression of Mrs. Kramer, Camp Williams's elderly proprietress, had her fellow counselors crying with laughter. Toni had *balls*. Way bigger balls than he did, for all Cassandra's kind compliments about his attributes. To Charles Braemar Murphy, Toni Gilletti was a trophy, a toy to be enjoyed over the summer. To Billy Hamlin, she was everything. Though he'd admitted it to no one, Billy was head over heels in love. He was determined not just to seduce Toni again, but to marry her.

*

14

Toni watched as Billy dived into the water. *Just look at that physique.* She loved the way the muscles rippled across Billy's broad swimmer's back and the way his powerful arms cut effortlessly through the water like twin scimitars slicing through silk. Charles Braemar Murphy was good-looking in a preppy, chiseled sort of way. But he had none of Billy's raw sensuality, none of that animal magnetism, that predatory, erotic hunger that oozed out of Billy's pores like sweat.

What Charles *did* have was a trust fund the size of Canada. With each passing day Toni Gilletti found it harder to decide which she wanted more: Adonis the Love God? Or Camp Williams's answer to Croesus?

Last night she'd fantasized about screwing Billy again while Charles was making love to her. Lying back on a cashmere blanket, with Charles diligently pumping away on top of her to a sound track of Todd Rundgren's "Hello, It's Me"—terrible song, but Charles had insisted on bringing along his portable eight-track to "set the mood"—Toni remembered what it felt like to be pinned beneath Billy 's powerful, masculine thighs. If he kept pursuing her like this she was bound to give in eventually. Toni Gilletti could no more stay faithful to an unsatisfying lover like Charles than a lioness could become vegetarian. Billy had been a wonderful lay. She needed fresh meat.

"C'mon, Toni! You're suppothed to be pothum. Try and catch the ball!"

Graydon Hammond looked up at her plaintively. He had his arm around Nicholas Handemeyer, another adorably geeky seven-year-old and the heir to a vast estate in Maine. Dark-haired Graydon and the angelically blond Nicholas were probably Toni Gilletti's favorite boys at Camp Williams. For all her carefully cultivated bad-girl ways, Toni was a

15

popular camp counselor and naturally maternal. Her own mother was so interested in shopping and vacations and spending Toni's dad's money, she'd have been hard-pressed to pick Toni out of a three-kid lineup. But in spite of this poor parental example, Toni warmed toward small children and found them a blast to be around: funny, energetic, loving. Best of all they didn't judge you. Toni loved them for that more than anything.

Today, however, hungover and in serious need of a line of coke, she could have done without the noise, and the questions, and the endless sweaty little hands pawing at her.

"I'm trying, Graydon, okay?" She sounded grumpier than she meant to. "Throw it again."

"Let me help."

Billy Hamlin had materialized beside her, his sleek blond head emerging out of the crystal-clear water like an otter's. After scooping up a giggling Graydon and Nicholas under each arm, he dropped them in the shallows, dividing the other boys up into teams and getting the game started. After a few minutes, Toni swam over, allowing her bare arm to brush against Billy's as she retrieved the ball. Just that small hint of physical contract was electric.

"Thanks." She smiled. "But go enjoy yourself. You only get a half day off per week, and I know you don't wanna spend it with my kids."

"That's true." Billy gazed unashamedly at Toni's breasts. "Tell you what. I'll make you a deal."

"A deal?"

"Sure. If I find a freshwater pearl in the next fifteen minutes, you spend the night with me tomorrow."

Toni laughed, enjoying the attention. "You've only found three pearls in the last month. You're hardly likely to scoop one up in fifteen minutes."

16

"Exactly. It's hopeless. So why not shake on the deal?"

"You know why not."

Toni glanced out to the harbor lanes, where the Braemar Murphys' yacht, *Celeste*, glittered in the afternoon sunshine.

"Oh, come *on*. Live a little," Billy teased. "You know he bores you. Besides, like you said, I'm hardly likely to find a pearl in a quarter of an hour, am I?"

"But if you do?"

Slipping an arm around Toni's waist, Billy pulled her close so their lips were almost touching. "If I do, then it's fate. We're meant to be together. Deal?"

Toni grinned. "Okay, deal. But it has to be at least the size of a pea."

"A pea? Oh, c'mon now. That's impossible!"

"A pea. Now get out of here! I've got some serious possum playing to do."

Billy swam out into deeper water, his shucking knife clamped between his teeth like a pirate's cutlass. He made a couple of dives, emerging each time with a large oyster shell and making a great theatrical show of prizing it open, but with no success, clutching his heart and swooning into the water, all for Toni's benefit.

Within a few minutes, a growing crowd of spectators had gathered to watch from the beach. The boy was an incredible swimmer and he was putting on quite a show.

Toni Gilletti thought, *He's funny, but he's getting way too big headed*. Turning away, she threw herself into the game with the boys, deliberately ignoring Billy's antics.

*

CHARLES BRAEMAR MURPHY WAS FEELING GOOD. He'd enjoyed a delicious lunch of fresh Maine lobster rolls on his parents' yacht, washed down with a couple of glasses of vintage Chablis. His old man had agreed to raise his allowance. And Toni had promised to wear the satin crotchless panties he'd bought her in bed tonight, a prospect that had had him in an almost constant state of arousal since daybreak.

Stretching out on a lounge chair on the upper deck, Charles felt his confidence returning. *I have to stop obsessing about the Hamlin kid. Sure he's after Toni. Everyone's after Toni. But he's no threat to me. She already had him and she tossed him aside.*

Toni would be on the beach now, building sand castles with her group of little boys.

I'll surprise her, Charles thought on a whim. *Bring her some chocolate-dipped strawberries from the galley. Chicks love that sort of meaningless romantic gesture. She'll be even more grateful in bed tonight than usual.*

He clicked his fingers imperiously at one of the deckhands.

"Get one of the tenders ready. I'm going ashore."

THE BOYS HAD TIRED OF POSSUM and were hunting for crab claws in the shallows. A collective gasp from the beach made Toni turn around.

Oh my God! Idiot!

Billy had swum out beyond the barrier that separated the swimming and harbor lanes. There were three large yachts moored offshore, and a host of smaller boats between them and the beach. A lone swimmer was as good as invisible amid such heavy traffic. Diving for pearls out there was preposterously dangerous.

Toni waved frantically at Billy, beckoning him over. "Come back!" she shouted into the wind. "You'll get yourself killed out there!"

Billy cupped a hand to his ear in a can't-hear-you gesture. Leaving the boys on the shore, Toni swam a few yards farther out and shouted again. "Get back here! You'll get hit."

Billy glanced over his shoulder. The nearest yacht tenders were at least fifty yards behind him.

"It's fine," he called back to Toni.

"It's not fine! Don't be a moron."

"Two more dives."

"Billy, no!"

But it was too late. With an effortless flick of the legs, Billy disappeared beneath the waves again, earning himself more gasps and claps from the beach.

Toni bit her lip, waiting anxiously for Billy to resurface. Ten seconds went by, then twenty, then thirty.

Oh, Jesus. What's happened? Has he hit his head? I should never have taken the stupid bet and encouraged him. I know how reckless he is. He's like me.

Then suddenly there he was, shooting up out of the blue like a dolphin at play, waving a huge oyster shell. The crowd on the beach whooped and cheered. Billy cut the thing open and pulled out a pearl, to even louder applause. But he shook his head sadly at Toni.

"It's too small. My princess needs a pea."

"Cut it out," Toni shot back angrily. The game wasn't fun anymore. Couldn't those idiots on the beach see how dangerous this was? "Get back here, Billy. I mean it."

Billy shook his head. "Two minutes left!" And with a deep gulp of air, he was gone again.

*

"Why don't you let me pilot the tender, sir. You sit back and relax."

Daniel Gray was an experienced crewman who'd spent the last twenty years working on rich people's yachts. The Braemar Murphys were no better or worse than most of the families Daniel Gray worked for. But their son, Charles, was an entitled little prig. He'd clearly been drinking, and should not be left alone at the wheel of an expensive piece of equipment like the *Celeste*'s tender.

"I'm perfectly relaxed, thanks," Charles Braemar Murphy drawled. "Just bring me the strawberries and champagne I asked for and let my mother know I'll be back in a couple of hours."

"Very good, sir."

Dickhead. I hope he runs aground and spends the next decade paying his old man back for the damage.

It took Billy Hamlin forty-five seconds to surface this time. He still seemed to think it was a joke, barely pausing before he went back down again.

Furious, Toni turned away—no way would she spend the night with him now, however big his damn pearl, or his damn anything else, might be. As she swam back toward the boys, she saw something out of the corner of her eye. It was a rowboat, a tiny, old-fashioned wooden affair. *What the hell is that doing out in the shipping lane?*

No sooner had the thought occurred to her than she saw two tenders, one gliding sedately through the water, the other, a few seconds behind it, going dangerously fast, churning up a choppy wake as it roared toward the shore. The first tender saw the wooden craft and veered to avoid it, changing course fairly easily. The second seemed totally unaware of the danger.

"Boat!" Toni waved frantically at the second tender. She

was in shallow water now and was able to jump up and down as she shouted and flapped her arms. "BOAT!"

CHARLES BRAEMAR MURPHY CAUGHT THE FLASH of blond hair and the familiar white bikini.

Toni was waving at him.

"Hey, babe!" He waved back, speeding up to impress her, but found he needed to clutch the wheel for support. That Chablis must have really gone to his head. "I brought you something."

It took a few moments for Charles to realize that people on the beach were waving at him too. Hadn't they ever seen a yacht tender before? Or maybe they'd never seen one as powerful as the *Celeste*'s.

By the time he saw the rowboat, and realized the danger, he was seconds away from impact. Crouched inside, two teenage boys huddled together in terror. Charles caught the look of pure panic on their faces as he hurtled toward them, and felt sick. He was close enough now to see the whites of their eyes and their desperate, pleading expressions.

Jesus Christ.

He lunged for the wheel.

THE TWO LIFEGUARDS LOOKED AT EACH other.

"Holy shit."

"He's gonna hit them, isn't he?"

Grabbing their floats, they ran into the water.

TONI WATCHED IN HORROR AS THE second tender sped toward the rowboat. As it got closer, her horror intensified. *Is that . . .Charles? What the hell is he doing?*

21

She opened her mouth to scream, to warn him, but no sound came out. Thanks to Billy's antics, she'd already shouted herself hoarse. That's when she realized with chilling finality: *Those kids are going to die.*

DEEP BENEATH THE WAVES, BILLY HAMLIN plucked a fifth oyster shell from the sand. It was cool and peaceful down here, and quite beautiful with the sun shining its dappled rays through the water, casting ethereal, dancing shadows across the bed.

The chances of him finding a pea-size pearl were almost nil. But Billy was enjoying showing off for Toni and the crowd on the beach. He felt at home in the water, confident and strong. In the real world he might be Charles Braemar Murphy's inferior. But not here, in the wild freedom of the ocean. Here, he was a king.

Grabbing the oyster tightly in his hand, he began to swim back up toward the light.

WRENCHING THE WHEEL TO THE RIGHT with all his strength, Charles Braemar Murphy closed his eyes. The tender banked so sharply, it almost capsized. Clinging on for dear life, Charles heard screams ringing in his ears. Was it the boys' terror he was hearing, or his own? He couldn't tell. Salt spray doused him, lashing his face like a razor. The tender was still moving at a terrific speed.

How had it happened so quickly, the shift from happiness to disaster? Only seconds ago he'd been deeply, profoundly happy. And now . . .

Heart pounding, teeth clenched, Charles Braemar Murphy braced himself for the blow.

*

THE CROWD ON THE BEACH WATCHED openmouthed as the tender careered uncontrollably to the right, farther into the shipping lanes.

At first the wake was so huge and the spray so high it was impossible to make out what had happened to the rowboat. But at last it emerged, bobbing wildly but still intact. Two boys could be seen standing inside, waving their arms frantically for rescue.

The relief was overwhelming. People cheered and cried and jumped up and down, hugging one another.

They made it! He missed.

Then, somewhere among them, a lone voice screamed. "Swimmer!"

FOR TONI GILLETTI, IT ALL HAPPENED in slow motion.

She saw Charles swerve. Saw him miss the rowboat by inches. For a split second she felt relief, so powerful it made her nauseous. But then Billy Hamlin shot up out of the water like a tornado, directly in the tender's path. Even if Charles had seen him, there was no way he could have stopped.

The last thing Toni saw was the look of shock on Billy's handsome face. Then the tender cut off her view.

Someone on the beach screamed.

Charles cut the engine and the tender sputtered to a halt.

Billy Hamlin was gone.

CHAPTER TWO

Charles Braemar Murphy was in shock. Slumped on the bench at the back of the tender, shivering, he stared at the water. It was calm now, silvery and still like glass.

The lifeguards splashed around, searching for Billy, taking turns plunging beneath the surface.

Nothing.

On the beach, people were crying. The boys in the rowboat had made it safely to shore, tearful after their own ordeal and confused by what was going on. In the shallows, the little Camp Williams boys from Toni's group huddled together nervously, frightened by the adults' panic.

In a complete daze, Toni swam back to them. Someone must have called for help, because the coast-guard officers were arriving from all sides, along with tenders from the other yachts moored offshore.

"Toni?" A shivering Graydon Hammond clung to Toni's leg.

"Not now, Graydon," she murmured automatically, her eyes still fixed on the point in the water where she'd last seen Billy.

He can't be dead. He was there, just seconds ago. Please, God, please don't let him be dead, just because he was playing the fool for me.

"Toni?"

She was about to comfort Graydon when she saw it. About fifty yards farther out to sea than the point where Toni had been looking, a dazed swimmer bobbed to the surface.

"There!" she screamed at the lifeguards, waving her arms hysterically. "Over there!"

She needn't have bothered. As one, the rescue boats converged on Billy, scooping him out of the water. Watching from his speedboat, Charles Braemar Murphy finally broke down in sobs.

It was over. The nightmare was over.

LESS THAN A MINUTE LATER BILLY was on the beach, smiling through the pain as a paramedic bandaged his head wound. Several people came over to shake his hand and inform him (as if he needed telling) how lucky he was to be alive.

"It was all for her, you know," he told his admirers, nodding at Toni, who was striding over toward him, an Amazonian goddess in her tiny bikini, with her long wet hair trailing magnificently behind her. "My princess needed a pea. What could I do? Her wish was my command."

Toni, however, was not in romantic mood.

"You goddamn fool!" she screamed at Billy. "You could have been killed! I thought you'd drowned."

"Would you have missed me?" Billy pouted.

"Oh, grow up. What happened out there wasn't funny, Billy. Poor Charles is in pieces. He thought he'd hit you. We all did."

"'Poor' Charles?" Now it was Billy's turn to get angry.

"That dickhead was piloting his boat like a maniac. Didn't you see how close he came to crashing into those poor kids in the rowboat?"

"They should never have been in the lanes," said Toni. "And neither should you."

Graydon Hammond had followed Toni out of the water and was tugging at her leg again, making whimpering noises.

"Graydon, *please*!" she snapped. "I'm talking to Billy."

"But it's important!" Graydon howled.

"Go ahead," Billy said bitterly. "It's clear you don't give a damn about me. Go comfort Graydon. Or better yet, Charles. He's the real victim here."

"For God's sake, Billy, of course I give a damn. Do you think I'd be so angry if I didn't care about you? I thought . . . I thought I'd lost you."

And to Toni Gilletti's own surprise, she burst into tears.

Billy Hamlin put his arms around her. "Hey," he whispered gently. "Don't cry. I'm sorry I scared you. Please don't cry."

"Toniiiiiiiiiiiiiiii!" Graydon Hammond's wails were getting louder. Reluctantly, Toni extricated herself from Billy's embrace.

"What is it Graydon, honey?" she said more gently. "What's the matter?"

The little boy looked up at her, his bottom lip quivering. "It's Nicholas."

"Nicholas? Nicholas Handemeyer?"

Graydon nodded.

"What about him?"

Graydon Hammond burst into tears.

"He swam away. When you were watching Billy. He swam away and he never came back."

CHAPTER THREE

IT WAS A QUARTER OF A mile back to Camp Williams from the beach, along a sandy path half overgrown with brambles. Toni's legs were scratched raw as she ran, but she was oblivious to the pain and deaf to the plaintive cries of the children struggling to keep up.

"My God. What happened to you? Forget your clothes?"

Mary Lou Parker, pristine in her preppy uniform of khaki shorts, white-collared shirt, and docksiders, looked Toni up and down with distaste. That bikini was really too much, especially with kids around. Mary Lou couldn't think what Charles Braemar Murphy saw in Toni Gilletti.

"Have you seen Nicholas? Nicholas Handemeyer?" Toni gasped. Belatedly Mary Louise clocked her distress and the muted sobbing of the children huddled behind her. They looked like they'd been to war. "Did he come back here?"

"No."

Toni let out a wail.

" I mean, I don't know." Mary Lou backtracked. "*I* haven't seen him, but let me go ask the others."

One by one the other counselors and Camp Williams

faculty emerged from their various cabins. No one had seen Nicholas Handemeyer. But Toni shouldn't panic.

He was bound to have gotten out of the water.

Little boys ran off sometimes.

He couldn't be far.

A group of the boys, including Don Choate, who was a varsity swim star, set off for the beach to help the rescue efforts. Billy Hamlin and Charles Braemar Murphy had stayed to help the coast guard, while Toni took the children back to camp.

Toni stood uselessly, watching them go. Not sure what else to do, she escorted the other boys back to camp, got them changed into dry clothes, and prepared some food for them. Mary Lou Parker arrived to find Toni mindlessly chopping cucumbers and staring at the wall.

"I'll take over here," said Mary Lou kindly. She didn't like Toni Gilletti, but everyone knew how fond Toni was of little Nicholas. You could see the misery in her eyes. "You go and clean up. I bet you he'll be back by the time you've had a shower. He's probably getting hungry by now."

Walking back to her cabin, Toni tried to make herself believe what Mary Lou had said.

He'll be back any minute.

He's probably getting hungry.

Other thoughts, horrific thoughts, hovered ominously on the edge of her consciousness, clamoring to be let in. But Toni pushed them aside. First the kids in the rowboat. Then Billy. Now Nicholas. The afternoon had been one long roller coaster of terror and relief. But it would end happily. It had to.

When Toni saw Nicholas she would hug him and kiss him and tell him how sorry she was for allowing herself to be distracted by Billy. Tomorrow they would catch crabs

28

together and play possum. They would build entire sand cities. Toni would not be hungover, or tired, or thinking about her love life. She would be with the children, with Nicholas, one hundred percent present.

She stopped at the door to her cabin.

The boys emerged from the beach path one by one. They walked with their heads down, in silence. Toni watched them, numb, aware of nothing but the distant lapping of the waves ringing in her ears.

In later years, she would dream about their faces:

Charles Braemar Murphy, her lover up until that day, ashen white and ghostly.

Don Choate, his lips set tight, fists clenched as he walked.

And at the rear, Billy Hamlin, his eyes swollen from crying.

Whoosh, whoosh, whoosh went the tide.

The boy's corpse hung limp in Billy's arms.

CHAPTER FOUR

"SO LET'S GET THIS STRAIGHT. WHEN did you first notice— first notice—that Nicholas was missing?"

Mrs. Martha Kramer cast her beady eyes from Toni Gilletti to Billy Hamlin. Both young people looked terrified. As well they might.

Martha Kramer had been running Camp Williams for twenty-two years now, first with her husband, John, and for the last nine years as a widow. Never, in all that time, had there been a single serious accident involving any of the boys in her care. Never. But now tragedy had struck. And it had struck on the watch of the carpenter's son and the electronics millionaire's daughter.

At only five feet tall, with perfectly coiffed gray hair and a pair of trademark pince-nez spectacles permanently suspended on a chain around her neck, Mrs. Kramer was considered a Kennebunkport institution. But her diminutive stature and soft-spoken, grandmotherly manner led many people to underestimate both her intellect and her business acumen. Camp Williams might sell itself as an old-fashioned, family-run retreat. But since her husband's death, Mrs. Kramer had doubled the prices and started strictly vetting the boys she admitted, ensuring her reputation as the owner of *the* elite summer camp on the East Coast. Teenage labor was cheap, overheads were low. She'd even gotten a great deal on the carpentry for last year's refurbishment project. Put simply, Mrs. Martha Kramer had been sitting on a cash cow. And these two irresponsible children had just slaughtered it.

"I told you, Mrs. Kramer. I had a concussion. Toni was looking after me. We thought all the kids were right there on the beach, until Graydon came over and said Nicholas was gone."

Billy Hamlin, the boy, was doing all of the talking. The girl, Gilletti, normally a chatterbox of the worst order, was curiously mute. Perhaps it was shock? Or perhaps she was smart enough not to say anything that might incriminate her later. Something about her eyes made Mrs. Kramer uneasy. *She's thinking,* the little minx. *Weighing up her options.*

Both Toni and Billy had gotten dressed since the beach, he in bell-bottoms and a Rolling Stones T-shirt, she in a floor-length skirt with tassels on the bottom and a turtleneck sweater that covered every inch of her skin. Again, the demure clothes were uncharacteristic of Theodore Gilletti's wayward daughter. Martha Kramer's eyes narrowed still further.

"And you raised the alarm right away?"

"Of course. The coast guard was already at the scene. I stayed to help them, and Toni came back here, just in case . . ."

Billy Hamlin let the sentence trail off. He looked at Toni, who looked at the floor.

"Miss Gilletti? Have you nothing to say?"

"If I had something to say, I'd have said it, okay?" Roused from her stupor like a sun-drunk rattlesnake, Toni suddenly lashed out. "Billy's told you what happened. Why do you keep hammering at us?"

"*Hammering* at you?" Martha Kramer drew herself up to her full five feet and glowered at the spoiled teenager in front of her. "Miss Gilletti, a child is dead. Drowned. Do you understand? The police are on their way, as is the boy's family. They are going to *hammer* at you until they know exactly *what* happened, *how* it happened, and *who* was responsible."

"No one was responsible," Toni said quietly. "It was an accident."

Mrs. Kramer raised an eyebrow. "Was it? Well, let us hope the police agree with you."

OUTSIDE MRS. KRAMER'S OFFICE, TONI FINALLY gave way to tears, collapsing into Billy's arms.

"Tell me it's a dream. A nightmare. Tell me I'm going to wake up!"

"Shhh." Billy hugged her. It felt so good to hold her. There was no more "poor Charles" now. He and Toni were in this together. "It's like you said. It was an accident."

"But poor Nicholas!" Toni wailed. "I can't stop thinking how frightened he must have been. How desperate for me to hear him, to save him."

"Don't, Toni. Don't torture yourself."

"I mean, he must have called out for me, mustn't he? He must have screamed for help. Oh God, I can't bear it! What have I done? I should never have left him alone."

Billy pushed the image of Nicholas Handemeyer's corpse from his mind. The little boy was floating facedown when Billy found him, in a rocky cove only yards from the shore. Billy had tried the kiss of life and the paramedics had spent

32

twenty straight minutes on the sand doing chest compressions, trying anything to revive him. It was all useless.

Toni said, "They'll send me to prison for sure, you know."

"Of course they won't," Billy said robustly.

"They will." Toni wrung her hands. "I already have two counts on my record."

"You do?"

"One for fraud and one for possession," Toni explained. "Oh my God, what if they drug-test me? They will, won't they? I still have all that coke in my system. And grass. Oh, Billy! They'll lock me up and throw away the key!"

"Calm down. No one's going to lock you up. I won't let them."

Billy was enjoying being the strong one. It felt good having Toni Gilletti lean on him. Need him. This was the way it was supposed to be. The two of them against the world. Charles Braemar Murphy wasn't man enough for Toni. But he, Billy Hamlin, would step up to the plate.

As he stood stroking Toni's hair, two Maine police squad cars pulled into the graveled area in front of the Camp Williams lobby. Three men emerged, two in uniform, one in a dark suit and wing-collared shirt. Mrs. Kramer bustled out to greet them, a grim look on her wizened, old woman's face.

Pulling Toni closer, Billy caught a waft of her scent. A surge of animal longing pulsed through him. He whispered in her ear.

"They're going to separate us. Compare our stories. Just stick to what you told Mrs. Kramer. It was an accident. And whatever you do, don't mention drugs."

Toni nodded miserably. She felt as if she might throw up at any minute. Mrs. Kramer was already leading the police toward them.

"Don't worry," said Billy. "You're going to be just fine. Trust me."

A COUPLE OF HOURS LATER, ONCE the little boys were safely in their beds, the rest of the Camp Williams counselors sat around a large cafeteria-style table, comforting one another. They'd all seen the ambulance arrive and drive away with little Nicholas Handemeyer's body. Some of the girls cried.

Mary Lou Parker asked, "What do you think will happen to Toni and Billy?"

Don Choate pushed a cold hot dog around his plate. "Nothing'll happen. It was an accident."

For a few moments they were all silent. Then someone said what everyone was thinking.

"Even so. One of them should have seen Nicholas leave the group. Someone should've been watching."

"It was an accident!" Don shouted, slamming his fist down on the table so hard it shook. "It could have happened to any one of us."

Don had helped carry Nicholas's body back to camp. He was still only twenty, and obviously traumatized by the whole episode.

"We shouldn't be throwing accusations around."

"I'm not throwing accusations. I'm just saying—"

"Well, don't! Don't say anything! What the hell do you know, man? You weren't there."

Sensing that the boys were about to come to blows, Charles Braemar Murphy put an arm around his friend and led him away. "It's all right, Don. Come on. Let's get some air."

Once they'd gone, Anne Fielding, one of the quieter Wellesley girls, spoke up.

34

"It's not all right, though, is it. The boy's dead. He couldn't have drowned in such shallow, calm water unless someone took their eye off the ball. For a long, long time."

"I can see how Billy might have been distracted," said one of the boys. "That bikini Toni was wearing was kind of an invitation."

"This is Toni Gilletti we're talking about," Mary Lou Parker drawled bitchily. "You don't need an invitation. It's first come, first served."

Everybody laughed.

"Shhh." Anne Fielding interjected, her face pressed to the window. "They're coming out."

The door to the administrative offices opened. Inside, Toni and Billy had both spent the last three hours straight being interviewed by the police. Toni emerged first, leaning on one of the uniformed officers for support. Even from this distance, you could see how smitten the young cop was with her, wrapping his arm protectively around her waist and smiling comfortingly as he escorted her back to her cabin.

"Well, *she* doesn't look like she's in too much trouble," Mary Lou Parker said caustically.

Moments later, Billy Hamlin came through the same door. Flanked by the plain-clothed detective on one side and the uniformed patrol officer on the other, he had his head down as he was marched toward the squad car. As he climbed into the backseat, the group in the cafeteria caught a glint of silver behind his back.

"They've cuffed him!" Anne Fielding gasped. "Oh my goodness. Do you think he's under arrest?"

"Well, I don't think they're taking him to an S-and-M club," one of the boys said drily.

The truth was, none of the boys at Camp Williams much liked Billy Hamlin. The carpenter's son was too popular with the ladies for their liking. As for the girls, although they humored him because of his charm and good looks, they too regarded Billy as an outsider, a curiosity to be played with and enjoyed, but hardly an equal. For those with a keen ear for such things, the sound of ranks closing in the Camp Williams dining hall was deafening.

"What do you think you're doing, gawking at the window like a gaggle of geese?" Martha Kramer's authoritative voice rang out through the room like an air-raid siren. Everybody jumped.

"If I'm not mistaken, you all have to be at work tomorrow."

"Yes, Mrs. Kramer."

"And it's vital that camp routines continue as normal, for the other children's sake."

Only Mary Lou Parker dared to pipe up. "But, Mrs. Kramer, Billy Hamlin—"

"—won't be helped by idle gossip." The old woman cut her off. "I hope I don't need to remind you that a child has died. This isn't entertainment, Miss Parker. This is tragedy. Now I want you all back in your cabins. Lights out at eleven."

CHAPTER FIVE

TONI GILLETTI WAS SURROUNDED BY WATER. Seawater. It was pitch-black and cold, and her saturated clothes stuck cold and clammy to her skin, like seaweed. Gradually it dawned on her. *I'm in a cave.* The water was rising, slowly but surely, each wave higher than the last.

Whoosh. Whoosh. Whoosh.

Blind, clawing at the walls, Toni groped desperately for an opening, a way out. How had she gotten in here in the first place? Had someone brought her here, to punish her? She couldn't remember. But if there was a way in, there must be a way out. She had to find it, fast.

The water was at her shoulders.

Her ears.

HELP!

Toni's scream echoed off the cave walls. Unheard. Unanswered.

Water was in her mouth, salty, choking. It flowed down into her lungs, robbing her of air, drowning her slowly. She couldn't breathe!

Please, somebody help me!

"Miss Toni. Miss Toni! It's all right."

37

Toni sat up in bed, gasping for breath. Wild-eyed and terrified . . . her nightdress soaked with sweat. "Carmen?"

The Gillettis' Spanish housekeeper nodded reassuringly. "*Sí*, Miss Toni. It's okay. Only you are dreaming. It's okay."

Toni slumped back against the pillows as reality reasserted itself.

She wasn't drowning.

She wasn't at Camp Williams.

She was in her own bedroom, at home in New Jersey.

But Carmen was wrong. Everything was not okay.

Billy Hamlin was going to be tried for murder.

The whole thing was ridiculous. So ridiculous that Toni had confidently expected to hear with each passing day that the charges were being dropped, that it was all a huge, horrible mistake. She'd had no chance to speak to Billy since his arrest, but she'd pieced together what had happened through the Camp Williams grapevine. Evidently Billy had told the cops that he had been in charge of Nicholas and the other boys when the accident happened, not Toni. He'd also admitted to having drugs in his system, presumably to deflect the heat from Toni, who he knew had prior convictions. That must have been what he meant when he told her he "wouldn't let" the police throw the book at her.

At first Toni was so relieved, she felt overwhelmed with gratitude. No one had ever stuck their neck out like that for her before, certainly not a boy. Boys all wanted to sleep with her, but none of them actually cared, not like Billy did. But it wasn't long before the romantic gesture turned hideously sour. The Handemeyer family, furious over the drug allegations and in desperate need of someone to blame for their son's death, insisted on pressing charges. Nicholas's father was a senator and one of the richest men in Maine. Senator Handemeyer wanted Billy Hamlin's head on a pike, and he was powerful enough to force the D.A.'s hand. Soon Billy's little white lie to protect Toni had become national news, and Toni's relief turned to constant, gut-wrenching fear.

Parents all over America identified with the Handemeyer family's grief. To lose a child was always horrific. But to lose an only son, at seven years old, and in such appalling circumstances; it was more than people could bear. And what did it say about modern society that a drug-addled teenager would be left in charge of a group of vulnerable children?

Overnight Billy Hamlin's handsome, nineteen-year-old face was on every news channel and in every paper as the poster child for a selfish, hedonistic generation. Of course he hadn't actually *murdered* the Handemeyer boy. Everybody knew that the case would be thrown out once it got to court, that in his grief Senator Handemeyer had gone too far. Yet people were pleased that the post-Vietnam generation should be somehow called to account. Two weeks before the trial, *Newsweek* ran an article about the trial with a shot of Billy, long-haired and bare-chested, next to a picture of dear little Nicholas Handemeyer in his school uniform, complete with tie. Below the images ran the simple, two-word headline:

WHAT HAPPENED?

They weren't asking what had happened on the beach that idyllic day at a children's summer camp in Maine. They were asking what had happened to America's youth. What happened to decency, to the nation's moral fiber.

Billy Hamlin's trial was set for October. As it drew nearer, Toni Gilletti's nerves stretched closer and closer to breaking point. She still didn't know if she would be asked to testify, and had no idea what she would say if she were. She knew she ought to come forward, to tell the world that it was she, and not poor, blameless Billy, who had allowed Nicholas Handemeyer to die. But every time she picked up the telephone to dial the D.A.'s office and tell the truth, her nerve failed her. When it came down to the wire, Billy was the one who had the strength, not Toni. She simply couldn't do it.

Meanwhile, the dreams got worse.

She longed to talk about them to someone, to unburden herself of the guilt and anguish, to talk openly about what had happened that fateful afternoon at the beach. But who could she talk to? Her girlfriends were all gossips and bitches. Charles Braemar Murphy hadn't called once since the day she left Camp Williams. As for her parents, her father was too obsessed with how the negative publicity might affect his business to give a damn about his daughter's emotional state. Walter Gilletti acted quickly to keep his Toni's name out of the papers, issuing preemptive injunctions against a number of media outlets and TV networks, and had kept Toni under virtual house arrest since she got home. But that was as far as his paternal support went. As for Toni's mother, Sandra, she was too busy shopping, playing bridge with her girlfriends, and self-medicating to question Toni about what had really happened on the beach that day, or how she might be feeling.

Forcing herself out of bed, Toni walked into the bathroom. Splashing cold water on her face, she gazed at her reflection in the mirror.

You left Nicholas Handemeyer to die, frightened and alone. You let Billy Hamlin take the rap for what YOU did.

You're a coward and a liar, and one day everybody will know it.

The trial would begin in six days.

CHAPTER SIX

"**H**OW DO I LOOK?"

Billy Hamlin turned to face his father. Standing in his sparse, six-by-eight-foot cell, his blond hair newly cut and wearing a dark wool Brooks Brothers suit and tie, Billy looked more like a young attorney than the accused in a major murder trial.

"You look good, son. Smart. Serious. You're gonna come through this."

The last three months had been a living hell for Jeff Hamlin. The carpenter from Queens could have coped with the malicious local gossip about his son. He could have dealt with the loss of half his customers and the judgmental glares of the women from his church, St. Luke's Presbyterian, the same church he and Billy had attended for the last fifteen years. But having to sit back impotently while his adored son's character was defiled on national television, torn to shreds by ignorant strangers who called Billy a monster and evil and a murderer? That broke Jeff Hamlin's heart. The trial itself might be a travesty—no one, not even the Handemeyers, seriously doubted that Billy would be acquitted of the murder charge—but whether the boy was acquitted

41

or not, the entire country would forever remember Jeff Hamlin's son as the druggie who let an innocent boy drown.

The worst of it was that Billy had done nothing of the kind. Unlike the police, Jeff Hamlin hadn't swallowed Billy's story for a second.

"He wasn't the one in charge of those kids," Jeff told Billy's lawyer, a state-appointed defender with the deeply unfortunate name of Leslie Lose. They were sitting in Lose's office, a windowless box of a room at the back of a nondescript building in Alfred, Maine, just a few blocks from the courthouse. "He's covering for the girl."

Leslie Lose looked at Jeff Hamlin thoughtfully. The truth was, it didn't much matter who had been supervising the children. What happened to Nicholas Handemeyer remained an accident. Any jury in the world would see that. But the lawyer was curious.

"What makes you think that?"

"I don't think it. I know it. I know my son and I know when he's lying."

"Really?"

"Really."

"Did you know that Billy likes to drink, Mr. Hamlin?"

"No," Jeff admitted. "I mean, you know, I assumed he had the occasional beer."

"Did you know he smokes marijuana?"

"No."

"Or that he's used hard drugs? Cocaine. Amphetamines."

"No, I didn't. But—"

"All those things were found in Billy's system the day Nicholas Handemeyer died."

"Yes. And *why* were they found?" Exasperated, Jeff Hamlin threw his arms wide. "Because Billy told the police to look for 'em. He *suggested* a blood test, for God's sake.

42

Why would he do that if he weren't trying to make himself look guilty?"

Leslie Lose cleared his throat. "I'm not suggesting Billy's guilty. This entire trial is a grudge match dreamed up by Senator Handemeyer, and the whole world knows it."

"I hope so."

"All I'm saying, Mr. Hamlin, is that once they're past the age of thirteen, none of us know our children as well as we think we do. The worst thing Billy could do right now would be to start pointing the finger at others, trying to shift the blame. He's admitted using drugs, he's admitted making a mistake. That doesn't make him a murderer."

Jeff Hamlin sat down wearily. "Billy's a good kid."

"I know he is." Leslie Lose smiled reassuringly. "And that's what's going to win us this case. That and the prosecution's total lack of hard evidence. The newspapers have demonized Billy. When the jury sees what he's really like, how different he is from the monster they've been expecting, they'll acquit for sure."

"But what about the damage to Billy's reputation? Who's going to pay for that?"

"One step at a time, Mr. Hamlin," Leslie Lose said gently. "Let's get your son home first. Once the criminal charges are dealt with, we can think about next steps."

Jeff Hamlin took comfort in the lawyer's certainty. Jeff might know his way around a lathe and a workbench, but he knew nothing about how to win over a jury, or what did or didn't constitute murder. Despite his name, Lose had a decent track record of winning cases a lot less cut-and-dried than Billy's.

A prison officer appeared at the door. "Time to go."

Billy smiled. He looked so happy and confident, even Jeff Hamlin relaxed a little.

"Good luck, son."

"Thanks, Dad. I won't need it."

IT WAS A SHORT DRIVE FROM the jail to the courthouse. Billy Hamlin gazed out of the rear window of the prison van.

He was excited, and not just because he was about to go free.

In an hour, I'll see Toni again. She'll be so happy to see me. So grateful. When it's all over I'll ask her to marry me.

He wondered if she would look different. If she'd cut her hair since the summer, maybe, or lost any weight. Not that she needed to. Toni Gilletti was perfect as she was.

She'd written him one short note while he was in prison awaiting trial. Billy had hoped for more letters, but Toni had kind of hinted that her folks were all over her and it was hard to make contact. She was especially nervous about putting anything in writing. Billy could understand that.

It doesn't matter anyway. Soon this nightmare will be over and we can start our lives together.

Although he was shocked when murder charges were brought against him, Billy didn't regret what he'd done. There was no danger of him actually going to jail, whereas if Toni had been on trial, with her prior record, anything could have happened. He knew he'd had some bad press—he hadn't seen a TV in months but one of the prison guards had showed him the *Newsweek* piece—but unlike his father, Billy wasn't overly concerned about his reputation.

Once the trial's over, people will forget. Besides, once they see what I'm really like, they'll realize I'm not the monster they thought I was.

He had youth on his side, and innocence, and the love of a truly extraordinary woman. One day he and Toni would

44

look back on this time and roll their eyes at the madness of it all.

The prison van rattled on.

BILLY HAMLIN'S TRIAL WAS TO TAKE place at the York County Courthouse in downtown Alfred. Superior-court judge Devon Williams would be presiding in Court Two, an elegant room at the front of the colonial-style building, with old-fashioned casement windows, wooden benches, and an original 1890s parquet floor, polished daily to an ice-rink-like sheen. The York County Courthouse represented all that was good and decent and traditional and ordered about this most conservative of states. Yet within its walls, all facets of human misery had come crawling. Grief. Corruption. Violence. Hatred. Despair. Behind the pleasant, white-pillared facade of the York County Courthouse, lives had been restored and destroyed, hopes fulfilled and crushed. Justice had been served. And in some cases, denied.

Toni Gilletti arrived at the courthouse flanked by her parents. A large crowd of spectators and reporters had gathered outside the court.

"Look at all those people," Toni whispered nervously to her mother. "Every hotel in Alfred must be full."

Sandra Gilletti smoothed down her fitted Dior skirt and smiled for photographers as the family entered the building. She was *so* glad she'd decided to go couture after all. Walter had worried it might be too much, but with the NBC news cameras trained directly on her, Sandra would simply have died if she'd worn something frumpy from a local department store.

"Well, the case *has* generated a lot of interest," she whispered back to Toni.

The way dog shit interests flies, Toni thought bitterly.

Her anger masked her fear. The prosecution had called her as a witness. She'd received the notice only a few days ago, much to her father's annoyance.

"Can't you get her out of it?" Walter Gilletti asked Lawrence McGee, the expensive Manhattan attorney he'd hired to advise them. "It's such short notice. She's had no time to prepare."

Lawrence McGee explained that Toni wasn't supposed to prepare. "All she has to do is stand up there and tell the truth. No one's contesting her evidence. Toni's police statement and Hamlin's tally exactly."

But of course, Lawrence McGee didn't *know* the truth. Nor did the police, or Toni's parents, or anyone except Toni herself and Billy. What if Billy changed his story under oath? What if his lawyer cross-examined her on the stand and bullied the truth out of her? Did Billy even know that the prosecution had called her as a witness? Would he hate her for testifying against him, for going along with the lie, or was that what he wanted? The mere thought of seeing his face again made Toni's heart race and her palms sweat, and not in a good way. She hadn't felt this frightened since Graydon Hammond had looked up at her with tears in his eyes and blubbered, "Nicholas has gone."

"Ooo, look. Those must be the parents." Sandra Gilletti sounded excited, like someone spotting at a celebrity wedding.

Toni spun around. She felt like she'd been stung. She'd seen pictures of the Handemeyers before, on the TV news, but nothing had prepared her for the reality. Ruth Handemeyer, Nicholas's mother, looked so like her son it was agonizing. She had the same butterscotch-blond coloring, the same saucerlike brown eyes. Except that where Nicholas's eyes had been playful and dancing, his mother's were glazed

46

and deadened with grief. Toni couldn't take her eyes off Ruth Handemeyer as she made her dignified way to her seat, escorted by her husband and daughter.

Senator Handemeyer was older than his wife, in his early fifties, with close-cropped gray hair and a face that looked as if it had been chiseled out of granite. Rage blazed out of his dark blue eyes, but it was a controlled rage, a determined rage, the rage of a powerful, intelligent man. Not for Senator Handemeyer the wild, impotent roaring of the wounded tiger. This was a man hell-bent on vengeance, a man who had set out methodically to bring those responsible for his son's death to justice. Surveying the courtroom as if he owned it, Senator Handemeyer fixed his gaze briefly on Leslie Lose, Billy's lawyer. Ruffled, the attorney looked away. Next, to Toni's horror, the senator caught her eye. She stared back at him like a statue, her stomach liquefied with fear.

Can he see the guilt in my eyes?

Can he guess the truth?

But when Billy Hamlin walked into the dock, all the senator's attention focused on him in a wave of such pure hatred, there was no room for anything, or anyone, else.

If Billy was unnerved by the senator's withering gaze, he didn't show it. Instead, scouring the room for Toni's face, he saw her and smiled broadly. It was the same boyish, open smile Toni remembered from camp. She smiled back, buoyed by his obvious confidence.

This is a court of law, Toni reassured herself. *Senator Handemeyer has a right to his grief, but Billy didn't murder anyone. The jury will see that.*

LESLIE LOSE FIDDLED NERVOUSLY WITH HIS gold cuff links. His client should not be smiling at the pretty prosecution witness like a lovesick puppy. Come to think of it, his client should not be smiling at all. A little boy had drowned. Guilty or not, Billy Hamlin ought to look as if he took that seriously.

Out of the corner of his eye, Leslie Lose saw Senator Handemeyer's broad shoulders tighten. His entire body was coiled like a spring, ready to wreak destruction on Billy Hamlin and, presumably, anyone who dared to help him.

For the first time since he'd taken the case, Leslie Lose began to wonder if he was out of his depth.

"All rise."

The proceedings got under way in what seemed to Toni like record speed. No sooner had both sides made their opening arguments than she found herself on the stand, being sworn in.

"Miss Gilletti, you were on the beach with the defendant on the afternoon in question. Did William Hamlin seem distracted to you?"

"I . . . I don't know. I don't remember."

She was so nervous, her teeth began to chatter. The entire room was looking at her. Terrified of accidentally making eye contact with Senator Handemeyer, or with Billy, she stared fixedly at the floor.

"You don't remember?"

Of course I remember. I remember everything. The rowing boat, Charles nearly killing those boys, Billy diving for pearls, disappearing under the water. I remember everything except Nicholas, because I wasn't watching. It was me! I let him die!

"No."

"Other witnesses have confirmed that William Hamlin was repeatedly diving for oysters that afternoon. That he was showing off for your benefit. Do you remember that?"

48

Toni looked down at her clasped hands. "I remember him diving. Yes."

"Despite being in sole charge of a group of young boys at the time?"

Toni mumbled something incoherent.

"Speak up, please, Miss Gilletti. You had originally been charged with taking the boys swimming that day. But you arranged to swap shifts with the defendant. Is that correct?"

No! Billy wasn't in charge. I was. It was my fault.

"Yes. That's correct."

"May I ask why?"

Toni looked up, panicked. Without thinking, she looked to Billy, as if asking for his help. *What should I say?*

"I'm sorry." She flushed red. "Why what?"

"Why did you agree to swap shifts, Miss Gilletti?"

For a horrible moment Toni's mind went blank. "Because . . ."

The word hung in the air, like a swinging corpse. The silence that followed felt endless. But at last Toni blurted out, "Because I was tired. I hadn't slept well the night before and I . . . I didn't want to take the boys when I wasn't a hundred percent focused."

She looked up at Billy again, who gave her an imperceptible nod. *Well done. Good answer.*

"Thank you, Miss Gilletti. Nothing further for now."

THE PROSECUTION'S CASE WORE ON. BILLY tuned in here and there, but mostly he just gazed at Toni.

She's even more beautiful than I remember her. We'll move to the West Coast after the trial. Start again, somewhere fresh.

He wished he could talk to her, tell her not to be afraid, that it was all going to be okay. The poor girl looked terrified, as if he were about to be led out to face a firing squad. It touched him that she cared so much. But there was really no need.

Billy knew he was going to be acquitted. Leslie, his lawyer, had told him so a thousand times. At the end of the day it didn't matter whether he or Toni had been watching Nicholas. What happened was an accident. Nobody murdered anybody. It was a mistake, a dreadful, tragic mistake.

The one thing that bothered him slightly was the number of witnesses who testified about his drug use. Yes, he smoked the odd joint and occasionally snorted a line or two of blow. But the "experts" on the stand made him out to be some sort of rampant addict, and Leslie didn't challenge their allegations.

Jeff Hamlin had the same concern. He took his son's attorney aside at the first recess.

"That drug counselor guy made Billy sound like a junkie. Why didn't you say anything?"

"Because the drugs are a distraction, Mr. Hamlin. A sideshow. We don't want to get drawn into that."

"Well, the jury was sure as hell being drawn in. Did you see the look on the foreman's face?" Jeff Hamlin protested. "And the middle-aged woman at the back? She looked like she wanted to string Billy up right here in the courtroom."

"Billy's drug use or otherwise has no bearing on the case."

"The prosecution obviously thinks it has some bearing."

"That's because they have no case," Leslie Lose said confidently. "A fact I will abundantly prove tomorrow when we start Billy's defense. Please try not to worry, Mr. Hamlin. I know what I'm doing."

THE PROSECUTION TOOK TWO DAYS TO present its case, which consisted of a thorough hatchet job on Billy Hamlin's character.

Much was made of the toxicology report, and Billy's "substance abuse problems." Still more was made of his promiscuity, with various girls from Camp Williams tearfully admitting under oath to being "seduced" by the charming carpenter's son. Combined with Billy's admission, backed up by Toni Gilletti's evidence, that he had been in charge of the boys that day, the consensus was that the district attorney's office had done enough to prove involuntary manslaughter. But for second-degree murder, they needed more. They needed negligence on a gross scale, and they needed malice.

"THE DEFENSE CALLS CHARLES BRAEMAR MURPHY."

Billy shot his attorney a puzzled look. *Had they discussed this?* Charles had never exactly been Billy's biggest fan.

"Mr. Braemar Murphy, you were present at the beach on the afternoon that Nicholas Handemeyer died, were you not?"

"I was." Charles nodded seriously. In an immaculately cut Halston suit and pale yellow silk tie, with his dark hair neatly parted to the side and a Groton class ring glittering on his little finger, he looked handsome, sober, and conservative—everything that the jury had been led to believe that Billy Hamlin was not.

"Tell us what you remember."

Charles took a deep breath. "I'd been on my parents' yacht for the day. I'm afraid I'd had a couple of glasses of wine, but I took one of the tenders over to the beach anyway, which was a stupid thing to do."

Toni watched the faces of the jurors, who were all listening intently. It was astonishing how forgiving they seemed to be of Charles's self-confessed drinking, in contrast to their disgust at Billy's supposed drug taking. Was alcohol just more socially acceptable? Or was it Charles's educated, upper-class manner that won them over?

Charles went on. "I was going at quite a clip, when I suddenly saw a rowboat directly in front of me, out in the shipping lanes. I swerved to avoid it and that's when I hit Billy. Not head-on, obviously. I'd have killed him. But I clipped him on the shoulder. I wasn't expecting to see a swimmer so far out."

"Where were the children at this point?"

"On the beach, playing," Charles said firmly.

That's odd, Toni thought. *I'm amazed he even noticed the boys from that distance and after the shock of what happened out in the lanes.*

"Was Nicholas Handemeyer with them?"

"I think so. Yes. There were seven boys, so he must have been."

A surprised murmur ran through the court. The Handemeyer parents exchanged distressed glances. Nicholas's elder sister, a pretty, dark-haired girl in her early teens, gripped her mother's hand. If Nicholas was safe and alive so late in the afternoon, whatever happened to him must have happened very quickly. Moreover, it probably happened when Billy Hamlin was on the beach, receiving medical attention. A mitigating circumstance if ever there was one.

"So your memory is that the children had been safe while in Billy Hamlin's care that day, until Billy himself was injured by your speedboat."

"Yes."

"Thank you, Mr. Braemar Murphy. No further questions."

It was all Jeff Hamlin could do not to punch the air in triumph. Good old Leslie knew what he was doing after all.

*

"A COUPLE OF QUESTIONS, MR. BRAEMAR Murphy." The prosecutor was on his feet. "I understand that you and Miss Gilletti were dating at the time of these events. Is that correct?"

"It is." Charles sounded perplexed. The question hardly seemed relevant.

"Other counselors at Camp Williams have testified that Miss Gilletti and Nicholas Handemeyer had a close bond. Is *that* correct?"

"All the boys adored Toni."

"But Nicholas Handemeyer especially?"

The furrow in Charles's brow deepened. "I guess so, yes. He wrote her these little love poems. It was sweet."

Toni dug her nails into her thigh so violently she drew blood. She did not want to think about Nicholas's poems, scrawled on slips of paper and pushed hopefully under her cabin door. Her heart might shatter.

"Mr. Braemar Murphy, did you consider William Hamlin to be your rival for Miss Gilletti's affections?"

"I'm sorry?"

"Were you concerned that Mr. Hamlin was attracted to your girlfriend?"

"Not concerned, exactly, no."

"Really? You knew the two of them had slept together?"

A disapproving murmur rippled through the court.

"Yes. But it was a one-night stand. It didn't mean anything."

From the dock, Billy Hamlin glared at Charles murderously. How dare the smug bastard say that what he and Toni had meant nothing? His fists were clenched and he looked fit to burst, but he managed to contain himself.

"So you weren't worried?" the prosecutor continued.

"No."

"Not even after Billy Hamlin made threats against your life?"

The jury jerked to life as if awoken from a deep slumber. Toni Gilletti sat bolt upright. From the dock, Billy glanced anxiously at his father.

"Several other Camp Williams counselors have given statements that the night before Nicholas Handemeyer's death, Billy Hamlin was vocally declaring his love for Miss Gilletti at a camp party and threatening to, quote, annihilate, unquote anyone who dared come between them. Wouldn't that include you?"

"Billy didn't mean that," said Charles. "He was high."

"Indeed." The prosecutor paused meaningfully. "As the court has heard. But I put it to you, Mr. Braemar Murphy, that Mr. Hamlin *did* mean it. I put it to you that William Hamlin was wildly, violently jealous of anyone whom Miss Gilletti loved. That his drug use merely unleashed feelings of rage and obsession that, in his more sober moments, he managed to keep hidden."

Belatedly, Leslie Lose got to his feet. "Objection! Conjecture."

The judge waved him away. Like the rest of the room, he wanted to see where this was going.

"I'll allow it."

The prosecutor continued. "I put it to you that Mr. Hamlin's violent jealousy was such that he even resented the affection shown to Miss Gilletti by a small boy."

A look of pain crossed Charles Braemar Murphy's face. Then, to Toni's astonishment, he said. "That may be true."

What? Of course it isn't true!

"Billy may have resented Nicholas."

"Indeed he may have! In William Hamlin's paranoid,

54

drug-warped mind, Nicholas Handemeyer wasn't an inno-cent, seven-year-old child at all, was he? He was a threat. Just like you."

"Maybe." Charles shook his head, as if willing it not to be so.

"A threat that needed to be disposed of. Neutralized. Annihilated."

"I hope not." Charles shuddered, as if the idea had never occurred to him. "Good God, I hope not."

Bastard! Toni thought. *Billy would never have hurt Nicholas and Charles knows it. He's just trying to get back at Billy for coming on to me.*

"Billy's a good guy." Charles twisted the knife. "But he was out of his depth at Camp Williams."

"In what way?"

"In every way. Socially, economically, educationally. The truth is, I felt sorry for him. We all did. He couldn't stand the fact that Toni chose me over him."

This was too much for Billy.

"Liar!" he shouted, jumping to his feet. His face was red with anger and the veins on his forehead and neck protruded as if they were about to explode. "Toni loves me, and I love her!"

The jury was not impressed. Billy looked like a madman, his hair a mess, arms gesticulating wildly, the flames of his obsession with Toni burning in his eyes. Toni felt like crying. Charles had provoked him, and Billy had fallen right into his trap. Worse, his lawyer had fallen with him.

"And that's *without* drugs in his system," the prosecutor said, sotto voce, accurately voicing the jurors' thoughts. "Thank you, Mr. Braemar Murphy. No further questions."

*

THE NEXT TWO DAYS WERE ABOUT damage control.

Leslie Lose wheeled out various witnesses from Billy's former life to attest to his good character: teachers, coaches, neighbors. The consensus was that the Billy Hamlin they knew would not knowingly have hurt a fly.

Jeff Hamlin pleaded to be allowed to take the stand, but Leslie Lose wouldn't allow it.

"You're too emotional. It won't help."

"Then let Billy speak for himself. He needs a chance to show people what he's really like."

That had been the original plan—for Billy to be his own secret weapon, for his affable charm and natural humility to change hearts and minds. But after Charles Braemar Murphy's evidence, that ship hadn't so much sailed as sunk without trace.

"The less Billy says the better," said Leslie. "From now on we focus on facts."

The facts were still in Billy's favor.

Had Billy Hamlin been negligent in taking his eye off a seven-year-old boy at the beach? Yes, he had.

Was he wrong to have used drugs and alcohol while working as a camp counselor responsible for young children?

Of course he was.

But had William Hamlin *murdered* Nicholas Handemeyer? Had he willfully caused the boy's death? Notwithstanding his disastrous outburst of jealous rage earlier, there was no proof that he had. There wasn't even any compelling evidence to suggest it.

Leslie Lose finished his summing-up with the words:

"Billy Hamlin isn't a murderer. Nor is he a monster. He's a normal teenage boy and a loving son. Let's not allow one family's tragedy to become two."

As he sat down, the lawyer was aware of Senator

Handemeyer staring at him. His skin prickled uncomfortably beneath his wool suit.

He prayed it was enough.

THE COURT ADJOURNED FOR THE NIGHT. Walter Gilletti spoke to his attorney outside the courtroom.

"What do you think?"

"Acquittal. No question. He didn't help himself with his outburst, but the prosecution hasn't proved a thing."

Listening in from a few feet away, Toni exhaled with relief. Her father's attorney was the best money could buy. Billy would be a free man by tomorrow. Of course, once he got out she'd have to talk to him about this marriage nonsense. Toni was fond of Billy and she owed him a lot, but matrimony was distinctly not on her agenda. Still, these would be good problems to have.

Her father was still talking.

"Good." Walter Gilletti's voice reverberated with authority. "If it's a done deal then I'd like to leave tonight. The sooner we're out of this circus the better."

"I can't leave, Daddy," Toni blurted. "I have to stay for the verdict. Billy needs me here."

Walter Gilletti turned on his daughter like a snake about to strike. "I don't give a damn what Billy Hamlin needs. We go when I say we go," he snarled.

IN THE END, THE GILLETTIS STAYED another night in Alfred.

On balance, Walter Gilletti decided it might look bad for business if they didn't.

CHAPTER SEVEN

S UPERIOR-COURT JUSTICE DEVON WILLIAMS TOOK HIS seat, surveying the sea of faces in front of him. A big man in his early seventies with a neatly clipped white beard and a snowy ring of hair around the tonsurelike bald spot on the crown of his head, Judge Williams had presided over many difficult cases. Thefts. Assaults. Arson. Murders. But few were as harrowing as this one. Or, in the end, as futile.

Nicholas Handemeyer's death was a tragedy. But it was plain to Judge Williams that no murder had been committed. Here, clearly, was an example of a case where public hysteria and outrage, fueled by one family's private grief, had gotten the better of common sense. Senator Handemeyer wanted heads to roll—the Hamlin boy's head in particular—and truth be damned. Once the emotion was stripped away, however, what mattered in this case—in every case—was the law. And the law was clear: if Billy Hamlin was guilty of murder, Judge Devon Williams was a monkey's uncle.

Of course, the law could not be taken in the abstract. It must be interpreted by the twelve men and women of the jury. Judge Williams watched them now as they filed back into court two. Ordinary men and women: ten white, two black, mostly middle-aged, mostly overweight, a snapshot of the great American public. And yet today these ordinary people bore an extraordinary responsibility.

Normally Judge Williams enjoyed the challenge of predicting a jury's verdict. How would *this* juror respond to *that* witness, or *that* piece of evidence. Who would react emotionally and who rationally. Whose prejudices or personality would carry the day. But as he called on the foreman to address the court, he felt none of the usual excitement or tension, only sadness.

A little boy had died. Nothing could bring him back. And now the unedifying spectacle of a murder trial that should never have made it to court was about to come to an end. It was obvious which way the coin would fall.

"Have you reached a verdict?"

"We have, your honor."

RUTH HANDEMEYER SQUEEZED HER DAUGHTER'S HAND. She was so tense she was barely breathing. Beside her she could feel her husband's anger and hatred coiled inside him like a spring. She had no idea how to defuse it, or what to say to comfort him. Since Nicko's death, they'd become strangers, separated by an ocean of grief.

The teenage girl squeezed back.

"Whatever happens, Mommy, we'll always love him."

Ruth Handemeyer stifled a sob.

JEFF HAMLIN LOOKED TO HIS RIGHT. Leslie Lose gave him an encouraging smile.

It's going to be okay, Jeff told himself for the hundredth time. He blamed himself for sending Billy to Camp Williams in the first place. How foolish he'd been, thinking his son would be able to make connections there to better himself! When the chips were down, the rich, educated classes stuck together. Old Mrs. Kramer, the Gilletti girl's family, even the Handemeyers, were all birds of a feather, looking for a sacrificial lamb to atone for a child's death. And who better than a carpenter's son?

Billy's in that dock because he's not one of them.

FROM THE DOCK, BILLY HAMLIN LOOKED at Toni Gilletti with eyes full of love.

Tonight he would be a free man.

Tonight it would all begin.

TONI'S STOMACH WAS CHURNING. SHE FELT guilty thinking it, after everything Billy had done for her, but the way he looked at her was starting to creep her out.

I have to talk to him right away. I can't let him leave here thinking we have a future together.

Whatever Toni Gilletti had once found attractive and exciting about Billy Hamlin had died along with poor Nicholas Handemeyer. From now on Toni would always associate Billy with that day. With terror and anguish. With tragedy and regret. With blood and with water. With death.

There could be no going back.

JUDGE DEVON WILLIAMS'S POWERFUL BARITONE CUT through the tension in the room like a power drill.

"And on the charge of second-degree murder, how do you find the defendant?"

Billy Hamlin closed his eyes. It was over at last.

"Guilty."

CHAPTER EIGHT

TONI RAN DOWN THE CORRIDOR, QUICKENING her pace. Her father was yelling at her to come back, but she didn't listen.

I have to see Billy. I have to tell him I'm sorry.

How had the jury found him guilty? It was impossible, ridiculous. The judge had clearly thought so too. You could see it in his eyes when he passed sentence: twenty years, with parole at fifteen, the minimum allowed for second-degree murder but still a lifetime.

"Sorry, miss." A court officer blocked her path to the holding cell. "Official visitors only."

"But he needs to see me!"

"Like hell he does."

Before Toni knew what was happening, Billy's father had grabbed her by the shoulders, throwing her back against the wall so hard she felt the breath leave her body.

"It was you, wasn't it? It was you! You let my boy take the fall for you, you rich, spoiled little bitch."

"Take your hands off my daughter."

For once, Toni was glad to see her father. Walter Gilletti was a slight man but he radiated authority.

"I understand you're upset," he told Jeff Hamlin. "But Toni had nothing to do with this."

"Yeah, right." Jeff Hamlin backed away with tears in his eyes. "Your daughter's shit don't stink. They gave my Billy twenty years. Twenty *years*!"

Walter Gilletti shrugged. "If he keeps his nose clean, he'll be out in fifteen."

The rich man's nonchalance was the last straw for Jeff Hamlin. Launching himself at Walter Gilletti with a mighty roar, he lashed out wildly with his fists as the policeman tried vainly to pry the two men apart. Seizing her chance, Toni bolted down the stairs toward the holding cell, but within seconds, another cop grabbed her.

"What the hell do you think you're doing, young lady? You can't just barge down here without authorization."

"It's all right, Frank. The boy asked to see her."

Leslie Lose seemed to have appeared out of nowhere. He looked white-faced and serious. Clearly the verdict had shocked him too.

Reluctantly, the guard stepped aside.

"Thank you," Toni said to Billy's lawyer.

"Please. It's the least I can do."

"It wasn't your fault, you know."

"Yes it was," Lose said quietly.

BILLY LIT UP WHEN TONI WALKED in.

"Thank God. I thought they might not let you come."

There she was. His Toni. His Helen of Troy. In a plain, knee-length shift dress in cream silk, teamed with low, kitten heels and a cashmere cardigan, she looked older than he remembered her. The outfit screamed rich (which she was) and demure (which she certainly wasn't). But nothing could hide the raw sensuality of the body beneath.

Billy moved toward her, drawn like a magnet to a piece of metal, or a helpless moth to the moon. "Hi."

Toni hugged him, squeezing tight as hot tears of guilt splashed onto his collar and trickled down his neck. "I'm so sorry, Billy."

"For what?" Billy forced a smile, determined to be brave in front of her. "This was my decision, not yours. And if I had the time over, I'd do it again, in a heartbeat."

"But Billy. Twenty *years*."

"Fifteen," he corrected her. "With parole."

"But you didn't do anything wrong."

"Neither did you."

"Billy, come *on*. I did. You know I did. We both know. Nicholas was in my group."

"It was an accident, Toni. An accident. Never forget that." Inhaling the scent of her skin, mingled with some faint lemony perfume, he felt overwhelmed with need for her. Despite his show of bravado, he was frightened. Frightened of jail, of a future without her. Desperately he pulled her closer, kissing her passionately, forcing his tongue into her mouth like a starving chick looking for food.

Toni recoiled. His breath was sour with fear.

"Come on." She tried to laugh it off. "This isn't the time."

"I think you'll find it's the only time we've got. They'll be taking me away in a minute."

"Do you know where?"

"The state prison, for the time being at least. It's in Warren, wherever the fuck that is." Billy laughed, but there was no joy in the sound. "My lawyer said he's gonna try to get me moved. It's a long way for my dad to come visit."

"Sure." Toni nodded lamely. If she were in jail rather than Billy, as she should be, would her dad even bother to come visit her? *I doubt it.* But she hadn't come here to talk about their respective fathers. She had to tell Billy the truth. To break things off between them. Under the circumstances she didn't know where to begin.

"Look, Billy," she started nervously. "I owe you so much I really don't know what to say."

"How about yes?"

He was looking at her with those puppy-dog eyes again. As if this were a movie, or a play, and any minute now they were about to walk offstage and go back to reality. And Nicholas would be alive and Billy wouldn't be going to prison and they would all live happily ever after.

Oh, Jesus. Toni's heart sank. *Is he getting down on one knee?*

"Say you'll marry me, Toni. Say you'll wait."

Toni opened her mouth to speak but he interrupted her.

"I know what you're thinking. But it might not be fifteen years. Leslie's gonna appeal. We might even get a mistrial."

"On what grounds?"

"I don't know."

For the first time since the day Nicholas died, Toni saw Billy Hamlin's facade of bravado and manly strength slip away. Looking into his eyes now, she saw a terrified kid. Scared. Alone. Out of his depth, just like she was.

"But Leslie says it's possible and I could be out in a couple of years. Then we could get married and . . . things."

He stopped talking suddenly. Could he read in her face how horrified she was? Belatedly, Toni tried to look the part of the devoted girlfriend. If Billy needed a fantasy to hold on to, something to get him through the nightmare of a life in jail, didn't she owe him that much at least?

"Please, Toni." The distress in his eyes was unbearable. "Please say yes."

Before she could stop herself, the words tumbled out. "Yes. I mean, of course. Of course yes! I wasn't expecting a proposal right this minute, that's all. But of course I'll marry you, Billy."

"As soon as I get out?"

"As soon as you get out."

Billy burst into racking sobs of relief. "I love you so much, Toni." Pulling her close again, he clutched her to his chest like a child with a teddy bear.

The guards arrived. "Time to go."

"I know it's gonna sound crazy," Billy whispered in Toni's ear, "but I mean it. This is the happiest day of my life. Thank you."

"Mine too," Toni assured him. "Be strong," she added as he was led away.

Toni Gilletti waited till the cell door closed behind him. Then she sank down onto her chair and wept.

She knew she would never see Billy Hamlin again.

THREE DAYS AFTER THE VERDICT, LESLIE Lose flew to Washington. He arrived at the secure underground parking garage at nine-fifteen at night, the agreed time.

He'd half expected his client to send a courier, someone anonymous to complete the transaction. Instead, slightly to Leslie's surprise, the client showed up himself. He was an important man, and his presence made Leslie feel important.

"Two hundred thousand. As agreed." Rolling down the smoked-glass window of his Lincoln Town Car, he handed Leslie a fat stuffed envelope. "You cut it fine."

"I knew what I was doing. It's all about knowing your jurors. Let's just say I knew mine *very* well."

"Clearly. I was sure they were going to acquit. But you pulled it off."

Leslie smiled, wrapping his sausagelike hands around the package greedily.

"You should have had more faith, Senator."

Senator Handemeyer smiled. "Perhaps I should have, Mr. Lose. Perhaps I should have."

Billy Hamlin's attorney watched in the dark as the Lincoln drove away.

PART II

CHAPTER NINE

"OH, MICHAEL! OH, MICHAEL, I LUF you, I luf you so much! Please don't stop!"

From his uncomfortable position in the backseat of his vintage MG convertible, Michael De Vere wondered, *Why do women say that? "Don't stop." Surely no one would stop at this particular juncture? Although presumably some men must; otherwise girls wouldn't bother to say it, would they?* As Michael's mind wandered, so his erection began to wilt. But once started, he couldn't seem to stop. What did Lenka, his latest conquest, think he was about to do? Whip out the *Racing Post* and start looking through the runners and riders for the four-fifteen at Wincanton? And if he *was* going to do that, what made her think that shouting "Don't stop" was likely to change his mind?

"You stopped." Lenka's voice trembled with reproach.

"Paused, darling. I paused."

It was four-fifteen on a glorious May afternoon and Michael De Vere was late. He was supposed to have dropped

Lenka at Didcot railway station an hour ago. But what with the sunshine and the blossoms bursting out of the hedgerows, and Lenka's impossibly short Marc Jacobs miniskirt riding up her smooth, brown thighs, one thing had led to another. Or rather, one thing had led almost to another.

Lenka pouted. "You don't find me attractive?"

"Darling, of course I do."

"You don't luf me."

Michael De Vere sighed. Clearly he was not going to be able to resume play. Pulling up his jeans, he started the engine.

"Lenka, you're an angel, you know you are. But if I'm late for Mother's dinner tonight, she'll be serving my balls deep-fried for pudding. I'm afraid that's what's putting me off."

The girl glared at him. "You lie! You are ashamed of me, this is the problem. You are embarrassed to introduce me to your mother."

"Nonsense, darling," lied Michael, glancing appreciatively at Lenka's underwear-exposing skirt and enormous silicone breasts bouncing happily beneath the skimpiest of PETA shirts. "Mother would adore you." *You'd be right up there with anthrax and Che Guevara.* "I simply don't think tonight's the right moment to introduce you, that's all."

TEN MINUTES LATER, WAVING LENKA OFF from the platform, Michael De Vere breathed a sigh of relief and cheerfully deleted her contacts from his cell phone.

Sexy, but way too high maintenance.

Michael had enough stress to contend with, what with his mother being appointed home secretary the very same week that he had decided to quit Oxford. Not just decided.

Actually done it. This morning Michael had gone to his tutor, signed the relevant forms, and packed up his gorgeous rooms in Chapel Quad, never to return. He planned to break the happy news to his parents over dinner tonight.

Naturally they would both have a fit, not least because his mother's new job meant that this was now a story. HOME SECRETARY'S SON FLEES BALLIOL TO BECOME PROFESSIONAL PARTY ANIMAL. The *Daily Mail* always used words like "*flee*." They were such arses. Michael felt bad about the inevitable negative coverage, but it couldn't be helped. He'd set up an events company last year with his best friend, Tommy Lyon, and the pair of them were printing money. The future was bright, and Michael De Vere could smell success from here. This was no time to be messing around analyzing T. S. Eliot.

Ironically, his mother's wrath would probably be as nothing compared to his father's. Teddy De Vere was a Balliol man himself, just as his father and grandfather and great-grandfather had been before him. Short of desecrating his grandmother's grave, or announcing he was gay, or (*unimaginable*) that he'd joined the Labour Party, in his father's eyes there was no worse crime that Michael De Vere could have committed than dropping out of Oxford.

Yes, tonight's dinner would be tricky enough, even without Lenka's histrionics. The only silver lining in the whole ghastly business was that Michael's sister, Roxie, would be there to support him.

"LAST CARD."

Teddy De Vere slammed the nine of clubs down onto the green baize card table with a theatrical flourish. It was a family joke that Teddy never won at cards, or indeed at anything: Monopoly, Pictionary, charades. You name it, Teddy lost at it, repeatedly and often quite spectacularly. As chief financial officer for a successful City hedge fund, not to mention a respected Oxford-educated historian, Teddy De Vere was no fool. But he played the fool to perfection at home, delighting in his role as the butt of family jokes, a sort of willingly tamed circus bear.

As usual, his daughter, Roxie, had gone out of her way this evening to give him an advantage in their predinner game of Oh Hell. For once, Teddy seemed genuinely to be winning.

"Oh, very good, Dad." Roxie smiled encouragingly. "All you need now's a two."

She placed the two of clubs gently on top of Teddy's nine.

Teddy frowned. "Hmm. Well, I haven't got a two, have I?"

"Then you have to pick up two, Daddy."

"Blast it."

"Last card."

"Now hold on just a minute . . ."

Roxie played the jack of clubs and sat back, triumphant. "I'm out."

Teddy's face was such a picture of outrage, she couldn't help but laugh.

"Oh, darling Dad, never mind. Maybe you'll win the next one."

Father and daughter were sitting in the library at Kingsmere, the De Veres' ancestral pile in North Oxfordshire. Since Roxie's "accident," her bedroom had been moved to the ground floor, with Teddy's old study converted into an en suite bathroom. As a result, the formal drawing room was now upstairs overlooking the deer park. But the library, a cozy, red-walled room with dark leather Chesterfield sofas, hunting paintings on the walls, and dog baskets nestled by the permanently crackling fire, remained exactly as it had always been. Roxie loved the room for that, for not changing. She loved it most of all when her father was in it.

"How about a nice, dry sherry before dinner." Teddy leaned back in his chair and stretched out his legs. He wore the same deep purple corduroy pants every evening, winter or summer, rain or shine. He had about a hundred pairs of them upstairs in his dressing room. To Roxie, everything about her father suggested familiarity and ritual, a comforting sameness in a bleakly changing world. "Your mother'll be home in a minute."

Roxie didn't need reminding. Turning her wheelchair around, she pushed herself over to the bar to fix Teddy's drink. Roxie rarely drank before dinner but tonight she made an exception, splashing the pale amber Manzanilla into two tumblers instead of the usual one. Mummy was bound to be unbearable tonight, gloating and full of herself after her big victory. *Home secretary.* The words stuck in Roxie's throat. How had her mother managed it? Why could others not see through Alexia the way that she, Roxie, could? Her mother would be the triumphant star of her own show at dinner, smug and unbearable. But then wasn't she always?

There had been a time, long, long ago, when Roxanne De Vere had loved her mother. Yes, Alexia had always been ambitious, self-contained, and distant in a way that other little girls' mothers were not. But even so, Roxie remembered happy times. Long summers spent on the beach together in Martha's Vineyard, eating picnic lunches and playing fairies-and-elves. Christmases at Kingsmere, with Alexia lifting Roxie up high to hang hideous, garish homemade decorations on the tree. She remembered wheelbarrow races in the garden, and—incongruously, for Alexia was a notoriously awful cook—making blackberry jam.

But then came Roxie's teenage years, and everything changed. From the first, mother and daughter battled. They battled about everything from politics to music, from fashion to religion, from which books they liked to the color of Roxie's hair. On the surface it was normal coming-of-age stuff. But over time, Roxie began to sense a deeper rift, something more disturbing.

Alexia, always considered a great beauty in her youth, seemed to become envious of her daughter's burgeoning good looks. Roxie couldn't pinpoint it exactly. It was hard to remember specific incidents, as Michael was forever asking her to when he leaped to their mother's defense. Nevertheless, Roxie developed a strong sense of her mother's resentment. She felt Alexia's eyes on her when she came out to the pool in a bikini, a gaze that blazed with a heat that was not admiration but rather a caustic, acid burn of envy on Roxie's skin. When Roxie started bringing boys home, things went from bad to worse. Alexia seemed to go out of her way to humiliate her, putting her down during family meals, or worse, taking over the conversation and ensuring that she, the great Alexia De Vere, was the center of attention at all times. She would grill Roxie's boyfriends about everything from their family backgrounds to their career ambitions—*God, she was such a snob!* No one was ever good enough.

Roxie's father, on the other hand, took a very laissez-faire attitude toward his daughter's dating. Naturally this drove Alexia to distraction.

"Can't you say something, Teddy?" she used to roar. "I know you don't approve. Why do I always have to be bad cop?"

But Teddy steadfastly refused to get involved, doing the best he could to keep the peace.

Until the day Roxanne De Vere met Andrew Beesley and everything changed.

ANDREW BEESLEY HAD BEEN HIRED AS Roxie's tennis coach.

He became the love of her life.

Roxie had loved Andrew deeply and passionately, but her mother was determined to destroy her happiness. Deeming Andrew unworthy and a gold digger, Alexia ruthlessly drove him away. Teddy, loving but weak in the face of his wife's determination, had failed to stand up to her. When Andrew returned to Australia, Roxie's heart shattered. In despair, she jumped from her bedroom window at Kingsmere, a sixty-foot drop that ought to have killed her. Instead, with bitter irony, Roxie survived the fall, only to be confined to a wheelchair for the rest of her life, doomed to remain her parents' dependent. She would never escape her mother, but would live out the remainder of her days a cripple under Alexia's roof.

There was nothing left for her mother to envy now. Alexia De Vere was once again the fairest of them all.

Roxie's accident was never referred to openly at Kingsmere, mostly because Teddy couldn't bear it. Of a different, older generation, Teddy De Vere buried his grief deep, preferring denial to the harsh light of truth.

Roxie could live with that. She loved her father. What she couldn't live with was the fact that her mother had never been punished for what happened. Never suffered, as she should have. Alexia De Vere was still happily married, still professionally successful, still famed for her beauty as well as her brains and, since Roxie's fall, for her resilience in the face of adversity. Actions should have consequences. But instead of suffering, Alexia De Vere sat back while yet more laurels were heaped upon her head. Her surprise appointment as home secretary was just the latest in a long line of unearned glories. It made Roxie sick.

"Cheers." She clinked her glass grimly against Teddy's.

"And to you, my darling. I know you're not looking forward to this evening. But try to keep things civil, for my sake, if not for your mother's. Being asked to be home secretary is a big deal, you know."

"Of course it is, Daddy."

Mummy's triumphs always are.

GILBERT DRAKE FELL TO HIS KNEES in the front pew of the tiny country church and made the sign of the cross.

He was frightened, despite the righteousness of his cause. How could he, one man, a lowly, insignificant taxi driver, deliver just retribution to the most powerful woman in England?

He prayed for courage, and a verse from Deuteronomy came to him, a gift from the Lord.

"Be strong and courageous, do not be afraid or tremble, for the LORD your God is the one who goes with you. He will not fail you or forsake you."

Sanjay Patel had been failed and forsaken. By his friends, by the courts, but most of all by that evil she-devil Alexia De Vere.

Gilbert Drake stayed in the church, praying, until darkness fell. Then he zipped up his hooded jacket and walked into the night.

"FOR WHAT WE ARE ABOUT TO receive, may the Lord make us truly thankful. Amen."

Alexia De Vere listened silently as her husband said grace.

When they had first married, Teddy's insistence on this arcane ritual used to irritate Alexia intensely. Neither of them was particularly religious, so why the pompous, public show of piety? But over time Alexia, like Roxie, had come to take comfort in Teddy's unchanging eccentricities. When the storms of her own life had raged, Alexia De Vere's husband had proved to be the rock she needed, the one, true, solid thing she could cling to. Very few politicians were so lucky.

"Well." Alexia smiled magnanimously around the table. "This all looks lovely. Anna has surpassed herself as usual."

"As have you, my darling." Leaning across the mouth-watering spread of roast beef, fresh tomato-and-basil salad, and home-baked bread, Teddy De Vere kissed his wife proudly on the cheek. "Home secretary! My goodness. I expect this means we'll see even less of you."

"Hopefully," Roxie muttered under her breath.

"You know, brown's really not your shade, darling," Alexia shot back, looking at Roxie's drab Next dress. No one was going to ruin this triumph for her, especially not her spoiled, self-centered daughter. "It makes you look like even more of a wet weekend than you usually do. Try a spot of color, next time. It might brighten you up. God knows you could use it."

Roxie flushed with anger and embarrassment but said nothing.

Eager to avoid further confrontation, Michael De Vere raised his glass.

"Congratulations, Home Secretary!"

Leaning forward, Michael helped himself to a mountain of beef. Bad news should never be broken on an empty stomach.

"Thank you, darling." Alexia beamed at her son. "You are sweet."

"Were you surprised they appointed you? I mean, it did come rather out of the blue."

"Nonsense," Teddy said loyally. "Your mother was the obvious choice for the job. After all her sterling work with the prison reforms."

"You're sweet, darling, but Michael's quite right. It was a complete shock. I mean, the PM and I do get along well on a personal level . . ."

"Yes, yes. As you've told us a thousand times," sniped Roxie, earning herself twin pleading looks from Teddy and Michael.

"But I never expected a promotion on this scale," Alexia went on regardless. "I don't think anybody else did either. It's ruffled quite a few feathers in the party, I can tell you. But then why be boring and play things by the book? You've got to take life's opportunities where you find them. Grab the bull by the horns and all that. And of course, if I can be of service to the country, then so much the better."

This was too much for Roxie. She knew she'd promised her father, but really. *Service?*

"Oh, please, Mother. At least have the decency to admit that this isn't about *service*. It's ambition that got you the job. Personal ambition. We're not journalists, we're your family. You don't have to lie to us, just because you lie to everybody else."

Teddy said reprovingly, "Roxie, love, steady on."

Alexia's chest tightened into a familiar ball of anger. *Steady on?* Was that all Teddy had to say? Why did he never stick up for her properly? Why did he kowtow to Roxie's victim complex by treading on eggshells all the damn time?

The girl used that damn wheelchair like a weapon, and Alexia for one was sick of it.

"Speaking of taking opportunities and grabbing bulls and . . . things," Michael began uncertainly. "I, er . . . I have some news."

"Don't tell us you've finally found a nice girl and are going to get married?" Teddy teased. "I thought we'd agreed. No weddings until you've finished Oxford."

"Don't worry," said Michael. "No weddings. At least none where I'm the groom. But I, er . . . well, that's the news. Part of it, anyway. I *have* finished Oxford."

Complete silence. You could have cut the atmosphere with a knife.

Alexia spoke first.

"What do you mean you've finished, Michael? You've only just started."

Michael looked at his mother plaintively. "Uni's not for me, Mum. Really."

"Not for you? Why on earth not?"

"Honestly? I'm bored."

"*Bored?*" Teddy erupted. "At Balliol? Don't be ridiculous."

Michael plowed on. "You remember Kingsmere Events, the company I started last year with Tommy?"

Tommy Lyon was Michael's oldest friend. The two boys had met at prep school and always remained close.

"Not really."

"Yes, you do. We threw a thirtieth birthday party for that Russian chap on a yacht in Saint-Tropez last summer?"

"Vaguely." Alexia looked at Teddy, whose usually jovial features were set like thunder.

"Well, anyway, we made twenty grand profit from that, just the two of us," Michael said proudly. "And we've had loads of inquiries since then, for corporate events, Bar mitz-vahs."

"Bar mitzvahs!" Teddy De Vere could take no more. "You're a De Vere, for God's sake, and you're halfway through a law degree at Oxford. You can't seriously expect your mother and I to agree to you throwing all that away to book clowns and balloons for thirteen-year-old Jewish boys from Golders bloody Green!"

"Their parents are the clients," said Michael reasonably. "And don't knock Golders Green. Some of these Jewish mothers are dropping half a million on little Samuel's big day."

"Half a million? Pounds?" Even Teddy was brought up short by this number.

"Think of the opportunity, Dad." Michael's merry gray eyes lit up. "Tommy and I can net eighty, a hundred grand in a *night*."

"Yes, and with a first from Balliol and my and your mother's contacts, you could be making tens of millions a year in the City a few years from now. I'm sorry, Michael, but it's just not on."

"Well, *I'm* sorry, Dad, but it's not up to you. I formally left college this morning. Gave in my keys and everything."

"You WHAAAAAAT?" Teddy's screams could be heard all the way to the Kingsmere gatehouse. Roxie tried to intervene and soon the three of them were shouting over one another like rowdy MPs at Prime Minister's Question Time.

Alexia De Vere closed her eyes. First bloody Roxie, getting out her violin again and scratching out the same, bitter old tune. And then Michael, dropping this bombshell. *So much for my celebration dinner.*

It was a relief when Bailey, the butler, tapped her on the shoulder.

"Sorry to interrupt your meal, ma'am. But there's someone at the gates wanting to see you."

Alexia looked at her Cartier watch, an anniversary present from Teddy last year. It was past nine o'clock. "It's rather late for house calls. Who is it?"

"That's the thing. They wouldn't give a name and they were acting, you know, erratically. Jennings wasn't sure what to do."

Alexia put down her napkin. "All right. I'll come."

ALFRED JENNINGS HAD BEEN THE GATEKEEPER at Kingsmere for almost forty years. At seventy years old, partially deaf, and with a weak heart, he was not much of a security guard. Michael had once described Jennings as being "as fierce as a newborn kitten," a phrase that Alexia had always thought summed up old Alfred perfectly. Unfortunately, because she was now home secretary, her security was no longer a laughing matter. Her controversial work as prisons minister had earned her a number of enemies, some of them potentially dangerous, others frankly deranged. Sanjay Patel, an Indian man who had taken his own life in Wormwood Scrubs when his sentence was extended, had a particularly vociferous and unpleasant group of supporters. Alexia De Vere didn't scare easily, but neither could she afford to be cavalier about unexpected "visitors."

The Kingsmere gatehouse consisted of an office-cum-sitting-room downstairs and a single bedroom and bathroom above. Jennings had made it cozy, his plug-in fake coal fire constantly burning.

"I'm so sorry to have bothered you, ma'am," he warbled feebly as Alexia came in. "Especially in the middle of dinner. Fella's gone now."

81

"That's quite all right, Alfred, better safe than sorry. Were the cameras on, by chance?"

"Oh, yes, ma'am." The old man wheezed, pleased to have gotten something right. "They's always on nowadays. Mr. De Vere, he's quite insistent about it. 'You switch them cameras on now, Mr. Jennings,' 'e says. They was on all right."

"Marvelous. Perhaps I could have a look at the tape?"

DINNER WAS OVER. TEDDY HAD STORMED off in a huff and Michael and Roxie were alone in the kitchen, making tea.

"Well," Michael quipped, "that went well, I thought. Dad was his usual calm, rational self."

"What did you expect?" Roxie said reprovingly. She loved her brother dearly. Everybody loved Michael, with his naughty-little-boy charm, his warmth, his humor. It was impossible not to. But it pained her to see their father so upset. "You know how much Balliol means to Daddy."

"Yes, but it's not 'Daddy' who has to be there, is it? It's me."

"It's only two more years."

"I know, Rox, but I'm bored out of my mind. I'm not really a lectures-and-libraries sort of bloke." Michael slumped down on the table with his head in his hands.

"Really? You don't say." Roxie raised a sarcastic eyebrow

"Ha ha. I'm serious. This business with Tommy, I honestly think I can make a go of it. Dad's an entrepreneur."

"Hardly."

"All right, well, he's a businessman at least. Surely there must be part of him that understands?"

"It's not that he doesn't understand. He doesn't want you to make a mistake, that's all."

"Yeah, well, I'm not. Mum gets it. Even though the press are bound to give her stick about it, she knows I have to find my own way."

"Alexia thinks the sun shines out of your arse and always has," Roxie said coldly. "She'd support you if you said you were off to join a Muslim Brotherhood training camp in the Kashmir mountains."

Michael frowned. He hated it when his sister called their mother by her first name. The rift between mother and daughter was obvious enough, but somehow that little verbal tic seemed to underscore it.

"She loves us both, Rox."

Roxie rolled her eyes.

"She does."

"Well, she has a funny way of showing it."

TEDDY FOUND ALEXIA IN HER STUDY. Sitting at the desk, an empty water glass in front of her, she was staring into space, twisting her wedding ring around and around on her finger.

"Are you all right?"

"Hmm? Oh, yes. Fine."

She forced a smile. Beneath the perfectly coiffed, politician exterior, Teddy could see how tired she looked. Alexia had been in her midtwenties when they met and her late twenties when they married, in a small Catholic chapel off Cadogan Street. Back in those days she was a raving beauty in the classic seventies mold. Very slender, with long, coltish legs and a mane of straggly blond hair that streamed behind her like the tail of a comet when she moved. But she was ambitious even then, and she'd changed very quickly, cutting her hair and adopting a more sober, suit-and-heels dress sense when she ran for her first London constituency seat.

Mrs. Thatcher had been elected leader a few years before Alexia De Vere became an MP, but the British Conservative Party remained a hostile place for a woman, especially one from a lower-middle-class background. Marriage to a British aristocrat had certainly helped Alexia's chances. Teddy had relinquished his peerage so that his young wife could have a shot at the Commons, but Alexia remained a De Vere, and De Veres had been part of the Tory establishment since time immemorial.

Teddy wasn't stupid. He was well aware that his name and his money and his family connections were a big part of the attraction for his brilliant, beautiful, pushy young bride. But he admired Alexia, and he loved her, and he was more than willing to offer up all that he had on the altar of her career. Before they met, Teddy De Vere's life had been grand, privileged, and deathly dull. Marriage to Alexia Parker had made it an adventure.

SITTING AT HER DESK TONIGHT, ALEXIA looked every inch the powerful, competent, wildly successful woman that she had become. From her subtle Daniel Galvin highlights, to her immaculately cut couture suit, to the diamonds glinting discreetly at her fingers, ears, and neck, Teddy De Vere's wife was a woman to be reckoned with. Watching her, Teddy could have burst with pride.

Home secretary. That was quite something.

We did it, my darling. We proved them all wrong.

Of course, the De Veres had had their fair share of trial and of tragedy, both as a couple and as a family. Teddy was intelligent enough to realize that the relationship between Alexia and Roxie would probably never recover, any more than his darling daughter's shattered legs. It had started so long ago, almost as soon as Roxie entered her teens, but of course that awful business with the Beesley boy had made it a thousand times worse. And Alexia had never been the touchy-feely type, the sort of mother who could give her daughter a hug and say "there, there." Teddy also knew that Alexia spoiled Michael rotten, partly in compensation for all that she'd lost with Roxanne. It drove him mad sometimes, but he understood. Teddy De Vere prided himself on the fact that he had always understood his wife. They were two sides of the same coin, he and Alexia. He loved her deeply.

"We missed you at dinner."

"Did you? I couldn't tell for all the yelling."

Walking up behind her, Teddy rubbed her shoulders. "I'm sorry things got so heated. Where did you disappear to?"

"Someone was at the gate, asking to see me. Jennings didn't like the look of them, but by the time I got there, they'd gone."

Teddy scowled. "I don't like the way these loonies keep following you around."

"We don't know it was a loony. It could have been anyone . . . a constituent, a reporter."

"Did you get him on tape?"

Alexia didn't blink. "No. The CCTV was acting up."

"Again?"

"I'm afraid so."

"For God's sake. What is wrong with that damn system? Can't you get MI5 to keep an eye on things, now that you're running the bloody country?"

Alexia stood up and kissed him. "Relax, darling. It was nothing. I'm sure I'll be given all the security I need, but we don't want to live like prisoners, do we?"

"Well, no."

"Good, then. Now, about Michael leaving Balliol."

Teddy held up his hands for silence. Few people could stop Alexia De Vere midsentence, but her husband was one of them. "Absolutely not," he said firmly. "We are not talking about either of the children anymore tonight. This was supposed to be your night. Let's go to bed and you can tell me everything about your first day in delicious, minute detail. Home Secretary." He gave her bottom a playful squeeze.

Alexia laughed. "All right. Bed it is."

Not for the first time, she thanked her lucky stars that she had such a wonderful, supportive husband.

If only I didn't have to lie to him.

The CCTV footage was poor quality. But it wasn't blank.

Tomorrow she would show the tape to Edward Manning. Edward would know what to do.

CHAPTER TEN

Sir Edward Manning was excited.

"Put your face on the table, you little bitch."

Having sex in the House of Commons always turned him on. There was something so deliciously illicit about having his way with the pliable, young serving staff in such an ancient, august setting. Tonight's twenty-year-old Romanian had been particularly accommodating, locking the door and stripping off to order as soon as the dinner was finished and the dull Chinese diplomatic party had returned to the embassy.

"Spread your legs."

Fine Waterford crystal wine goblets etched with *House of Commons* shook perilously on the table as it rocked back and forth. Sir Edward Manning, his trousers around his ankles but his black tie still perfect, thrust harder and faster till wet patches appeared through his starched dress shirt.

"Not so rough, Edward, please! It hurts."

"'Sir Edward' to you, my dear. And I want it to hurt. That's the whole point."

Pushing the young Romanian farther onto the table, Edward hoisted himself up onto the polished wood, squatting over his lover like a toad as he forced himself inside the deliciously soft, twenty-year-old body. Sir Edward Manning didn't pine for his own youth, but he still appreciated the delights of youthful flesh, especially when it was so freely offered. A crystal goblet fell and shattered loudly on the parquet floor. Then another. Sir Edward quickened his pace. It was one in the morning and the door was locked, but they didn't want to be disturbed.

At last, with a stifled cry of pleasure, he came, liberally spilling semen all over the Romanian's smooth bare buttocks before sliding off onto the floor. Pulling up his trousers and straightening his hair, he admired his conquest, still spread-eagled on the table.

"Don't worry about sweeping up the mess, Sergei. The stewards will do it in the morning."

Sergei Milescu turned and looked up at the old man he'd just serviced. Sergei Milescu hated Sir Edward Manning with a burning, murderous intensity. But he hated himself more for the huge erection between his legs. The things the Englishman did to him were disgusting and painful and shaming. But Sergei had come to enjoy them almost as much as his abuser did.

Not that he was with Sir Edward Manning for the sex. Manning was a powerful man with powerful contacts. He was also wealthy, wealthy beyond Sergei Milescu's wildest dreams. One day Manning would pay for the humiliation he'd inflicted on Sergei over the last six months, for the bruises and tears to his body that would never fully heal.

"Come here."

Sir Edward Manning stroked his hair, petting him like a dog, his bony, old man's fingers tracing languid lines along Sergei's smooth cheeks.

"You enjoyed that, didn't you?"

Sergei nodded. "You know I did. But must it always be in here, where I work? Can't we go to your place sometimes? I feel like such a . . ."

"Such a what?" Sir Edward purred, his hand reaching down for the boy's rock-hard cock.

"You know what," Sergei moaned. "A whore."

"Ah, but my dear boy, that is the whole point of the matter. You are my little whore."

I hate you, thought Sergei, twitching against his lover's fingers.

He was on the point of orgasm when, without warning, Sir Edward Manning released him.

"All right," he said, to Sergei's surprise. "If it makes you happy. Next time we'll do it at mine."

It does make me happy. Very happy indeed.

"Really?"

"Really." Sir Edward blew him a kiss. "Don't forget to turn the lights out when you leave."

LATER THAT MORNING, RESTED AND SHOWERED and smelling of Floris aftershave, Sir Edward Manning sat at his desk rereading his new boss's file.

Alexia De Vere (née Parker), MP North Oxfordshire. Born April 8, 1954. Married 1982 Lord Edward, Stanley, Ridgemont De Vere. (Title renounced 1986.) 2 children; Roxanne Emily (1983), Michael Edward Ridgemont (1985). 6 years Trade and Industry. 2009–present, Junior Minister for Prisons.

There was little in the new home secretary's file to excite interest. But that was exactly what interested Sir Edward Manning. By the time somebody arrived in his office (like all senior civil servants, Sir Edward Manning considered the Home Office to be his fiefdom. Ministers came and went, but Sir Edward and his staff remained permanent fixtures. It was they who actually ran the country), they usually had an MI5 file as thick as the Koran and a lot more salacious. Sir Edward had served under five home secretaries, Labour and Conservative, and all five had had more rattling skeletons in their closets than in the average London plague pit. Nothing had ever been proven against any of them, of course. It was Sir Edward Manning's job to see that it wasn't, one of the few areas in which his interests and those of his political masters were aligned. In Westminster's version of Snakes and Ladders, only the snakes got to the top, men and women who sloughed off scandal effortlessly like eels in a sea of oil.

Alexia De Vere was different. Her file was so thin it was practically a pamphlet. Up until last year, when her sentencing reform bill had made headlines in all the wrong ways, Mrs. De Vere had been as good as invisible. There was nothing at all in her records prior to her brief stint as a Liberal MP's secretary as a young woman. Since then, an uneventful few years in local politics had been followed by a spectacularly good marriage to a wealthy British lord and a free pass into the uppermost echelons of the social and political establishment. There were two children, one of them a dud. (Roxanne De Vere's rumored suicide attempt over a broken love affair was the only hint of color in an otherwise storybook-perfect family life.) A modestly successful political career had no doubt been boosted by Mrs. De Vere's personal friendship with Henry Whitman, the new prime minister. (Something else that bothered Sir Edward Manning. What on earth did the nearly sixty-year-old Mrs. De Vere have in common with the young, newly married head of the party? There must be a connection, but Sir Edward was damned if he could see it.)

But there was nothing, absolutely nothing, to indicate why Alexia De Vere had been plucked from the lowly Prisons Ministry and appointed to the position of home secretary.

Where are the dead bodies, the enemies she's seen off along the way as she shimmied so silently up the greasy pole?

Where are the land mines, the tangled web of unexploded bombs for me to dodge and weave my way through?

Alexia De Vere's file was not interesting for what it contained, but for what it omitted.

She's keeping secrets from me. But I'll find her out. If I'm going to protect this office and our work, I need to know who she is, and what the hell she's doing here.

"Good morning, Edward. You're in early."

A lesser man would have jumped. Sir Edward Manning merely closed the file calmly, slipped it into his desk drawer, and composed his hawklike features into a smile.

"Not at all, Home Secretary. It's almost eight o'clock."

He had told his new boss to call him Edward and to dispense with the title, but he found it irritated him every time she did so. Perhaps it was the grating, pseudo-upper-class accent. Or perhaps it was simply because Alexia De Vere was a woman. Sir Edward Manning had worked for women before, but never by choice. Discreet about his own sexuality, the truth was he found women quietly repulsive.

"I wish you'd call me Alexia."

"I know you do, Home Secretary. If I may say so, you look a little tired."

Alexia caught a glimpse of her reflection in the office window and winced. He wasn't kidding. Her eyes were puffy and swollen, her skin dry, and every line on her face was etched visibly deeper than it had been a week ago. *They say high office ages you. Maybe it's starting already.*

"I had a difficult night last night."

"I'm sorry to hear that."

"Somebody showed up at my house. A man. He wanted to talk to me, but by the time I got down to the gatehouse he'd gone."

Sir Edward frowned. "You don't know who it was?"

"Not for sure, no. But I have my suspicions." Alexia filled him in briefly on the Sanjay Patel case, and the threats she'd received afterward. "We did get some footage of him on tape, although the quality's awful." Pulling a silver disc out of her briefcase, she handed it over.

"Excellent. I'll send this directly to the Met. We're scheduled for a review of your security arrangements anyway this Friday at three. Can it wait until then?"

"Of course," Alexia said brusquely. "The whole thing's a distraction anyway. I'm not worried. Now let's get to work."

HE HEARD VOICES IN HIS HEAD.

Some were voices that he recognized, voices from the past.

His best friend.

His wife. Ex-wife.

His daughter.

His daughter's voice always calmed him, made him smile. But never for long. Because then there was *the* voice.

Sometimes he thought it was the voice of the Lord, full of righteous anger. At other times it sounded more like the devil: distorted, sinister, inhuman. All he knew for sure was that it was the voice of fear. It told him terrible things, and it demanded terrible things from him. It was a voice that must be satisfied, must be obeyed. But how could he obey if he couldn't even get to see her?

Alexia De Vere was untouchable.

"Did you say something, dear?"

Mrs. Marjorie Davies eyed her latest paying guest suspiciously. During her twenty-five years running a bed-and-breakfast in the Cotswolds, Mrs. Davies had seen all sorts of oddballs come through her door. There was the couple from Baja California, who'd brought crystals down to breakfast every morning and arranged them in a circle around their sausages and beans, "for positive energy." Then there were the French queers who'd refused to pay the bill because they'd found a spider in the bath, not to mention the born-again Christians from Canada who'd ordered and eaten four full cream teas (each!) in a single sitting. But this latest chap was more than just eccentric. He was downright strange, talking to himself and wandering around the house at God knows what time of night, spouting religious claptrap. This morning he'd come down to breakfast in a stained T-shirt, and he clearly hadn't shaved. Mrs. Davies wondered, belatedly, whether he might actually be dangerous.

"I'm sorry," the man mumbled. "I didn't realize I'd spoken aloud."

Definitely a nutter. Mrs. Davies held up her teapot like a weapon.

"More Earl Grey?"

"No, thank you. Just the bill, please. I'll be checking out after breakfast."

Good riddance.

Mrs. Davies had noticed the Didcot-to-London railway timetable wedged under the toast rack and had hoped as much.

"Oh, I'm sorry to hear that," she said on autopilot. "Have you enjoyed your stay in Oxfordshire?"

The man frowned, as if he didn't understand the question. "I need to see Alexia De Vere."

93

"I beg your pardon?"

"I said I need to see the home secretary!" He banged his fist on the table. "She's expecting me. We're old friends."

Marjorie Davies backed away. The man returned to his breakfast, and she rushed out to reception, quickly printing out his bill. His suitcase was already in the hallway, a good sign. As soon as he finished eating, she returned to the table.

"I think it's best if you leave now. We take Visa or MasterCard."

She was surprised by the firmness in her own voice. But she wasn't about to spend another minute in the company of a card-carrying lunatic. Certainly not in her own home.

The man seemed unfazed. He signed the bill, took his suitcase, and left without another word.

After he'd gone, Mrs. Davies looked at the signature on the credit card, half wondering whether she'd hear the name again on the news one day, linked to some awful crime or some plot against the government.

Mr. William J. Hamlin.

Hamlin.

She would have to remember that.

CHAPTER ELEVEN

Prison life suited Billy Hamlin.

It was a bizarre thing to say, but it was true. The regularity, the routine, the camaraderie with the other inmates all suited Billy's easygoing, follow-along character to a T once he got used to it.

The first year was the toughest. Having been transferred to a facility closer to his father, Billy was devastated when Jeff Hamlin died suddenly of a heart attack just three months into his sentence. Billy tried to tell himself that it wasn't the stress of his arrest and trial that had destroyed his father's health, but deep down he knew the truth. Guilt gnawed at him like a dog with a bone.

Meanwhile, Leslie Lose, Billy's lawyer, would leave messages from time to time about an appeal. But as the weeks passed, then the months, and finally the years, with no date set, Billy resigned himself to the fact that he would serve his full sentence.

Twenty years was too painful to contemplate. Even fifteen with good behavior was a bitter pill. Billy Hamlin decided to focus on the one positive he had left in his life: Toni Gilletti.

When I get out, Toni will be waiting for me.

It was a sweet, addictive fantasy, and Billy Hamlin clung to it like a life raft.

When I get out of here, Billy told himself in his cold, lonely bunk each night, *I'm gonna make love to Toni every night, five times a night. I'm gonna make up for lost time.*

He fell asleep dreaming of Toni's soft, sensual teenage body and woke up with the smell of her skin in his nostrils, the soft caress of her silken blond hair on his chest. As the years rolled by and he heard nothing from Toni whatsoever—no letters, no visits, no calls—he made up a series of stories to explain her absence.

Her father was keeping her from him.

She was traveling, somewhere remote—trekking in the Andes maybe—trying to put him out of her mind until they could be together again.

She was working, quietly saving money for the house they were going to buy together when Billy got out.

As the fantasies grew more ludicrous, even to himself, Billy stopped talking about Toni with his fellow inmates. Instead he compartmentalized her, packing her away in a mental box to be opened joyously in secret, once the lights were out and he was alone. Sustained by these romantic dreams, by day Billy determined to get the most out of prison life, enrolling in science and mechanics classes and working long hours on the prison farm, which he enjoyed. In normal circumstances child killers were considered the lowest of the low in jail, ostracized and often physically assaulted by fellow inmates. But there was something about Billy's kind, relentlessly cheerful nature that the other men all warmed to.

The bottom line was that no one believed Billy Hamlin had murdered Nicholas Handemeyer. His trial had been a travesty.

The day Billy walked out of East Jersey State Prison, after fifteen years inside, nobody was waiting to greet him. His father was dead and he had no other close family. There were a few people he knew from back home, acquaintances he could call. But he realized with a pang of fear that all of his *real* friends were behind him, on the other side of the penitentiary's huge, locked steel gates. Billy Hamlin wasn't ready to face the outside world, not on his own.

So he did the only thing he could.

He went looking for Toni Gilletti.

Billy's first stop was Toni's parents' mansion in New Jersey. He'd never been there before, but he'd long since memorized the address, and he'd seen pictures of the place in a fancy *Dream Homes* magazine.

The maid who opened the door was kind. Her brother Tyrone had spent eight years in jail for petty theft, and she knew what a long stretch inside could do to a man's soul. But she told Billy he had a wasted journey.

"Old Man Gilletti sold this place eight years ago. My people, the Carters, been here since then."

Billy bit back his disappointment.

"Do you know where the Gillettis moved to?"

"I don't. Back to New York City, I think. But Walter Gilletti lost a lotta money when his business went broke. There were debts, to partners, to the bank. That's why he sold up here. They was in real trouble."

Billy remembered Walter Gilletti as the arrogant, bullying, cock-of-the-walk figure who'd been so dismissive toward his father at the trial. Toni's dad was not a man who would have coped well with such a huge reversal of fortune.

With a little research and a few calls to some of Walter's ex-employees, Billy found the Gillettis' new home, a clean but modest apartment in a midrent part of Brooklyn. When he got there it looked as if he'd had another wasted journey. An ancient, wizened crone in a dirty velour leisure suit answered the door.

"What the hell do you want?"

It was only when her mean eyes narrowed and she rasped, "Billy Hamlin? Are you out already?" that Billy placed her as Toni's mother.

"Sandra?"

"Mrs. Gilletti to you, boy."

Jesus Christ, thought Billy. *She's aged thirty years. More.*

"I—I was looking for Toni," he stammered. For some reason, the old woman made him nervous.

"You and the rest of the world." Sandra Gilletti cackled grotesquely. Billy recognized the rattle of emphysema in her chest. He hoped the old adage wasn't true, about all girls eventually turning into their mothers. "Toni's gone, kiddo. And she ain't coming back."

For a hideous moment Billy thought she meant that Toni was dead. In fact, Sandra Gilletti explained, her daughter had taken off shortly after the trial, informing both her parents coolly that she wanted nothing more to do with them and that she was starting a new life.

"Just like that," the old woman wheezed. "After twenty years of love and affection, she just ups and leaves, and Walter and I never hear a peep from her again."

Billy cast his mind back to his one, magical summer with Toni and the long conversations they had had about her parents. *Love* and *affection* had not been words he had ever associated with the Gillettis. He remembered feeling sorry for Toni, and grateful for his own, warm relationship with his father.

Mrs. Gilletti went on. "Of course, Walter lost everything. You probably know that. Died of a stroke just months after we moved in here. Left me without a penny, the tightfisted son of a bitch."

Billy looked past her into the clean, comfortable apartment. It wasn't the Ritz-Carlton, but he would have killed to have a place like that to come home to.

"You seem to be doing all right to me, Mrs. Gilletti."

Sandra Gilletti's upper lip curled. "That's because you have low standards. Probably why you fell for our Toni in the first place. She never came back for the funeral, you know. Never even sent flowers. Heartless bitch."

Billy left the apartment feeling deeply depressed. In prison, at least he'd had his fantasy, his little box of dreams to keep him going. Now even that was disintegrating, rained on and destroyed like everything else in his life.

And not just his life. The Gillettis had clearly lost everything too. It was as if everyone connected with that awful summer in Kennebunkport had been cursed. Billy might have been the one sent to jail, but everyone had been punished. Everyone had suffered in their own way. Billy tried not to think of the Handemeyer family, and their never-ending grief. Had they been torn apart by this too? He wondered what had happened to them after the trial. Had his imprisonment given Senator Handemeyer the closure he craved? Somehow Billy doubted it.

For the next few months Billy searched tirelessly for Toni Gilletti, but it was like trying to catch a ghost with a butterfly net. He even spent a thousand dollars of the small amount of money his father had left him on a private detective, but it was to no avail. Toni's poisonous old witch of a mother was right.

She was gone. And she was never coming back.

It wasn't until a few months later that Billy Hamlin recognized the emotion building up inside him for what it was: relief. He had let go of the dream, let go of his parachute, and discovered to his astonishment that he hadn't plummeted to his doom after all. In fact, he felt as if a huge burden had been lifted from his shoulders.

Walking out of jail had not made Billy Hamlin a free man. But giving up on Toni Gilletti had. At last he could begin to build himself a life.

He'd qualified as mechanic in jail, and spent the last of Jeff Hamlin's money buying a stake in a run-down body shop in Queens, in partnership with an old buddy from high school, Milo Bates. Milo had followed Billy's trial on TV and had always felt bad about what had happened to him. Still living in the Hamlins' old neighborhood, Milo was now married to a sweet local girl named Betsy and the two of them had three kids. The Bates family took Billy Hamlin under their wing, and it was their friendship more than anything that helped turn Billy's life around.

It was Betsy Bates who introduced Billy to Sally Duffield, the woman who was to become his wife. Billy and Sally hit it off immediately. Sally was a redhead with incredible ice-blue eyes and skin like an old-fashioned porcelain doll. She had a small waist, large breasts, and a full-throated, infectious laugh that could fill a room. She was kind and maternal and had a steady job as a legal secretary. Billy wasn't in love with her but he liked her a lot, and he wanted children. So did she. There didn't seem any reason to wait.

For the first five years the marriage was happy. Both Billy and Sally were busy, Billy with the car-repair business and Sally with their baby daughter, Jennifer. Jenny Hamlin was the apple of both her parents' eyes, as round and fat as a dumpling, permanently covered in floury talcum powder and cooing adorably at anyone who cared to smile at her. Billy's only sadness was that his father, Jeff, hadn't lived long enough to meet his granddaughter and to see his son so happy and settled. As Jenny Hamlin grew, strong and pretty and funny as all hell—no one was faster on the draw with the one-liners than Jenny—so her parents' love for her grew as well.

Unfortunately their love for each other, never really more than a friendship to begin with, began to fade. When Sally went back to work and fell for one of her colleagues, it wasn't so much the affair that upset Billy as the fact that he didn't care about it. At all. When another man sleeping with your wife is a matter of complete indifference to you, something is probably wrong. And so quietly, amicably, and without an iota of drama, the Hamlins divorced.

Years later, when Billy asked his daughter earnestly whether the split had affected her, the twelve-year-old Jenny Hamlin looked her father in the eye and said, deadpan: "Dad. I've seen eggs separate with more emotion."

When her mom asked her the same question, Jenny stood up and gasped melodramatically, clapping a hand over her mouth.

"What? You mean you guys are *divorced*?!"

The truth was that Jenny Hamlin was a happy, secure, resourceful kid. Her mother was blissfully remarried, and although Billy remained single, he was perfectly content with his business, his buddy Milo, and his season ticket to Yankee Stadium.

Then the voices started.

It began as mild depression. Billy and Milo's business started to struggle, then fail. The debts piled up, and Billy no longer had Sally's income to cushion the blow. When Milo and Betsy Bates's marriage also fell apart, Billy took it hard. He couldn't put his finger on it, but it felt as if the whole world were coming unglued. He started to drink, a little at first, then a lot. Somewhere along the line, the boundary between reality and Billy's increasingly doom-ridden imagination began to blur. Eventually it disintegrated altogether.

Milo Bates left town, abandoning Billy to face their debts alone. Billy convinced himself that Milo had been abducted and murdered.

He told the police, "He wouldn't leave me. Not Milo. He's my best friend. They've taken him. They've taken him away and killed him."

When asked who "they" were, Billy Hamlin could only reply "the voice." An evil voice had apparently told Billy Hamlin that "they" had kidnapped Milo Bates. Billy described vivid, nightmarish fantasies of Bates being tortured and killed by this anonymous individual, and demanded that the police investigate.

Desperately worried, Bill's ex-wife, Sally, called in the social workers. Billy was diagnosed as schizophrenic and prescribed medication. When he took it, things got better. When he didn't, they got worse. Much, much worse.

He would disappear for months on end on mysterious "trips," not telling anyone where he was going and refusing to discuss where he'd been once he returned. "The voice" would tell him where to go, and Billy would follow its instructions, clearly terrified. Nobody knew where he got the money for these trips, and Billy himself seemed vague about it, insisting that funds had mysteriously appeared in his bank account. Sally and Jenny begged him to get help but Billy refused, convinced that if he didn't do what "the voice" asked, if he allowed the voice to be silenced by doctors or psychiatrists, something quite terrible would happen.

Occasionally he got fixated on specific people. Some

were locals, people he knew from the neighborhood whom he believed to be in danger. Others were public figures. Baseball players. Politicians. Actors.

Most recently, and most bizarrely, Billy Hamlin had become obsessed with the new British home secretary, Alexia De Vere. *Time* magazine had run a picture of Mrs. De Vere as part of its profile on women in power, and Billy had fixated on it, spending hours and hours on his computer "researching" the British politician's background.

"I have to warn her," Billy told his daughter, Jenny.

Not again, thought Jenny. *He seemed so much better lately.*

"Warn her about what, Dad?" She sighed. "You don't know this woman."

"That's not the point."

"But, Dad . . ."

"She's in grave danger. The voice said so. I have to warn her. I have to go to England."

No one, not even Jenny Hamlin, thought that her father was actually going to go.

TEDDY DE VERE CAME INTO THE kitchen at Kingsmere looking upset.

"What's the matter, Daddy?" Roxie asked. "As Granny used to say, you look like you've lost a shilling and found sixpence."

Teddy didn't laugh. "Have you seen Danny?"

Danny was the ancient family dog, a wire-haired dachshund with the IQ of a cabbage to whom all the De Veres were devoted. Especially Teddy.

"I called him this morning for his walk and he never came. Can't find him anywhere."

"He's probably asleep somewhere," said Roxie. "Or

waddled off to the gamekeeper's cottage for some free sausages. Do you want me to look for him with you?"

"Would you mind? Silly, I know, but I'm worried about him."

Half an hour later, so was Roxie. They'd searched the entire house, twice, and all the likely places in the grounds. No doubt about it, the dog was gone.

"Might Mummy have let him out by mistake when she left for London this morning?" Roxie asked. "Should we call and check?"

"Done it already. She said she didn't check his basket but she doesn't remember seeing him, and he definitely didn't get out."

"Your lordship."

Alfred Jennings hovered in the kitchen doorway. Teddy De Vere had given up his title decades ago, when Alexia first stood for Parliament, but Alfred was congenitally incapable of addressing a De Vere in any other way.

"Have you found him?" Teddy's round face lit up with hope.

The old gatekeeper stared at his shoes. "Yes, your lordship. I'm afraid we have."

ALEXIA DE VERE PEELED BACK THE Frette sheets on her London bed and slipped inside. It had been a long day—since her appointment as home secretary, all the days were long—and the soft touch of Egyptian cotton against her bare legs felt wonderful. Alexia usually wore silk Turnbull & Asser pajamas to bed, but London was enjoying a three-day heat wave, and the one luxury that the De Veres' Cheyne Walk house lacked was air-conditioning.

"I'm buggered if I'm paying for that nonsense when

we're away all summer," Teddy insisted. "If it's hot, we can open the bloody window."

He can be so English sometimes, Alexia thought affectionately.

Teddy had called her earlier from Kingsmere. Sir Edward Manning had passed on three messages, but Alexia literally hadn't had a single free moment to return his calls. The phone rang just as she was reaching for it.

"Darling. I'm so sorry. You wouldn't believe how hectic things have been here, I've had two select committees, my first full cabinet meeting, I've—"

"Alexia. Something's happened."

Teddy's tone stopped her instantly. Horrors flashed through her mind. *An accident. Michael. Roxie.*

"Somebody's poisoned the dog."

For an instant Alexia felt relief. *It's only Danny. Not the children.* Then the full import of what Teddy was saying hit her.

"Poisoned him? Deliberately?"

"I'm not sure. But none of the gardeners are admitting to putting rat poison down and the vet says his stomach was full of it."

"*Was* full of it? Is he dead?"

"Yes, he's dead! That's what I've been trying to tell you. All damn day."

Alexia could hear Teddy's voice quavering. He loved that dog. Suddenly she felt afraid. The mystery caller. Danny being found dead. There was probably no connection. But what if there was? What sort of psychopath would kill a sweet little dog?

After a few minutes comforting her husband, Alexia De Vere hung up. As soon as she did so, the phone rang again. She snatched it up, silently praying that it wasn't her mother-in-law, who often called late at night. The Dowager Lady De Vere was ninety-six and profoundly deaf, a disability that had in no way reduced her enthusiasm for the telephone as a means of communication. She particularly enjoyed shouting recipes down the line at her daughter-in-law, conveniently ignoring the fact that Alexia had never cooked so much as a piece of toast in her six decades on this earth, and was probably even less likely to do so now that she had the small matter of a country to run. A typical call would begin, "Teddy's very keen on eels in aspic. Have you got a pen and paper handy?"

But it wasn't Teddy's mother. The faint click on the line told Alexia immediately it was a long-distance call, but there was no voice on the other end.

"Hello?" Sometimes there was a delay on the line, especially with calls from the U.S. "Lucy, is that you?"

Lucy Meyer, Alexia's summer neighbor from Martha's Vineyard, was the only other person she could think of who might call her at home at this hour. With the holidays approaching, Lucy had been in closer touch, a welcome reminder of the peaceful life that existed outside of politics. *If only Lucy lived in England, how much easier my life would be.*

"If it's you, Luce, I can't hear you. Try again."

But it wasn't Lucy Meyer. It was a low, synthesized growl. "The day is coming. The day when the Lord's anger will be poured out."

The voice distorter was designed to frighten. It worked. Alexia tightened her grip on the handset.

"Who is this?"

"Because you have sinned against the Lord, I will make you as helpless as a blind man searching for a path."

"I said who is this?"

"Your blood will be poured out into the dust and your body will lie rotting on the ground. Murdering bitch."

The line went dead. Alexia put the phone down, gasping for breath.

She closed her eyes and the view from her office window popped into her mind: the silver Thames and its deadly currents snaking their way around her, cutting her off like Rapunzel in her tower.

Somebody out there hates me.

The waters were rising.

CHAPTER TWELVE

ALEXIA DE VERE TAPPED HER DESK impatiently with a Montblanc silver fountain pen. Commissioner Grant, the senior Metropolitan Police Officer in charge of her personal security, was late for their three o'clock meeting. If there was one thing Alexia disliked, it was lateness.

Her first boss in politics, an odious Liberal MP named Clive Leinster, had been a stickler for punctuality and it was a lesson that had remained with Alexia throughout her career. *God, Clive was an asshole, though!* Working as his personal assistant had changed Alexia's life, but he himself had been a horror. In his midforties, married, and an appalling letch, even by Westminster standards, Clive Leinster was short and wispily bald, with knock knees, bad breath, and a receding chin to match his hairline. It was a miracle to Alexia Parker (as she was then) that Clive Leinster had found one woman prepared to sleep with him, never mind several.

"Power'th an incredible aphrodithiac, Alexia," Clive would breathe huskily over her desk after one of his long, boozy lunches. After a month it was painfully clear that the type of personal assistance Clive Leinster was looking for was not the sort that Alexia was prepared to offer. "You'll never get ahead in Wethtminthster if you're not prepared to play the game, you know," Clive sneered as Alexia packed up her desk.

"At least I can say 'Westminster,'" Alexia shot back. "And I've every intention of playing the game. Just not with you."

Marching out of Leinster's office with her head held high, Alexia was convinced she'd get another job in a heartbeat. In fact, she spent the next six months back behind a bar at the Coach and Horses on Half Moon Street.

"No MP will touch me," she complained to one of her regulars, a shy young financier named Edward De Vere. "It's like I've got the plague or something. That fucker Leinster must have poisoned the well."

"I can ask a few questions at the Carlton Club, if you like. See if there are any rumors knocking around."

"You're a member of the Carlton?" It was the first time Alexia had realized that Edward De Vere must be well connected. Politically well connected, that is. The Carlton Club was an exclusive—*the* exclusive—Tory Party members club in St. James's. Like all would-be Conservative politicians, Alexia would have sold her soul to have access there, but there were no women allowed. Even if there had been, unknown barmaids with no family or connections to recommend them were probably not at the top of the Carlton membership committee's wish list.

Two nights later, Edward De Vere was back in the bar.

"So, did you hear anything?"

"As a matter of fact, I did."

"Well?" Alexia leaned forward across the bar, accidentally affording her customer an excellent view of her breasts. "Don't keep me in suspense."

"I'll tell you on two conditions."

"Conditions?" She frowned.

"Actually three conditions."

"Three?"

"Three."

"And they are?"

"The first is, don't shoot the messenger."

Shit, thought Alexia. *He must have heard something bad. Really bad.*

"I would never do that. Go on."

"The second condition is that you call me Teddy. 'Edward' makes me sound like such a stiff."

Alexia laughed. "Okay. Teddy. And the third?"

"The third is that you agree to have dinner with me on Friday night."

Alexia considered for a moment. She already had a date on Friday night, with a dancer from the Royal Ballet named Francesco. Her gay colleagues at the pub were beside themselves with excitement about it.

"Lucky you," the Coach and Horses landlord had cooed, staring unashamedly at Francesco's crotch in the promotional pictures Alexia showed him. "He certainly carries all before him, doesn't he?"

"It was love at first tights!" Stephane, the bar manager, giggled.

By contrast, Edward De Vere—Teddy—looked like a gauche little schoolboy. Ruddy-cheeked, awkward, and painfully reticent around women, Teddy was the archetypal British upper-class male, and not in a good way. And yet he had plucked up the courage to ask Alexia out. And he was funny. And a member of the Carlton Club. More important than all of this, he knew why Alexia was being blackballed by Westminster MPs and he wasn't going to tell her unless she agreed to have dinner with him.

"All right, fine. I'll have dinner with you."

"On Friday."

"Yes, on Friday. Now, for pity's sake, what did you hear?"

Teddy De Vere took a deep breath.

"Clive Leinster told the entire House of Commons bar that he slept with you and you gave him crabs."

"I . . . he . . ." Alexia spluttered, too outraged for speech. "Fuck! How dare he? The lying little . . ."

"I'll pick you up at seven." Teddy beamed. "We'll go to Rules."

RULES WAS UNLIKE ANY RESTAURANT ALEXIA had ever been to. Since moving to London, she had occasionally been taken out to smart establishments where they served champagne and oysters, and where pretentious maître d's lorded it over their wealthy clientele by denying them the best tables.

Rules was in a different class to any of those places. Yes, it was expensive, but the menu read like a boarding school lunch board: toad in the hole, spotted dick, jugged hare, steak and kidney pudding, jam roly-poly. The average age of the waiters must have been eighty if they were a day, all of them men and dressed as if they'd walked off the pages of a Dickens novel, in long black aprons and stiffly starched shirts. Everything about the place, from the overcooked vegetables, to the smell of beeswax on the polished wood floors, to the cut-glass accents ricocheting off the walls, was as upper-class English as Buckingham Palace.

The moment she walked through the door, Alexia realized two things.

The first was that she did not belong here.

The second was that Teddy De Vere did.

"You're not still miffed about the crabs thing, are you?" Teddy asked, in a voice Alexia could have wished were at least a decibel lower.

"No, I am not miffed," she whispered back. "I'm furious. Everyone knows the only way in to the Commons for a woman is as a secretary. I'm wildly overqualified, but now, thanks to that asshole, I don't stand a chance. I mean, as if anyone could *give* Clive Leinster crabs! As if he isn't alive with them already, the revolting little pervert."

Teddy De Vere chuckled. "You know you have a marvelous way with words, Alexia. You should be a politician."

Alexia prodded her unappetizing Yorkshire pudding. "One day."

"Why not today? There's a seat going begging in Bethnal Green."

Alexia laughed. "It's not begging for me."

"It could be," Teddy said seriously. "I put some feelers out at the Carlton Club the other night, in between spying for you. They're looking for someone different to contest that seat. A 'younger, more modern face' was how Tristan put it."

"Tristan? As in Tristan Channing?"

Teddy De Vere nodded. "We were at Eton together."

Of course you were. Tristan Channing ran Conservative central office. He was the closest thing to God within the party. "Young and modern is one thing. But do you really think a woman from my background has a chance in that seat?"

"Why not?" Teddy shrugged. "There's only one way to find out, isn't there? Forget all this nonsense about being a

112

secretary and throw your name in the hat. What's the worst that can happen?"

It was hard to believe that that conversation had taken place more than thirty years ago. And now here she was, home secretary. *I always had ambition. But Teddy was the one who pushed me. He gave me the confidence and he opened the doors.*

"Home Secretary? Commissioner Grant has arrived."

Alexia's permanent private secretary, Sir Edward Manning, broke her reverie. Immaculate as ever in a bespoke three-piece suit, with his hair smoothed flat against his scalp, Edward smelled faintly of the same Floris aftershave that Teddy wore.

"About bloody time. I'm supposed to meet the Russian ambassador at four-fifteen, you know. My day just got completely squeezed."

"I know, Home Secretary. This shouldn't take too long."

A couple of influential Russian oligarchs based in London were spitting teeth at the new regulations Alexia had proposed to Parliament, designed to close tax loopholes for the super rich and to prevent Russian money from being laundered through the City. As a result, the ambassador had demanded a meeting, and Sir Edward had granted it. Russian oligarchs were not the sort of people whom the Home Office wanted as enemies. Commissioner Grant was going to have to cut to the chase.

"Home Secretary, I do apologize. We had a developing situation to deal with in Burnley this morning, a possible Islamic terrorist cell."

Commissioner Grant was in his late forties, overweight and altogether unattractive, with a pale, doughy face, piggy little eyes, and thin lips that he permanently wetted with a nervously darting tongue. Next to Edward Manning he

113

looked horribly disheveled in a crumpled nylon suit, his cheap Tie Rack tie splattered with coffee stains.

Alexia was not reassured. *I hope his mind is less disordered than his dress sense.*

"Is this something I need to be aware of?"

"Yes, ma'am. The threat has been neutralized but your office has been given a full briefing."

"I thought we'd go through everything after this meeting," Sir Edward Manning said smoothly.

"Surely a terror threat takes priority over a few nutters showing up at my house or making crank calls?"

"As I said, Home Secretary, the threat isn't active. And your security is vitally important. If I may . . ."

Without waiting for approval, Commissioner Grant pulled a laptop out of his briefcase and plunked it down on Alexia's desk. Pushing a stack of documents to one side, he launched directly into a PowerPoint presentation.

"As prisons minister, you received more threats last year than any other Tory politician."

It was a punchy opening. Alexia thought, *He's not frightened of me. That's good.*

"I did upset a few people."

"More than a few, Home Secretary. This is a list of incidents relating to your security. Everything from protest marches to egg throwing to hate mail is listed here, in order of seriousness. My job is to isolate the genuine danger from the, er . . ."

"General sea of loathing?" Alexia smiled. The commissioner smiled back.

"I was going to say 'from the merely unpleasant.'"

"Right. How can I help?"

"If I understand correctly from Sir Edward, there have been three specific incidents since your appointment as home secretary. The individual who tried to gain admittance to your country residence. The poisoning of your husband's dog. And the threatening phone call made to your London home."

"That's correct. Do you think the three are linked?"

"No."

Alexia raised an eyebrow. It was a more unequivocal response than she'd expected.

"At least, the death of the dog *may* be connected to the late-night visit to Kingsmere. But the phone call we're treating as a separate incident. Here's what we know so far."

With a click of the mouse, Commissioner Grant brought up a new screen. Alexia found herself looking into the face of a man about her own age. He had thinning blond hair, striking azure-blue eyes, and a gentle, if somewhat confused, expression on his face.

"William Jeffrey Hamlin. We're pretty sure this is the man who came to Kingsmere the other night."

Alexia sounded suitably amazed. "How on earth do you know that?"

"Our technicians did some work on the CCTV footage. We got a partial on the face. Your gatekeeper remembered that the man had an American accent, so we sent the images to our friends at the State Department and the FBI on the off chance. We got lucky. If he hadn't had a prison record, we'd never have found him."

Sir Edward Manning asked, "What sort of prison record?"

"Second-degree murder."

Alexia bit her lower lip nervously.

"It's not as bad as it sounds. A child drowned, back in the early 1970s, while in Hamlin's care. He got out in the

115

late eighties. No history of violence, no subsequent offenses. From everything we know, I'd be highly surprised if he poisoned your dog, Home Secretary."

Alexia looked at William Hamlin's kind eyes and agreed.

"What's he doing here?" asked Sir Edward. "In this country, I mean."

"We don't know. He may just be on vacation. What we do know is he has a long history of psychiatric problems." The commissioner turned to Alexia. "Home Secretary, are you aware of any reason why this man might be interested in you?"

Alexia shook her head. "None whatsoever."

She gazed at the face on the screen. There was some-thing so sad about it.

"And the name William Hamlin means nothing to you?"

"Sorry. No."

Sir Edward asked, "Is he dangerous?"

"Probably not. As I say, he has no history of violence. But with schizophrenics, you don't take any chances. We believe he's still in this country, and if he is, we need to find him. More concerning is the phone call you received at Cheyne Walk."

The screen switched again. William Hamlin's face was gone, replaced by the angry, heavy-set features of another middle-aged man. This man Alexia did recognize. Instinctively her jaw tightened.

"Gilbert Drake."

"Indeed."

Sir Edward Manning looked concerned. "Who's Gilbert Drake?"

"He's a taxi driver from East London," said Commissioner Grant.

"And a *friend* of Sanjay Patel," Alexia added bitterly.

"Ah."

Sir Edward knew about the Patel case. Everyone in Britain knew about the Patel case. It was this case, more than any other, that had dogged Alexia De Vere as prisons minister, and that for a while had threatened to derail her career completely.

Whatever human sympathy Alexia herself might once have had for Sanjay Patel had long since been replaced by cold anger. Not only were Patel's supporters threatening and aggressive, but the tabloid press, and in particular the *Daily Mail*, blathered on about the man as if he were Gandhi.

"Fill me in on Drake," said Sir Edward.

"He's has been cautioned twice before over threats made toward Mrs. De Vere," Commissioner Grant explained. "He's also spent four months inside on a separate charge of firearms possession."

"And you think Gilbert Drake made the phone call last week?"

"It's possible."

"How would a taxi driver from East London have obtained the home secretary's private home number?"

Commissioner Grant frowned. "That's of paramount concern to us obviously. We don't know that it was Drake. But certain things do point toward him. He's known to have issued threats before. The caller last week also used biblical references."

Alexia's skin prickled at the memory. "That's right."

"We know that Drake has become active as a born-again Christian. He's written numerous blog posts using similar language. He's also made two unexplained trips to the home secretary's Oxfordshire constituency in the last month. So his interest in Mrs. De Vere must be assumed to be ongoing and active."

Alexia stood up and walked to the window. The distorted voice from that phone call had frightened her more than she liked to admit. The idea that a crass bully like Gilbert Drake could have been behind it offended her pride as much as anything.

"I don't think it was Drake."

"May I ask why not?"

"I'm as sure as I can be that the call was placed long distance. Plus the fact that it was untraceable and the use of the synthesized voice both show a sophistication that Gilbert Drake simply doesn't have. He's a rock thrower, not a strategist."

Commissioner Grant mulled this over. "You may be right, Home Secretary. I hope you are. But we should talk about the Patel case."

Alexia rolled her eyes. "Must we? I am so tired of hearing Sanjay Patel's name, I can't tell you. Anyone would think he was a saint, not a convicted drug dealer and human trafficker who was punished appropriately and in accordance with British law."

Commissioner Grant thought, *They're right about her.* He liked Mrs. De Vere more than he'd expected to, but she was as tough as old boots.

"Talk me through the case, ma'am. From your perspective."

"It's not a question of perspective, Commissioner. Facts are facts. What happened is a matter of public record."

"Humor me, Home Secretary. We're on the same team here."

Alexia sighed. "Fine. A man named Ahmed Khan was arrested in Dover in 2002. He'd arrived in this country with twelve other men, as part of a shipment of illegal immigrants. Drugs, specifically heroin, were found in the van used to transport Khan. When questioned, Khan told police that he was in

118

fear of his life in Pakistan—of course, they all say that—and that his cousin, Sanjay Patel, had arranged to have him brought to England. He denied any knowledge of the heroin.

"None of the other refugees in the case had mentioned any specific individuals. Patel's was the only name put forward, and he had also recruited the driver. Patel was arrested, and confessed to having helped his cousin, Khan, but feigned ignorance about the heroin. Anyway he was tried and found guilty of drug smuggling and human trafficking. The judge sentenced him to a minimum term. I believe it was twelve years."

"Fifteen," Commissioner Grant corrected her.

"Was it? Right. In any event, his appeal had been scheduled for June 2004, but after my sentencing reforms came in, it was scrapped and Patel's sentence was retrospectively raised."

"To twenty-two years."

"That's right."

"Quite a steep hike."

Alexia's eyes narrowed. "You sound as if you sympathize, Commissioner."

"I do to a degree, Home Secretary. Everybody needs hope, even criminals. Take that away and you get some very desperate people."

For a moment a tense silence hung in the air. Then Alexia smiled broadly. It was refreshing to have someone stand up to her for a change, or at least to hold their ground. Commissioner Grant was quite wrong, of course. But Alexia found she liked him increasingly.

"Well," she said convivially, "Sanjay Patel clearly agreed with you. He hung himself in his cell on Christmas Day 2008. His supporters have blamed me for his death ever since."

If she felt any guilt about this, or any regret, she didn't show it. Sir Edward Manning had worked with politicians for thirty years. Rarely had he seen one quite so ruthlessly without emotion.

"Am I correct in thinking that Sanjay Patel always maintained his innocence?" Commissioner Grant asked.

"Convicted criminals usually do, in my experience."

"Yes, but in Patel's case the evidence against him was felt to be particularly weak."

"Felt by whom? The *Daily Mail*?"

Sir Edward Manning watched the two of them square off, like a pair of expert fencers.

"Wasn't Patel convicted purely on Khan's statement? No DNA or prints ever linked him to the drugs, nor were any middlemen ever found or any evidence linking Patel to any sort of drug deal."

"Clearly the jury considered the evidence sufficient. It is not for me, or indeed you, Commissioner, to question their verdict."

"No indeed, Home Secretary. It's for the court of appeal. Only there was no appeal in Patel's case."

"No."

"Because of your sentencing reforms?"

"Because of the reforms passed into law by a majority of MPs and overwhelmingly supported by the British public, yes." Alexia smiled. "Is there a point to all of this, Commissioner?"

"Only that we consider Sanjay Patel's supporters to be a genuine potential threat to your security. From now on we will be treating them on an equal risk level with the other terror threats made against the Home Office, or against you personally."

"Okay." Alexia nodded seriously. This was no longer a

game of verbal dexterity. The commissioner meant what he said. "What about William Hamlin?"

"We'll keep an eye on him too. Once we find him. Hamlin and Drake are persons of interest. We'll keep you informed."

"Please do. And on Danny's poisoning too."

For a moment the commissioner looked confused. "Danny?"

"Our dachshund. I realize it may have been an accident. But he was a dear little dog. I'd like to know what happened."

Outside in the lobby, Sir Edward Manning spoke to Commissioner Grant privately.

"Do you really think these Patel people are dangerous?"

"I think Gilbert Drake could be, given the right set of circumstances. And there may be others. Some of the anonymous letters she received last year didn't mince their words. Slitting throats and rivers of blood and what have you. Then again, putting something on paper, or saying it over a telephone line, and actually doing it are two very different things."

"And the American man?"

"Harmless. I did want to ask you something, though, Edward. Off the record."

"Yes?"

"This business with the dog. I'm playing it down in front of the home secretary. No need to create undue anxiety. But I don't like it."

"And you have no leads?"

"No. What do you know about the family dynamic?"

"Not as much as I'd like to," Sir Edward said truthfully. "Mrs. De Vere is a frustratingly closed book. I know the rumors. There's tension with the daughter. Apparently she loathes her mother, but that may be exaggerated. She still lives at home."

Commissioner Grant rubbed his chin thoughtfully.

"So did the dog."

CHAPTER THIRTEEN

SERGEI MILESCU REARRANGED THE PILLOWS ON the bed. Lying back, he checked the angle of the flat-screen television over the fireplace, making sure that any images would be clearly visible to someone lying flat on their back. This would be the first time he'd had sex in Sir Edward Manning's flat. Everything had to be perfect.

Sergei glanced at the clock on the wall: 6:23 P.M. Edward would be home soon, awaiting his pleasure. He'd given Sergei his keys this morning.

"Get everything ready. The game starts the moment I walk through the door."

Sergei could hardly believe it when Edward had suggested a night of role reversal. For months Sergei been angling to shift the dynamic between them, to establish himself as more of a boyfriend and less of a plaything. Just when he'd begun to think it was hopeless, that the old bastard would never change, Edward had not only agreed to have sex at home but had actually *offered* to let Sergei dominate. For days now, the young Romanian had been quivering with excitement at the prospect. But as the moment of truth drew nearer, he shook as much from fear as from arousal.

What if I fuck it up?
I can't. I can't fuck it up.
This may be my only chance.

The door to the apartment opened, then closed. Sergei heard the thud of Edward's briefcase hitting the floor, followed by the quiet rustle as he removed his jacket and shoes.

"Where are you?"

"In here."

Sir Edward Manning felt a frisson of excitement shoot through him as he entered his bedroom. How long had it been since he'd brought a lover back here? Years, certainly. He couldn't remember the last time. But neither could he remember the last time a boy had excited him as much as Sergei. It was that intoxicating combination of hatred and desire that did it. Sergei Milescu thought he hid his hatred, but it was as obvious to Sir Edward Manning as the rock-hard dick between the young Romanian's legs, and every bit as arousing.

Am I being foolish, bringing him here? Allowing him to take the lead?

Probably. But it's the danger that makes it so sweet.

"Nice place."

"Thank you."

"Take your clothes off and lie down on the bed."

Edward hesitated, taking in the various props around the room. There was a video camera on a tripod in the corner, and a spool of rope in plain view on top of the dresser.

"No filming. In my position I can't allow—"

The slap came out of nowhere, hard and sudden. "I said get undressed."

Sir Edward Manning did as he was told.

I'm going to enjoy this.

124

For the first thirty minutes he did. Sergei was such a natural submissive, it was incredible how readily and skillfully he took to the dominant role. Tying Edward to the bed, first by his wrists alone and later by his ankles as well, he did things to his body that Edward had never even imagined. Probing, teasing, hurting occasionally but never to the point where it became a turnoff, the boy had the energy of a young bull and the ingenuity of a chess grand master. Time after time Sergei brought Edward to the brink of orgasm, only to deny him the ecstasy of release. After a long, difficult day of serving the needs of his demanding new female boss, this night of unbridled male pleasure was exactly what Edward needed. *Why would anyone want to come out of the closet when life inside was as exquisitely pleasurable and verboten as this?*

"Stay there. I've got a little something I want you to watch."

Spread-eagled on his back, with patches of still-warm wax congealing around his nipples and groin, Edward had no choice but to comply. He hoped the porn would be good. Generally speaking, he wasn't a fan, preferring his own imagination to the crassly performed scenarios of the "actors" on-screen. But perhaps this was more of a young man's thing, a price one paid for having such delectably nubile lovers.

The film began predictably enough, with a young hitchhiker servicing an improbable-looking group of truck drivers at a truck stop. But about ten minutes in, things became too violent for Edward's taste. The boy was being choked, and was clearly in distress.

"This isn't working. Turn it off."

When Sergei turned around there was no mistaking the wild arousal in his eyes. For the first time Edward felt a flicker of real fear.

"Turn it off? How about I turn *you* off, old man."

Pulling a rolled-up pair of socks out of the top drawer of Edward's dresser, Sergei stuffed them into the civil servant's mouth. Then, as casually as if he were snuffing out a candle, he closed Edward's nostrils, pinching them between finger and thumb.

The panic was immediate and total.

He's going to kill me.

Edward struggled wildly, aware that his efforts were futile but unable to stop himself from straining at the ropes. He could hear the blood in his brain, the pressure building up like a swollen dam. He felt as if his skull would explode, imagined his eyeballs popping out of their sockets. He was aware of losing consciousness, of the white stucco ceiling above his antique mahogany bed blurring then turning to black. He braced himself for death.

"There now. No more talking. We watch."

Miraculously, incredibly, the boy let go of his nostrils and pulled the balled-up running socks out of his mouth. Air rushed painfully into Edward's lungs and tears streamed down his cheeks.

"Jesus!" he sobbed. "That wasn't funny. I thought you were going to kill me."

Sergei Milescu looked at him and smiled.

"Maybe I am."

HENRY WHITMAN FELT THE SWEAT POURING down his back as he increased the incline on his running machine. The prime minister's daily workouts were grueling, but did wonders for his stress levels.

"Prime Minister? Sorry to disturb you, sir. But I have the home secretary on the line."

Henry scowled at his secretary, Joyce Withers. "Can't she wait?"

"Apparently not, sir."

Henry hesitated, aware how foolish he must look in front of Joyce. *I'm the damn prime minister. Alexia De Vere works for me, not the other way around.* But he took the call. He was too afraid not to.

Afterward he ran and ran until his legs shook with exhaustion. But his frustration lingered. How had he gotten himself into this situation?

More importantly, how the hell was he going to get himself out?

SIR EDWARD MANNING STARED AT THE laptop, wide-eyed with terror. On a pillow in front of him, Sergei Milescu had arranged Edward's own top-of-the-line Japanese chef's knives into the shape of a fan.

"You see, *that's* what I call true love," Sergei was saying. "Not just being willing to die for someone. But being cooked and eaten. Would you do that for me, Eddie? Do you love me that much?"

The images on the laptop weren't graphic. Sergei was showing Edward a CNN news report from a few months ago of a famous case in which a gay psychopath had murdered, dismembered, and ultimately eaten his boyfriend in the ultimate snuff movie. The boyfriend was filmed willingly consenting to the entire affair, prompting a flurry of philosophical hand-wringing about the dangers of sadomasochism, and whether voluntary killing could ever be classed as murder.

It was the look in Sergei's eyes that terrified Edward, turning his bowels to liquid and making sweat stream in little rivers down his back and chest.

"Now. Where shall we begin? Here, perhaps?" Picking up a serrated fruit knife, Sergei pressed it against Edward's left nipple. The old man shrieked into his gag.

"Or here?" He moved the knife over an index finger. With a flick, he sliced into the skin. Edward screamed, his pupils dilating wildly with terror and pain. The cut was small but deep. Blood was everywhere, soaking the sheets in a deep, plum-red pool.

"Or here?" Slowly, relishing each second, Sergei dragged the point of the knife onto Edward's belly, tracing a line downward till the blade brushed the top of his penis. "Would you like that, Eddie? Would you like me to cut?"

Sir Edward Manning strained wildly, pulling so hard that the ropes at his wrists and ankles drew blood.

Death was coming. He knew that now. It wasn't death that scared him as much as the torture that would precede it. He wasn't very good with pain. Never had been.

How could I have been so stupid? Risked so much, and for what? For sex?

In his terror, he thought about his mother. He thought about Andrew, his college boyfriend and the only man he'd ever really loved.

"Close your eyes, Eddie," Sergei whispered in his ear. Through his tears, Sir Edward Manning did as he was told. He felt the cold blade against his genitals and wondered when, or even if, he would pass out.

"Let's get some sound effects, shall we?" Leaving the knife resting on Sir Edward's groin, Sergei untied his gag. "I want to hear you beg for your life."

"Please!" Sir Edward hated the sound of his own voice, but he couldn't help himself. "Don't do this. You don't have to do this! I'm a rich man. I . . . I can pay you."

"Pay me? Pay me what?"

"Whatever you want! Anything. Name your price."

"Name my price? You *still* think I'm your whore, don't you?" Grabbing a second, larger knife from the pillow, Sergei slashed like Zorro across Sir Edward's chest. The old man let out a bloodcurdling scream.

"No, please. Please! Tell me what you want. I'm sorry! Just tell me what you want, for God's sake!"

"All right," said Sergei. "I'll tell you what I want." To Sir Edward Manning's astonishment, the Romanian got up off the bed and began getting dressed. Scooping up the knives, he rattled them close to Sir Edward's face, laughing loudly as the old man cowered, then leisurely carried them back into the kitchen.

For the first time since he was a child, Sir Edward Manning prayed.

Please, please let it be over. Please don't let this be a trick, a way to prolong the agony.

He tried to fight back hope but it was impossible. He wanted so very, very desperately to live.

Sergei came back into the bedroom and smiled. Sir Edward Manning smiled back.

Then he realized that the boy had something behind his back.

"No, please! Don't hurt me. PLEASE!" Sir Edward Manning felt black despair overwhelm him.

Sergei came closer. "Too late!" He laughed. "Bang bang!"

By the time Sir Edward realized it was an iPhone in Sergei's hand not a gun, he'd already lost control of his bladder.

"First," said Sergei, "I'm going to take some pretty pictures of you, Eddie. So I need you to smile for the camera. Can you do that?"

Sir Edward nodded furiously.

"I'm going to send these pictures to some friends of mine. If anything happens to me—or if you don't do exactly as I ask—they're going to wind up online for the whole world to enjoy. Do you understand?"

Another nod.

"And after that, my friends will kill you. They will slice off your dick and roast it with rosemary and they will eat it." Sergei Milescu's upper lip curled. "Do you believe me, *Sir* Edward?"

"I believe you." Sir Edward Manning felt nauseous with relief. "I'll do anything you say, Sergei. Anything."

"That's good. My friends will be happy to hear it. They'll be even happier when you get them the information they need."

"Information?"

"About your boss. But shush now." Sergei smiled, laying a finger over Sir Edward's lips. "First it's picture time. Say 'cheese.'"

CHAPTER FOURTEEN

BILLY HAMLIN WAS SITTING ON THE train on his way into London. Outside, a steady, gray drizzle had set in, sluicing the train windows with a grimy film of water. There was water everywhere, sucking him down, drowning him. An endless current that, no matter how hard or how fast he swam, he could never escape.

"You off up to London sightseeing?" The young mother next to him made conversation. "Heard your American accent earlier. You on your holidays?"

The woman was attractive but looked tired. She had two small, sticky-fingered kids with her, and was no doubt hoping Billy might provide some adult distraction. Taking in the normality of her life—the restless children, the stained raincoat, the bags of groceries wedged into the seat beside her—Billy felt a pang of envy so sharp it was like a knife in the heart.

"Actually, no. I'm on my way to visit Alexia De Vere."

The young mother laughed. "Really? I'm off to see the Queen meself. Straight to Buckingham Palace once we get in to Paddington, aren't we, kids?"

"I'm serious," said Billy. "I have to warn Alexia De Vere."

"Warn her? Warn her about what?"

Billy looked at the woman as if she were mad. "The voice. I have to warn her about the voice."

The young woman turned away, drawing her children closer to her, protecting them.

She could see it now. The madness blazing in Billy Hamlin's eyes.

"Excuse me." Billy pressed his cell phone to his ear. "I have to take this. Hello?"

An eye for an eye, Billy. An eye for an eye.

Billy felt his throat go dry and his stomach turn to water.

Who will be the next to die?

The voice. It was back.

Billy started begging. "Please don't hurt her!"

Hurt who, Billy? Your daughter?

"No, not Jenny."

Or Mrs. De Vere?

"Neither of them."

You choose.

"But they're both innocent! Why are you doing this? Please, please just leave me alone."

I can't do that, Billy.

"Then tell me what to do."

You know what to do.

"I need more time. It's not that easy. She's the home secretary! It's not like I can walk up to her in the street."

"Are you all right?" A young man, a commuter, put a hand on Billy's arm. He was looking at him curiously, the same way that the young mother had a few moments earlier.

He thinks I'm crazy, thought Billy. *They all do. They don't understand.*

"I'm fine," he said patiently. "I'm on the phone."

"There's no reception here, mate," the man said kindly. "We're in a tunnel. See?"

Billy looked through the grimy windows into the blackness. Panicked, he shouted into his handset.

"Hello? HELLO?"

The young man was right. The line had gone dead.

The voice was gone.

THE SELECT COMMITTEE MEETING WAS GETTING heated.

"With respect, Home Secretary . . ."

"Don't talk to me about respect, Giles," Alexia De Vere said curtly. "That's the whole point, isn't it? These people have no respect. Not for our values, not for our institutions, not for our flag. And we're too cowardly to stand up to them."

"Cowardly?" the minister for agriculture muttered under his breath. "What the hell would a woman know about fighting for the bloody flag."

Alexia turned on him like a rattlesnake. "What was that, Charles?"

"Nothing."

"No, please. If you have something to say, do share it with all of us."

The six men seated around the table eyed one another nervously, like schoolboys who'd gotten on the wrong side of their teacher. They were here to discuss the problem of migrant agricultural workers demonstrating in Parliament Square. The protests were becoming increasingly unruly. Last week two Albanian beet pickers had urinated on the Union Jack, an incident that had made the national news and ignited a renewed debate on immigration that the Home Office could have done without. Everyone was on edge, but the home secretary seemed to be particularly waspish this

133

morning. Poor Charles Mosely, the agriculture minister, looked as if he were about to have his balls cut off.

"Do you think I'm some sort of second-class citizen, Charles?"

"Of course not, Alexia." *I think you're a first-class bitch, and so do the rest of the cabinet.*

"Good. Because the last time I checked, women and men were considered equals in this country."

"I appreciate that, Home Secretary. The point is that none of us feels that throwing the book at these two young men is going to solve anything."

"They're very poor." The trade and industry secretary spoke slowly, as if explaining something very simple to a small child. "Destitute, effectively."

"Irrelevant," Alexia said witheringly. "They're criminal vandals and they're pissing on the hand that feeds them. They're turning this government into a laughingstock."

Walking over to the water cooler, she filled a plastic cup, willing herself to calm down. She knew she was overreacting. Taking everything too personally. But she'd had a frustratingly sleepless night, fretting over yesterday's meeting with Commissioner Grant, and for some reason the six unfriendly, embittered faces watching her around the table this morning were bothering her more than usual.

Alexia had played things cool yesterday, refusing to show weakness in front of Sir Edward Manning and the commissioner. As a woman in politics, one couldn't afford to let one's guard down, ever. But the truth was, she was frightened, filled with a deep sense of foreboding that she couldn't seem to shake. She'd received threats before, of course, as prisons minister. But this business with William Hamlin and the fire-and-brimstone voice on the phone was different.

And the dog. She felt awful about the dog.

Normally Alexia would have been completely unfazed chairing a meeting in which every man in the room was against her. The envy and hostility around the table this morning was palpable, but it was nothing new. But today she felt tired and vulnerable. To make matters worse, when she finally got to sleep last night, she had a terrible nightmare, of the kind she hadn't had in years—the drowning dream. Strong, dark currents pulling her under. Lungs filling with water, unable to breathe. Poor Teddy had done his best to calm her down, fetching her a glass of water at four in the morning. Afterward he'd fallen back to sleep, but Alexia had lain awake, watching the dawn break over the river with exhausted, bloodshot eyes.

Parliament broke for the long summer recess in a couple of weeks' time. It couldn't come soon enough for Alexia. Just thinking about her summer house on Martha's Vineyard and spending time with Lucy Meyer, her only real girlfriend, filled her with a longing she could hardly describe.

"Alexia? Are you with us?" Giles Fring, from the immigration think tank Borders, was talking to her.

"I'm sorry, Giles. What were you saying?"

"We need to draft a statement, Home Secretary." Fring's irritated sigh spoke volumes. "We must reach some sort of consensus."

"We have a consensus."

"No we don't," the trade and industry secretary said bluntly.

"Yes we do, Kevin. This is my department, my call. I decide a course of action and you agree to it. Voilà. Consensus."

The men around the table exchanged despairing glances.

"Our statement is as follows: 'The government will not tolerate acts of violence or hatred toward Great Britain or her people. It will be up to the courts to decide the fate of

Mr. Silchek and Mr. Vladmizc. But the home secretary hereby authorizes the immediate clearing of Parliament Square. Moreover, the work visas of all those involved in last week's rallies will be reviewed, with immediate effect.'"

The room erupted.

"You can't be serious, Alexia! Revoking visas? What about freedom of speech?"

"Not revoking. Reviewing."

"But with a view to deporting people! For peaceful protest."

"There was nothing peaceful about what happened to that flag, Kevin."

"The prime minister will never allow it."

Alexia smiled thinly. The trade and industry secretary was really beginning to get on her nerves. "Oh, I think you'll find he will. Henry's support is nothing if not staunch."

Throwing his papers down on the table in a petulant rage, Kevin Lomax stormed out.

Charles Mosely said, "If nothing else, Home Secretary, I would suggest you reconsider the tone of the statement. It sounds . . ."

"Strong?" Alexia suggested.

"I was going to say 'Stalinist.' Put bluntly, it won't win us any votes."

"I beg to differ."

"But, Alexia, be reasonable. We all—"

"Meeting adjourned. Good day, gentlemen."

TEN MINUTES LATER, IN THE BACK of her ministerial Daimler, Alexia kicked off her shoes, sighing heavily.

"What's wrong with these men, Edward? They're all such cowards."

Sir Edward Manning shifted uncomfortably in his seat. He had bandaged the wound on his finger, explaining it away as a kitchen accident, but the lines that Sergei Milescu had sliced into his chest were far harder to dress. Not only were they agonizingly painful, but they put him in a constant state of fear that blood was about to seep through his shirt. Sergei wanted information on Mrs. De Vere, something scandalous enough and serious enough to have her forced out of her job. Right now Edward had no idea how he was going to get it. All of which made it extremely difficult to concentrate.

"I mean, you tell me, Edward. Have they forgotten how many men died for that flag?"

"I highly doubt Charlie Mosely's forgotten," Sir Edward said through gritted teeth. The pain was almost unbearable. "His son was killed three years ago in Helmand. Blown to bits by some roadside bomb."

Alexia gasped. "Oh God. Really? I had no idea."

"It was in your briefing notes, Home Secretary."

"Was it? Shit. No wonder he was so touchy about the flag thing. Why didn't you stop me, Edward?"

They both knew this was a rhetorical question. For a few minutes the Daimler glided on in silence, each of them lost in their own private thoughts.

Alexia watched Sir Edward Manning as he stared out of the window. *He looks even stiffer and more controlled today than usual.*

I don't trust him.

The realization was instant and unexpected, but it was also total, an instinctive reaction rather than a critical judgment.

I don't trust him but I need him. If I'm going to survive in the snake pit of this job, a good PPS is essential. We have to find a way to work together.

"Do you have any suggestions, Edward?"

"Suggestions for what, Home Secretary?"

"For how I make things right with Charles Mosely. I used the word 'cowardly' to a man who lost his son in action."

"In my experience, Home Secretary, an apology is usually the first step."

"Should I call him?"

"I would write. A letter, not an e-mail. A formal, hand-written apology smacks of an appropriate degree of contrition."

Alexia De Vere smiled.

"Thank you, Edward. That's what I'll do."

IT TOOK LESS THAN AN HOUR for Henry Whitman to hear about the fireworks at the Home Office. Charles Mosely gravely offended. An incendiary statement being drafted for the press, without his knowledge or consent. It was only a week since Alexia De Vere had gravely offended the Russians with a stupid, throwaway remark to Parliament about money laundering. And now this.

He was furious.

"Should I get the home secretary on the line, Prime Minister?" Joyce, Whitman's secretary, asked eagerly. Alexia De Vere was even less popular with Tory women than she was with the party's ruling males.

"Yes." Henry Whitman hesitated. "I mean no. Just put a call through to central office and make sure no statement is released to anybody until I've seen the wording and approved it."

Joyce raised an eyebrow. "You *don't* want to talk to Mrs. De Vere, sir? Are you quite sure?"

"That's what I said isn't it?" Henry Whitman snapped.

The secretary left. Alone in his office at Number Ten, Henry Whitman made a call from his private cell phone.

"I need that information."

"You'll get it."

"When? I'm being made to look like a laughingstock here. I need something I can use."

"Soon."

"Your source had better be good."

"My source is impeccable. Very well placed. Very motivated." There was a pause on the line. "Would you like to see a picture of him?"

"A picture?" Before Henry Whitman could answer, an MMS image appeared in his in-box. He clicked it open, and really wished he hadn't.

"Jesus Christ."

"JESUS CHRIST, OUR LORD AND FATHER, welcomes you into his heart."

"Hallelujah!"

The young female minister was new to St. Luke's Church and she was going down a storm. Gilbert Drake was normally not a fan of women priests, but even he was prepared to make an exception for this girl, with her loose blond hair, trim figure, and girlishly freckled cheeks.

"Jesus Christ forgives your sins and washes you in the holy water of His love."

"Hallelujah!"

"Godparents and sponsors, if you would now submerge the postulants."

Gilbert Drake put a hand on the young boy's shoulder and pressed down, till his head was completely beneath the waterline of the baptismal pool. For a few seconds Gilbert watched the boy's jet-black hair swirl upward, lifted from his scalp by the water like the hair of a corpse.

How easy it would be to drown someone. To drown a child. All you had to do was stand there.

It was a sinful thought. Gilbert dismissed it.

"In the name of the Father, and of the Son, and of the Holy Spirit."

"Amen."

"Now raise the postulants up, cleansed of sin, into the Light of the Lord."

The children came out of the water as one, gasping a collective breath. The congregation cheered. In the pool, wet hugs were exchanged. Gilbert Drake's godson looked up at him, gap-toothed and triumphant, his smooth Indian skin the only flash of brown among the other pasty-faced, East End boys.

"I did it, Uncle Gil! I did it!"

Gilbert Drake's eyes filled with tears. "You did it, Nikil. Your big brother would've been so proud."

THE ROOM BILLY HAMLIN RENTED IN King's Cross was dark and dank and depressing. A bare lightbulb hung pathetically from the ceiling, the plastic window blinds were broken, and the squalid single bed smelled of cigarette smoke and sweat.

Billy didn't care. He lay down on the bed and closed his eyes and a feeling of peace washed over him.

In a few days he would see her.

In a few days it would all be over.

He slept.

CHAPTER FIFTEEN

ROXIE DE VERE OBSERVED HER NAKED body in the mirror and frowned. A small curve in her midriff bothered her.

I'm getting fat. If I stuck it out far enough, I'd look pregnant.

She tried it, edging forward in the wheelchair the physical therapists at Guy's Hospital had designed especially for her, to enable her to take showers by herself. Turning sideways, she stroked her bloated stomach and struck a maternal pose.

"It's as close as I'll ever come," she said out loud.

Roxie's hatred for her mother was like a thing then, solid and physical, a teddy bear that she could clutch to her chest and nurture. At other times it felt more like a rock, something heavy and grounded that she could chain herself to while she screamed. One day she would do it. She would hurl that rock into the ocean of her own self-pity and drown. Then her mother would be sorry.

Or would she? Roxie didn't know anymore.

All she knew was that Andrew Beesley was the only man she would ever love. And that thanks to her mother, Andrew was gone.

Wheeling herself into her bedroom, Roxie got dressed.

It took a long time, but thanks to the inventiveness of her medical team, and the hundreds of thousands of pounds thrown at the problem by her father, Roxie could now manage almost all of life's daily tasks for herself.

"You could live independently, you know," Marie, Roxie's chief physical therapist, had told her repeatedly. "Get your own place. You don't *have* to live at home if you don't want to."

Roxie told Marie that she stayed on at Kingsmere for her father's sake. "Mummy's away so much. Darling Daddy would be desperately lonely on his own." But the real reason she stayed was to spite her mother. As much as Roxie loathed living under the same roof as Alexia, she knew that Alexia hated it even more.

Why should that bitch have a peaceful, happy life with Daddy after what she did to me?

She should be punished. She should suffer.

Roxie pulled her blond hair back into a ponytail and dabbed blusher on her cheeks. She was still a beautiful young woman, despite her ruined body. Parliament's summer recess was coming up. As usual, the De Vere family would decamp to Martha's Vineyard for the holidays, with Alexia jetting back and forth to London as needed.

If only there were a way I could really hurt her, thought Roxie. The only thing Alexia had ever truly cared about was her career. By rights, that was what she should lose. Unfortunately, Roxie's mother had an almost supernatural gift for political survival.

Still. *One day . . .*

In her study at Cheyne Walk, Alexia De Vere flipped through the file that Sir Edward Manning had given her. She'd requested the information only yesterday, but with

142

typical efficiency, Edward had had the file on her desk by eight o'clock this morning. It was a lot thicker and more detailed than she'd expected.

"You got all this from the U.S. State Department?" she'd asked.

"I got it from a reliable source, Home Secretary."

"And nobody else knows I requested it? You didn't discuss it with Commissioner Grant?"

Sir Edward Manning looked affronted. "You asked me not to, Home Secretary. Of course I didn't."

Alexia thought, *Perhaps I was wrong to distrust him. He's loyal to the department, if not to me personally. As long as I make sure our interests are aligned, Edward's going to be a useful ally.*

"Are you sure you're feeling quite well, Edward?" she asked, putting the report aside. "You look as if you're in pain. Your chest."

Belatedly, Sir Edward Manning realized that he was clutching the wound again. He'd had to change his shirt three times yesterday and was crunching down ibuprofen tablets like M&M's. Sergei Milescu had stopped by last night, to ask about "progress." He'd insisted on sex, which was agony for Edward, and left with the unspoken threat of violence hanging heavy in the air.

"My friends are not patient people, Eddie. They want results."

"But I don't even know what I'm looking for!" Sir Edward Manning had pleaded. "I need time. I need to gain her trust. Can't you explain?"

Sergei Milescu shrugged. "Not my problem. I'll see you soon, Eddie."

Sir Edward looked at Alexia De Vere. "I had a minor accident, Home Secretary. I fell off my bike on the way into work."

Alexia looked horrified. "When?"

"Oh, a few days ago. At the end of last week."

"Well, why on earth didn't you say so? You must go home and rest."

"There's no need, Home Secretary."

"There is need. You're in your sixties, Edward. You must take these things seriously."

"It's only a few scrapes and bruises. I'm perfectly fit to work."

Alexia shook her head. "I won't hear of it. I'm working from home myself this afternoon, so there's no need for you to be here. Go home. I'll have my driver take you."

Rereading the report Edward had given her in her home office, Alexia wondered whether her PPS *had* actually gone to bed, or whether he'd sneaked back into the office to work. Career civil servants like Sir Edward Manning—"lifers," as they were known in Parliament—were almost all workaholics, addicted to their jobs and the buzz of Westminster life. But she quickly forgot Edward as his report once again engrossed her.

CONFIDENTIAL PSYCHIATRIC EVALUATION:
WILLIAM J. HAMLIN.

The patient displays classic paranoid schizophrenic symptoms, including delusions and auditory hallucinations, frequently triggered by the telephone or television. He claims to hear one specific voice, a classic dominant negative hallucination combining critical commentary with specific instructions to the patient. He intermittently describes this voice as female. (Mother?? Deceased during patient's infancy. Patient alluded in treatment to feelings of abandonment and betrayal.) Generally suffers from

144

obsessional thoughts about women, mostly nonsexual/ family-oriented, e.g., acute anxiety about his daughter. His divorce also seems to be an underlying factor in his delusional thinking and psychosis, although relations with ex-wife appear good.

Intermittent depression but no suicidal thoughts. No self-aggrandizing. No recorded violent tendencies. Very limited aggression.

The patient's condition is manageable with medication and home care, <u>when accepted.</u> Atypical antipsychotics have been highly effective in this patient's treatment, esp. Geodon (ziprasidone). Unfortunately his track record of staying on meds is poor. Alcohol abuse remains an ongoing aggravating factor.

The psychiatrist had signed and dated the report eighteen months ago. Alexia read the doctor's notes again and again, trying to piece together William Hamlin's tortured inner life both from what was written and from what she gleaned between the lines: Who *was* this man who was looking for her?

And what did he want from her?

He has close relationships with women, his wife, his daughter—yet women are at the root of his mental instability.

He feels abandoned and betrayed by women. And yet this is not an angry man, not a violent man.

He hears voices, frightening voices.

Alexia smiled. *I guess that's one thing we have in common. Only* my *voices are real. No amount of ziprasidone is going to make* them *stop.*

145

On balance, everything she read in Sir Edward Manning's file confirmed Commissioner Grant's view. William Hamlin had not poisoned Teddy and Alexia's dog. Nor, in all likelihood, did he mean Alexia any harm. Even so, the thought of him out there, wandering confusedly around England looking for her, hunting her down, was not a happy one. Commissioner Grant had gotten no further in locating him.

"It's very difficult with psychiatric patients. Unless they actively seek help, or offend, they quickly slip off radar. As a tourist with no National Health Service number, no fixed address, no National Insurance, Hamlin's effectively a ghost here."

Alexia De Vere was afraid of ghosts.

It was time to see just how far Sir Edward Manning's loyalty might stretch.

JAMES MARTIN, DOWNING STREET'S CHIEF OF communications, put his head in his hands.

Henry Whitman asked, "How bad is it, James? Honestly."

"Honestly, Prime Minister? It's not good. I hesitate to use the word 'disaster,' but . . ."

The two men sat at a round conference table with a sea of this morning's newspapers spread out in front of them. Alexia De Vere's statement on the agricultural workers affair had caused an uproar in the liberal press. It had also lit a fire under the more right-wing elements of the British public, inciting racist violence and public unrest on a scale not seen since Enoch Powell's famous "Rivers of Blood" speech in the 1960s.

"There's been looting in Burnley, an arson attack at an immigration holding facility in Dover, and violent protests at the docks in Southampton. The British National Party are calling for simultaneous mass rallies in London, Manchester, and Birmingham on Saturday. They're calling themselves the 'Reclaim Britain Movement.'"

"Jesus. What do the newspapers say?"

"Nothing you want to hear. The *Guardian* calls Alexia a 'loose cannon.' The *Times* wonders whether the Home Office is running the government and the *Indie* thinks the home secretary should be charged under the Incitement to Racial Hatred Act. Then you have the *Sun*, hailing Alexia as a hero. Oh, and this cartoon from the *Telegraph*."

James Martin handed his boss the relevant page. It showed Alexia De Vere, dressed as Britannia and seated on a throne, with the prime minister as a lapdog under her feet. Alexia was offering Henry a bone, labeled *European Union*. The caption read *Chew on that, boy.*

"I thought you told her to tone the statement down."

Henry Whitman said grimly, "I did."

"We can't go on like this, Prime Minister. You must be seen to regain control."

"I'll fly up to Burnley this morning. Can you organize a press conference for six o'clock tonight here?"

"I can. But I suggest we do it this morning, as soon as possible. The one thing you don't want is for the Home Office to get in there first."

ALEXIA TOOK THE CALL IN THE car.

She'd expected the prime minister to be angry. But not this angry.

"I told you, I expressly told you, to tone the statement down."

"And I did tone it down."

"You changed one word! Have you seen what's going on

147

out there? It's a major public order situation, Alexia. People are going to get killed."

"People are angry, Henry," Alexia said coolly, "and I don't blame them. The British public are tired of being held hostage by a bunch of disrespectful immigrants who sponge off our benefits and piss on our flag. I'm standing up for ordinary voters."

"Horseshit. You're trying to make personal political capital. If you want to indulge in some power struggle with cabinet colleagues, do it in private."

"But, Henry—"

"Be QUIET!" It was the first time Henry Whitman had ever raised his voice to her. "You say NOTHING, do you understand? Nothing. Not to me, not to the press, not to anyone. You lay low and you let me handle this mess. Are we clear?"

Alexia was silent.

"Have you any idea how many people are calling for your resignation, Alexia?" The prime minister's frustration was palpable. "How much pressure I'm under to rein you in?"

"No idea whatsoever," Alexia said defiantly. "Nor do I care."

"Well, you should care. I can be pushed too far, you know, Alexia. Remember that."

"So can I, Henry. Perhaps *you* should remember that."

She hung up. Sitting beside her, Sir Edward Manning noticed that her hands were shaking. Whether it was from fear or anger, he couldn't tell.

"Can I help, Home Secretary?"

"No. Thank you, Edward. I'm fine."

They drove on in silence. The traffic eased as they merged onto the Embankment. In a few minutes they'd be at Parliament Square.

148

"There *is* one thing, Edward. It's about the file you gave me last night, on our friend Mr. Hamlin. The American."

Sir Edward Manning's ears pricked up. The prime minister had clearly just ripped Mrs. De Vere a new asshole. Her career was on a knife edge over this immigration furor. And yet her prime concern seemed to be a single, harmless crackpot.

Why?

"What about him, Home Secretary?"

"Well, the police have had no success in tracking him down. I wondered if you might know of any . . . alternative channels."

"I see."

"I'd like to locate him."

Sir Edward paused for just a moment, as if about to ask a question, but he obviously thought better of it.

"Of course, Home Secretary. Consider it done. Oh, goodness!"

The scene in Parliament Square was chaotic. *Mob* would be putting it too strongly, but there were angry groups of protesters from all sides of the debate waving placards and shouting competing slogans. Alexia's photograph was being held aloft like an icon, triumphantly by some groups and ironically by others. One gathering of mostly male, Eastern European faces had drawn devil horns on the home secretary's head. Through the Daimler's blacked-out windows Alexia heard the abuse, both the English chants of "racist bitch" and the hate-loaded shouts in various Slavic languages.

"Go around," Sir Edward Manning hissed to the driver. "We'll go in the back entrance."

"We will do no such thing," Alexia said firmly. "Stop here." And before Sir Edward could restrain her, she had opened the car door and stepped outside.

"Home Secretary!" he called after her but it was useless. The noise of the crowd was deafening. Once people realized who it was, pandemonium broke loose. Luckily, two policemen swooped in to protect the home secretary, one on either side of her, but they offered little protection against the swelling mass of bodies.

For the second time that day, Alexia felt frightened. The prime minister's phone call earlier had frightened her, although she hadn't shown it, either to Henry Whitman or to her own staff. *Never show weakness. Never back down.* When cornered, she had a tendency to fight even harder. She knew with hindsight that her statement on the flag affair had been mistaken. But she would never admit it, especially now, when the stakes were so high. She must appear strong, to Downing Street, to the cabinet, to everybody. Strength was what Alexia De Vere did best.

But this was different. This was physical fear. She'd acted on impulse, jumping out of the car, but she knew now it had been a mistake. *I should have listened to Edward and gone around the back. This is dangerous.*

Aware that she might be being photographed, she held her head high as she was hustled through the jeering crowd, almost all of them men. But she was afraid. The men's physical closeness was intimidating. Alexia could smell their foul breath, soured by bitterness, and felt suddenly nauseous. Then, out of nowhere, she felt herself being grabbed by the arm and pulled forward. She couldn't see her rescuer, but she knew he was dragging her toward the private members' entrance to Parliament, toward safety.

My security detail. Thank God. I must be more careful next time.

Relaxing her body, she allowed herself to be pulled closer, tuning out the angry faces on either side of her, focusing only on the door ahead. At last the danger was past. A wall of police moved in behind her, forcing the protesters back. The hand that had been gripping her arm let go and Alexia looked up for the first time into the eyes of her savior.

"You!" she gasped.

"Me."

Billy Hamlin smiled. Then he said two words that Alexia De Vere had thought she would never hear again. Two words that brought the past rushing back and that filled her heart with utter, abject dread.

"Hello, Toni."

PART III

CHAPTER SIXTEEN

TONI GILLETTI THOUGHT DISAPPEARING WOULD BE difficult.
In fact it was frighteningly easy.

A few days after Billy Hamlin's trial, she sneaked out of
her bedroom window in the wee hours of the morning and
ran. She ran and she ran and she didn't look back. When
she could run no more she waited. For retribution. For her
father, Walter, to come for her. Or her friends. Or the police.
Or Billy's lawyers, already busy working on an appeal. Surely,
eventually the truth would catch up with her? She would
be hauled back to jail and left to rot.

But nothing happened. No TV appeals, no expensive
private detectives on her tail. No one came for Toni Gilletti.
No one cared.

Well, not quite no one. The one person who *did* care
had sacrificed his freedom for Toni Gilletti and allowed
himself to be branded a murderer. In return, Toni had promised to marry him, to give him her life just as he had given
her his. An eye for an eye.

But when push came to shove, Toni couldn't do it. She
couldn't sacrifice her whole life on the altar of one teenage
mistake. Not for Billy Hamlin. Not for anyone. Once she

realized this, her path was clear: there was nothing left for Toni Gilletti to do but to run.

She spent the first two years of her new life in that mecca of lost souls: Las Vegas. Nevada was like another planet, hot and dry and soulless and sleepless and as good a place to get lost as any. It was 1975 and business was booming, with new hotels and casinos popping up out of the ground every month like vast, concrete krakens rising from the waves. Everybody was hiring, and nobody cared about your past. If ever there was a place to reinvent yourself, it was Las Vegas in the midseventies. Toni Gilletti did just that. Rechristening herself Alexia Parker (her best friend in grade school had been called Alexia and she'd always loved the name. Parker just sounded unobtrusive and real), she started working as a bartender. She had no papers and no Social Security number, but Vegas employers were happy to pay cash. Alexia Parker was a sexy girl, which the customers liked. She was also hardworking and reliable, which the club owners loved. Sexy girls were a dime a dozen in Vegas, but Alexia Parker combined her good looks with abstinence, neither drinking nor doing drugs. That was a whole lot rarer. She also appeared to have taken a vow of celibacy, never dating customers or other bar staff.

Toni Gilletti had been a party girl. But Toni Gilletti was dead. Alexia Parker lived to work. In two years she'd earned enough of a nest egg to put herself through college. She applied to UCLA, intending to major in political science.

Unfortunately, unlike the Vegas bar owners, UCLA *did* need papers. Alexia Parker had no Social Security number, no passport, no birth certificate, no history of any kind. It was a problem.

Alexia solved the problem by moving to L.A., breaking

her vow of celibacy, and sleeping with Duane from the Social Security office on Santa Monica Boulevard.

"I could get fired for this. I could go to jail," Duane moaned, typing Alexia Parker's fake details into the state records while she gave him expert head under the desk.

"So could I," Alexia said, spitting out Duane's twitching cock like a chick rejecting a worm. "Which means we'll both keep the secret, right?"

"What are you doing? Don't stop now!"

"I *said*, we'll both keep the secret. Right, Duane?"

"Right, yes, of course. You got it. I ain't gonna tell nobody. Just please, please don't stop."

Alexia Parker left Duane's office with a newly minted Social Security card and a backdated birth certificate. Her SAT results she forged herself.

Alexia did not consider herself a dishonest person. She simply did what she had to do. She looked forward, never back, and she solved problems as they arose, using her natural talent for acting and mimicry to help her forge a new identity.

First rule of politics: *be pragmatic.*

Only two years later, as she was working her ass off, she graduated UCLA summa cum laude and boarded a plane for London. There was no way she could pursue a political career in Washington, not without her past coming back to haunt her. But politics was in her blood now. It was time for another new chapter.

Alexia Parker landed at Heathrow Airport with no friends, no connections, and two hundred pounds of cash in her pocket.

She was twenty-three years old.

*

BILLY HAMLIN'S GRIP ON HER ARM was tightening.

"Please, Toni. I need to talk to you."

Her heart pounding, Alexia wrenched herself free.

"I'm afraid you're confused. I don't know any Toni. Excuse me."

The members' entrance to Parliament was only a few feet away. She stumbled toward it desperately, afraid for her life. But Billy Hamlin lunged for her, grabbing her again.

"Toni, for God's sake, it's me. It's Billy."

Alexia looked into his eyes and saw the confusion written there, the desperation. *What are you doing here, Billy? Don't you understand? Toni's dead. She died years ago. I'm Alexia now, a new person, a phoenix risen from the ashes of a ruined life. I can't let you drag me back there!*

"Let go of me."

"I know you're busy." Tears welled in Billy Hamlin's eyes. "But this is important. It's life or death. My daughter's in terrible danger."

"Step back please, sir." Finally, a policeman managed to pull Billy away. Dizzy with relief, Alexia almost fainted. Thankfully Sir Edward Manning reappeared just in time, grabbing Alexia's hand and helping her through the gate and into the building.

"Are you all right, Home Secretary?"

Alexia nodded. She was still shaking. Through the closed door, she could hear Billy's screams. Sir Edward Manning heard them too.

"Toni, please! It's my daughter. My daughter! Why are you doing this? I KNOW WHO YOU ARE!"

They waited for the commotion to calm down and silence to fall. Then Sir Edward Manning said, "I think we need to talk, Home Secretary. Don't you?"

*

158

THEY RETREATED TO ALEXIA'S PRIVATE OFFICE. Sir Edward Manning shut the door and locked it.

"That was him, wasn't it? That was William Hamlin."

Alexia nodded. "I think so. Yes."

"He knew you. You knew each other."

Alexia looked past Sir Edward out of the window. Two barges were making their stately way down the Thames, as leisurely and untroubled as a pair of drowsy swans.

This is reality. London, Parliament, my life with Teddy. The present.

I am Alexia De Vere. I am the home secretary of Great Britain.

The past is gone.

Only the past wasn't gone. It was outside in Parliament Square, grabbing hold of her in broad daylight, demanding to be heard. It was threatening everything she had become, everything she had worked for.

"Home Secretary?" Sir Edward Manning disturbed her reverie. "What is your connection with William Hamlin?"

"We have no connection, Edward."

"I don't believe that, Home Secretary," the civil servant said bluntly. "What you tell me will go no further than these four walls. But I need to know what's going on. I can't do my job otherwise."

Alexia's mind raced.

Should she trust him?

Did she have a choice?

"We knew one another slightly. As kids. That's all. I haven't laid eyes on Billy in almost forty years."

"But you chose not to share this information with the police. Why?"

"Because I was born in the United States and grew up there. Nobody in this country knows that—not the media, not the party, not even personal friends—and I'd like it to stay that way."

Sir Edward Manning took this in. It was quite a revelation. To have made it as far in public life as Alexia De Vere, and to have successfully concealed such a big piece of one's past, was quite a feat.

"May I ask why you chose to conceal this, Home Secretary? After all, being American is hardly a crime."

"Indeed. But I'm not American, Edward. I renounced my citizenship years ago, before I stood for Parliament. My whole adult life has been spent in this country and I consider myself completely English. Besides, I didn't conceal anything. I've never been asked about my childhood other than in the most generic of ways. It's never come up, that's all."

"But it's coming up now."

Alexia sighed. "Yes. That night, at Kingsmere, the figure on the CCTV footage. There was something familiar about him. I couldn't put my finger on it at first. But then it came back to me."

"You recognized Hamlin?"

"Not definitively. I didn't know it was him. I wasn't sure. Like I say, I hadn't seen him since we were children. But as soon as Commissioner Grant mentioned the name . . ."

She left the sentence hanging.

"Did you know he'd been in prison?"

Alexia hesitated for a moment. Then she said, "Yes. The case was in the news at the time."

"About the child who drowned."

"Yes." Alexia shivered. Just hearing the word *drowned* still made her blood run cold. "But I knew nothing about what had happened to him since. His mental illness, the delusions, all of that stuff."

160

Sir Edward Manning asked, "Why do you think Hamlin would want to contact you now?"

"I have no idea. You saw his file. He's had business and financial problems, as well as his mental health issues."

Sir Edward Manning cast his mind back. He did remember reading something about bankruptcy. Hamlin's auto-repair business going under during the recession.

"You think he may be after money?"

Alexia shrugged. "Like I said, I have no idea."

"Were you lovers?"

The question was so blunt, for a moment Alexia was blindsided.

"I . . . we . . . does it matter? For heaven's sake, Edward, it was forty years ago!"

"It may matter, Home Secretary. Does Hamlin know anything that he could use to blackmail you?"

Alexia looked away. "No. Not that I can think of."

"What about sexual peccadilloes, things of that nature?"

"No." Alexia shot her PPS a look that could have frozen fire.

"Drugs?"

"No! I mean maybe the odd joint. It was the sixties." She ran a hand through her hair. "Look, when Commissioner Grant confirmed that the man at Kingsmere that night was Billy Hamlin, I was curious as much as anything. That's why I asked you for his file, privately. But what I read disturbed me. Clearly Billy isn't well. He's psychotic, he develops weird obsessions with famous individuals. And now he shows up here, in England, behaving in a very confused, aggressive manner toward me. I don't like it."

"Nor do I, Home Secretary," Sir Edward Manning said with feeling. "Nor do I."

For a few moments silence fell. On one level, Alexia had told Edward the truth. She didn't know what Billy Hamlin wanted from her. He'd mentioned his daughter being in danger, but according to his psychiatrist's report, unspecified threats to the lives of loved ones were a common delusional theme. Or perhaps it was money he needed. Who knew?

What Alexia did know, with certainty, was that she wasn't about to let Billy Hamlin destroy her life. She'd worked too hard for her career, and her marriage, to allow them to be threatened by a ghost from the past, a past to which she no longer felt any connection. Not while she still had breath in her body.

Besides, the girl that Billy Hamlin was looking for was already dead.

Alexia De Vere had buried Toni Gilletti a long, long time ago.

"Edward?"

"Home Secretary?"

"I'd like you to get rid of him."

The hairs on Sir Edward Manning's neck stood on end. He looked at his boss with new eyes.

There's a determination there, a ruthlessness that I didn't appreciate before. She's a street fighter. A survivor.

Just like me.

What had Hamlin shouted at Alexia, when the police dragged him away?

I know who you are.

Sir Edward Manning wished he could say the same. Not least because his own survival might now depend on it. He thought about Sergei Milescu and the faceless people paying him. He remembered the sharp pain of the kitchen knife as it cut through his skin, the cold terror of being tied to his own bed, helpless, with the blade hovering over his genitals. He remembered the camera and the awful, degrading things that Sergei had made him do.

Edward Manning had secrets of his own.

For a tense few seconds the civil servant and the cabinet minister eyed each other across the desk like two desert lizards. Unblinking, cold-blooded, and as still as statues, each assessed the other's intentions. Were they to be hunting partners, ranged against Billy Hamlin? Or was one of them the predator and one the prey?

"Yes, Home Secretary. I can get rid of him. If that's what you want."

"It is, Edward. It is."

"Then consider it done." Sir Edward Manning got up to leave the room. When he reached the door he turned. "Just one small question, Home Secretary. I heard Hamlin calling you 'Toni.' Why was that?"

"It was a nickname I had as a little girl," Alexia answered unhesitatingly. "To be honest with you, I can't remember why. So strange, hearing it again all these years later."

Sir Edward Manning said, "I can imagine."

The door closed and he was gone.

IT WAS ALL OVER SO QUICKLY.

There were no lawyers, no phone calls, no court appearances or appeals. After Alexia De Vere refused to see him, the police threw Billy Hamlin into the back of a van with six other protesters and kept him in a cell at Westminster police station. A few hours later a smartly dressed man arrived to claim him.

"Mr. Hamlin? There's been a misunderstanding. You can come with me."

The man seemed avuncular and kind. He had an educated accent and was wearing a suit. Billy felt quite safe getting into his chauffeur-driven car, assuming that they were heading straight to the Home Office. In fact, as soon as the car door closed, Billy was restrained and injected with some sort of sedative. He was dimly aware of being transferred from the fancy car to an anonymous-looking white van and driven to Heathrow. After that, it was like a dream. His passport was taken, then returned with various hostile-looking stamps in black ink on its last pages. He was escorted, luggageless, onto an ordinary Virgin Atlantic passenger plane, strapped into his seat, and, as he fought the drug-induced sleep that inevitably claimed him, launched into the gray, drizzly sky. When he awoke, he was in New York, dumped penniless and alone back on U.S. soil like an unwanted package returned to sender.

Dazed, he found an airport bench to sit on and rummaged through his pockets for his cell phone.

Gone.

No! It couldn't be gone! What was going to happen when the voice called? Who would answer?

Billy Hamlin started to shake.

Why hadn't Alexia De Vere listened to him? Why hadn't he made her listen?

He had failed. Now there would be blood, more blood, and it would be on his hands.

He wept.

"Mr. Hamlin?"

Billy looked up, defeated.

He didn't struggle as the strong arms gripped him and carried him away.

CHAPTER SEVENTEEN

"Okay. So we have nine lobsters, six pounds of crayfish, fresh Adams Farm tomatoes for the salad. How many of those?"

Lydia, the Meyer family's Filipina cook-cum-housekeeper, held up an enormous, groaning burlap sack. "Plenty. Enough to feed an army, Mrs. Lucy."

"Good. Because we're going to *be* an army. Now what else? Beef?"

"Already in the oven, slow-cooking."

"Fresh bread?"

"Got it."

"Strawberries? Tonic water for Teddy's G-and-T? Oh, darn it." Lucy Meyer clapped a hand dripping in diamonds to her fevered brow. "We're totally out of gin. I'll send Arnie into town to get some. Do you think the A&P's still open?"

"At one o'clock in the afternoon? Yes, Mrs. Lucy. Definitely." The housekeeper put a reassuring hand on her boss's arm. Lydia liked working for Mrs. Meyer. "Try to relax. The dinner's going to be just perfect."

Lucy Meyer hoped so. She liked things to be perfect, from her dinner parties, to the just-so caramel highlights in her hair, to the updated-every-season soft furnishings of her Martha's Vineyard summer home. During her childhood, Lucy's family summered on nearby Nantucket. She remembered her mother's picnics from those vacations as things of exquisite beauty, from the colorful salads and fresh seafood to the chicly mismatched French chinaware and the crisp white linen cloths thrown over the picnic blankets. As for evening dinners, those were nothing short of spectacular. Lucy remembered long, antique tables, sparkling with cut crystal and the finest silverware. Back then the men all wore tuxes to dinner and the ladies dazzled in chiffon and sequins and silk and lace and jewels. Lucy and her little brother would watch the preparations in awe, before being hustled upstairs to the nursery by their nanny.

Of course, things had changed since the sixties. As an adult, Lucy preferred Martha's Vineyard over Nantucket, partly because it had more life to it and felt less starched. Everything on the Vineyard was about cookouts and pool parties and sustainable, locally caught seafood. But that didn't mean an effort shouldn't be made, especially for Alexia and Teddy's welcome-back dinner.

Wandering into her huge, vaulted drawing room, Lucy replumped the already perfect cushions on her Ralph Lauren couches and tried to take her housekeeper's advice.

Relax. It's just a party. Everything'll be fine.

How on earth her friend Alexia De Vere coped with the stresses of running a country, Lucy Meyer had no idea. She found running a home quite exhausting enough.

Alexia De Vere's world was as far removed from Lucy Meyer's as it was possible to be. But what made the friendship work was that neither woman would have traded her life for the other's. Lucy loved being a homemaker and a hostess every bit as much as Alexia loved politics and the trappings of power. Both women excelled at what they did. And despite their different lives, they did have some things in common. Both were married to wonderful, supportive husbands who worked in the finance industry. Teddy De Vere was a hedge fund manager, with a niche but lucrative European business. Arnie Meyer was a venture capitalist with stakes in funds across the continental United States as well as in Asia and now the growing Middle Eastern market. The two men had never worked together directly, but they understood each other's business. From day one they had gotten along like a house on fire.

It was hard to believe that more than twenty years had passed since Arnie Meyer sold the De Veres their summer home. The Gables was a comfortable, midsize property on the edge of the Meyer's Pilgrim Farm estate, with a pool, a small guesthouse, and an attractive backyard filled with clematis and roses and towering hollyhocks. Arnie and Lucy lived in the much grander "big house," a spectacular eighteenth-century farm with high ceilings, original wide oak floorboards, and vast, airy rooms filled with light. Alexia and Lucy had both been young mothers when they met, the summer that Teddy bought The Gables. Lucy remembered her first meeting with Alexia as if it were yesterday. Already a British MP, she was clearly extremely ambitious even then. But no one, least of all Lucy Meyer, imagined that her new neighbor would one day reach the dizzying heights of power that she now occupied.

My friend the British home secretary.

Lucy quite literally never got tired of saying it.

Tonight was an extra-special occasion. Not only because Alexia and Teddy were back on the island for the summer after Alexia's triumphant appointment. But because Michael, their ridiculously good-looking son, was joining them for the first time in many years. Roxie always came out for the summers. Poor girl, she had nothing else to do, and of course, since the accident, she and her father had become pretty much inseparable. But Michael De Vere hadn't been to the Vineyard since his teens. Lucy Meyer couldn't help but think how wonderful it would be, how darling and perfect and just wonderful, if Michael De Vere were to fall in love with her daughter, Summer. *Then we could all be one, big, happy family.*

Lucy's twenty-two-year-old daughter had recently broken up with her college boyfriend, the dreadful, pompous Chad Bates. (*Chad. I mean, really. Who has a perfect little newborn baby boy and calls him Chad?*) In Lucy's book, this meant that Summer was ripe for a new romance. And just imagine if Summer and Michael got married and had babies! Lucy and Alexia could be the doting grannies together.

It could happen. Lucy Meyer could make it happen.

And it all starts tonight.

MICHAEL DE VERE SAT IN THE back pew of Grace Church on Woodlawn Avenue, snoring loudly while the congregation sang "Bind Us Together."

"Wake *up*!" His sister, Roxie, nudged him in the ribs. "People are staring."

Michael jerked awake. Immediately a wave of nausea hit him like a punch in the gut. What the hell was he doing here? What madness had possessed him to come, not just to this church full of uptight Episcopalian Americans, but to this island?

He knew the answer, of course. He was here in an effort to appease his father. Teddy had been so furious about Michael dropping out of Oxford that he'd threatened to disinherit him.

"I'll leave every penny to your sister! Don't think I won't!"

But Michael had stood his ground, pressing ahead with his plans for Kingsmere Events and renting office space in Oxford with his friend Tommy. By an incredible stroke of luck they'd immediately landed a huge gig in the Hamptons, organizing a sixtieth birthday party for a billionaire real estate developer on his new Oceano superyacht. Just forty-eight hours ago, Michael had been lying back in a luxury tender with a supermodel under each arm, gazing up at a hundred grand's worth of fireworks exploding across the East Hampton sky and mentally calculating his profit. (Okay, so perhaps "supermodel" was pushing it. The girls were actually high-class Russian hookers, but they charged like supermodels and looked like goddesses, so who was counting?) The last thing on earth Michael wanted to do the next morning was catch a plane over to sleepy Martha's Vineyard, the island with the world's biggest stick up its ass. But Teddy had insisted. "It would mean a lot to your mother if you came out this year."

For all his apparent independence of spirit, Michael De Vere was devoted to his mother, and to his inheritance. He had no intention of losing either. So here he was, hopelessly hungover, trussed up like a Christmas turkey in a jacket and tie, trying not to puke during the Lord's Prayer.

At long last the service was over. Michael pushed Roxie's wheelchair out into the bright sunshine, wincing in pain behind his Ray-Bans.

Alexia slipped a slender arm around his waist. "Are you all right, darling?" she asked. "You don't look well."

"I'm fine, Mummy, thanks."

"He's hungover," growled Teddy.

"Lovely service." Michael forced a pious smile, but Teddy wasn't buying it.

"Please. Pull the other one. I can smell the booze on your breath from here."

In his regulation corduroy trousers, sport jacket, and brogues—Teddy De Vere wore the same clothes to church every Sunday of the year, and saw no reason to change because he happened to be in America, or because the temperature was nudging well into the nineties—Michael's father was like Lord Grantham from *Downton Abbey*, as English as PG Tips tea and cucumber sandwiches. If Disneyland had an England theme park, Teddy De Vere could have been one of the characters.

Alexia winked at Michael. "Hungover or not, we're glad you made it, darling. Aren't we, Teddy?"

"Humph."

"Now we must go and say hello to Father Timothy. We'll see you two at dinner tonight."

"Dinner?" Michael frowned.

"At the Meyers'," said Alexia, kissing him on the cheek and wiping off a lipstick mark with her handkerchief. "Drinks are at six."

"No kiss for me?" Roxie said sarcastically.

Alexia yawned. "Do change the record, Roxanne. I wonder sometimes if you have any idea how boring you can be."

"Bitch," muttered Roxie under her breath as her mother walked away.

Michael winced. He hated the conflict between his mother and sister more than anything. Pushing Roxanne's wheelchair across the street to the Even Keel coffee shop, a favorite hangout since their teens, he bought her a conciliatory frappucino.

"I suppose you're going to defend her now, are you?" said Roxie.

170

"No. I'm going to keep out of it."

"You and Dad are as bad as each other. You never stand up to her."

"I seriously don't know if I can make it to the Meyers' drinks party this evening," said Michael, adroitly changing the subject. "My head feels like someone dropped an anvil on it."

"Yes, well, *I'll* drop an anvil on it if you abandon me tonight. You can't leave me to cringe through hours of Mummy's boasting on my own: G7 Summit this, Ten Downing Street that. Lucy Meyer lapping it all up like a poodle. Blech."

Michael frowned but said nothing.

"Summer's flying in specially for it, you know," Roxie teased. "I know you wouldn't want to miss *her*."

Michael rolled his eyes to heaven. Summer Meyer had been his and Roxie's childhood playmate. She'd always had a quiet but burning crush on Michael. Shy even as a little girl, as a teenager poor Summer had gained a huge amount of weight. The last time Michael saw her, she must have been seventeen, weighed around a hundred and eighty pounds, and was so silent in his presence she was borderline autistic. The thought of sitting through a four-hour dinner trying to make polite conversation with a sweet but mute Rosie O'Donnell look-alike was stomach-churning. And Michael De Vere's stomach was already churning.

"If I come, will you make Dad put me back in the will?"

Roxie laughed. "No. But if you don't come, when I have all the family money and you're completely financially dependent on me, I'll send you to the workhouse."

"Fine. I'll come. But I am *not* sitting next to Summer Meyer and that's final."

*

"MICHAEL. YOU'RE SITTING *THERE*. NEXT TO Summer. If she ever gets here."

Lucy Meyer pointed to an empty chair on Michael's right. Roxie De Vere collapsed into giggles, earning herself a death stare from Michael. Talk about the hot seat! On Michael's left sat Vangie Braberman, the stone-deaf widow of Senator Braberman, who owned one of the smaller cottages on the Pilgrim Farm estate. Vangie was in her late seventies and had a complex series of ailments that provided her with inexhaustible conversational material. Michael De Vere had known her since his childhood, and at this point probably knew as much as Vangie Braberman's doctor about the old lady's irritable bowel syndrome, and certainly more than he wanted to. Vangie refused to wear a hearing aid, but carried an ear trumpet that had once belonged to her grandmother, which made her look like something out of a Victorian picture book. She was fond of hitting young people with it if they insisted on mumbling, something that, according to Vangie, Michael's generation did "CONSTANTLY!"

On Michael's right, an empty chair sat reserved for Summer Meyer. In the faintest wisp of a silver lining to the cloud currently looming over Michael's head, Summer's plane had been delayed out of Boston, so he'd be spared her shy, burning stares for the first course at least. But she was expected to arrive in time for dessert. If Michael's memory served, no force on earth could keep Summer Meyer away from a good dessert. The prospect of Lucy's tiramisu would be enough to have her swimming across the sound from Boston. *The first whale sighted off the Vineyard this summer.*

Meanwhile Summer's mother, Lucy, trim and pretty in a plain white shirtwaist dress and raffia wedgies, was on her feet, relishing her role as hostess. Lucy Meyer had a motherly, nurturing way about her that Michael's own mother had always lacked, but she also managed to keep herself in great shape. As a boy, Michael used to fancy Lucy Meyer as the ultimate yummy mummy. He was pleased to see that she hadn't changed.

"Now, if we're all seated, before we start I'd like to say a few words." Lucy's tinkling, feminine voice rang out around the room. "All of us here tonight have known one another a long time. Arnie and I like to think of this as the Pilgrim Farm family. Every one of you is dear to our hearts. But one member of our party deserves special mention tonight."

All eyes turned to Alexia, who blushed becomingly at the chorus of "hear, hears."

"Not content with going into the British Parliament, our very own Mrs. De Vere decided that she should run the whole darn country."

"And who better?" Teddy chuckled, beaming with pride.

"Who indeed? So as well as a welcome-home party, tonight we would like to say a belated congratulations to the lovely Alexia. You may be a rabid Republican—"

"Conservative," Alexia corrected.

Lucy's father had been a politician and her family were all staunch Democrats.

"—but we love you and we could *not* be more proud. To Alexia!"

"To Alexia!"

Fifteen glasses were raised, the antique crystal clinking and dazzling in the candlelight. During the melee Michael stole a glance at his sister. Roxie's glass was also raised, but her once-soft face was set like flint. Michael thought sadly, *You could strike a match off her rage. There's murder in those eyes.*

"Sorry I'm late."

Everyone looked up. A tall, dark girl had walked into

the room during the toast, dropping her backpack with a thud on the wooden floor. She wore a simple pair of faded Levi's and a white T-shirt, the neck scooped low enough to show the tan lines from her bikini. Her long mane of chestnut hair was tied back in a ponytail and her makeup-free face glowed with health and youth, despite her obvious tiredness. She was, quite simply, stunning.

"Summer, darling!" Arnie Meyer stood up to hug his daughter.

"At last." Lucy clapped her hands "Come and sit down, sweetheart, over here. You're next to *Michael.*"

Summer blushed and shot her mother a look. Talk about mortifying! Lucy had all but patted the chair!

"Aren't you going to say hello?"

"Hi." Summer nodded awkwardly at Michael. "It's been awhile."

"Yes."

He wanted to say something suave, but he was too busy picking his jaw up from the table. *Bloody hell. If Arnie hadn't said her name out loud, I wouldn't even have recognized her.*

"Are you on the island for long?" Summer asked Michael politely.

"Erm . . . I, erm . . ."

"Unfortunately not." Alexia answered for him, telling the table at large: "Michael's just founded a new business back in England. We feel lucky he was able to make it out at all, don't we, Teddy?"

"Hmm." Teddy grunted disapprovingly.

"He has to fly back in a couple of days."

"Well, I . . . not necessarily," Michael stammered. His eyes were fixed on Summer's cheekbones and translucent, bronzed skin. And her lips, soft and the palest of pinks, parting invitingly as she took a sip of chilled white wine.

174

Had she always had those lips? Why had he never noticed them before? "I might be able to stay a bit longer. Tommy can hold the fort for a while. You know. If necessary."

"Really?" Alexia brightened. Having Michael here made everything so much easier at home. "That's wonderful. Are you sure you can spare the time?"

"Of course, Mum. Anything for you."

Roxie De Vere wondered how her brother managed to keep a straight face.

LATER, IN THE KITCHEN, ALEXIA HELPED Lucy prepare coffee.

"Dinner was a triumph, Luce. Thank you so much."

"It was all Lydia's doing. Anyway, dinner schminner," said Lucy, setting rose-printed coffee cups carefully onto bone-china saucers. "Talk to me. What's it like? I mean what's it *really* like?"

"The job? It's exciting." Alexia smiled but there was a wariness in her eyes. She was holding something back.

"But?"

"No buts. It's a great honor to have been appointed. And a huge challenge, of course."

"Honey," said Lucy kindly, "you're not on Fox News now. You don't need to give me the party line. Heck, I can't even vote in Merry Olde England, so you may as well tell me the truth."

Alexia smiled. "That's true, I suppose. Well, the job's terrific. But it's been stressful. I've had one or two unpleasant incidents."

"Which in English means . . . ?"

"Threats. There was a phone call, a few weeks before I got out here." Alexia told her about the sinister, distorted voice and the fanatical, fire-and-brimstone cursing.

175

"Something about shedding my blood in the dust. I don't know."

"My God," Lucy gasped. "How terrifying."

"I wouldn't go that far. But it bothered me that this wacko had my home number."

"I'll bet it did," Lucy said quietly. "Does Teddy know?"

"He knows about that phone call."

Lucy knew her friend well enough to read between the lines.

"But there's more. Something that you haven't told him."

The understatement made Alexia smile. "There's so much I haven't told him, Luce! Believe me, you have no idea. There are things that, if he knew, he'd leave me in an instant."

"Teddy? Leave you? Never!"

"He would."

Alexia sank down into the rocking chair in the corner. Here, in this familiar kitchen with her closest friend, so far from London and Westminster and everything that had happened, she felt an overwhelming urge to unburden herself. To have someone, one other person on this earth, know the whole truth about her past. Who she was—who she had been—and what she'd done. To have someone forgive her.

Could Lucy Meyer be that person?

Putting down the coffee cups, Lucy moved to her friend's side.

"Alexia, you're shaking, honey. What on earth's the matter? Whatever it is, you can tell me. It can't be that bad."

Can't it?

"Someone tried to contact me a few weeks ago. Someone from my past."

"What sort of someone? A boyfriend, you mean?"

"Of sorts, I guess." Alexia put her head in her hands.

"I want to tell you. I do. But I don't know where to start. There are things you don't know about me. Things nobody knows. Terrible things."

Lucy Meyer took this in. She understood instinctively that she shouldn't push, that she should let Alexia share her secrets in her own time.

"But this man from your past . . . he knew?"

"Yes. He came to see me. He'd been in prison and he has a history of mental problems."

"My *God*, Alexia. You *have* to tell Teddy. This man sounds downright dangerous."

"Yes, well, I dealt with it."

"How?"

"I had him deported."

"Good."

"Was it? You see, now I don't know if it was the right thing. I owe this man, you see. He did something for me once, something kind and noble, at great cost to himself. But when he needed me, I turned him away." To Alexia's own astonishment, she found herself starting to cry. "I just felt under so much pressure! The telephone threats, Billy turning up like that out of the blue . . ."

"His name's Billy? The man from your past."

Alexia nodded. "And there've been other things too. The whole cabinet hates me. I know I'm being briefed on an almost daily basis. Then there was that awful business with our dog being poisoned. Teddy's dog, really."

Lucy looked suitably horrified.

"Sometimes it feels as if it's all connected, all the hatred. But I don't know what the connection is. That's the awful thing. I don't know, and the not knowing is driving me mad. This ought to be the happiest time of my life, but instead I feel like I'm going crazy."

"Well," Lucy said reasonably, "it sounds as if this Billy guy may be at the root of it. Now that you've had him deported, things will start to get better, I'm sure."

"I hope so." Alexia sniffed. "But what if it's nothing to do with him? Anyone could be behind these threats. It could be one of the prisoners whose sentences I increased, or one of their family members. So many people hate me, Lucy. Even my own daughter hates me. Let's face it, if anyone wants my blood shed in the dust, it's Roxanne."

"That's not true," Lucy said loyally, although she suspected it was. She couldn't help but notice Roxie's brooding at supper, the way the girl had literally recoiled at the sound of Alexia's voice, as if bitten by a snake. Things had clearly got worse on that front since Lucy had last seen the De Veres. But Alexia could be terribly caustic toward her daughter too, a fact she seemed completely blind to.

Arnie Meyer poked his head into the kitchen and was amazed to find his wife on her knees, comforting a sobbing Alexia De Vere. Arnie had never seen Alexia cry in his life. Not even when Roxie was in the hospital, fighting for her life.

"What on earth's the matter?"

"It's nothing," said Alexia.

"Can I help?"

"Yes," said Lucy practically. "You can take the coffee things out to the table. We need a minute here."

"Should I get Teddy?"

"No." Alexia shook her head vehemently. "Poor Teddy's stressed enough as it is. Let him relax. Honestly, Arnie, I'm fine. I just got a little emotional."

Pulling a perfectly pressed white linen handkerchief out of a drawer, Lucy Meyer passed it to her friend.

"We can't talk now. There are too many people here."

"I know. I'm sorry. I ruined your dinner."

"Nonsense. It was *your* dinner anyway."

"'It's my party and I'll cry if I want to'?"

"Exactly!" Both women laughed. "I was going to say we should take a walk together tomorrow. I know a great secluded beach on the north of the island. If we leave early enough, we'll have the place to ourselves."

"Sounds heavenly. But I can't tomorrow. Teddy's flying back to London for a big business meeting on Tuesday and I promised him we'd spend tomorrow together. We're sailing."

"Next week, then. After he's gone. I'm not going anywhere."

Alexia squeezed Lucy's hand. She felt profoundly grateful for her friendship. "I'd like that."

"Then you can tell me everything."

If only I could.

"Now, come on," Lucy said briskly. "We can't keep moping around in here. Let's go and see if that divinely gorgeous son of yours has finally fallen for my daughter. I've got my wedding outfit all planned, you know. Had it in my closet for years."

Alexia laughed aloud.

Thank God for Lucy.

CHAPTER EIGHTEEN

THE MORNING AFTER LUCY'S DINNER PARTY, Michael De Vere asked Summer Meyer out on a date.

"I booked us the best table at Marco's. Saturday night, eight o'clock."

"That's sweet of you," said Summer. "But I just got out of a relationship. I'm not ready to start dating again."

"How about eating?" said Michael. "Are you eating yet? Because food's important, you know. It's right up there with water. And breathing air. You do breathe air?"

Summer laughed. "Yes, Michael. I do breathe air."

"Thank God. So anyway, back to food. Marco's food is the best on the island. That's all I'm saying."

"Really? Thanks for the tip. I must get some takeout and try it one night. *Alone.*"

She hung up.

THE NEXT MORNING, MICHAEL DE VERE showed up on the doorstep at Pilgrim Farm.

"I brought you a present."

He thrust a neatly wrapped package into Summer Meyer's hands.

She opened it. It was a cookbook.

Meals for One.

"How thoughtful." She tried not to laugh but it was impossible.

"I am *very* thoughtful," said Michael. "How's the heart-break coming along?"

"Slowly."

"Wanna speed it up?"

"Good-bye, Michael. Thanks for the book."

AT TWO O'CLOCK THE NEXT MORNING, Summer was roused from a deep sleep by a sharp rap on her bedroom window. Staggering out of bed, she opened it, narrowly missing being hit in the face by a pebble.

"What are you *doing*?" She rubbed her eyes blearily.

Michael grinned up at her in the moonlight. "Trying to get your attention. Is it working?"

"No."

"I brought a guitar."

"You did *not*."

"Would you like me to serenade you?"

"No! I'd like you to go home, you lunatic. It's the middle of the night."

"All right. I won't sing, *if* you agree to have dinner with me."

"Michael, we've been through this."

"You can cook dinner for one and I'll eat half."

"I'm in love with someone else!"

"I know. Chad Bates. Your mother told me."

"Well then."

"Well then, what? You broke up. I know Barry Manilow, you know." Michael shook his guitar mock-threateningly. "And I'm not afraid to use him."

181

Summer burst out laughing. "My God. You don't take no for an answer, do you?"

"It's a family trait."

"Fine. I'll have dinner with you. But as an old friend, nothing more. Now for heaven's sake go home and let me get some sleep."

Michael De Vere went home. But Summer Meyer didn't sleep. She lay awake thinking about Chad, Chad whom she'd loved so hard for so long and whom she really believed she was going to marry until he'd told her back in May that he "needed space" and never called her again. Chad was serious and cerebral and a genius. Chad was going to be an important journalist one day.

Then she thought about Michael, in his leather bomber jacket with that ridiculous guitar slung over his shoulder, Martha's Vineyard's answer to John Mayer. Michael was sexy and immature and impulsive. Michael had given up Oxford to become a professional partier.

There's your answer, Summer told herself. *Michael De Vere is not the sort of man I need in my life.*

Absolutely, categorically not.

"I WROTE YOU A POEM."

They were having dinner, not at Marco's but at a little, nondescript café by Eastville Point Beach. Summer had finished a delicious burger and fries, washed down with two Sam Adams, and was just starting to relax about the evening (*Of course, two old friends can have dinner together. It doesn't have to be a big deal*) when Michael pulled the envelope out of his pocket.

Summer's face fell. "A poem? I thought we agreed. I meant it when I said I'm not ready to start dating again. And even if I were, I'm not really a poetry sort of girl."

"How do you know? You haven't read it yet."

Summer opened the envelope and read aloud.

"There once was a loser named Bates.
Who danced the fandango on skates.
But a fall on his cutlass
Has rendered him nutless,
And practically useless on dates."

Summer grinned. "Very romantic."

"You like that?" Michael smiled back. "I made up a whole bunch of limericks, but I thought that was the best. He never deserved you, you know."

"How would you know? You never even met him!"

"I know, but come on: *Chad*. What kind of a name is that?"

"It's a perfectly normal name."

"Let's be honest, it's not a name one can imagine screaming in ecstasy, is it? *'Chad! Oh, Chad! Harder, Chad!'*"

"Stop!" Summer feigned indignation. "I suppose 'Michael' would sound so much better, wouldn't it?"

"Naturally. It just rolls off the tongue. I'll show you later if you like."

Summer cocked her head to one side and studied him closely. In faded brown Abercrombie shorts, flip-flops, and a Balliol Boat Club T-shirt, with his Hamptons tan and dark curly hair grown out, rocker-style, Michael looked even more handsome than usual. Ever since he was a kid, he'd been beautiful. But was there any substance behind the pretty face?

"I had the biggest crush on you when I was little."

"I had an inkling," said Michael.

"This is the part where you're supposed to say you always liked me too," Summer teased him. "Didn't you?"

"The thing is . . ." Michael swirled the beer around the bottom of his bottle thoughtfully. "You weren't that little."

"Hey!"

"No, really. You were absolutely enormous."

Summer picked up a piece of bread from the basket between them and threw it at him. "That's not very gentlemanly!"

"It's true, though." He laughed. "You were massive, and you never said anything. You just stared at me, like a hippo about to charge. Scared the shit out of me, if you must know."

It was pretty much the rudest thing anyone had ever said to her, but somehow, coming from Michael, it was funny.

"How did you lose the weight?"

"I ate less."

"Good strategy."

"Thanks." They both smiled. "I don't know," said Summer. "I got happier, I guess."

"You know what's funny?" said Michael, finishing his beer and ordering another.

The fact that I'm supposed to be heartbroken, but at this moment I feel totally happy?

The fact that I know you're a player and you're full of shit, but I still want to go to bed with you?

"No. What?"

"I've known you since you were five years old. But I don't really know you at all."

Reaching across the table, Michael touched Summer's hand, flipping it over and slowly caressing the inside of her wrist with his thumb. Chad Bates had never done that. Summer felt the blood rush to her groin like it had a plane to catch.

Michael grinned. "Let's go to bed."

*

"WHAT ARE YOU THINKING?"

Teddy De Vere looked over at his wife. In the moon's half-light, Alexia's skin looked flawless, like it used to when they were courting. The night's shadows had erased the wrinkles and age spots, leaving nothing but the beautiful profile he remembered: strong jaw, long, aquiline nose, high brow. Alexia was nearly sixty, but she was still a sensual, desirable woman, at least in Teddy's eyes. He had loved her for most of his adult life, and she had changed his life, completely. If he could choose only one word to describe her, it would be *strength*. The beauty of Alexia's strength was, it was contagious. She had made him strong. Teddy loved her for that.

The De Veres were having dinner on the deck at The Gables, just the two of them. A crescent moon hung in a star-flooded sky, and bullfrogs croaked sleepily from the pond at the bottom of the property. The guesthouse lights were still on, but neither of the children was home. Roxie was having supper with a friend, a rare occurrence indeed these days, and Michael was somewhere with Summer Meyer. Ever since Lucy and Arnie's dinner party Michael had been following the Meyer girl around like a lost puppy. Though it pained Teddy to admit it, it was rather sweet. He couldn't remember ever seeing his son so besotted, unless you counted Michael's infant crush on his mother.

Alexia let out a long sigh.

Teddy asked, "What was that for? Something on your mind?"

"No, not really. I was just thinking how lovely it is here. How peaceful."

She was right. It was a perfect Martha's Vineyard night, warm, the air slightly sticky and sweet with the scents of roses and violets and lavender, competing with the succulent

185

aroma of lemon-garlic chicken wafting out through the kitchen window. Even so, Teddy sensed that Alexia was only half in the present.

"You're worrying. I can tell. What is it, my darling?"

Cupping her glass of Pellegrino in both hands, Alexia drew her knees up to her chest. "Is it that obvious?"

"Only to me."

"If I tell you, do you promise not to overreact?"

"I'll do my best. What is it, Alexia?"

"Do you remember that man who came to the gates at Kingsmere, the night after I was elected?"

"Dimly. I remember you left the table. But didn't you say it was nothing?"

"It *was* nothing. It probably still is nothing."

Teddy raised an eyebrow. "Probably?"

"I didn't tell you, but a few weeks ago in London, I saw him again. The same man."

"But . . . you never saw him. I remember now. He'd gone by the time you got to the gate, and the camera wasn't working."

"It *was* working," Alexia said sheepishly. "I lied because I didn't want to worry you."

"For God's sake, Alexia. I'm not a child. I want to know these things."

"I know. I'm sorry. Anyway, I gave the footage to the police and they found out who it was."

"Well? Who was it?"

"An American. He's an ex-con with a history of mental illness."

"Jesus Christ."

"It's not as bad as it sounds. He's not violent or anything. But the thing is, he turned up again. In Parliament Square, a couple of weeks before the summer recess. He grabbed me as I was getting out of the car with Edward. We—"

"Whoa, whoa, whoa, hold on." Teddy sat up. "He *grabbed* you? What do you mean? Did he hurt you?"

"No. I was shocked, but no."

Teddy absorbed this information. He hated it when Alexia kept secrets from him, especially secrets like this. It was his job to protect her. His duty. He felt completely emasculated.

"Where were the police when all this happened? Your so-called security?"

"They were there. They pulled him off me."

"I hope you pressed charges."

Alexia looked uneasy. Teddy's eyes widened.

"You *did* press charges?"

"I didn't need to. Edward dealt with it."

"How?"

"We deported him. Quietly. I didn't want the press to make a story out of it. I just wanted him gone."

Teddy nodded approvingly. This was the one reassuring thing he'd heard all evening. For a few minutes he sat in silence, sipping his Bordeaux contemplatively. Then he asked Alexia, "What was his name?"

She seemed surprised by the question. "Does it matter?"

"It matters to me, yes. I'd like to know."

"I'm afraid I can't tell you."

Teddy looked at her, disbelieving. "What? Don't be silly, darling. Who was he?"

"I would if I could, Teddy. But I can't. You're just going to have to trust me on this one."

"Trust you? That's rich! You clearly don't trust me enough to confide in me." Teddy stood up angrily and began pacing the deck. Suddenly all the peace and ease of the evening had gone. He felt like he'd been punched in the stomach.

Alexia pleaded. "Don't be angry. You knew what we were getting into when I put my name forward for this job."

Did I? thought Teddy bitterly.

"I'm not some back-bench MP anymore. I'm the home secretary."

"I know your job title, Alexia." It was unlike Teddy to lose his temper, especially with her, but he couldn't seem to help himself.

"Then you should also know that there are going to be things, many things, that I'm not able to share with you." Alexia fought back. "It's just the way it is."

"So why tell me anything? Why tell me you're worried about this man and then not let me help?"

Alexia sensed the frustration in his voice, and the hurt. Perhaps she shouldn't have said anything. But after the other night, in Lucy Meyer's kitchen, she'd felt a growing need to talk about her fears.

"I told you because you asked. And because I wanted to be honest, as honest as I can be."

"Yes, well. It's not bloody good enough!"

Standing up, she wrapped her arms around Teddy's waist and pressed her body against his. It was an affectionate gesture. Vulnerable. Needy. Contrite. Despite himself, Teddy felt his heart melting.

Turning around, he pulled her into his arms.

"I want to protect you, Alexia. That's all. Can't you understand that?"

"You *are* protecting me." Alexia whispered. "Right now. I need you so much, Teddy. I couldn't do any of this without you."

Teddy kissed her hard on the mouth. He would never stop wanting her.

Never.

*

188

Lying naked and sated in bed, wrapped in Michael De Vere's arms, Summer Meyer stared at the ceiling, grinning from ear to ear.

It was official.

She was over Chad Bates.

Michael's breath tickled her ear and the warm weight of his body pressed against her back. He smelled of sweat and cologne and sex, and Summer didn't think she had ever wanted a man quite so badly. Kissing him, she whispered, "I was thinking about what you said before."

"You mean about your arse being the eighth wonder of the world?" Michael's hand crept downward.

"No, not that." Summer giggled.

"Because it is, you know. Honestly, if you were English, I'd be having that thing preserved for the nation. Of course, you Yanks have no sense of heritage."

"I mean what you said about us not really knowing each other, even after all these years."

"Oh. That."

"It's true."

"Well, hopefully it's a little less true now."

Reaching for her breasts, Michael lazily traced a line around her nipples with his index finger. Summer moaned with pleasure. His hands on her body were pure bliss. She shuddered to think of where and how he had picked up his technique.

"I'm serious. I mean I know your whole family better than I know you. Your mom's a machine. Your dad's a saint."

"I wouldn't go that far," muttered Michael.

"And Roxie was always so happy-go-lucky and sweet . . . before, you know."

"Yeah." Michael smiled sadly. "She was."

"But I don't know anything about you. Not really."

189

Michael lay back, throwing his arms wide, like a hot version of Jesus. "Ask me anything. I'm an open book."

"Okay." Summer propped herself up in bed. Michael loved the way her long chestnut hair spilled over her shoulders onto his sheets.

"Why did you quit Oxford?"

"That's easy," said Michael. "It was boring. Next question."

"Are you easily bored?"

"Very. This is fun."

"By women?"

"If they're boring, yes. Don't worry. You're not boring."

He reached between her thighs. Summer firmly removed his hand.

"I'm not worried. And you're not boring either. Yet."

Michael grinned. He liked a challenge.

"Any more questions, Miss Meyer, or can the witness be excused?"

"Plenty. Why do you always defend your mother when she and Roxie fight?"

Michael frowned. "Do I?"

"You did at supper the other night."

He thought for a while, then said, "I suppose I defend her because nobody else does. I love Roxie as much as anyone, and we all feel terrible about what happened to her. But she can be very unfair to Mummy. She blames her for everything."

"Isn't your mother to blame, though?" Summer asked.

"She can be cruel to Rox at times," Michael admitted. "She's to blame for that."

"But wasn't she the one who drove Roxie's boyfriend away? That's what I heard."

"You can't drive someone away who doesn't want to be driven. He was a grown man, not a goat."

Michael was angry, but he wasn't sure why. He'd never really talked about this with anyone, not even with Tommy, his best friend. No one in the family talked about it. But perhaps, he realized, that was part of the problem, part of what gave Roxie's tragedy its power. The fact that it had become taboo.

"I'll tell you what happened. Mum hired a tennis pro one summer, a guy named Andrew Beesley." Michael spat out the name as if it were poison.

"You didn't like him."

"No, I didn't. Not from the start. He was a snake. Good-looking, but by God he knew it."

Look who's talking, thought Summer, but she wisely said nothing.

"All Beesley was interested in was screwing women. I don't think he ever really cared about Roxie, but she fell for him hard."

"And your mother didn't approve?"

"Neither of my parents approved. Nor did I, nor did most of Rox's friends. By the time Roxie and Andrew got together, he'd already shagged half of Oxfordshire."

And I'll bet you shagged the other half.

"Anyway, he and Rox became an item. After a few months Andrew proposed. Roxie was beside herself with joy. She accepted right away. But Mum was worried he was a gold digger, with good reason, as it turned out. She invited him out to lunch one day, when Roxie was up in London. As I understand it, she offered him money if he would break off the engagement, move to Australia, and never contact Roxie again."

"She bribed him."

"Yes. Against my father's wishes."

"How much money did she offer him?"

Michael shrugged. "Dunno. Enough to set him up in a private coaching business. I suspect a few hundred grand. Anyway, whatever it was, he took it. Pretty much bit Mummy's hand off apparently, which in my book goes to show how little he cared about Rox in the first place. All Andrew Beesley ever wanted was a slice of my sister's inheritance. When Mum made it clear she wouldn't get a penny if the marriage went ahead, he was out of there faster than Boris Becker could drop his trousers in a broom cupboard.

"Roxie blamed Mummy entirely. Said she shouldn't have interfered, that she'd poisoned Andrew against her. I believe she even accused Mummy of sleeping with him at one point, that's how unhinged she'd become." He shook his head sadly. "It was awful."

"I'm sure." Summer's sympathy was genuine. She could imagine how painful it must have been, for all of them.

"The truth is, Rox had totally lost her marbles at that point. She was so in love with this bastard, so totally, hopelessly, dangerously in love. It broke her when Andrew left, it really did. I don't think even Mummy expected her to take it as hard as she did."

There were tears in his eyes. Tentatively, Summer reached out a hand and stroked his face.

"Don't go on if you don't want to."

Michael grabbed her hand and kissed it. "No. It's good to talk about it, actually. It's a relief. About two weeks after Beesley took off, I got a call from Dad telling me Roxie had jumped out of her bedroom window at Kingsmere.

"She definitely intended to die. It wasn't a cry for help or any of that bollocks. She left a note eviscerating poor Mum."

"How horrendous. For all of you."

"Yes," said Michael. "But, you know. She didn't die. It could have been worse."

"*Something* died, though."

"Yes. Something died. The girl that she was died. The family that *we* were. It's so fucking sad, but there was nothing I could do about it then, and there still isn't."

Summer wrapped her arms around him, cushioning his head against the soft pillow of her breasts. "Of course there isn't. It's not your fault, you know."

"It's not Mum's fault either. Not entirely, anyway. But she doesn't help herself. After Roxie's fall, Dad was so loving and sympathetic, and Mum just . . . wasn't. It's not that she doesn't care. She's just not very expressive when it comes to emotions."

She's a total fucking machine, thought Summer. Alexia had always intimidated her, and still did to some degree. They didn't call Michael's mother the Iron Lady for nothing. She'd always had an edgy relationship with Roxie, even before the boyfriend came on the scene.

As if reading Summer's mind, Michael said, "Mum's not a warm and cuddly person like your mother. She's practical and she gets on with things. She doesn't like wallowing."

"She thinks Roxie's wallowing? That's a little harsh under the circumstances, wouldn't you say?"

"Not really," Michael said defensively. But then he relented. "I don't know. Maybe. She's tough, my mother, and Roxie isn't tough, and I think fundamentally Mum just couldn't understand why Roxie did what she did."

"What about you?" Summer asked.

"What about me?"

"Do you understand it?"

"No. I've tried to. But I don't. I understand loving someone, but not losing yourself to that degree. It's not healthy."

No, thought Summer, *it's not. But it's human*.

She wondered if Michael De Vere had ever been in love. But that was one question she was too afraid to ask.

CHAPTER NINETEEN

Alexia De Vere closed her eyes and tried to enjoy the feeling of the salt breeze in her hair and the warm sand between her toes. For years, her entire twenties, she had avoided beaches. It was the sounds that bothered her most: the rhythmic lapping of the waves, the distant peal of children's laughter. Just thinking about those sounds made her feel sick and anxious. But since Teddy had persuaded her to buy The Gables in the early nineties, she'd slowly rediscovered her love of the ocean. The irony was that Teddy, probably the most English man in the world, had chosen to buy in the States. But Arnie Meyer had offered him a deal he couldn't refuse, and over the years both he and Alexia had come to love Martha's Vineyard.

These days, Alexia found the vastness of the ocean calming rather than frightening. She enjoyed the sense of nature being so big, and her own life and struggles so small by comparison. All her life, Alexia De Vere had struggled to *be* someone, someone important, someone whose life mattered. A little boy had lost his life because of her, and a decent man had had his life destroyed. She owed it to both of them to make her own life count, to achieve something significant. So it was ironic in a way that the feeling of *in*significance the ocean gave her should bring her such profound peace.

"Spit spot, no dawdling!" Lucy Meyer's Mary Poppins impression was embarrassingly bad, but it always made Alexia laugh. Because Lucy truly *was* Mary Poppins, in so many ways. "We'll never get to the beach by lunchtime if you keep standing there with your eyes closed like Kate Winslet on the *Titanic*."

It was an unfortunate allusion. Too often these days Alexia felt as if she were aboard the *Titanic*, sailing inexorably toward her doom. She'd worked things out with the prime minister before Parliament broke for the summer—at least she thought she had. And despite the storm of disapproval within the party over her handling of the flag-burning affair, in all the opinion polls Alexia's popularity rating was high. Even the *Daily Mail* was changing its tune in support of her tough-on-immigration stance. But the turmoil in her personal life had stopped her from savoring these successes. Not being able to talk properly to Teddy about the pressure she was under was the hardest part of all. Just alluding to Billy Hamlin the other night had sent Teddy into a full-fledged panic. If she hadn't known it before, she knew it now: she had to solve her problems on her own.

"Sorry," she called ahead to Lucy. "Lead on."

Lucy and Alexia had finally found time for their much-postponed hike to the Gay Head Lighthouse. Perilously close to the ever-eroding cliffs, the current redbrick structure had been built in 1844 to replace a wooden tower authorized by President John Quincy Adams, and was a popular tourist attraction on the island. With her encyclopedic knowledge of Martha's Vineyard's sandy tracks and back roads, however, Lucy had devised a route where no other sightseers would bother her and Alexia.

Since their tête-à-tête in Lucy's kitchen two weeks earlier, neither woman had alluded to the "secrets" of Alexia's past. They'd been walking for over an hour now, and still Alexia had said nothing, leaving Lucy to fill the silence with excited prattle about Michael and Summer's burgeoning love affair.

"I'm telling you, I hear wedding bells."

"You always hear bells." Alexia laughed. "You're Quasimodo."

Alexia wanted desperately to talk about Billy Hamlin and her past. But starting the conversation was harder than she'd thought it would be. Back at Pilgrim Farm that first night, buoyed by everybody's kindness and warm wishes, the subject had all come up naturally. Now, in the cold light of day, she would have to begin again.

How does one do that, after forty years of silence?

In the end, Lucy broke the ice for her.

"So," she said, when they finally stopped for lunch at a clearing on top of the cliffs. "Do you still want to talk to me about Billy?"

She remembers the name. She's been thinking about it.

"It's fine if you don't. I just thought I'd ask. In case it's still bothering you."

Lucy said it so casually, between mouthfuls of an egg and watercress sandwich. Even her choice of words was harmless. Billy Hamlin had been "bothering" Alexia. Not terrorizing. Not haunting. *Bothering.* Like a fly, or a hole in one's sock.

Alexia bit her lip nervously. It was now or never.

"What would you say if I told you I'd once done something terrible? Something that I would give anything to take back, but that I can't change."

Lucy tried not to betray her own nerves when she answered.

"I'd say welcome to the human race. We all have regrets, Alexia. Especially at our age."

196

Regrets. Bothering. Lucy made it all sound so acceptable, so normal. But then Lucy didn't know the truth. Not yet.

"This is more than a regret. It's something I've buried for almost forty years. Nobody knows about it. Not even Teddy. And if it ever became public, it would mean the end of my political career. Maybe even the end of my marriage."

Lucy Meyer took a deep, steadying breath.

"I'm listening."

TEDDY DE VERE LEANED BACK IN his first-class seat and closed his eyes as the 747 shuddered upward over Boston. He worried about leaving Alexia on her own, especially with Roxie still being so difficult. But his business couldn't completely run itself for an entire summer. Besides, he had other things to deal with in London.

As home secretary, Alexia was a public figure. A certain amount of unwanted attention was inevitable. But she was also Mrs. Edward De Vere, a wife, a mother, and a member of one of the oldest, grandest families in England. Protecting the De Vere family name was Teddy's job. And he couldn't protect it if he only knew half the facts.

It was time for a little chat with Sir Edward Manning.

"HOW WAS YOUR HIKE?"

Summer Meyer was in the kitchen at Pilgrim Farm, arranging the latest bouquet of flowers that Michael De Vere had brought her, when her mother walked in. In her yellow sundress and flip-flops, her newly washed hair hanging damp down her back, Summer was a vision of happiness. But Lucy was oblivious, walking straight past her toward the stairs.

"Mom? Is everything okay?"

"Everything's fine," said Lucy.

She went upstairs to her bedroom and closed the door, sinking down onto the bed. The story Alexia had told her had shaken Lucy deeply. She was grateful to be alone, grateful that Arnie wasn't here to pester her with questions. She needed to think.

She thought about Teddy De Vere. According to Alexia, Teddy knew nothing of her past. Lucy had no reason to disbelieve this. But still the thought of it shocked her to the core. A thirty-year marriage, a rock-solid marriage to all appearances, but built on a sham! Alexia De Vere wasn't a real person at all. She was a character, a fake, an impostor created out of willpower and dust by a girl named Toni Gilletti, almost forty years ago.

An American girl.

A "bad" girl.

A girl with no hope, no future, no prospects.

Lucy Meyer would never have become friends with Toni Gilletti. Never in a million years. And yet Alexia had been her closest friend, almost a sister, for half of her adult life.

In the moment, when Alexia had poured out her confession, Lucy had remained calm and practical, reassuring her that deporting Billy Hamlin had been the right thing to do.

"You did what you had to do to protect yourself and your family. That's it, end of story."

"But he gave up so much, Lucy, to protect me."

"That was his decision. He's responsible for his actions. You're responsible for yours."

Outwardly, Lucy hoped, she'd been supportive, unruffled, staunch. But inside, her emotions raged and roiled like a violent, stormy sea.

There was a tentative knock on the door.

"Only me. Are you sure you're okay?" Summer walked

in with a jug of peonies held out like a peace offering. "Can I help?"

Lucy painted her usual smile back on.

"I'm fine, sweetie. I think maybe Alexia and I overdid it on our hike, that's all. I'm really bushed."

"Do you want me to run you a bath?"

Lucy kissed her on the cheek. "No, honey. I'm not that old. I can do it. You should be down at the beach with Michael, having fun."

At the mention of Michael's name, Summer's face lit up like the sun.

Lucy thought: *Young love. How wonderful it is!*
And how dangerous.

It was young love—Billy Hamlin and Toni Gilletti's—that had caused the tragedy that was to define Alexia De Vere's life. Alexia herself may have thrived and prospered. But other lives had been ruined. Lucy thought about the little boy who drowned. Nicholas. He was the true victim here, not Billy Hamlin, for whom Alexia seemed to feel unaccountably sorry, and certainly not Alexia herself. But somehow Nicholas's story had gotten lost, overshadowed by Alexia De Vere's fame and success. He'd become part of the wallpaper, the backdrop for what happened next.

For what Alexia became. What Alexia achieved. What Alexia now stood to lose, if Billy Hamlin or her other myriad enemies had their way.

Lucy Meyer would remain loyal. There was no question about that. Sisters must always remain loyal. They must stand by their siblings through thick and thin. Lucy Meyer had been raised to believe in family, and she believed in it to this day.

Lucy would keep Alexia's secret.

But after today's revelation, nothing would ever be quite the same between them again.

CHAPTER TWENTY

IT WAS A TYPICAL LATE-SUMMER NIGHT in London: rainy, gray, and cold. As a result, all the pubs were full.

At the Old Lion on Baker Street, Simon Butler was working his usual shift behind the bar when a disoriented man rolled in.

"Watch that one." The landlady, Simon's boss, saw the man too. She immediately recognized the stooped shoulders, staggering gait, blank stare, and unshaven hopelessness of the long-term homeless. "He looks like he's had a few too many already."

The man made a beeline for the bar. "Pint, please." He pushed a handful of dirty change in Simon's direction.

"Coming up."

He's not meeting anybody. He's here to drink. To forget.

As Simon pulled the man his beer, he noticed him muttering to himself. Quietly at first, but then in a more agitated way, the classic confrontational, paranoid ramblings of the schizophrenic. Simon's brother Matty had been schizophrenic. Simon recognized inner hell when he saw it.

"Booze isn't the answer, you know," he said gently, handing the man his beer. Close up he looked even worse than he did from a distance, all sallow skin and bloodshot eyes. He smelled of desperation and dirt, a wisp of unhappy smoke floating aimlessly on the wind.

"She was going to marry me."

The man wasn't talking to Simon. He was talking to himself, to nobody, to the air.

"She loved me once. We loved each other."

"I'm sure you did, mate. I'm sure you did."

Poor bastard. He wasn't dangerous. Just pathetic.

It was a cruel world.

BROOKS'S IS ONE OF THE MOST exclusive gentlemen's clubs in London. Standing on the west side of St James's Street, it was founded by four dukes and a handful of other aristocrats in the 1760s, and began life as a political salon for Whigs, the liberals of the day.

Nowadays it has a broader membership, but is still heavily frequented by diplomats, politicians, and civil servants. The only true, unspoken conditions of membership are that applicants be male, British, and unquestionably upper class.

Teddy De Vere was not a member, belonging as he did to the Tory Carlton Club just across the street. The two institutions consider themselves gentlemanly rivals, and membership in both clubs is quite unheard of. Teddy was, however, a frequent guest at Brooks's, so today's lunch was nothing out of the ordinary.

"De Vere."

Sir Edward Manning, Alexia's permanent private secretary, greeted Teddy warmly. With the home secretary herself, Sir Edward maintained an appropriately formal distance. But Alexia's husband was another matter. The two men knew each other slightly. As social equals, meeting privately, familiarity was perfectly appropriate.

"Manning. Thanks for seeing me. I'm sure your schedule must be jam-packed."

"No more so than yours, old man."

They ordered gin and tonics, and a pair of rare filet steaks with Brooks's famous crispy fries. Teddy got down to business.

"It's about Alexia."

"I rather assumed it might be. What's on your mind?"

"It's a bit awkward. She alluded to me that she'd been having trouble with a chap she knew years ago."

Not by a flicker did Sir Edward Manning betray his surprise that Alexia had chosen to confide in her husband about Billy Hamlin. The deportation order had been executed so swiftly and secretly that not even the home secretary's own security detail had been informed of it. And at Alexia's request! If Hamlin held a dark key to the home secretary's past, Sir Edward imagined that the very last person she would wish to know it would be her husband, the nice but dim Teddy.

"She suggested this man has been harassing her."

Again, Sir Edward said nothing. Teddy De Vere had not asked a question. He had made a statement. Sir Edward Manning had not risen to the highest ranks of the British Civil Service by responding to statements.

"The bugger of it is, Alexia won't give me the fellow's name. All she'll say is that you've 'dealt with it.'" Teddy sliced off a succulent bite of steak and put it in his mouth. "So what I want to know is: have you?"

"Yes," said Sir Edward, in his usual measured tone. "As far as I'm able."

"What does that mean?"

"Off the record?"

"Of course."

"The man the home secretary is referring to is an American citizen."

"She told me. She also said he was an ex-con and a lunatic."

Sir Edward Manning raised a laconic eyebrow. "I'm not sure I'd go that far. The point is, due to his nationality, our powers, though considerable, are limited."

"Alexia said you deported him."

"That is correct. He was deported and his passport's been red-stamped so it's impossible for him to reenter Britain legally. I had a quiet word with some of our American friends and I understand that he has also been sectioned. As far as I know he remains in a secure facility somewhere on the Eastern Seaboard."

Teddy De Vere did not look reassured. "As far as you know? *'Somewhere'?*"

"It's not perfect," Sir Edward admitted. "But given that this was all done under the radar, so to speak, it's the best we can do without putting the Home Office at risk. One always needs to think, what would one say to the press if it *did* get out? How far can one go? Having a schizophrenic ex-convict who harassed the home secretary deported and institutionalized would be acceptable to the majority of voters, in my view, were the story ever to leak. Especially as the man concerned is an American. Nobody likes Americans."

"Indeed," Teddy agreed. "Is the story likely to leak?"

"Leaks are never likely. Unfortunately they happen on a daily basis."

Teddy nodded knowingly.

Sir Edward went on. "Your wife's appointment upset quite a number of people, as you know. There was some unseemly briefing against her during the whole flag-burning crisis. Plenty of people are hunting feverishly for a chink in her armor. We don't want to give them one."

For a few minutes both men returned to their steaks. Then Teddy said, "So this nutter could still enter the country illegally?"

"Anyone can do anything illegally." Taking a sip of Burgundy, Sir Edward dabbed his mouth daintily at the corners with a monogrammed napkin.

"And if he did? What would happen then?"

"Then we would arrest him, like any other illegal immigrant, and deport him again. Look, De Vere, I understand your concern. I'd feel the same if it were my wife."

Teddy tried and failed to picture the utterly effete Sir Edward Manning having a wife.

"But I honestly don't think either you or the home secretary has reason to be concerned. This man is ill. He has no source of funds. Trust me, I've met him and he is no criminal mastermind. He simply lacks the wherewithal to get himself back to Britain."

They finished their meals. Teddy ordered a sticky toffee pudding with butterscotch sauce. Sir Edward, conscious of his waistline, had a double espresso. Sergei Milescu liked him to stay in shape. Soon, Edward hoped, he would be able to give Sergei what he wanted and get him off his back forever, literally and metaphorically. Until then, dessert menus must remain resolutely closed.

Sir Edward signed the bill. Both men retrieved their coats.

Sir Edward asked Teddy, "When are you headed back to Boston? You're still on holiday, aren't you?"

"On and off. I'm flying back tonight actually. I want to get back to Alexia. Things are still tricky at home with our daughter and I don't like to leave her on her own."

For the second time in an hour, Sir Edward Manning hid his surprise. He'd understood that the bad blood between Mrs. De Vere and her daughter, Roxanne, was a taboo subject, but Teddy had just brought it up quite openly.

"Well, do give my best to the home secretary," he said politely. "We're looking forward to having her back."

"I will," said Teddy. "And many thanks for lunch. Oh, one last thing," he added casually.

"Yes?"

"I don't suppose I can persuade you to give me this chap's name, can I?"

THE MAN CAME TO THE PUB every day for the next week. Always sat at the bar, always nursed two beers, no more, and never spoke to a soul other than Simon Butler.

Simon Butler and the voice in his head.

Simon now knew a little about him. He was in London visiting a friend. He loved cars. He had a daughter. Someone had been going to marry him, but they had changed their mind. This much Simon thought was true. But a lot of what the man said was pure paranoia.

The British government was on his tail.

The home secretary was trying to silence him.

A trained killer wanted him dead and was picking off his loved ones one by one.

Every night the man told Simon Butler about "the voice." On the telephone. In his head. In his dreams. Telling him what to do. Terrorizing him. No one believed him. But the voice was real.

He didn't want to tell Simon his name. That was part of the paranoid delusions. No one could be trusted. But he did mention a daughter, Jennifer, over and over again.

One night after work, Simon told his landlady, "I'd like to try and find her. She's obviously his only family and the guy needs help. She's probably worried sick."

The landlady looked at the young barman with affection. He was a good boy, Simon Butler. Kind. Not like her own son, Arthur. It pained her to say it but Arthur and his mates were delinquents. "It's a nice idea, Si. But you've only a first name to go on. That's not going to get you very far, is it?"

Simon shrugged.

"If you're really worried you'd be better off calling Social Services. Maybe they could help him."

"Maybe," said Simon. "I'd need an address, though."

It wasn't a hospital. It was a prison.

Yes, there were doctors, the proverbial men in white coats. But they didn't want to help him. They wanted to control him. To trap him. All Billy Hamlin remembered was being locked in, strapped down, and doped up to the eyeballs with God knows what. Things to make him forget, to make him relax, to keep him in a permanent state of inertia.

The voice was gone. The doctors called that progress.

But Billy's panic grew.

Time was running out.

As much as it terrified him, Billy needed the voice. He needed it to tell him what to do next. To give him another chance. Jenny's life depended on it.

Ironically, it was Jenny who saved him. She was still safe—so far—and once she tracked him down, she came to visit every day. Billy couldn't tell his daughter the whole truth about the voice. The truth would terrify her, and he didn't want that. But he talked to Jenny about the drugs, about the cotton-wool clouds in his head, numbing every sense and emotion. About his longing to be free. Eventually, Jenny had convinced the doctors that she could care for him, that he would be safe at home with her. Little did she know that it was really he, Billy, keeping *her* safe, watching her night after night while she slept, on constant vigil at her modest Queens apartment.

He hadn't wanted to leave. To sneak out like a thief in the night, without explanation, without saying good-bye. But the voice had called and left him instructions. And the voice must be obeyed.

Balling his hands into fists, Billy pressed them to his eyes, willing himself not to cry. He had to stay focused. And positive. Focused and positive, that was the key.

He was here, after all, in London. He'd made it. That in itself was no mean feat. But the first thing he learned when he arrived on British soil was that Alexia De Vere was not here. Parliament was on its long summer recess, and the home secretary was on a three-week break in Martha's Vineyard of all places, less than a hundred miles from the hospital where Billy had been locked up. He could have stayed where he was! The irony was so bitter it choked him, a cold hand of fate closing around his throat.

Alexia De Vere was gone. But she would be back.

There was nothing for it but to wait.

Simon Butler was furious. Social Services was about as much use as a water pistol in a forest fire.

"We've got some leaflets," the bored moron on the so-called help line informed him, unhelpfully. "Or you can go on our Web site for details of your nearest local drop-in center."

Simon remembered this same, not-my-problem attitude from when his brother Matty had been ill. "What's your

Web site," he asked tersely. "Www-dot-I-don't-give-a-shit-dot-com?"

"I understand your frustration, sir—"

Simon Butler hung up. There had to be a better way.

BILLY HAMLIN WAS FEELING BETTER.

The sun had come out, and London no longer looked like a study in gray. Women put their short skirts back on, people smiled at one another in the street, and the pub crowd had spilled onto the pavements, people perched on picnic tables smoking and laughing and enjoying the novelty of having their evening tipple "alfresco."

Parliament reconvened in nine days but Alexia De Vere was due back in six.

It was almost over.

He usually went to the Old Lion on Baker Street. It was busy and anonymous, with more passing trade than regulars, and Billy liked the barman there. He was friendly but not intrusive, and he slipped Billy chips and peanuts for free. But the Old Lion had outdoor seating, so today Billy made an exception and went to the Rose and Crown in Marylebone instead.

For the first two beers he was fine. But as the afternoon turned to evening and he kept on drinking, his mood darkened.

"She was going to marry me, you know."

"Who was?"

A group of young men sat next to him at the bar, smartly dressed City types. *How long have they been there?* Billy wondered. He hadn't noticed them before.

"Toni. Toni Gilletti."

"Right. Okay." The young men turned away.

For some reason, Billy felt slighted. He grabbed one of them by the arm. "I know things, you know. I know things about the home secretary. I could bring the British government down. That's why they're after me."

"What's your problem, asshole?" The trader shook his arm free, accidentally pushing Billy back off his bar stool in the process. Losing his footing, Billy crashed into a nearby table of diners, sending plates and cutlery flying. Somebody screamed.

The next thing Billy knew he was on his feet. Someone, one of the diners, had thrown a punch. Panicked, he lashed out wildly, kicking and shouting as the bar staff manhandled him onto the street.

"Come back and I'll call the police," the landlord shouted after him. "Fucking loon."

It wasn't until he started walking home, weaving his way through unfamiliar streets, that Billy realized how drunk he was. His lip was split, he felt nauseous and dizzy, and one of his eyes appeared to be starting to close. Worse, he had no real idea where he was. The smiles he'd seen on the streets earlier had all gone now. People he passed glared at him, their expressions ranging from distaste to outright hostility.

They're afraid of me.

The thought made him sad.

By the time he made it back to his guesthouse, one of a row of nondescript Victorian houses along the Edgeware Road, it was close to midnight. Wearily, he tramped up the stairs. A stranger was standing outside his door.

"Billy Hamlin?"

Like a trapped rat, Billy looked from left to right, hunting for an escape, but there was none. "Who are you? What do you want?"

"Don't worry, Billy." The stranger smiled. "I'm not from the police. You're not in any trouble. I'm here to help."

Beneath the posh British accent, Billy recognized the earnest, concerned tone of the professional social worker. He'd heard it so often back in the States, it was depressingly familiar. But who would have reported him here? Who even knew he was in England?

"Look, I'm fine. I don't need help."

"We all need help, Billy, now and then. It's nothing to be ashamed of."

"I don't know who sent you. But I'm fine. Please leave me alone." Billy fumbled in his pockets for his door key.

"Here." The stranger came up behind him. "Let me help you with that."

The knife was so sharp, Billy Hamlin barely felt it slice between his shoulder blades and puncture his heart.

CHAPTER TWENTY-ONE

Alexia De Vere sipped her iced cranberry juice as she gazed out of the plane window. On her lap, a thick ministerial brief lay open reproachfully. *Immigration Solutions for 21st-Century Britain*. Somehow even the title sounded dispiriting, a glass of cold water in the face. Alexia couldn't face it just yet.

Her vacation on Martha's Vineyard had done her a world of good. Lucy Meyer in particular had lifted her spirits and strengthened her resolve. Alexia *had* done the right thing by closing the door on Billy Hamlin and her past. Lucy had confirmed it. No good could come of her and Billy meeting now, of conjuring up the ghost of Toni Gilletti and the life she, Alexia, had worked so hard to leave behind. Gradually she started to rewrite the story in her head. She hadn't callously turned Billy Hamlin away. Billy was ill, and she had gotten him help. Edward Manning had dealt with things, and Alexia trusted Edward Manning. It was time to move on, and get on with the business of government. As for Teddy, put simply, what he didn't know wouldn't hurt him.

Teddy was asleep beside her now, snoring peacefully with a half-drunk glass of Glenfiddich in one hand and yesterday's edition of the *Times* in the other. With typical thoughtfulness Teddy had flown back to Martha's Vineyard for the final days of their holiday last week rather than staying on in London and waiting for Alexia there. *How many other political husbands would clock up eight thousand air miles in a week just so they could keep their wives company?*

Alexia had particularly enjoyed having Teddy with her because Roxie and Michael had both returned to England the week before. Poor Michael had torn himself away from sweet little Summer Meyer with infinite reluctance in order to get back to Tommy and the business. Roxie, not wanting to stay on without her brother, had flown home too. The last few days at The Gables had been like a second honeymoon for Teddy and Alexia, memories that Alexia would cherish for a long, long time.

I wasn't in love with him when we married, Alexia thought. *But I love him now. I love our life together, everything we've built.*

Easing the newspaper out of Teddy's hand, being careful not to wake him, she flipped through the home news pages. Edward Manning had briefed her by e-mail twice daily during her vacation, so she was already up to speed on all the news that mattered or that required a statement or action from her. But she hadn't actually held a British paper in her hands for three weeks.

UNEMPLOYMENT FIGURES RISING

The headline irritated her. *Bloody* Times *leader writers.* It was shameless the way they manipulated that data. Jobs were actually being created across the public and private sectors, a point Alexia had made on the *BBC News at One* via satellite link only yesterday. The *Times* might be a Murdoch-owned paper, but as far as Alexia could tell, all the journalists who worked there were bloody Trotskyites.

She flipped to page two, and a dull piece about wind farms. Renewable energy bored Alexia rigid, but green issues were important to the PM, so like the rest of the party, Alexia paid lip service. She wondered whether any of the rest of the cabinet knew about Henry Whitman's affair with Laura Llewellyn, the very beautiful, very married eco-lobbyist whose husband, Miles Llewellyn, was the Conservative Party's single largest financial donor? Alexia doubted it. She'd only found out herself by chance, running into Henry and Laura quite by accident at an obscure Yorkshire hotel the week before last year's party conference in Blackpool. If gossip had been flying around, Alexia would probably have been the last to hear of it. Her so-called colleagues in the cabinet were the most standoffish bunch of bastards it had ever been her misfortune to work with. And Alexia De Vere had worked with a great many bastards.

As she turned to page four, a small, single-column story caught her eye.

FATAL STABBING YIELDS NO CLUES

Alexia began to read.

> Police currently have no leads into the fatal stabbing of an American man in Edgeware Road on Friday night. William Hamlin, a convicted killer with psychological problems . . .

Alexia clutched her seat arm for support.

213

. . . who had been denied a visa and entered the United Kingdom illegally, was found dead outside his flat with a bread knife still lodged in his heart.

No. It can't be true. Not Billy! He's in America. He's safe. Edward took care of it.

She read on.

Simon Butler, bar manager of the Old Lion in Baker Street, where Hamlin had become a regular over the summer, described the murdered man as "a lost soul." Mr. Butler had recently contacted Social Services regarding Hamlin's volatile mental state, but claims to have been "given the brush-off" by staff. Police are appealing for witnesses.

The print blurred before Alexia's eyes. Her heart was pounding and her mouth and throat felt dry, as if she'd swallowed sand. She shook Teddy awake.

"Look at this!"

Teddy De Vere sat up abruptly, spilling his whisky down his shirt. "Damn and blast it. What is it, darling?"

"Look." Alexia pointed at the picture of Billy, a mug shot that must have been taken well over a decade ago. "That's him."

"That's who?"

"The man I was telling you about."

"Please don't speak in riddles, Alexia. I'm half asleep."

"William Hamlin!" Alexia said exasperatedly.

"Ah. So that's his name. You wouldn't tell me before, remember?"

"*Was* his name," said Alexia. "He's been killed. Murdered."

"I thought you said he'd been deported?"

"He had. He must have come back, somehow. And now he's dead. Read the article."

Teddy read. As he did so he thought back to his conversation with Sir Edward Manning, only a week earlier.

"Trust me. He doesn't have the wherewithal to get himself back here."

So much for that. Teddy shuddered to think of how close this madman had come to contacting Alexia a second time, perhaps even to hurting her.

"The journalist doesn't mention you." He handed the paper back to her.

"No. No one seems to have made the connection."

"Good." Dabbing the amber liquid off his shirt with a napkin, Teddy rolled over, replumping his pillow. "Then you've nothing to worry about. Good night."

Alexia was shocked. "Nothing to worry about? Teddy, he's been murdered."

"Exactly. So he won't be bothering you again, will he? That's good news in my book."

"Why are you being so callous?" Alexia asked angrily. "He didn't deserve to die. He was ill. Confused."

Teddy sat up wearily. "Look, Alexia, the man threatened you. You can't expect me to like people who threaten my wife, or to feel sorry for them. I'm not going to be so hypocritical as to feign grief for a complete stranger just to salve your conscience."

"You're right. I'm sorry." Leaning over, she kissed him on the cheek. "I'm shocked, that's all. He was a sweet boy once."

"So was Hitler," said Teddy robustly. "Try to get some rest."

Within minutes he was snoring loudly.

The flight attendant came over to Alexia. "Can I bring you something to eat, Home Secretary? A cheese plate perhaps, or some fruit? I know you said you wanted a light meal."

Alexia pulled herself together. Teddy was right. What had happened to Billy was awful, but it *did* draw a line under things. And wasn't that what she wanted, deep down? It wasn't as if his death was her fault, or her responsibility. As tragic as it was, maybe it was for the best.

She smiled at the flight attendant. "I'll have the cheese, please. No blue. And a strong cup of coffee. I have a lot of work to get through before we land."

CHAPTER TWENTY-TWO

THE NEXT YEAR WAS A TRIUMPHANT one for Alexia De Vere. As Britain's economy rebounded, so the nation's collective spirit blossomed like a daffodil bursting through the frost after a long, cold winter. A Gallup Poll ranked Henry Whitman the most popular sitting prime minister since Churchill, and the rest of the cabinet basked contentedly in Henry's reflected glow. As for Alexia De Vere, the home secretary's personal popularity almost rivaled that of the prime minister.

How had it happened? Only a couple of years ago, Alexia De Vere had been one of the more loathed figures of minor British politics, a throwback to the bad old days of heartless Conservatism. When people thought of Alexia De Vere (if they thought of her at all), they associated her with prison riots and knee-jerk, throw-away-the-key justice. The fact that she was stinking rich, spoke with a plum in her mouth, and had married into a family posher than the Windsors did little to endear her to ordinary voters. But after a year and a half in the job that no one, including Alexia herself, had ever expected her to get, and despite her early hiccups over immigration, Mrs. De Vere had succeeded in winning over the hearts and minds of the British public in a spectacular *coup de grace*. People respected the way she had strengthened the police force and put more coppers back on the beat. They approved of her defense of hospitals, of her libertarian stance on education and support for parent-run schools. They liked her Care Homes Act to protect the elderly from exploitation and abuse. Yes, Alexia De Vere was tough. But she was also hardworking, efficient, and ballsy enough to fight for traditional British values and institutions. The Rottweiler of old had transformed herself into a British bulldog for the modern age. Her enemies could do nothing but sit back and watch.

After brokering a deal to establish a vast Renault car plant in the East Midlands, creating tens of thousands of new jobs, Alexia received an invitation to tea at Ten Downing Street.

"I should have made you foreign secretary." The prime minister stretched his legs while a butler poured the tea. "The French think the *soleil* shines out of your derrière. You're the toast of Paris."

"I don't know about that," Alexia said modestly. She never quite knew where she stood with Henry Whitman. Cabinet colleagues complained that he supported her unreservedly, but Alexia often felt an undercurrent of dislike beneath the prime minister's smiles.

"Try the chocolate cake," Henry urged her. "It's from Daylesford. Tastes like heaven."

"Thanks, but I'll pass." Alexia enjoyed being a size eight far too much to indulge her sweet tooth. "You should be careful not to let Ian hear you take his job in vain. He's doing well at the Foreign Office, isn't he?"

"He is," Henry admitted. "But no one's putting Ian James's ugly mug on the front page of *Le Figaro*, let's put it that way."

Alexia laughed. It was true that her photogenic looks and brusque, no-nonsense manner had helped make her a popular figure in France and a great ambassador for the British government. But she couldn't imagine that Henry Whitman had summoned her to Downing Street merely to flatter her.

"Was there something in particular you wanted to see me about?"

"Not really." Whitman sipped his tea. Alexia felt his eyes on her, studying her. There was a distrust there, a wariness that she didn't understand. *What does he want to know? And whatever it is, why doesn't he just ask me?* "Do you have any plans for the summer? You'll be heading back out to the States, I presume."

The interview was getting stranger and stranger. *Why does Henry Whitman care where I take my vacation? Is he trying to get rid of me?*

"Actually no, not this year. We're staying in England. This ridiculous party Teddy's organizing at Kingsmere, it's more work than the G7 Summit."

"Ah, yes." Henry nodded. "*The* party."

By now the whole of Westminster knew that Alexia De Vere's charming old duffer of a husband was celebrating three hundred years of De Vere family history with a huge event at Kingsmere, arguably one of the most exquisite houses in England. Anyone who was anyone in European politics would be attending, as well as the great and the good from the entertainment and business worlds. It would be like Elton John's White Tie & Tiara Ball, minus the vulgarity factor.

"You're coming, I take it?" Alexia asked.

"Of course."

"With Charlotte?"

Henry Whitman's brow knit into a frown. "Naturally with Charlotte. I'm not in the business of attending social events alone, Alexia."

"Of course not."

There it was again. The chill.

"We get back from Sicily the night before, but we'll definitely be there."

After an awkward silence, the prime minister asked some polite questions about Alexia's upcoming trip to Paris with Kevin Lomax. As trade secretary, Kevin's department had also been involved in the Renault deal, although everybody knew it was Alexia who had clinched it.

"How are things between the two of you these days?" Henry Whitman asked.

"Fine," Alexia lied. "Cordial." Everybody knew that Kevin Lomax wanted her head on a pike, so much so that she wondered why Henry had even asked the question.

"You don't foresee any problems on the trip?"

"No, Prime Minister. None whatsoever."

"Good."

Henry Whitman stood up, signaling that their awkward interview was over. But as Alexia reached the door, he called after her.

"There was one more thing I wanted to ask."

Alexia stopped. "Oh?"

"Your PPS. Are you happy with him?"

Alexia looked surprised. "With Edward? Absolutely. He's fantastic."

"Good." Henry Whitman smiled. "Terrific."

"Why do you ask?"

"Oh, no reason, no reason. I think of the Home Office as the government's mother ship, that's all. Just checking that things are steady belowdecks."

Alexia raised an eyebrow. "Why wouldn't they be?"

"No reason at all. Honestly. You're reading too much into it. I simply want to make sure that you have the support you need. If that's Sir Edward Manning, then fine."

"It is Sir Edward Manning."

"Fine!" The PM laughed. "Then there's no problem."

"No problem at all, Henry."

FIVE MINUTES LATER, ONCE ALEXIA HAD left the building, Henry Whitman made a phone call.

"It's me. She just left. I think we have a problem."

MICHAEL DE VERE BOUNCED DOWN THE Broad in Oxford with a spring in his step, whistling happily.

It was strange, but in the two years he'd spent at Balliol, Oxford's glorious Baroque architecture and fabled "dreaming spires" had completely passed him by. All Michael remembered were dry-as-dust lectures, rain, and a lot of dreary nights at the Old Boar Inn, with girls who talked too much and didn't believe in shaving their armpits. But now that he was a free man—Kingsmere Events was thriving, so much so that even his father had finally started to come around—Michael appreciated all that the city had to offer. Today, with the sun out and the cherry trees in bloom, the feeling of optimism and energy on the streets was palpable. Like all university towns, Oxford belonged to the young. As he walked past Exeter and University colleges, Michael felt all the joy of being in his twenties and successful, building a business that he loved and was good at. When they started the company, Michael and Tommy had rented office space in Oxford to avoid paying London rents. Now, with eight full-time employees and big-money assignments rolling in, they could easily have afforded to move, but neither of them wanted to. Life didn't get any better than this.

Michael checked his watch. *Twelve-fifteen.*

Mustn't be late.

He was headed to San Domingo's, probably the most expensive restaurant in Oxford, for a lunch date with his mother. Michael would pay, then bill it back later under *Client Expenses Misc.* Having one's parents as clients had its advantages. To Michael's shock and delight, Alexia had persuaded Teddy to let him and Tommy organize the Kingsmere summer party. They'd put the event together on the cheap, slashing their usual rates—Teddy De Vere would have had a coronary had Michael charged him the sort of fees he charged wealthy London clients for similar dos—but the PR for Kingsmere Events would be priceless.

Michael's partner, Tommy, had marveled at the updated entertainment list only this morning.

"Have you seen this? Mick Hucknall's coming out of retirement to perform a live solo, Princess Michael of Kent's proposing the toasts, and Nigel Kennedy's just given a yes to a violin recital on the terrace during the predinner drinks. And we have your mother to thank for all of it."

"Actually, *I* got Kennedy," said Michael. "We hit it off last year at the book launch for his autobiography."

But he took Tommy's point. The Three Hundred Years of Kingsmere celebrations might have been Teddy's idea, but it was Alexia's social and political pulling power that was going to make this a major media event. Thanks to Michael's mother, the guest list read like the love child of *Vanity Fair*'s "100 most powerful" and Debrett's, with just a splash of *Hello!* magazine glamour thrown in for good measure. Henry Whitman and his wife would be rubbing shoulders with the

French president and the crown prince of Spain. At another table, Simon Cowell, Gwyneth Paltrow, and Sir Bob Geldof would be sharing after-dinner coffee with the Dowager Duchess of Devonshire, Nicola Horlick, and Sir Gus O'Donnell, former head of the Civil Service in Whitehall and popularly known by his initials: *GOD*. Michael thought it a safe bet that if Jesus Christ were alive today, He would make room in His miracle-working schedule for the Kingsmere summer party. After all, if it was good enough for Matthew Freud and Elizabeth Murdoch . . .

San Domingo's was full—San Domingo's was always full—but Michael was shown to a spacious table by the window, overlooking the river and the famous Magdalen College deer park. He'd just had time to sit and order a bottle of sparkling water when Alexia swept in, looking powerful and glamorous in a dark green Prada pantsuit and cream silk blouse, a ministerial briefcase in one hand and a BlackBerry in the other.

"Darling. Have you been waiting long?"

"Not at all. You look fabulous as ever, Mum."

She gave him an "oh, this old thing" eye roll, kissed him on both cheeks, and sat down, ordering the steamed monk-fish and a green salad without so much as glancing at the menu. Michael plumped for his usual steak and fries. "Sorry to seem so rushed," Alexia said. "But unfortunately—"

"You *are* so rushed."

"Yes. I've got this bloody Paris trip tomorrow with the trade secretary, who loathes me. I've barely had a second to read the brief, and now your father's insisting I spend the night in Oxfordshire before I leave."

"Why?"

"He feels your sister and I must spend more time together. As if time's going to solve anything."

Michael had been so busy working this year, he'd seen very little of Roxie, which he felt guilty about. On the rare occasions when he took a break from the business, he tried to spend as much time as possible with Summer, although even that was difficult, what with Summer finishing her journalism degree at NYU and Michael based three thousand miles away in Oxford.

"Are things no better on the Roxie front, then?"

"Things are the same. I open a door, your sister slams it." Alexia smiled thinly, but Michael could see the pain behind the smile.

"Are you really opening doors, though, Mummy?" he asked cautiously. "You can be pretty short with Rox at times, you know."

"I know." Alexia sighed. "She frustrates me so much, sometimes it's hard to keep my temper. But I *am* trying. I don't want to give up on her, Michael, but it's as if she's given up on herself."

"I know." Michael sighed.

"Anyway, enough of that nonsense. How are *you*, my darling? How are things going with Daddy's party?"

"Wonderfully, thanks."

"Anything you need from me?"

"Nope." Michael sipped his water. "You've done more than enough already. Tommy says to tell you if you ever tire of running the country, there's a guaranteed job for you with us."

Alexia laughed loudly. "How sweet of Tommy. Do give him my best."

"You mustn't give up hope with Rox, you know," Michael said abruptly. "Look how much better things are with Dad and me now, versus a year ago."

"That's hardly the same."

"It is in some ways."

224

"Your sister's never going to get over Andrew Beesley leaving her. I don't know if she even wants to get over it, to tell you the truth. Sometimes I think she's more comfortable being a victim than she is being happy." Alexia took a bite of her fish. "Does that sound terribly harsh?"

It did sound harsh, although Michael had had the same thought himself, many times. Roxie liked being a victim and Teddy liked having a victim to care for. In some sick, twisted way, tragedy suited the two of them.

Michael's face darkened. "I hate Andrew Beesley. I hate him so much it's like a pain in my chest."

Alexia looked at her son intently. "Do you?"

"Yes. I think how different things would be if Roxie had never met him. Don't you?"

"No," Alexia said truthfully. "I never think about the past. What happened, happened. It can't be changed."

"So you don't hate Andrew Beesley?" Michael sounded disbelieving.

"No, I don't hate him."

"Because it would be okay to hate him, you know. It would be normal."

Alexia laughed, more from nerves than amusement. Something about Michael's tone disturbed her. "Would you *like* me to hate him?"

"No. All I'm saying is, I wouldn't judge you if you did. Some people are just bad people. They deserve to suffer. They deserve to die."

The mood at the table had shifted. Michael had been all sunshine and smiles when she walked in. Now suddenly he was so cold, Alexia felt a shiver run through her. She'd had the same feeling at Number Ten, when Henry Whitman had been so cryptic about her relationship with Sir Edward Manning.

225

Had Henry been trying to tell her something? Was Michael?

"How's Summer?" Alexia asked, changing the subject to what she hoped would be a happier topic.

"Fine, I think."

"What do you mean you *think*? Don't you know?"

Michael fiddled uncomfortably with his napkin. "I haven't seen her for a couple of months, to be honest. She's in New York. I'm here. It's not easy."

"But you speak on the phone? You Skype?"

Michael nodded noncommittally.

Oh dear, thought Alexia. *Trouble in paradise?* She did hope not.

In the beginning Alexia hadn't particularly shared Lucy Meyer's enthusiasm for their respective children to become an item. But Summer had been good for Michael. She'd calmed him down and brought peace and contentment to the point where Alexia had begun to hope that perhaps the kids *would* get married. Certainly Summer Meyer would make a far more acceptable daughter-in-law than the motley parade of cocktail waitresses, models, and Lithuanian "students" that Michael had been dating before they got together.

"You're still happy together, though, aren't you?"

"Mmm-hmm." The napkin twisted tighter.

"And she's coming to the party?"

"Uh-huh. She's flying over with Lucy and Arnie. Can we change the subject?"

"Of course." Mother and son chatted happily for the rest of the meal, both making fun of Teddy's utter obsession with the Kingsmere celebrations and with the great De Vere family history. By the time Alexia had to leave, Michael's earlier odd mood had evaporated. He hugged her with his usual carefree grin.

"So, Paris tomorrow?"

"Paris tomorrow." Alexia sighed. "I can't remember the last time I had this much work on."

"Can't you?" Michael smiled to himself. His mother had been a rabidly ambitious workaholic since the day he was born, and almost certainly long before that. "Listen, Mum, I meant what I said about Roxie. Don't give up hope. Deep down she still loves you. I know she does."

Alexia kissed him on both cheeks. "Sweet boy."

She swept out of the restaurant and didn't look back.

THE PARIS TRADE MEETINGS WERE AS dull as trade meetings always were, at least during the morning sessions. In France, everybody drank wine with lunch, making the afternoons slightly more bearable for most. Unfortunately, Alexia was a teetotaler, a concept so alien to her Parisian hosts that it became quite a talking point.

"But of course you 'ave wine in the evenings, madame?"

"No, no. I don't drink."

"Ah, *oui, je vois*. You are not drinking at work. I understand. This is a British habit, *n'est-ce pas*?"

"I actually don't drink alcohol at all."

"No, I am sorry. I don't understand."

"I don't enjoy it."

"Don't enjoy it?"

"No. It's not to my taste."

"Ah, *d'accord*. But you will 'ave a little Château Latour, of course? This is not alcohol, madame. This is a great wine."

Alexia was as sure as she could be that Kevin Lomax was behind the rumor that she didn't drink because she was an alcoholic. But the last thing she wanted was to be drawn into a slanging match with Kevin, so she let it slide. Meetings with Lomax were stressful at the best of times, and the alcohol issue didn't help. It was a relief to be able to escape for a couple of hours. While the trade and industry secretary toured the Renault Headquarters and enjoyed the CEO's *"déjeuner de bienvenue"* alone, Alexia had taken herself off for a spot of shopping on the avenue Montaigne. No doubt the other delegates would be three sheets to the wind by the time she got back to the committee rooms. It did irritate her that so little was achieved in afternoon sessions, but she tried to focus on the job at hand: choosing a dress for Roxie. The assistants at Christian Dior were all male, all impeccably dressed in dark suits like nineteenth-century butlers, and had all mastered the art of efficiently unobtrusive service.

"'Ow may I help you, madame? You are looking for professional wear, or something for the evening perhaps?"

"Actually I wanted something for my daughter," Alexia said. "A gift."

She'd taken Michael's advice to heart and decided to make more of an effort with Roxanne. Since communication of a personal, emotional nature had never been Alexia's strong point, she thought she'd start with a peace offering. A present.

The assistant took her arm. "Well, madame, we 'ave some classic silk scarves, of course. Very chic, very beautiful. And our new collection of *sacs à main* is just arrived."

"I thought perhaps a dress? We've a summer party coming up and my daughter will want to look her best. She's the same size as I am."

"And as beautiful as madame, I am sure," the assistant said smoothly.

An old feeling of irritation rose up within Alexia, but she suppressed it. It was not an attractive trait, to feel jealous of one's own daughter's youth and beauty, and she disliked herself for it. When all was said and done, she did love Roxanne and always had.

Hands were clapped, fingers clicked, and immediately Alexia found herself surrounded by swathes of rustling fabric, cotton and toile and slub silk and velvet and lace in every conceivable cut and color. It had been a long time since Alexia had shopped for clothes. These days she ordered everything from Net-A-Porter, or got her PA to pick things up for her. She realized she'd forgotten how much fun nonvirtual fashion could be.

She'd also forgotten just how obnoxious Americans could be, especially when on vacation abroad. In the dressing room next to Alexia's, a very loud, very vulgar Texan woman was shouting at her husband to turn off his iPad and pay her some attention.

"I swear to Gaaawd, Howie, if you don't turn that thing off right now, I'm gonna spend so much money in here you won't be able to afford a cab back to the Georges V." She pronounced it "George Sink," which made Alexia cringe. Having eradicated her own American accent forty years ago, she recoiled at Americanisms now like a reformed smoker wrinkling her nose at others' cigarette smoke. Clearly this woman felt the need to ensure that the entire store knew that she and "Howie" were staying at the most expensive hotel in Paris.

"Would you shut the fuck up, Loreen?" her husband replied boorishly. "I'm tryin' to listen to the news here."

"There's news at the hotel. I am *tryin'* to shop."

"I mean real news, not that French communist baloney."

"Real news" turned out to be Fox, probably Alexia's least favorite media outlet. But, like the rest of the store, she soon found herself being deafened by the noise from Howie's iPad, turned up to maximum volume, presumably to make a point and show his strident young wife who wore the pants.

The Dior staff, as ever, were scrupulously polite.

"Sir, I'm afraid we're going to have to ask you to turn that off."

"Ask away, Pierre," the Texan said rudely. "I'm listening to the news and that's that. Do you have any idea how much money I've spent in your store in the last forty-eight hours?"

"No, sir, I don't."

"Yeah, well. It's more than you make in a year. I pay your fucking wages, okay, Pierre? So back off."

"Howie! Stop being such an asshole and help me pick a dress."

As the marital argument wore on, Alexia found herself tuning in to the headlines on autopilot. The U.S. president had delivered a popular speech on the first day of his trip to Israel. American defense spending was up again, for the third quarter in a row. *That's a mistake*, Alexia thought. The euro was down against the dollar. A flamboyant Miami businessman had thrown his name into the hat for the Republican presidential nomination next spring. But it was the last item, added by the newscaster almost as an afterthought, that made Alexia De Vere catch her breath.

"The mutilated body of a young woman washed up on the Jersey shore yesterday morning has now been identified as that of Jennifer Hamlin, a twenty-two-year-old secretary from Queens, New York."

Jennifer Hamlin!

The name rang in Alexia's ears like a hideously clanging bell. Her mind flashed back to last year. Billy Hamlin standing in Parliament Square, calling her Toni, begging her to acknowledge him. Alexia heard his voice now, as if he were standing right beside her.

230

"Toni, please! It's my daughter. My daughter!"

He was frightened, frightened for his daughter, and he needed my help. But I turned him away. And now his daughter's dead. Murdered, just like poor Billy.

In her guilt, Alexia clutched at straws. Perhaps it was a different Jenny Hamlin? Not Billy's daughter at all? But she knew in her heart that the coincidence was too great. She remembered the file on Billy Hamlin that Edward Manning had compiled for her. Billy had had one daughter, Jennifer. The family was from Queens. *What did Billy want to tell me, about his daughter? What was it that I was too afraid, too self-interested, to listen to? Could I have saved her? Saved both of them?*

Alexia handed the dresses back to the assistant and left the store in a daze.

Outside on the avenue Montaigne, she made a phone call.

"Billy Hamlin's daughter's been murdered."

On the other end of the line, Sir Edward Manning betrayed no emotion. "I see." He'd been exactly the same after Billy Hamlin was found dead last year, a case that the police had closed without identifying a single suspect. Cool. Calm. Unruffled. It was what Alexia expected of him, what she wanted, in a way. And yet, unreasonably, it still upset her.

"Is there anything you'd like me to do, Home Secretary?"

"Yes. Get me all the information on the case. All of it. Talk to the U.S. police, to the State Department, to the FBI. I don't care how you get it and I don't care who knows. I want a report on Jennifer Hamlin's murder on my desk by the time I get back to London."

"And if people ask why the British Home Office is so interested in an obscure American murder inquiry?"

231

"Tell them to mind their own damn business."

Alexia hung up, shaking. Suddenly the trade talks and the stupid Kingsmere summer party didn't matter at all anymore. All she could think about was Billy Hamlin and his poor daughter. Just as it had last summer, Alexia's past had emerged to reclaim her. But this time she couldn't resist it. She couldn't stick her head in the sand and simply run away. People were dying. *Because of me?*

Alexia De Vere caught the Eurostar back to London that night, with a deep sense of foreboding in her heart.

Roxanne De Vere never did get her peace offering.

CHAPTER TWENTY-THREE

LUCY MEYER SAT DOWN ON THE end of the bed and began carefully unpacking her suitcase.

"Why are you doing that?" Arnie asked her. "I'll get the front desk to send up a maid."

"And have some barely trained Eastern European slip of a girl put grubby finger marks all over my vintage Alaiia? No thank you," huffed Lucy. "I'll do it myself."

Arnie laughed. It amused him that even here, at London's *über*-luxurious Dorchester Hotel, where he'd booked them into one of the two royal suites (a genuine royal was apparently in the other), his wife was too distrustful of foreigners to let the staff help her unpack. Arnie had been married to Lucy for a long time, and had learned to find her idiosyncrasies endearing rather than annoying. At the same time, as an international financier who spent half his life in other cultures, he found it baffling that his wife could be so resolutely narrow-minded about all things European. As far as Lucy Meyer was concerned, if a thing wasn't done *exactly* as it was done in America, then it was done wrong.

The Meyers had flown in for the De Veres' summer party at Kingsmere next weekend. All the Pilgrim Farm neighbors knew that Teddy and Alexia were skipping their annual trip to the Vineyard this year because of some big bash of Teddy's back in England. But it wasn't until they landed in London that Lucy and Arnie realized exactly how high profile next weekend's event was going to be. The British prime minister and his wife, Charlotte, were flying back from their holiday in Sicily in order to attend. Every English newspaper was running paparazzi shots of the various international celebrities congregating in London like exotic pigeons, all at the behest of Britain's glamorous home secretary. Even more exciting, quite a number of said celebrities were spending the nights before the party at the Dorchester, getting over their jet lag and generally being seen. Lucy Meyer had already spotted Prince Albert of Monaco at the bar downstairs, and the Spanish prime minister and his wife had checked in immediately before her and Arnie. *Literally next to us at the front desk!* as Lucy had written excitedly on her Facebook page.

"I hope Summer's gone formal enough with her dress," Lucy fretted as she hung up her own floor-length silver gown. "Do you remember last Christmas, at the White House Correspondents' Dinner, when she went knee length?" She gave a small, involuntary shudder at the memory.

"Summer always looks wonderful," Arnie Meyer said loyally. "Besides, Michael's organized this thing, hasn't he? I'm sure he'll have filled her in on the dress code."

"I hope so." Lucy sounded worried. "Even so, I think I might pop over to Harrods before she gets here and pick up a couple of backups for her, just in case."

"Only a couple?" Arnie teased. "Wouldn't it make more sense to buy up the whole designer-wear floor, honey? You don't want to leave anything to chance."

"You may laugh." Lucy scooped up her quilted Chanel

purse from the table by the door. "But it's very important for a woman to look the part at these things."

"I know that, sweetie."

"After all, Summer's attending as a potential daughter-in-law. Let's not forget that."

Arnie Meyer rolled his eyes.

Forget it? With Lucy's wedding fever as strong as ever, there was no chance of that.

SUMMER MEYER WAITED BY CAROUSEL NUMBER eight for her bag to arrive.

And waited.

And waited.

Finally she went to the help desk.

"Are you sure everything's been taken off the plane?"

"I'm afraid so, miss. Do you have your baggage tag handy? It should be on the back of your ticket."

Summer scrabbled around in her purse. As usual it was a total mess, full of makeup and pens and half-eaten candy bars and scraps of paper with ideas for feature articles scrawled across them. But no boarding pass.

"I must have left it on the plane."

The man at the desk was sympathetic, taking down the description Summer gave him of her untagged suitcase ("black" and "large") without so much as a smirk. But they both knew it would be a miracle if she saw the bag again. Exhausted and defeated, she caught the first Heathrow Express train to London, sinking down into the window seat, close to tears.

What the hell's wrong with me? I've really got to pull myself together.

An impartial observer could have answered her first

question at a glance. The dark shadows under her eyes and sickly pallor of her skin showed just how little Summer had slept in the last month. Her journalism program at NYU was intense and required a lot of late-night cramming and long hours in the classroom or chained to her intern's desk at the *Post*. But the true reason for her sleep deprivation lay closer to home.

Michael was acting strange. He had been for months. When it started, shortly after Christmas, Summer had put it down to the pressure of work. Kingsmere Events was still a new business, and Michael and Tommy both worked like galley slaves to get it turning a profit. Often that meant grueling foreign travel, with a party in Cape Town one night and another in London or Paris or New York the next. Understaffed and running on adrenaline and espresso, it was no wonder Michael had little time left for romance.

On top of all that, there was the long-distance thing. Summer had her own commitments in New York, her own dreams and ambitions. She couldn't keep flying to England to play the little wife to Michael De Vere. And yet Michael's hot-and-cold behavior was more than that. The awkward phone calls, the canceled trips, the uncharacteristic fits of temper when they were together, followed by wallowing bouts of guilt. Call it woman's intuition, or a journalist's nose for the truth. But Summer Meyer knew there was something going on, something Michael wasn't telling her. And it didn't take Einstein to figure out what that something might be.

Michael De Vere had always been a womanizer. Even as a teenage boy, he'd had a whole raft of girlfriends on permanent rotation. Summer knew that about him. She'd gone into this thing with her eyes wide open. But like a fool, she'd thought he could change. *Worse, I thought I could change him. Talk about a cliché.*

Yesterday, right before she left for the airport, he had telephoned.

"I've been thinking. Why don't you stay with your folks at the Dorchester for the first couple of nights. I'm going to be snowed down here with last-minute preparations. You'd have much more fun flexing Arnie's AmEx on Bond Street than hanging around my flat in Oxford while I work."

Summer had agreed—what else could she do without making herself look desperate?—but inside, her heart sank. She and Michael hadn't seen each other for months. But instead of counting the hours until they reunited, he was putting her off.

If he's changed his mind about me, why doesn't he just break up with me? Why drag out the torture?

She hated Michael for this, but she hated herself more for not having the guts to call him on it. Summer didn't know when, or why, or how it had happened. But she had fallen so deeply in love with Michael De Vere, she was as helpless as a kitten blown into a lake, splashing and mewling to no avail as the waters rose around her.

"Next stop, London Victoria. The train will terminate here."

Would Summer and Michael's relationship terminate at the Kingsmere summer party? Or before?

She couldn't bear to think about it.

MICHAEL DE VERE WAS IN A foul mood.

"I don't care, Ajay, okay? The frame was supposed to be here yesterday." Shouting into a walkie-talkie, he paced the grounds of his family's estate like a hungry tiger looking for lunch. "I'm sitting here with a hundred grand's worth of flowers, enough to fit out a Royal Navy fleet, and a melting

237

ice sculpture delivered two days early, and I have no motherfucking marquee. I'm not paying you a penny unless your guys are here within the hour."

Kingsmere's grounds looked glorious in June, a riot of apple blossoms and roses and scented buddleia bursting with life and color. At six o'clock, the house was bathed in a honey glow of late-afternoon light, as warm and inviting as it was architecturally magnificent. Teddy had bustled outside earlier, a proud Mr. Toad observing the party preparations at Toad Hall without actually understanding a bit of what was going on. What Teddy saw were gratifying numbers of lithe young people scurrying hither and thither with silverware, china, balloons, and the like. He'd been apprehensive about allowing Michael and Tommy to organize such a prestigious event, and one on which so much De Vere family honor rested. But the boys had been nothing if not diligent, showing up before dawn this morning to check on the delivery of the fancy Porta Potties and generally running what appeared to be a tight ship.

Michael smiled at his father and gave a confident wave. Little did Teddy know it was the wave of the proverbial drowning man. With less than seventy-two hours to go until his mother's A-list guests started arriving, Michael De Vere was standing in a garden full of workmen, food, and props, with no freaking tent. Meanwhile Alexia, who'd returned from her trip to Paris looking as white as a sheet, had gone completely AWOL, holing up in London and not returning Michael's calls. Roxie was being more than usually needy as the prospect of an evening in the public eye drew nearer. And to top it all, Summer had landed in England today, and naturally expected to spend some quality time with him.

Michael thought, *I'm being cowardly. I should be straight with her, not just keep putting her off with no explanation.* But there was only so much stress he could take. It was an odd feeling, longing to see someone and dreading it at the same time. Work was a welcome distraction.

His cell phone buzzed. Michael read the text and grinned, checking his watch.

"In a hurry, are we?" Tommy Lyon, Michael's partner and best friend, said archly. "I hope you're not thinking of sloping off."

"Give me a break. I spent half the night here last night," Michael said reasonably.

"Working on the pagoda? Yes, I saw that. You seem to have spent the moonlit hours digging a big hole and filling it with concrete. Looks fabulous, by the way."

"Ha ha."

The "pagoda" Tommy was referring to was supposed to have been the centerpiece of Kingsmere's three-hundred-year celebration. Teddy De Vere had ordered the construction of a Greek Revival pillared folly out near the lake, but the project had been beset by one problem after another, from poor drainage to sinking foundations. In the end, Michael had taken over. This late in the day he'd been forced to implement a policy of damage control, pouring concrete over the half-finished foundations. With luck, the concrete should be dry by tomorrow. Then Michael and Tommy's landscape guys would cover it with huge potted olive trees, string up a few fairy lights, and voilà, an impromptu Florentine garden.

"I won't be long," Michael assured Tommy. "Forty minutes. An hour, tops."

"Is that all you give them these days?" Tommy teased. "Poor girl. Whoever she is, she has my sympathy."

Michael made a face.

"Just cover for me, would you?"

"All right. And if your girlfriend shows up, wondering where you've got to?"

"She won't. She's in London. Shopping."

Tommy Lyon watched his friend hop onto his new Ducati motorcycle and speed off down the drive. One of these days, Michael's wicked ways were going to catch up with him.

Tommy Lyon didn't know how he did it.

ARNIE MEYER HAD BOOKED A TABLE for three at Scalini. The spaghetti *alle vongole* was the best in London, you could order a bottle of Sangiovese and get a second for free, and it was close enough to Harrods for Lucy to roll out of Marc Jacobs evening wear without bothering to go back to the hotel in between. Knowing Summer would be tired and hungry after her flight, Arnie made the reservation early: seven-thirty.

What with all Lucy's shopping and excursion plans, Arnie Meyer felt as if he'd barely spent five minutes with his wife since they got to London. He was looking forward to tonight's dinner. Summer's presence would be an added bonus.

"Your usual table, sir?"

"Yes, please, Giacomo."

Arnie smiled. He hadn't been to Scalini for over four years, but these people made an effort with the service. "And a gin and tonic while I wait for the ladies."

"Of course, Mr. Meyer."

Arnie Meyer loved England. He was glad he'd made this trip, glad Teddy De Vere had badgered him into coming. Once his two favorite girls arrived, the evening would be just about perfect.

*

SUMMER WOKE AS THE TRAIN RATTLED to a halt. *Has an hour gone by already?* Her chestnut hair was greasy and matted and stuck to her cheek, and there was a deeply unattractive wet patch on her shoulder from where she'd drooled onto her T-shirt.

She longed to shower and change, crawl between a pair of newly laundered sheets, and sleep for about a year. Instead she was supposed to be at a fancy Italian restaurant in less than fifteen minutes. With her suitcase lost over the Atlantic, she didn't even have the option to change in the station bathrooms. At this point even a clean T-shirt and a spritz of perfume would have been a luxury.

If only she could ditch this damn dinner. But Summer knew what her father would say if she wimped out now. *"Are you a Meyer or a mouse?"* Thinking of Arnie's silly expressions, imagining his voice in her head, she started to laugh, then cry.

I really do have to get a grip.

LUCY MEYER ARRIVED AT SCALINI'S BREATHLESS, weighed down with bag after bag of expensive clothes.

"Sorry I'm late." She kissed Arnie on the cheek.

"*Really* late."

"I know, honey. I'm afraid I got a little carried away." She smiled sheepishly.

Arnie bit back his irritation. He didn't know how Teddy De Vere did it, constantly waiting around for his wife, playing second fiddle. The man must be a saint. Then again, at least Alexia had better excuses for her lateness than an extended shopping spree in Harrods.

"Where's Summer?" Lucy asked, apparently oblivious to her husband's bad mood.

"You tell me. I guess she inherited her mother's sense of punctuality."

"I'm sure she'll be here in a minute. Why don't we order some appetizers while we wait. All that shopping's gone and worn me out."

Yup. A saint.

Definitely a saint.

SUMMER WAS LATE.

The PA who'd given her directions to the restaurant was either confused, or deliberately messing with her because in *no sense* was the restaurant "a straight shot" left from the railway station. Nor had any of the people Summer stopped on the street heard of it, despite the PA's insistence that it was "a landmark. Really famous."

At last, at almost nine o'clock, she found herself standing outside. The place looked cozy rather than fancy, entirely lit by candles and with an inviting smell of garlic and truffle oil floating out to the street through the open windows. Inside, a low hum of laughter and conversation added to the warm, relaxed atmosphere.

If only I felt warm, or relaxed. But I'm here now. It has to be done.

Painting on a smile and holding her head high, Summer walked in. She saw the table immediately, walked over, and sat down.

"Summer! Oh my God, w-what are you doing here?"

The blood drained from Michael De Vere's face like water out of a bath.

"I think we need to talk, Michael. Don't you?"

*

242

Arnie Meyer hung up.

"Well, at least she's safe. She's in Oxford with Michael."

Lucy's eyes widened. "Oxford? That's kind of last minute, isn't it? I wonder why she didn't call to let us know."

"Because she's twenty-three and about as considerate of the needs of others as a particularly vacuous fruit fly?"

Lucy laughed. "I guess that must be it. Did she say . . . I mean, do you think things are okay between them?"

Arnie rolled his eyes. "Who the heck knows? She said they were 'talking things through,' whatever that means. You want some tiramisu?"

Lucy shouldn't, not if she was going to get into her dress on Saturday. Then again the dessert trolley did look good. And she had had an exhausting afternoon.

"Oh, go on, then." She winked at her husband. "You only live once."

Summer lay in Michael's arms feeling foolish. When the clueless Kingsmere PA, Sarah, had told her Michael had reservations at Bepe in Oxford at eight—a table for two— Summer was convinced he was meeting another woman. On a whim she'd jumped on the first train from Paddington intending to confront him, only to arrive at the restaurant and find Michael alone.

"Where's your date?" she asked sarcastically.

"In the loo."

"I see. You won't mind if I wait, then? I'm dying to meet her."

"You are?"

Michael had seemed more confused than panicked. When his companion returned from the bathroom, Summer could see why. She found herself being introduced to a

243

perfectly charming Indian gentleman. Ajay Singh was in his early fifties, smelled faintly of turpentine, and was one of Michael and Tommy's key suppliers.

"I thought I told you I had to work tonight," Michael said later as the two of them walked back to his flat along the backs. It was a dreamy night in Oxford, warm and cloudless, with a blanket of stars twinkling over the river like fireflies. Undergraduate couples punted past them in the darkness, and in the near distance the bells of Christchurch Cathedral chimed midnight, as they had done every night for the last eight hundred years.

"You did." Summer took Michael's hand. "But I really wanted to see you. Aren't you happy I came?"

"You haven't come, yet." Pulling her to him, he kissed her roughly on the mouth. It was a passion she hadn't felt from him in months, that she'd feared was gone forever. "But you will."

Michael was as good as his word. In bed later, their lovemaking was intense, wild and wonderful, the way it was last summer when they first got together back on Martha's Vineyard. As soon as Michael touched her, Summer felt her tiredness lift and her misery of only a few hours ago evaporate like raindrops in the sun.

It was all in my head. There's nothing wrong. He's been working too hard and we've been living oceans apart. Everything will be fine now that we're back together.

Stretching out a lazy arm, she stroked Michael's bare back.

"Are you nervous about Saturday night?"

"Nervous? I'm terrified. Tommy came up with a great expression yesterday. He said he was 'shitting porcupines.' I'm about the same."

Summer laughed, because it was funny, and because it

was such a relief to be Summer and Michael again, and not the suspicious strangers they'd become.

"I'll have to remember that one. Work it into a political piece at the *Post:* 'Senator Brownlow "Shitting Porcupines" over Upcoming Iowa Primary.' Yeah, I like it. I think it's gonna catch on. How about your parents. Are they calm?"

"Mother is. Mother's always calm."

Was it Summer's imagination, or had a slight edge crept into Michael's voice?

"And Teddy?"

"In Dad's mind, this party is all about family honor. Three hundred years of the De Veres at Kingsmere. That's all he cares about. I don't think it's registered how much more than that it's become, how much it means for Mummy's career. I mean, it's Mummy they're all coming to see. No one gives a rat's arse about the De Vere family tree."

Without thinking, Summer blurted out, "I thought you were with someone else tonight. Another woman. I thought I'd catch you out."

"Oh." Michael frowned. "Is that why you came?"

Summer nodded, biting her lower lip and willing the tears not to flow. "I'm sorry. It's just things have been so . . . so *off* between us lately. I've felt so distant from you."

Michael put a finger to her lips. "Shhh. Don't let's talk about it. I'm sorry too. I love you."

They kissed again. Summer felt overwhelmed with relief, as if she'd been holding her breath for the last six months and had finally been allowed to exhale. When at last they pulled apart she said, "I don't want us to have secrets from each other. I want us to know each other completely."

"I'm not sure that's possible."

Summer raised an eyebrow. "You don't think honesty is possible?"

245

"To a point it is," said Michael. "But everyone has secrets, don't they?"

"Do they?" Summer was starting to feel uneasy.

"I think so. But that doesn't have to be a bad thing. Secrets can be a burden. I mean, once you know something, that's it. You can never un-know it. You can never take that knowledge back. The innocence you had before, it's gone. You shouldn't inflict that on someone unless you really have to. Especially not someone you love."

Summer sat up. "Okay, now you're scaring me. Is there something you want to tell me, Michael?"

"No! That's the whole point. There isn't."

"All right, is there something you *don't* want to tell me? Something specific?"

"I should never have got into this, should I?" He tried to laugh it off, but the ease of a few moments ago had gone. "Look, really, you're getting worked up over nothing. This isn't about us. Okay?"

"Okay," Summer said warily.

"I'm talking purely hypothetically. Let's say you knew a secret. Something bad that someone has done."

"All right."

"I mean something *really* bad. And let's say you loved the person who's done it."

"But we're not talking about us, right?"

"We're not talking about us. Would you tell the person that you knew? Would you confront them?"

Summer thought about it. "It depends on the person. And the secret."

"That's not an answer."

"Well, yours wasn't a question! It was a riddle. Okay, I'll give you an answer. The answer is, you follow your conscience. You do what feels right in your gut."

Michael turned and looked at her. The shadows under her eyes were darker and heavier than usual. She looked tired—*is that because of me?*—but still so beautiful. He'd forgotten just how beautiful she was.

I'm an idiot. A total idiot.

"Do you know what feels right in *my* gut?" he asked.

"What?"

Grinning, he rolled on top of her. "This."

Michael was glad Summer had come to Oxford. He was even gladder she'd decided to surprise him at Bepe's, and not at his flat a few hours earlier. What a horror story that would have been. Guilt gripped him for a moment, but he batted it aside. What was done was done. Once this crazy party was over, he would focus on Summer more, make up for all his bad behavior.

As for his secrets, those would go with him to the grave.

CHAPTER TWENTY-FOUR

AT LAST THE DAY OF THE Kingsmere summer party arrived. Alexia De Vere awoke before dawn after another night of broken sleep. Creeping into the bathroom so as not to wake Teddy, she peered at her reflection in the mirror. A hag stared back at her. Wisps of gray were fighting their way through the blond, her skin looked dry and flaky and old, like stale pastry, and lines of exhaustion and stress ran in deep grooves, fanning out from her eyes and lips.

This wouldn't do.

Switching on her BlackBerry, Alexia fired off an e-mail to her personal assistant, Margaret, arranging for a hairdresser and makeup artist to come to the house in the early afternoon and fix the damage. Sir Edward Manning ran Alexia's political life, but when it came to personal matters, Margaret French was her right-hand woman. Having sent the e-mail, Alexia pulled her cashmere dressing gown tightly around her and went downstairs to her office.

"Good morning, madam. You're up early. Can I bring you some coffee?"

Thank God for Bailey. Good butlers were a dying breed, but Kingsmere's was the absolute best.

"Oh, please, Bailey, that would be lovely. As strong as you can make it, with warm milk and sweetener on the side. And some rye toast."

"Slightly burned, ma'am. I should hope I know how you like it by now."

What a relief to be home, in a place where little rituals mattered and the fundamentals of life never changed. Ever since Paris, and the awful afternoon in Dior when she'd heard about Jennifer Hamlin's murder, Alexia felt as if the world—her world—had gone mad. By day her schedule at the Home Office was as crammed as ever. Education Committee meetings here, hospital openings there, white papers to be digested on everything from scrapping jury trials for terrorists to the increasingly contentious and unpopular U.S. extradition treaty. But all the time, in the back of her mind, Billy Hamlin's fate, and that of his daughter, haunted her. When Alexia ate lunch, or went to the bathroom, or slept, or turned on the television, there was Billy's face like Banquo's ghost, demanding her attention, demanding justice.

I came to you about my daughter.

I needed your help.

But you turned me away.

Every day, guilt came knocking like a beggar at the door of Alexia's heart, demanding to be let in. *You owed Billy Hamlin so much. And you gave him so little.* But every day, with a supreme effort of will, she turned it away. The crimes of the past were Toni Gilletti's crimes and Toni Gilletti was dead. She was Alexia De Vere: a loving wife, a competent mother, and a committed politician, changing her adopted country for the good. Alexia De Vere hadn't killed anyone. It wasn't her fault.

Guilt may have been forced out, but curiosity was

249

allowed in, and soon it was running rampant. Who had killed Billy and Jennifer Hamlin, and why? Were the deaths connected to each other, or to her, or were they in fact merely random acts of violence, two isolated incidents of cruelty in a cruel, cruel world? More importantly, had everything possible been done to try to bring their killer, or killers, to justice? Throughout her political career, Alexia De Vere had championed the victims of violent crime, urging evertougher sentences for those who terrorized the weak. Billy and Jennifer Hamlin had been weak.

Toni Gilletti hadn't helped Billy Hamlin when he needed her. But perhaps Alexia De Vere could use her influence to help him now . . . ?

The coffee and toast arrived. Revived by both, Alexia opened her briefcase and pulled out the file Sir Edward Manning had compiled for her on Jennifer Hamlin's murder. Edward had really gone the extra mile, calling in favors from the FBI and Interpol. He'd spoken to New York journalists, sliding through a sea of off-the-record information like a diligent and determined eel, condensing and refining his search so as to present only the most relevant, verifiable facts to the home secretary. As ever, Alexia was impressed and grateful. Edward had become her closest political ally, closer even than family at times. One day she must thank him properly.

The first six pages were pictures of Jennifer Hamlin's grotesquely mutilated corpse. Alexia had seen them many times now, but their power to shock had not diminished. *What sort of animal did this?* Billy at least had died cleanly, executed by a single knife wound to the heart. But his poor daughter had clearly been tortured. Each of Jennifer's limbs was covered in burn marks, and ligature bruises were visible on her wrists, ankles, and neck. According to the autopsy, however, Jenny Hamlin had been alive when she hit the water. The official cause of death was drowning.

Drowning.

Alexia shook her head, forcing the unwanted images out. Was it a coincidence? Or was the manner of Billy's daughter's death as significant as the fact of it?

It struck Alexia that all she really knew about Jennifer Hamlin was that she'd been murdered. Her life, her character, remained opaque. Jenny's mother, Sally, and her friends all painted the same picture to the police of a quiet, thoughtful girl, happy in her job as a legal secretary, and secure in her relationship with her boyfriend, a local baker named Luca Minotti. Partners were always the first suspects in murders involving young women, but there was no question about Minotti's innocence. He was in Italy visiting relatives the week Jenny disappeared, and more than thirty customers confirmed his presence at the bakery the day she died.

Poignantly, Jenny Hamlin had been pregnant when she was killed. Luca Minotti knew about the baby and was apparently ecstatic at the prospect of fatherhood. He and Jenny had been saving up for their wedding. It was all just too awful. No one could think of anyone who might conceivably have wanted to hurt this gentle, family-oriented young woman.

No one, that is, except Billy Hamlin.

Billy had been convinced for years that Jennifer was in danger. For two years prior to his own death, he had plagued the NYPD, FBI, local newspapers, and anyone else who would listen with complaints about threatening phone calls. "The voice" was going to hurt him. It was going to kill his daughter. Unfortunately, Billy also told police that numerous public figures were in danger. These included two prominent baseball players, the governor of Massachussets, and an

Australian swimsuit model named Danielle Hyams, with whom Billy had been briefly obsessed during his last spell of severe depression. Not unsurprisingly, his claims were dismissed as symptoms of his mental illness. Police could find no record of suspicious calls on his cellphone or landline records, and Billy failed to produce a single recording in evidence. Jennifer Hamlin herself was never contacted, and neither were any of the other individuals Billy mentioned.

Alexia jumped. Her BlackBerry was ringing. It was barely after six. Who on earth would be calling at this time in the morning?

"Alexia? It's Henry. Did I wake you?" The prime minister's voice sounded strained.

"No. No, I'm up. Is everything all right?"

"It's fine. No crisis. I probably shouldn't have called so early. I just wanted to let you know that I'm afraid Charlotte and I won't be able to make it tonight after all."

"Oh." Alexia swallowed her disappointment and her annoyance. If there was no crisis, it was inexcusable to pull out so late in the day. "That's a shame."

"Yes. Something . . . personal's come up," Henry said awkwardly. Alexia wondered whether the "something" was a certain donor's wife by the name of Laura Llewellyn, but she said nothing. "I'm sorry."

Alexia hung up. Her initial anger gave way to unease. The prime minister had been behaving distinctly strangely around her recently. She sensed a caginess in Henry Whitman now that hadn't been there before. *Those bastards in cabinet would do anything to see me fail. Have they got to him? Perhaps Edward Manning knows something? That might be why Henry was asking me about him the other day, almost pushing me to get rid of him as my PPS.*

Or maybe Charlotte Whitman was the problem. Wives

often became jealous of their husbands' professional relationships with other women. *But I'm far too old to be considered a threat.*

Perhaps it really IS Laura Llewellyn? It must be something serious for Henry to perform such a public U-turn on a long-standing commitment.

It was only after five minutes of prolonged and fruitless speculation that Alexia pulled herself up short. *You're being paranoid. You're letting the stress get to you.* The Hamlin murders had been giving her sleepless nights, to add to the anxiety of tonight's party and the daily battles of life as a woman at Westminster. What Alexia really needed was a break.

Her phone buzzed again. This time it was a text, from Lucy Meyer.

Can't wait to see you!! it read, followed by a string of smiley, excited, and kissy-face emoticons. *Party's gonna be awesome!!!*

Alexia laughed out loud. She'd missed Lucy this year, with her relentless good spirits and her endless enthusiasm. The woman would have exclamation marks carved into her gravestone.

Carefully lifting the Hamlin file, Alexia slipped it into her desk drawer and locked it away.

Screw Henry Whitman. Teddy and I are going to see our friends tonight and relax.

It's going to be fun.

MICHAEL DE VERE REVVED HIS NEW Ducati Panigale superbike, letting the roar of its powerful engine drown out the tumult of thoughts in his head.

He knew the route from Oxford to Kingsmere like the

back of his hand, but today he'd deliberately taken obscure back roads, through Witham Woods, the ancient forest bordering North Oxford and into the Evenlode Valley beyond. It was a perfect day—how could it be anything other for his mother's perfect party?—blue-skied and sunny and clear. On either side of the lane, high hedgerows teemed with life, honeysuckle and bumble bees and butterflies of all sizes and colors frothing like a fountain of buzzing, sweet-scented energy. Frightened by the noise of Michael's motorbike, starlings and blue tits and lapwings took to the sky as he passed, in a stunning aerial salute. In other circumstances, Michael would have felt exhilarated, racing through the landscape that he loved with the wind in his face and the sun on his back. As it was, he felt agitated and jumpy, angry at the emotions whipsawing him as he leaned into each bend.

Some of them were easy to identify. Guilt, for example, squatting like a fat toad over his heart, suffocating his happiness. It had been a close call with Summer last night. Too close. He hated himself for lying to her, for becoming the cliché of the unfaithful boyfriend, a parody of the very worst side of himself. When they were apart, he told himself that he had things under control. That he could compartmentalize his relationship with Summer and his life here in England. That it would all be all right. Last night had brought home to him what a hollow self-deception that was.

I love her.

I love her and I'm an idiot and this has to stop.

Michael's tangled love life was far from the only thing on his mind. For weeks now he'd been acting as if everything were normal. As if he didn't *know*. He'd driven back and forth to Kingsmere, installing lighting and working on the ill-fated pagoda, as if nothing had happened.

But something *had* happened. Something terrible.

And Michael De Vere hadn't the first idea what to do about it.

He needed to talk to someone. But who? Talking to his mother was impossible. Even if he knew what to say, Alexia's schedule was so jam-packed there was simply no opportunity to get her alone and focused. As for his father, Teddy De Vere had always lived in his own world, a fantasy of past family glories attached to some archaic concept of chivalry that Michael had never fully understood. Teddy could no more handle the truth than a four-year-old child could handle Michael's new gleaming red Ducati. The truth would break him, shatter him into a thousand shardlike fragments like a dropped Christmas tree ornament. Michael couldn't tell his father.

Which left him with Roxie.

Angrily Michael twisted the bike's handlebars, pumping more gas into the already shrieking engine. Poor Roxie, his once-vivacious, outgoing sister, reduced to a lonely, embittered cripple for the sake of a worthless former lover. If Roxie were to suffer any more, it wouldn't be because of Michael. She too was a closed door.

Last night he'd come close to confiding in Summer. But he'd stopped himself before he went too far. Saying the thing out loud, talking to another person about it, would have made it real. Michael De Vere had realized with sudden clarity last night that he did not want this to be real. He wanted it to be gone, hidden, buried, as it had been for so long. He wanted his innocence back, but he couldn't have it, and it made him so mad he wanted to scream and scream and never stop.

I have to get through the party. Make it a success, smile through it for all our sakes. After that, I'll deal with this. Decide what the hell to do.

He was approaching the top of Coombe Hill. From the

peak one could see the spires of Oxford on one side and the slumbering Cotswolds on the other, mile after mile of honeyed villages and lush green valleys, still dotted with the white sheep that had once been the region's lifeblood and primary source of income. Glancing down at his speedometer—he was already doing sixty, but it felt much faster on such narrow, deserted roads—Michael twisted the gas again, accelerating on the climb so that his wheels briefly left the ground as he cleared the top of the hill. He remembered the rush from childhood, doing wheelies off of humpback bridges with Tommy on their BMX push bikes. But the Ducati was a different beast altogether, wild and dangerous, like riding a leopard bareback.

Luckily, Michael was a skilled rider. Bringing the bike back down with ease, he leaned gracefully into the turn as the ground fell away beneath him. As the gradient grew steeper, he eased off the gas, but the speedometer needle kept rising, propelled by the Panigale's own momentum. Michael squeezed lightly on the front brake. Nothing happened. Surprised but not especially alarmed, he squeezed more forcefully, instinctively pushing down on the front wheel with his body weight to slow the bike's progress.

Nothing. What the hell?

The bottom of the hill was fast approaching. Adrenaline began to course unpleasantly through Michael's veins. Mercifully there were no other cars on the road, but the bend at the valley floor was almost forty-five degrees, after which the lane almost immediately fed into a T-junction with the busy A40. Forcing himself to stay calm, he looked at the speedometer again.

68 mph.

71 mph.

At this speed, using the rear brakes alone could be highly

dangerous, with bikes tending to skid out of control, but there was no other option. *What were you supposed to do to keep control in a rear-brake skid?* He willed himself to remember. *That's it. Keep your eyes on the horizon.*

He looked up, but as he did so tears of panic stung his eyes. The horizon was no longer a placid, flat line. It was a tidal wave of fields and sky, hurtling toward him at breakneck speed.

78 mph.

82 mph.

Michael's arms and legs shook as he gripped the rear-wheel brake, abandoning caution and wrenching it toward him with all his strength. His whole body tensed, waiting for the skid, for the jolting halt, but there was nothing. The brake rolled loose and limp in his hands.

That was when he knew.

Jesus Christ. I'm going to die.

A strange peace came over him, slowing his heart rate and reactions and immersing all his senses in a sort of muffled slow motion. He knew it was the end. But it was as if it were happening to someone else. As if someone else were watching the trucks on the main road race closer and closer, unable to stop or move or even swerve aside, passively succumbing to the inevitable like a paralyzed spectator.

The last thing Michael De Vere thought was, *I left Summer this morning without saying good-bye. I should have said good-bye.*

Then came the impact and the blackness and there were no more thoughts and nothing mattered anymore.

ROXIE DE VERE GAZED AT HER reflection in her dressing room mirror.

She claimed not to care about her appearance. There would never be another man for her after Andrew. Even if her body weren't broken and useless, she had no heart left to give, no sexual desire, no appetite for life or love and the inevitable pain that came with both. And yet, on a night like tonight, with the whole world watching, Roxie took a certain perverse pleasure in making herself look beautiful. If there was anything more poignant than a young girl confined to a wheelchair, it was surely a ravishing beauty confined to a wheelchair. More importantly, Roxie knew that when she looked her best, even now, it irritated her mother.

She'd pulled out all the stops tonight. Her naturally thick, blond hair was swept up into an elaborate chignon, fixed in place with antique Victorian hairpins studded with prettily colored glass beads. Her drop diamond earrings had once belonged to Teddy's grandmother, Lady Maud De Vere. The light they reflected contrasted perfectly with Roxie's smooth, softly sun-kissed skin. Her gown was simple, nothing like the fancy Dior confection that Alexia had been planning to buy for her in Paris. Left to her own devices, Roxie had opted for a plain, cream silk column that discreetly covered her shattered legs while encasing her full, smooth breasts in a subtly boned corset. The result was both inno-cent and sensual, an effect that Roxie highlighted with subtle makeup—palest pink lips and cheeks flushed with a dusting of shimmery peach blush. A simple, heart-shaped gold pendant hanging sweetly at her neck completed the picture.

Pushing herself over to the window, Roxie looked down at the legions of liveried staff running back and forth like ants. Tommy Lyon was striding around the grounds, a worried general in the hours before battle, shouting and gesticulating and generally marshaling the troops in Michael's absence. Very unusually, Michael had failed to show up at Kingsmere on this most crucial of afternoons. Tommy had no idea where he was, and Michael's cellphone, usually glued to his ear, was switched off. With the firsts guests due to start arriving in an hour, tensions were understandably running high. Roxie hoped that her friend Summer Meyer's unexpected appearance in Oxford last night wasn't behind her brother's disappearing act. If Summer had caught Michael in flagrante with one of his bimbos, anything could have happened. Not that he wouldn't deserve everything that was coming to him. But Roxie liked Summer and she liked Summer and Michael together. She'd be sorry to see Michael fuck that one up.

Back on the dressing table, Roxie's cellphone rang. Michael's name flashed across the screen. *Speak of the devil*.

"You better have a good excuse, Houdini. Poor Tommy's about to have a breakdown out there."

"Miss De Vere?"

The voice on the line wasn't Michael's. "Yes. Who is this?"

"Oxfordshire police. I'm afraid there's been an accident."

"How do I look?"

Alexia twirled in front of Teddy like a high school senior on prom night.

Teddy puffed out his chest happily. "You look perfect, my dear. I could die of pride."

Good, thought Alexia. Perfect was what she'd been aiming for.

Gone was the haggard crone of this morning. Gone also the frightened woman haunted by pictures of Jenny Hamlin's mutilated corpse. Or the paranoid politician, looking over her shoulder for imagined enemies. There would be no enemies tonight. No death. No fear. No surprises. The prime minister and his wife might have let Alexia and Teddy down, but Alexia intended to make sure it was the Whitmans who regretted their absence at tonight's party, not the De Veres. The party was, as Lucy Meyer had predicted, going to be "awesome."

Dresswise, Alexia had changed her mind at the last minute, opting for a dramatic dark green gown in heavy, structured jacquard silk with a high, Oriental collar. It had a touch of the Cruella De Vil about it, but not in a bad way, and it was utterly elegant and restrained. The pearl-and-diamond choker was less restrained, but at Alexia's age, a choker covered a multitude of sins, and it was a De Vere family heirloom, which naturally delighted Teddy. With her hair recolored, styled, and sprayed into place, her skin revivified, and her makeup flawlessly applied by the incomparable Marguerite, Alexia both looked and felt a million dollars. *Battle-ready*, as Teddy would have called it.

"Blast this bloody, buggery thing. Where is Bailey?"

Teddy fumbled with his bow tie in front of the mirror. A regular attendee of black- and white-tie events for well over forty years, Teddy nevertheless approached each bow tie as incompetently as if it were his first.

"You don't need Bailey." Alexia tutted, patting his hands away and taking charge herself. "Over, around, under, through. There. It's not rocket science, darling."

Slipping both arms around her waist, Teddy pulled her to him. Closing her eyes, Alexia inhaled his familiar smell, a combination of Floris aftershave, Pears soap, toothpaste, and polished shoe leather. *Safety. Home.* She had never been attracted to Teddy sexually, not even when they were young. But she had found his physical presence comforting, pleasant rather than exciting, like cuddling a slightly worn but much-loved teddy bear. She felt the same way now. She wished she could bottle that feeling somehow, keep it to savor when she was alone, when the stresses of the present and horrors of the past became too much for her.

"I love you."

Teddy De Vere had been married to Alexia for more than three decades. He understood his wife well enough to know that verbal expressions of affection were not her usual style.

Reaching out, he put a concerned hand on her forehead. "Are you feeling quite well, old girl?"

Alexia batted his hand away, embarrassed. "Stop making fun. Can't I tell my own husband how much I love him from time to time?"

"I'm not making fun." And suddenly she saw that he wasn't. "Darling, darling Alexia," Teddy whispered urgently. "If you had any idea how much I love you, how far I'd go to protect you . . ."

"What?"

"You'd be terrified."

He kissed her then, passionately, thrusting his tongue into her mouth like a teenager in the back row of a movie theater. Alexia was so shocked she responded in kind. It was exciting, like kissing a stranger, but after a few moments she was aware of being watched. Pulling away, she saw Roxie, her wheelchair parked in the master bedroom doorway. She looked stunning in a cream silk dress. At least she would have done if it weren't for the look of revolted horror on her face.

Alexia lost her temper. "What *is* the matter, Roxanne? Haven't you seen a husband and wife kiss before?"

"Steady on, darling," murmured Teddy, but Alexia was on a roll.

"No, I'm sorry, Teddy, but I won't 'steady on.' How dare she look at us like that! I'm tired of creeping around my own house, my own husband, like I'm walking on eggshells. Your father and I love each other, Roxanne. We are happy together, blissfully happy, and if you don't like it . . . well, I'm afraid that's simply too bad."

Roxie opened her mouth to say something, then closed it again. For what felt like an eternity, she sat frozen in the doorway. When she did finally speak, her voice came out as a croak.

"It's Michael."

Cold fear flooded Alexia's heart. "Michael? What about Michael? Has something happened?"

"That's what I came to tell you." Tears streamed down Roxie's face. "There's been a terrible accident."

CHAPTER TWENTY-FIVE

SUMMER MEYER LEAPED OUT OF THE taxi and ran through the electric double doors into the John Radcliffe Hospital. Situated out in Headington, a few miles north of Oxford city center, the Radcliffe was home to one of the busiest accident and emergency departments in the country. It was still only late afternoon, but the sun was out, it was a Saturday, and the pubs were open. This being Oxford, Summer found herself fighting her way to the reception desk through a sea of drunken students, noisily bemoaning their mostly self-inflicted injuries.

"Michael De Vere," she said breathlessly. "Motorcycle accident. He came in a few hours ago."

Please, please hold on, Michael. Please don't die.

A litany of hideous coincidences had prevented Summer from arriving earlier. Roxanne was listed in Michael's wallet as his next of kin. When Roxie heard the news she'd called Summer immediately. Unfortunately Summer's U.S. cell-phone battery died, and she'd left Michael's flat to go makeup shopping just minutes before Roxie called and left her voice mail. Summer finally heard Roxie's message almost two hours later. She would not forget it as long as she lived.

Coming back to the flat and hitting play, expecting to hear Michael's voice, she had found herself listening instead to Roxie. Choking with sobs, Roxie told her that Michael had been "crushed" by a truck in a horrific accident, and was on his way to hospital. But it was the last five words of Roxie's message that had branded themselves eternally on Summer's memory:

"He might not make it."

Summer ran out into the street, still barefoot and with her long hair dripping from the shower, but it took her fifteen minutes to find a free cab, and a further five to convince the driver to take her in her half-dressed, hysterical state. Once they did get going, the traffic on the beltway was terrible.

The receptionist in the emergency room typed Michael's name into her computer.

"De Vere. Yes, here we are."

"How is he? Is he in surgery?"

The receptionist looked up from her screen. "And you are?"

"Summer. Summer Meyer."

"Are you family?"

"I'm his girlfriend."

"Sorry. Family only."

"But I just told you. I'm his girlfriend."

"Y'gan be my girrrlfren, 'fyou want . . . gorgeous fucking arse." A revolting, paralytically drunk man in a suit careered into Summer from behind, groping her as he tried to steady himself.

Turning around, Summer pushed him off hard, sending him flying back into a nearby group of patients. "Fuck off!"

"Look," she implored the receptionist, "Michael's sister called and asked me to come. She's his next of kin. Please. I *am* family. I have to see him."

"Wait here a moment."

Getting up, the woman conferred with a colleague in whispered tones. Summer saw the pained, serious looks on their faces and drew the obvious conclusion. *I'm too late. He's dead.* She wanted to ask the question outright, but found that the words refused to come. Instead she stood mute and helpless as the receptionist returned, handing her a slip of paper with a number on it.

"If anyone asks, say you're related. Critical care, fourth floor, lift bank C. This is your pass."

"Is he dead?" Summer finally blurted it out.

The receptionist looked down, unable to meet her eyes.

"They'll explain everything to you on the fourth floor, my love."

"Please! Just tell me. Is he dead?"

The receptionist exchanged an anxious glance with her colleague. "Look, we're not supposed to say anything," she whispered to Summer. "But according to my notes, Michael De Vere *was* pronounced dead about an hour ago. I'm so sorry. Critical will tell you more."

Summer pushed her way through the swing doors in a daze.

Michael's dead.

Dead.

I'm too late.

An orderly stopped her. "Are you all right, miss? Can I help?"

Summer held up her piece of paper like a zombie. The orderly waved her on. Elevator bank C was over there. Turn right for trauma, left for critical care. Reception up the stairs. Summer was aware of people moving around her, nurses and patients and visitors and doctors. There was piped music and a coffee shop selling plastic-wrapped sandwiches and a big fish tank with a gang of bored children hovering around it and huge glass windows with light streaming through them. But for her, everything had stopped. She moved through the corridors like a ghost, numb and silent.

He's dead. Michael's dead.

Bizarrely, she found herself thinking about the party. What was happening at Kingsmere while Michael's private tragedy unfolded? Would the event still go on as planned? Or would heads of state arrive and be turned away? She tried to picture the scene.

"I'm so sorry, Your Highness. There's been a tragedy. The hosts' son has been killed."

"You going up, love?"

Michael's dead, we can't go ahead.

That rhymes.

"Fourth floor. Doors opening."

Michael's dead, in a hospital bed, we can't go ahead.

"This is critical care. Can I help you?"

"Summer." Teddy De Vere's voice was the first thing to reach her. She turned around and there he was. It took a few seconds for the fog to clear, for the shock to fade enough for her to recognize Michael's father's kind, familiar features.

"Teddy." She burst into hysterical tears.

"Now, now." Teddy wrapped comforting, paternal arms around her. "Don't cry. It's all right."

"All right? It's not all right," Summer wailed. "He's dead!"

Teddy looked perplexed. "No, he isn't."

Hope rose up in Summer's throat like vomit. "Michael's not dead?"

"No, my dear. Who told you that?"

"The receptionist. Downstairs."

266

She felt her knees start to give way. Teddy helped her into a chair.

"She must have been confused. He was *pronounced* dead by the ambulance team initially. But when they got him here, the doctors were able to restart his heart."

"So, he's okay?"

It was too much to take in. The roller coaster of hope and despair had left Summer's head reeling.

"I wouldn't say that. He's in a coma. That's all we know. They operated for three hours and what can be done has been done."

"But he's going to be okay."

Teddy rubbed his eyes with exhaustion. "I honestly don't know, Summer. Alexia's been talking to the doctors. You'd best talk to her. She's with Michael now."

A nurse showed Summer in. Michael's room looked more like the deck of the starship *Enterprise* than a hospital room. Machines and wires and lights were everywhere—against the walls, on stands next to Michael's bed, even suspended from the ceiling.

Then, there was Michael himself.

As soon as she saw him, Summer's hand flew to her mouth in shock. There was no blood. But he'd been cleaned up so thoroughly, and he lay so utterly still, he barely seemed real. His body was covered with a white sheet, and the upper part of his face was swathed in bandages. Only his chin and mouth were visible, and those were half obscured with bulky tubes and a breathing apparatus that attached to a respirator behind the headboard. The wheezy *wheesh*, *whoosh* of the machine as it pumped air in and out of his lungs gave the otherwise high-tech room a distinctly old-fashioned feel. Summer half expected a dwarf to jump out from behind the bed with a pair of bellows or an accordion. Instead, Alexia stood up to greet her.

"Summer. How are you?" Alexia extended a perfectly manicured hand for Summer to shake. Her fingers were ice cold. "So sweet of you to come."

Summer looked at her blankly. *Sweet of me?* Alexia was greeting as her as if this were a cocktail party she'd been kind enough to attend. Did she not realize how serious the situation was?

"What's happening, Alexia? What are all these machines? Teddy said you spoke with the doctor."

"The surgeon, yes, Dr. Crickdale. Terribly nice man."

Summer waited. *And . . . ?*

"We've met before, as it happens," Alexia rambled on. "I know him from the local constituency party. His wife's done stalwart work as a fund-raiser."

Summer wanted to shake her. *I don't give a fuck about the constituency party and neither should you. Your son may be dying!* Instead, fighting to keep her voice steady, she asked, "What did Dr. Crickdale say about Michael?"

"Ah yes, well. Michael's in a coma, which was medically induced."

Summer looked horrified. "You mean the doctors did this to him?"

"They had to. There was no way they could have operated on his brain without it."

"They operated on his brain?" Summer's insides began to liquefy with fear. For the second time in as many minutes she found she needed to sit down.

Alexia said, "Yes. They think he was going over eighty when he hit the lorry. It was a side impact, but at that speed it's a miracle he survived at all. Both legs and arms are broken, and there's some internal bleeding, but the main concern is the head trauma. Dr. Crickdale removed sixteen separate shards of bone from his right ventricle."

It was like listening to a weather report. Alexia sounded so calm, so chillingly controlled.

"There's been considerable swelling and bleeding in the brain. Unfortunately the first scans showed a very poor level of activity. We're waiting on the later ones, but Dr. Crickdale doesn't hold out much hope."

"Will he live?" Summer whispered.

"They can't say at this stage. He may. But that may not be the best outcome."

Summer looked at Alexia incredulously. Michael's mother had always intimidated her. Summer had long thought of Alexia as a cold fish, but she'd never imagined her capable of such callousness toward her own son. Roxie, maybe. But Michael had always been the apple of her eye.

"What do you mean it 'may not be the best outcome'? You don't want him to live?"

"Not as a vegetable, no. I'll stay with him tonight." Alexia turned regally away, resting her diamond-encrusted hand on Michael's limp one. "You can come back in the morning."

It was a dismissal, an empress shooing away her ladies' maid. Summer's shock at Alexia's detachment turned to anger.

"I want to stay. Michael would want me here."

"No." The steel in Alexia's tone left no room for nego-tiation.

Summer opened her mouth to protest but Teddy wisely put a hand on her arm. "Not now," he whispered. Outside in the corridor, he spoke more openly.

"You mustn't judge her too harshly, my dear. She's in shock. We all are."

"But she's so *cold*, Teddy!"

She hadn't meant to speak so bluntly, but the words just came out.

269

"I know it seems that way," Teddy said kindly. "But that boy means everything to her."

He means everything to me, Summer thought desperately.

"Can't you convince her to let me stay? What if . . ." She started to cry. "What if he dies in the night?"

Teddy gave her a look of infinite kindness.

"If he dies in the night, he won't need either of you. Will he?"

THE NEXT MORNING'S SUNDAY PAPERS WERE full of pictures of the Kingsmere party-that-wasn't, and lurid accounts of Alexia De Vere's son's near-fatal motorcycle accident. The *Sun on Sunday* was the first to coin the expression that was to haunt Alexia over the coming months, with its questioning headline: THE CURSE OF THE DE VERES? With this latest juicy tragedy to chew on, the tabloids delighted in dredging up all the old rumors about Roxie, and the "real story" behind the home secretary's daughter and her mysterious three-story fall. Pictures of a wheelchair-bound Roxie were run alongside images of the John Radcliffe, where Michael De Vere remained "critical but stable." Even the old, infamous shots of Sanjay Patel, taken before his imprisonment and subsequent suicide, were given a fresh airing. Instead of sympathy, the fickle British public seemed to react angrily towards Alexia, interpreting her stoicism (about Michael's accident) as cold-heartedness, a reverting to type. Overnight, it seemed, the positive image that Alexia had worked so hard to build with voters all year began to unravel. She was more alone than ever.

AT HOME IN EAST LONDON, GILBERT Drake devoured the coverage with gleeful relish.

Just as in Exodus, when the Pharaoh refused to release God's people and the Lord killed every firstborn, both man and animal, in retribution, so Alexia De Vere had been punished for keeping poor Sanjay behind bars.

"She will sacrifice the first male offspring of her womb to the Lord."

I must guard against the sin of pride, Gil warned himself. *Vengeance is the Lord's, not mine. I am but his instrument.*

Gilbert Drake prayed for guidance. *Show me your will, O Lord. Show me the way from here.*

Retribution had begun at last. But it was far from finished.

Two weeks after Michael's accident, Alexia met with the prime minister.

"You are entitled to compassionate leave, you know," Henry Whitman told her. "No one would blame you if you felt you needed to step down for a while, to be with your family."

Alexia's eyes narrowed distrustfully. Senior cabinet ministers did not step down "for a while." They clung to their jobs or they lost them. Henry Whitman knew this as well as she did.

"Trying to get rid of me, Henry?"

"Of course not," Whitman blustered. "I wouldn't dare!"

"Good," Alexia said, not returning the prime minister's smile. "Michael hasn't regained consciousness since it happened. According to his doctors, he's highly unlikely ever to do so."

"I'm so sorry."

"Please, spare me the sympathy." Alexia sounded almost angry. Henry Whitman hoped it was grief talking, but it was hard to tell. "If it were up to me, we'd turn off the damn machines tomorrow. It's Teddy who insists on keeping them going. But I've no intention of wasting my life in a hospital room holding my son's utterly unresponsive hand when I could be here, being useful, simply because it makes some judgmental hag at the *Daily Mail* feel better."

"No one's suggesting that, Alexia."

"Aren't they? I'll bet Kevin and Charles have been helpfully pointing out how negative my press has been since this happened."

"Not at all," Henry Whitman lied. Alexia's enemies in cabinet had indeed wasted no time renewing their attacks. But Henry hardly needed his cabinet to tell him that which he could read for himself. Whatever her true feelings, Alexia De Vere had come across as cold and heartless in the extreme in the wake of her son's accident, insisting on "business as usual." The effect on her image had been catastrophic, and the bad press was rubbing off on the entire Conservative Party.

Charlotte Whitman, the prime minister's wife, had said as much to him last night in bed. "She's making you look bad, Henry. You need to get rid of her."

"I know, but what can I do? I can't tell the woman how to grieve for her own son."

"Grieve?" Charlotte let out a mirthless laugh. "If that's grief, I'm a monkey's uncle. You're the prime minister, darling. Reshuffle."

If only it were that easy! If only Alexia De Vere didn't have him over the proverbial barrel! Although neither of them ever spoke of it, the elephant in the room was alive and well, and protecting Alexia, even now.

Alexia looked at Henry Whitman and thought, *He's hiding something.* The vague sense of unease she'd had before Michael's accident had now grown into something closer to full-blown paranoia. Where did Henry Whitman fit into it all? He'd pulled out of the Kingsmere party at the last minute, mysteriously; hours later, Michael was in a coma. There was no earthly reason to connect those two events, and yet Alexia found herself searching for meaning, sinister meaning, in everything. Everywhere she turned, she sensed enemies lurking. Enemies from her past and enemies from her present. Enemies at home and enemies at work. Her career was collapsing around her ears. Michael was fighting for life. Billy Hamlin and his daughter were dead. Her own daughter hated her. It felt as if some evil, unseen hand were demolishing her life brick by brick, destroying everything she'd worked for, everything she'd become. Had it not been for Teddy's unflinching support—Teddy's and Lucy Meyer's . . . Lucy had been a rock through this entire nightmare—Alexia would honestly have feared for her sanity.

Back at her parliamentary office, she confided in Sir Edward Manning.

"They're all out to get me, Edward. All of them. Henry's just waiting for his chance to strike, I can tell."

"I doubt that's the case, Home Secretary," Sir Edward said smoothly.

"It is, believe me. You're the only one I trust, Edward. I need your help now more than ever."

"And I'm delighted to give it, Home Secretary. Quite delighted. Try not to worry. We shall weather the storm together."

LUCY MEYER WAS IN OXFORD, HAVING coffee with Summer. It had been two weeks since Michael's accident, and Lucy and Arnie were preparing to head back to the States. Lucy was eager for Summer to join them—*"you can't stay here forever, darling"*—but so far at least, Summer was insistent that she couldn't leave Michael's bedside. Unlike some people she could mention.

"Do you realize Alexia hasn't visited him once—not once—since the day after it happened? She just disappeared."

Lucy sipped her coffee. "I'm sure she has her reasons."

"She does. Selfishness," Summer said furiously. "It's like you have a total blind spot with that woman. Why do you always let her off the hook?"

"What hook?" said Lucy. Much to Summer's chagrin, Lucy had had lunch with Alexia in London yesterday and tried to offer a shoulder to cry on. "Honestly, sweetheart, I know you want someone to blame. But what happened to Michael was not his mother's fault. It was an accident."

"Maybe."

"What do you mean, maybe? It was an accident!"

"Michael was a good driver," said Summer. "An experienced driver. It was an empty road in broad daylight. Why would he suddenly career out of control?"

"Because he was going too fast," Lucy said reasonably.

"Yes, but why?"

"Young men on powerful motorbikes *do* sometimes drive too fast, honey. They don't need a reason."

"Sure, but not that fast. He must have been distracted. He was acting so strange the night before it happened. He kept talking about a secret and asking me weird questions. Like if I knew a secret about someone I loved, would I tell?"

Lucy put her coffee cup down. "What sort of secret?"

"That's just it. I have no idea. He was so cryptic about it. But it was obviously something bad. I got a strong sense it was about Alexia."

Lucy twisted the ring on her right hand thoughtfully. It was a family ring, a gift her father had given her when she was young. She'd always used it like a worry bead, to calm her nerves and help her think. Lucy had encouraged Summer's romance with Michael De Vere. But now that tragedy had struck, she just wanted her daughter home, back in the States and far away from all this mess. Lucy already knew more about the De Vere family's secrets than she wanted to. Summer, at least, should be spared such knowledge.

Summer finished her double espresso. "I have to find out what Michael meant. What was distracting him when he . . ."

She realized guiltily that she was about to say *died. I mustn't give up on him. Not when everybody else already has. Where there's life there's hope.*

"When he had his accident."

Lucy said, "Has it occurred to you that maybe he didn't want you to know? This secret, whatever it was. He had a chance to tell you, and he didn't. Maybe Michael wants you to let it be. To move on with your own life."

"I am moving on with my life," Summer said defiantly. "Being here for Michael. Supporting his recovery. That is my life."

"Summer, sweetheart . . ."

"Hadn't you better go, Mom? You don't want to miss your flight."

Lucy Meyer looked at her watch. She did have to go. As much as she wanted Summer to come with her, she knew couldn't live her daughter's life for her.

"All right. I'll go. But we need to talk more about this."

"Sure," Summer said dismissively.

"Your father already called the dean's office at NYU. He

275

persuaded them to grant you a compassionate study leave, but at some point they're going to want to know when you're coming back."

"Of course. I'll let you know. Bye, Mom."

Summer watched her mother leave.

I'm never coming back. New York and college and my internship at the Post. *They're all part of another life. Meaningless and puerile. None of it matters without Michael.*

SUMMER TOOK THE LONG WAY BACK to Michael's flat, through the maze of alleyways that ran behind Exeter and Lincoln colleges down toward Magdalen and the river. Her mother's visit had left her feeling anxious and unhappy, unable to enjoy the warmth of the late-summer sun on her back or the beauty of the spires that towered above her. The streets of Oxford were filled with smiling lovers in shorts and sunglasses, taking pictures of themselves amid the "dreaming spires" or kissing on the ancient bridges. As Summer walked, willow trees bathed their branches languidly in the Cherwell's gently flowing waters. Children ate ice cream cones and skipped and cooled their toes in the water, as a family of swans glided regally by.

Everybody's happy. Everybody's living their lives as if nothing has happened. As if the world hasn't stopped.

Summer looked at strangers with wonder and then with anger, an irrational resentment taking root in her heart. *How dare life go on? How dare it? With Michael fighting for breath just a few miles away.*

But another voice in her head, her mother's, was equally insistent.

What happened to Michael was an accident.

It was nobody's fault.

Just come home.

Was her mother right? Was Summer looking for meaning in what was really a simple act of fate, a motorcycle accident, an everyday cruelty that happened to millions of people all over the world? Maybe. But right now she needed to believe there was a reason Michael had crashed that day. There was something she needed to know, something she was supposed to find out. Whether Michael wanted her to or not. She would look at it like a job, like a story she'd been assigned to investigate.

All her investigative instincts told her to start with Michael's mother, the steely, ruthless Alexia De Vere.

Back at the apartment, Summer kicked off her shoes and padded into Michael's study. His computer was still on the desk, set to hibernate, as if he might walk back in at any moment and pick up where he left off. Next to it, messy stacks of paper spilled everywhere—receipts, lists, bills, most of them having to do with the Kingsmere party. More were stuffed into the various drawers, or piled on top of the printer, chair, and sofa that filled the small work space. Clearly, Michael hadn't been a big believer in filing. Summer wondered idly how on earth he'd managed to run a successful business amid such chaos, and whether Tommy Lyon's desk looked the same. Or perhaps Tommy was the sensible one, the one who held it all together while Michael shot off ideas and plans and concepts like fireworks from his brilliant, scattered mind?

I must call Tommy.

Sitting down in Michael's chair, she was surprised to feel her heartbeat spike when she turned on his computer. Was it really only a couple of weeks ago that she'd taken the train up to Oxford, convinced she'd catch Michael cheating on her? He'd reassured her that night, made her believe in him again, believe in the two of them as a couple. But now, alone in his study as she was, doubts began to creep back in. Did Summer really want to go through Michael's in-box, his photos, his Facebook contacts? What if she couldn't handle what she found?

Password. The screen blinked at her demandingly.

Stupid of me. Of course, the computer's password-protected.

She typed in Michael's pin number: his zodiac sign and date of birth. *Obvious, but you never know.* No joy. Next she tried various permutations of his family members' names, adding her own name on a whim, but again, nothing. *Oh well. I'll have to get a professional to hack into it later. Unless maybe Tommy or Roxie knows.*

Pushing the laptop to one side, Summer began to leaf through the nearest pile of papers. Not knowing what she was looking for, and with nothing better to do, she began to sort them methodically into piles. Invoices to the right, receipts to the left. She divided everything into business, personal, or junk, running to the kitchen for a trash bag to use for envelopes, flyers, and other rubbish. The work was consuming. By the time she looked up, it was already six P.M. and the sun was beginning its long, slow descent into the horizon, casting orange beams through the shutters and onto the study floor.

Summer stood up and stretched like a cat. She was just about to fix herself a drink when a box in the corner of the room caught her eye. Everything else in Michael's home office was messy to the point of being deranged, but this box—crate really—had been carefully divided into color-coded sections, with newspaper and magazine clippings as well as photocopied letters stacked sensibly together. It had also been wedged between the bookcase and a large fire extinguisher, not hidden exactly, but definitely moved to a safe place, out of plain sight and where it wouldn't be contaminated by the general mayhem.

Carefully, Summer pulled out the box and carried it into the kitchen. The clippings were organized by date. Almost all of them related to cases affected by Alexia's sentencing reform laws.

Some of the stories were genuinely harrowing.

Daya Ginescu, a Romanian immigrant originally given four years for shoplifting but who'd seen her sentence increased to seven years, had not been allowed to be at her son's bedside when he died of leukemia.

Others were cheap sob stories, whipped up to tragic proportions by the press. Summer found it hard to feel much compassion for Darren Niles, for example, a career burglar whose fiancée had jilted him at the prospect of a further eighteen-month wait for their wedding date.

But the overwhelming bulk of the coverage related to one man, Sanjay Patel. Convicted for drug trafficking on what his supporters clearly believed to be trumped-up evidence, Patel had hanged himself in prison in despair over a lengthening of his sentence.

Summer traced her fingers over the pictures of Patel's face. There was something sweet about him, sweet and gentle and sad. If Sanjay Patel *had* smuggled heroin, she could see why the cartels chose him. He had the perfect face for a drug mule, utterly guileless, his dark eyes shining with innocence and integrity even from beyond the grave.

His so-called friends, however, were far from innocent. Next to the Patel clippings, Michael had kept photocopies of three threatening letters sent to his mother. Two of them were handwritten, if you could call it writing—the spelling and grammar would have made a five-year-old blush—and were clearly from the same individual. A man, judging by his liberal use of the C-word and other explicitly sexist, borderline gynecological slurs. But it wasn't the language in the letter that shocked Summer so much as the hatred resonating from each line. The writer wanted to slash Alexia's "throte" until she screamed like a "squeeling fucking pig." He looked forward to "slicing" her tits off, making her pay "for what you done, you stinking c—t." The third letter was much more erudite, liberally quoting scripture and invoking the wrath of a vengeful God, in punishment for Alexia's "sins." Summer didn't know which of the letters chilled her more. She was no fan of Alexia's, especially not at the moment. But the letters made even her blood run cold.

She wondered how Michael had gotten hold of them and why he kept them. Were they connected to this secret, whatever it was, this "bad thing" that someone close to him had done? Or was he merely concerned about his mother's safety generally, or her security at the Kingsmere party in particular?

Possibly. But that didn't really add up either. As home secretary, Alexia had plenty of police and secret-service protection at her disposal 24/7. She wouldn't have needed Michael's amateurish efforts. Something wasn't right.

There were other things in the box that Summer found curious. In the middle of the file, diligently tagged with dated yellow stickers, was a stack of documents relating to the prime minister. Some were letters that Henry Whitman had written to Alexia around the time of her appointment as home secretary. Others were copies of replies that Alexia had sent him. Still others bore no obvious relation to Alexia at all. There were articles about Whitman opening a hospital, about his wife, Charlotte, attending a charity event. Innocuous pieces about the prime minister's commitment to renewable energy projects, each one carefully cut out, dated, and filed. Michael—or someone—must have thought them significant.

Why?

The telephone rang, scaring her half to death. Who on earth would be calling here? As far as she knew, no one used Michael's landline number as a contact number for her. Except the hospital. For emergencies. *Oh God, no.*

"Hello?" The panic in her voice was audible.

"You sound terrible, my dear. Is everything all right?"

"Teddy!" She let out a long breath. *Thank God.* "I'm fine. I thought it might be the hospital calling."

"No, no. Only me. Now listen. Your ma rang earlier and asked me to keep an eye on you while you're in Oxford. I'm to make sure you're not wasting away in that gloomy flat or starving to death on hospital food."

Summer laughed. "You can tell my mother I've been cooking for myself for some time now. Years, actually."

"Be that as it may, I was hoping you might want to join us at Kingsmere for dinner."

Join "us." Did that mean Alexia too?

As if reading her mind, Teddy said, "Alexia's away in London, so Roxanne and I are rattling around here on our own like two lost pebbles. You'd be doing an old man a favor."

Suddenly Summer wanted to see Teddy and Roxie, kind, familiar faces of people who loved Michael as much as she did. They too were infrequent visitors at the hospital, but somehow Summer could tell that their absence at Michael's bedside was born of heartache, not callousness, like his mother's.

"All right. That would be lovely, thanks. What time would you like me to arrive?"

"Now, my dear. My driver should be with you at any minute."

"Now? But I haven't changed or showered or—"

281

"Never mind that. Just pack an overnight bag and hop in the car."

An overnight bag? Summer considered protesting but changed her mind. Why not get away for a while? As long as she was back in Oxford by tomorrow night, in time for her daily visit to Michael.

Throwing some clothes into a bag, she waited for the doorbell to ring. *How thoughtful of Teddy to send a driver.* He really was the kindest man in the world.

CHAPTER TWENTY-SIX

Gravel crunched satisfyingly beneath Summer's feet as she pushed Roxie De Vere's wheelchair down the long drive at Kingsmere.

"It's so beautiful here. You must wake up every morning and pinch yourself."

Roxie smiled. "Not exactly. But it *is* lovely. I'm not sure I could live anywhere else."

After a hearty breakfast of kedgeree and strong black coffee, the girls were out for a morning walk. Whether it was the cloud-soft, goose-feather bed in the guest room, last night's wonderful food and wine, or the simple pleasure of being in the company of old friends, Summer didn't know, but she felt revived and refreshed this morning in a way she hadn't felt in a long time. The blue sky, and slight crispness to the air, somehow brought a sense of hope, and the rooks cawing in the treetops seemed to be heralding a new start.

The two girls reached the end of the drive. A winding country lane snaked in front of them, bordered by tall hedgerows and overhung with ancient oaks, giving it the feel of a tunnel.

"Left or right?" asked Roxie.

"What's the difference?"

"Left is the village, right is the farm."

"Left then," said Summer. "Your father said he wanted a newspaper, and I've never seen the bright lights of downtown Kingsmere."

Roxie was pleased Summer had agreed to spend the night. The two girls had been close as children, although, of course, they had both changed so much since those innocent, carefree days. The Summer that Roxie remembered from holidays on Martha's Vineyard had been fat and withdrawn and painfully, agonizingly shy. Back then she, Roxie, had been the confident one, not to mention the great beauty. But now it was Summer Meyer who had the world at her feet. How strange life was.

"You must think I'm awfully heartless," Roxie blurted out. "Not going to visit Michael."

"I don't think any such thing," Summer assured her.

"The truth is, I simply can't cope with it. Hospitals still give me dreadful panic attacks. That hospital in particular."

Summer had forgotten that Roxie had recuperated at the John Radcliffe after her suicide attempt. No wonder she couldn't face the place.

"I totally understand. And so would Michael."

"Daddy's been twice, but he hates it too. He says he feels like a spare part. He doesn't know what to say or do."

"I'm not sure it matters what you say. And he's doing something just by being there."

"Spoken like a true woman. But you know men, especially British men. They want to 'fix' things. I don't think Daddy can stand the fact that he can't fix this for Michael. Just like he couldn't fix things for me. He thinks it's history repeating itself."

"The curse of the De Veres," Summer mumbled under her breath.

"The only curse on this family is my bitch of a mother," Roxie said bitterly. Pushing the wheelchair from behind, Summer couldn't see the cloud of hatred contorting Roxie's face.

They walked on in silence. Eventually the village hove into view, a pretty cluster of wisteria-clad, stone cottages huddled around a triangular green, in the shadow of a squat Saxon church. A sleepier, more idyllic spot than Kingsmere would have been hard to imagine. Summer half expected Mrs. Tiggy-Winkle to emerge from one of the cottages, or to discover that Jemima Puddle-Duck was the proprietress of the village store.

This isn't a place where bad things are supposed to happen.

In reality, the village store was owned by a grumpy old woman with prodigious facial warts, called Rose Hudgens. Rose nodded a curt acknowledgment to Roxie when they walked in, but blanked Summer completely when she bought Teddy's paper, returning her smile with a sullen scowl.

"Is she always like that?" Summer asked Roxie after they left the store.

"I'm afraid so. Rose isn't too keen on newcomers. Especially Americans."

They'd been walking for an hour and Summer still hadn't broached the subject of Michael's list, or of the mysterious secret he'd alluded to the night before his accident. Now seemed as good a time as any.

"I've been meaning to ask you, did Michael say anything to you, anything unusual, in the run-up to your father's summer party?"

Roxie looked up sharply. " 'Unusual' in what way?"

"In any way."

"No, I don't think so. Why?"

285

"It's probably nothing. But the night before his accident, when I came to Oxford to see him, he said something to me about a secret. He said he was talking hypothetically, but I got the feeling that he wasn't. That he'd found something out and that it was worrying him deeply. I thought he might have mentioned it to you."

"No. He never said anything like that. All he talked about was the party, to be honest. He was consumed by it in those last few weeks, especially building this ridiculous folly for Dad. That was stressing him out, because it was all going wrong and he didn't want Dad to worry. Do you think that could have been it? Although I can't see why it would have been a secret."

"Like I say, it was probably nothing." Summer smiled reassuringly. It wasn't fair to burden Roxie with her fears and suspicions. Not unless she had hard evidence to back them up. Whatever Michael's dark secret was, clearly he had not confided in his sister.

Back at the house, Roxie delivered Teddy his *Times* while Summer went upstairs to make her bed and pack. She'd just zipped up her overnight bag when a voice behind her made her jump.

"You will stay for lunch?"

Teddy stood in the doorway. He was wearing a yellow sweater stretched tightly over his paunch, giving him the look of an elderly Winnie-the-Pooh. It occurred to Summer for the first time that he looked absolutely nothing like Michael. Not one grain of De Vere genes seemed to have been passed down from father to son.

"You scared me! I thought you were downstairs with Roxie."

"I was, but she told me you were leaving, so I came up straightaway. Surely you don't have to disappear so soon?"

"I'm afraid so. You've been incredibly kind and hospitable, but I have to go and see Michael."

"Yes, but that won't take all day."

"I also have things to do back at the flat."

"What things?"

"Just paperwork. But there's a lot of it, believe me." She yawned loudly. Teddy enveloped Summer in a big, paternal bear hug.

"If I may say so, my dear, I think you're overdoing it. Your parents are right, you know. You should go back home to America."

"I couldn't possibly leave Michael." Summer sounded shocked.

Fighting back his emotion, Teddy said, "Michael's gone, Summer."

"He isn't gone."

"Not in body, perhaps. But in every way that really matters. His mother's right."

"His mother is *not* right!" Hot tears stung Summer's cheeks. "I'm sorry, Teddy. I know you love Alexia. But she's *not* right about this. She wants to turn off those machines because it would be easier for her. Because it would put an end to a situation she doesn't want to deal with."

"That's not true, my dear."

"It *is* true. She's too busy trying to hang on to her glittering career to be concerned with a little thing like her son."

Teddy shook his head. "Alexia may not be demonstrative. But she loves Michael dearly. The doctors have told all of us that there is almost no chance of Michael ever regaining consciousness."

"*Almost. Almost* no chance. That means there *is* a chance, right? Who's going to fight for him, Teddy, if not us?"

Teddy stroked Summer's hair tenderly. She was a sweet girl. Misguided but terribly sweet. "When you reach my age, Summer, you learn that there are some fights you simply cannot win."

"If you really believed that, you'd do what Alexia wants and turn off Michael's life support. But you haven't."

"I do believe it," Teddy said soberly. "I'm just too weak, too sentimental, I suppose, to act on what I know is the truth."

"I guess no one could accuse Alexia of being weak and sentimental," Summer said bitterly.

"Alexia prefers to remember Michael the way he was. You mustn't hate her for that, just because you want someone to blame."

They were the same exact words her mother had said to her yesterday. It baffled Summer that Alexia De Vere seemed to inspire such deep loyalty in those closest to her. Teddy. Michael. Even Summer's own mother, Lucy. What had Alexia ever done to deserve such devotion? Of her inner circle, only Roxie appeared to be able to view her mother as she really was.

Teddy was still talking, his eyes misting over with love as he spoke of his wife.

"Through all the tragedies of her life, Alexia has found solace in her work. It gives her a sense of meaning, a purpose and a function that transcend the pain. You could do worse than follow her example."

"Go back to work, you mean?" said Summer.

"Yes. Go home to America. Go back to college, back to your job in New York. Don't sacrifice yourself for my son, my dear. It won't help Michael, and it will most certainly harm you. Why blight two lives, instead of one?"

Because I can't. Because I can no more leave Michael and

288

go back to New York as if nothing's happened than I can fly to the moon.

"At least say you'll think about it."

"I'll think about it," Summer lied.

Teddy carried her bag downstairs. "You will come again, won't you?"

"Of course I will." Summer kissed him on the cheek. "And I'll give Michael your love . . . Oh." An envelope on the hall table caught her eye. Addressed to Michael, it had the red-and-black Ducati logo embossed on the back. "Is he still getting mail sent here?"

"Occasionally," said Teddy. "I believe we've always been his permanent address for passports and licenses and things like that. This only arrived this morning. I assume it's the registration papers for that damn-fool motorbike."

"Do you mind if I take it? I'm doing all Michael's filing at the moment. Gives me something to do between visits. You wouldn't believe what a mess his flat's in."

"Oh, indeed I would." Teddy chuckled, handing her the Ducati envelope. "You should have seen his childhood bedroom. It looked like the wreck of the *Hesperus*."

A few minutes later Teddy watched from the doorstep as Summer's car pulled away.

Poor child.

Young love was so very hard. And loss at that age was quite unbearable.

The sooner Summer Meyer went home and forgot all about Michael, the better. For all of them.

MICHAEL DE VERE LAY PRONE AND all but lifeless on his hospital bed. Tubes ran from his nostrils and mouth to a ventilator at his side. Two round electrical pads just above his nipples sent a read of his heart rate to the beeping monitor at the foot of the bed. Amid all the high-tech equipment, Michael looked as white and peaceful as an alabaster statue, still and silent as the grave.

Summer Meyer held his hand, stroking each limp finger like a child caressing a favorite doll.

"I'm here, Michael," she murmured, over and over. "I'm here."

I'm here, but where are you, my darling? That's the question. Everyone tells me you've gone. But I feel you here, with me. Don't leave me, Michael. Please, please don't leave me.

She would find out the secret.

She would find out the truth.

Then, if she had to, she would let him go.

CHAPTER TWENTY-SEVEN

Alexia De Vere flipped grimly through the *Telegraph*'s three-page spread.

"I've seen worse."

"So have I." Sir Edward Manning handed her the remainder of the morning's newspapers in a thick stack. "The *Sun*'s calling you a lame duck. The *Guardian* predicts you'll be out of a job by Christmas. And the *Mirror* likens you to a Gestapo agent."

"Isn't that actionable?"

"Probably. But a lawsuit won't help you keep your job, or win back voters. Much more of this and the prime minister will announce he's giving you his 'full support.' Then you're really done for."

In normal circumstances, Alexia would have laughed at that. But the strain of the last month had really taken its toll. Her honeymoon period as home secretary was well and truly over. Public criticism of her perceived lack of grief over Michael's accident had been relentless and quite poisonous. Last night, against her better judgment, Alexia had appeared on a popular television talk show to discuss it, a move central office had dreamed up to help soften her image. Unfortunately the program had the opposite effect, with viewers and critics universally branding Alexia "cold" and "unfeeling." *Remorseless* was a word that had come up more than once, which really made Alexia's blood boil.

"I wish someone would explain to me what exactly it is that I'm supposed to be sorry for," Alexia complained to Edward. "Not being sorry enough, I suppose?"

Most of this morning's pieces eviscerating her character had focused on her answer to the talk-show host's question "What is your biggest regret?" To which Alexia had replied pithily: "I don't do regret, David. I don't have time," a sound bite that had alienated what few supporters she had left.

"If I were a man, people would be praising my for my strength."

"Very possibly, Home Secretary. Unfortunately, you are not a man."

"No, Edward. I'm not."

"Conservative voters expect their female politicians to display certain maternal instincts."

"Oh, for God's sake. What nonsense!"

"Unfortunately, Home Secretary, it's the sort of nonsense that wins votes, not to mention friends within the party. It wouldn't have killed you to tone your responses down a little," Sir Edward Manning admonished. "Especially given today's significance."

Alexia rubbed her eyes wearily. "What significance?"

"The anniversary of Sanjay Patel's suicide, Home Secretary. Surely you haven't forgotten?"

Oh, shit. Alexia had completely forgotten. Distracted by the furor over her public image, and desperate to think about anything but Michael, she'd been spending every waking moment not devoted to Home Office business researching Jennifer Hamlin's murder. The New York police had all but given up on the case. As with Billy's murder in London a year earlier, it seemed to Alexia that remarkably little effort had been made. Nobody was arrested in either case, let alone charged. Surely it wasn't right that such wanton brutality should go unpunished? But while nobody cared about the Hamlin murders, it seemed that the damn Patel case refused to die.

The anniversary of his death was always a bad day for Alexia. There were bound to be crowds of protesters outside her Westminster office later, and probably a fair few at her Chelsea home as well. This year, no doubt, they'd be even more vociferous, sensing that her political star was on the wane.

If they think they're going to bully me into quitting my job, or admitting some sort of guilt, they're in for a rude awakening. Bastards.

Alexia knew her approval ratings were at an all-time low, and that her cabinet colleagues wanted to be rid of her. It wasn't just the embittered trade and industry secretary and his cronies anymore. It was all of them. Henry Whitman had protected her so far, but his support would not stretch indefinitely. Alexia tried hard to put the malicious whispers out of her mind and focus on the job. Contrary to popular opinion, she did have feelings. The criticisms, pressure, and above all the isolation were beginning to get to her.

If only Teddy could stay with her in London, perhaps things might be easier. But he insisted on spending at least half his time at Kingsmere ("The estate won't run itself, you know, darling") with Roxie attached to him like a limpet. Last week she'd received another threatening phone call at Cheyne Walk, the same Bible-bashing lunatic who'd called the last time. She'd told Edward Manning about it, but refused to alert her security, in case the story leaked and people thought she was trying to garner sympathy for herself. If there was one thing Alexia objected to more than being unfairly hated, it was being pitied.

Sir Edward Manning's voice fought its way through the fog in Alexia's brain. "Perhaps you should take a holiday, Home Secretary?" Sir Edward's was an archetypally English voice, clipped and brittle and staccato, like Teddy's. A voice that commanded authority without even trying.

"A holiday?" Alexia looked at him disbelievingly.

"A sabbatical, if you prefer. On compassionate grounds."

"Have you been talking to Number Ten?"

Sir Edward Manning looked suitably offended. "Of course not, Home Secretary."

"Henry Whitman said exactly the same thing to me last week. He's trying to get rid of me, you know."

"Perhaps he's trying to help you."

"By sacking me?"

"You can't keep carrying on as if nothing has happened, Home Secretary."

"Can't I, Edward? Why not?"

"Because"—Sir Edward pointed exasperatedly to the newspapers—"much more of this coverage will finish your political career completely. Go on as you are and Whitman will dump you in the next reshuffle anyway. I'm sorry to be so brutal, but one must face facts."

Alexia stared blankly out of the window. "Yes," she murmured, to no one in particular. "I suppose one must."

An hour later, alone in a nondescript Italian restaurant in Chelsea, Alexia forced herself to eat lunch. She'd lost too much weight since Michael's accident. Since her trip to Paris, in fact, when she first heard about Jenny Hamlin's murder, her appetite had deserted her. As for sleep, she was lucky if she got more than three hours a night, so relentless were the dark thoughts dancing through her mind. Plowing on with her job at the Home Office, fueled on coffee and adrenaline and a desperate fear of stopping, Alexia knew that the moment she did stop, the dark thoughts would rush in like floodwaters and drown her. When she did sleep, the drowning dreams were back with a vengeance: rising waves, riptides sucking her in, pulling her under, starving her lungs of air.

"Your cioppino, Mrs. De Vere. Enjoy."

Alexia stared down at the lumps of monkfish and squid bobbing grotesquely in the saffron-scented soup and felt sick. Pushing the bowl aside, she tried to eat some bread, but she felt weak and nauseous with stress.

Maybe Edward's right. Maybe I do need a break. I'm so desperately worried about Michael and paranoid about being pushed out of my job. But maybe the PM really is trying to help me.

Suddenly an image of Martha's Vineyard and The Gables floated into her mind. She pictured the wisteria trailing over the trellis in her backyard; the pitch-black night sky full of dazzling stars; the low, growly croak of the bullfrogs, lazily mating.

That's where I should go. I feel safe on the island. Safe and sane and rested.

It would mean leaving Michael. But Alexia was no good to her son at the moment. If she didn't take some sort of a mental and physical break soon, she'd be no good to anyone. *I'll wind up in hospital myself.*

Lucy Meyer was in Washington with Arnie at the moment, but Alexia wondered if she could persuade her friend to fly out and join her? It wasn't as if Lucy had a job or any real commitments at home, especially now, with Summer away. How wonderful it would be to talk to Lucy, with no husbands or children around to distract them!

The two women had spoken by phone about Michael's accident. Unlike the rest of the world, Lucy had understood instinctively why Alexia had to work afterward. Why she had to keep going. Why she couldn't break down and be the weak, hair-tearing mother the British public seemed to demand she be. Alexia had even confided in Lucy about Jenny Hamlin's murder, and her fears of being the target of some sort of bizarre conspiracy, some nameless evil that she couldn't put her finger on. Colleagues would have laughed, or thought she was losing her mind. But Lucy didn't judge her, any more than she had judged her when Alexia told her about her dark past. She simply listened, as silent and patient and unchanging as a stone.

Teddy loved her. But he didn't know her the way that Lucy Meyer did. With Lucy—*only* with Lucy—Alexia could let go completely and be herself. That was what she needed, now more than ever.

Alexia's soup had grown cold. She asked for the bill. She had a Select Committee meeting at two-thirty and a vote at four. After that she would go home and sleep. Then she would call Lucy, arrange to take this break that everyone seemed to want her to.

It will be all right, she told herself. *It will all be all right.*

"FORGET IT, MATE. THAT'S MY SPOT."

The burly photographer pushed his colleague out of the prime position on Cheyne Walk, directly opposite Alexia De Vere's house.

"Says who?"

"Says me. I've been 'ere since ten o'clock this morning. I only nipped over the road for a packet of fags."

"That's your problem."

As the two men noisily fought out their turf war, a growing crowd of protesters lined up along the home secretary's Chelsea Street house, waving placards imprinted with Sanjay Patel's face. So far the anniversary of Patel's death had been a subdued affair. The dead man's supporters were being respectful of the police line keeping them twelve feet back from the De Veres' property, even though it was only marked with tape. But as afternoon turned to evening, the chants of "No Regrets, No Reelection" and "De Vere OUT!" grew louder and less good-natured. The home secretary was due home any minute. Despite the presence of both police and television crews, the potential for violent confrontation hung in the air like a rotten smell.

In the middle of the crowd, Gilbert Drake said a silent prayer.

May it be as Isaiah said: *"I will punish the wicked for their iniquity. I will cause the arrogance of the proud to cease, and lay low the haughtiness of the terrible."*

Alexia De Vere's son might be on life support, but that wasn't punishment enough for the suffering she'd caused poor Sanjay, and so many others. All Alexia De Vere cared about, all she had ever cared about, was herself, her own self-serving, godless life. *That* was what she had to lose.

An eye for an eye.

Beneath his parka, Gilbert Drake lovingly fingered the cold metal of his gun.

HENRY WHITMAN WAS ON HIS PRIVATE line.

"How many of them are out there?"

"About fifty or sixty, Prime Minister."

"Is that enough? It doesn't sound like much of a crowd."

"It's enough."

"So we're a go?"

The voice on the other end of the line sounded amused.

"That's up to you, Henry. You're the boss, remember?"

Henry Whitman closed his eyes and made a decision.

"I don't like it, Alexia. I don't like it at all." Teddy De Vere's voice was full of concern. "I saw some of them on the television earlier and they looked distinctly aggressive. Can't you come back here tonight, to Kingsmere?"

In the back of her ministerial car, Alexia pressed the phone to her ear, trying to conjure up Teddy's presence, the comfort of his arms. *I must spend more time with him. Lean on him again like I used to.* Her committee meeting had dragged on longer than expected—didn't they always?—and the vote was interminable. The brief peace she'd felt at lunchtime, planning her escape with Lucy Meyer, was all gone now. She wished Teddy were with her. But the thought of schlepping all the way out to Oxfordshire, not reaching her bed till ten or eleven at night, made her want to cry.

"I truly can't, Teddy. I'm exhausted. Anyway, Edward's briefed me, there are plenty of police at the house. If things get rowdy, they'll simply clear people out."

"Why risk it, though, my darling? You can sleep in the car if you're tired. Please come down, Alexia. I miss you."

"I miss you too." Changing the subject, Alexia said, "I've been thinking of taking some holidays."

"Really? That's marvelous." She could practically hear Teddy's smile all the way from Oxfordshire. "When should I start packing?"

"Actually I thought I might take a short break with Lucy. Hole up on Martha's Vineyard for a while. Would you mind?"

There was a split second of hesitation. Then Teddy said, "Of course not, my darling. I think it's a wonderful idea."

"Great. I'll clear it with Henry tomorrow. I'd better go now, darling. We're here."

The line went dead before Teddy had a chance to say good-bye.

THE DAIMLER PULLED UP OUTSIDE THE house, its occupants hidden behind the smoked-glass windows. Gilbert Drake slipped the safety catch off his pistol and gripped it tightly. It was hard to tell which were louder, the jeers of the protesters or the *click, click, whir* of multiple camera shutters as Alexia De Vere stepped out of the car.

The day of the Lord is at hand, when destruction comes from the Almighty.

They were about to get one hell of a picture.

HENRY WHITMAN TURNED ON THE TELEVISION. He watched Alexia De Vere step out of her car, excruciatingly thin, like a couture-clad skeleton.

"My God," said his wife. "She looks ill."

"Yes."

"Why doesn't she just resign? Why does she cling like this? It's pathetic."

"Yes," said Henry. But he wasn't really listening. He was watching the protesters on the screen booing his home secretary as she walked past. *They really do hate her.*

He was beginning to hate her himself.

*

In Michael De Vere's hospital room, Summer Meyer was also watching the news.

The nurse who was plumping Michael's pillow said cheerfully, "That's his mum, isn't it? She's dead glamorous. Bit skinny, though."

That's an understatement, thought Summer. Alexia looked as frail as a bird as she stepped out of her car. Her black Chanel suit with gold bouclé detailing hung off her like rags on a scarecrow.

"Crowd don't like her much, do they?"

"No. They don't."

"You'd think they'd give her a break, what with her son being so ill and that. Still, it's a rough old game, isn't it? Politics."

Summer focused on the screen, tuning out the nurse's prattle. Just as Alexia was about to reach the safety of the police cordon, something caught her eye. A glint of silver, flashing at the front of the crowd.

"Oh my God!" Summer said aloud. "Oh my *God*!"

ALEXIA LOOKED STRAIGHT AHEAD AS SHE walked toward her front door, ignoring the shouts and chants and angry faces surrounding her.

"OUT, OUT, OUT!" they yelled. But Alexia wouldn't be pushed out, not by her enemies in the cabinet and certainly not by this ignorant rabble.

Just keep walking. It'll be over soon. Oh, look, there's Jimmy.

Her secret-service officer smiled as Alexia reached the line of tape dividing the pavement from her private property. Alexia smiled back. The cameras instantly caught the exchange, clicking frenziedly like a swarm of cicadas.

It was a strange thing—a split-second thing—but one of

the clicks sounded different from the others. Searching out the noise, Alexia spun around. She found herself staring into two eyes alight with raw hatred.

"I've got something for you, Home Secretary."

The shot rang out as loudly as a thunderclap. Alexia felt a sharp pain and a moment's intense surprise.

Then everything went black.

CHAPTER TWENTY-EIGHT

"Alexia! Alexia, can you hear me?"

Sir Edward Manning's voice sounded very far away. Alexia thought, *How strange that he's using my first name. He never uses my first name. Something serious must have happened.*

Opening her eyes, Alexia found her vision was distorted. She could make out Edward's concerned features, and a sea of other, blurred faces behind him. But everything was lurching, as if they were on a ship on the high seas. She had no idea where she was. The light hurt her eyes, and a wave of nausea combined with a searing pain in her side.

Then the blackness returned and she felt nothing at all.

Henry Whitman spoke grimly into the phone.

"Is she alive?"

"Yes, Prime Minister."

For a brief, unworthy moment, Henry Whitman felt disappointed.

"He shot her at close range, but somehow the bullet lodged in her ribs. They're operating now, but I understand she's going to make it. She was incredibly lucky."

Yes, thought Henry Whitman. *She usually is.*

"They arrested the man?"

"Yes, sir. Gilbert Drake. A cabbie from North London, no prior record. He was a friend of Sanjay Patel's, apparently. Gave himself up, no trouble."

"All right. Keep me informed."

The prime minister hung up, poured himself a whisky, and took two long, deep swallows. *Gilbert Drake.* What kind of an idiot must the man be to have missed at point-blank range? Henry Whitman hoped they locked Drake up and threw away the damned key.

BLACK BECAME WHITE. WHITE WALLS, WHITE ceiling, white bed, white light.

Am I dead?

Alexia blinked against the brightness. Slowly reality reasserted itself.

A hospital. The pain in her side was gone, replaced by a warm, fuzzy feeling she hadn't felt since her teens. *Morphine.* She looked down. Sure enough, there were the tubes, pumping some unnamed painkiller into her arm.

Suddenly it all came back to her.

The Patel protesters. The clicking cameras. The eyes full of hatred, blazing out at her.

"WHAT HAPPENED?"

The words came out so faintly she could barely hear them herself, but they were enough to bring the staff nurse running.

"You were shot, Mrs. De Vere, but you're going to be fine. Try not to panic."

Alexia smiled wanly. "I never panic. Will I need an operation?"

"You've already had it. Everything went perfectly. Try to rest. I'll page the surgeon now and he'll come and explain things."

The nurse ran out. Almost immediately there was a knock on the door.

"Mummy?"

Roxie looked awful. White as a sheet and with her mascara running all over her face, she had clearly been crying. She wheeled herself over to Alexia's bedside.

"I saw it on TV. I thought you were dead." To Alexia's astonishment, her daughter reached over the bed and took her hand. For a moment Alexia was too stunned to respond. It was the first genuinely kind gesture Roxie had made toward her in so many long years. But then she pulled herself together and squeezed back, caressing her daughter's fingers as though they were precious jewels.

"You've been crying," she said gently.

Roxie nodded. "I've already lost Michael. I . . . I can't lose you too."

Alexia's eyes welled up with tears. All the emotion she'd repressed since Michael's accident erupted out of her now, like floodwaters breaching a levee.

"You're *crying*!" Roxie sounded astonished.

"It's the drugs." Alexia laughed, then winced as the pain in her side reasserted itself,

"What the devil's going on here?" An overbearing man in a three-piece suit, obviously a surgeon, came storming into the room. "I gave very clear instructions. You need rest. No visitors."

Roxie swiveled around in her chair. "Bugger off," she said firmly. "I'm her daughter and I'm not going anywhere."

"Oh, yes you are, young lady."

Watching the two of them argue, Alexia felt suffused with happiness.

Her daughter had come back to her.

Nothing, absolutely nothing else mattered anymore.

CHAPTER TWENTY-NINE

THE MECHANIC LOOKED AT THE MANGLED Ducati Panigale and shook his head sadly.

"That's a shame, that is. A real shame. Beautiful bike."

Summer begged to differ. As far as she was concerned, Michael's bike was the ugliest thing she'd ever seen, a hideous, lethal weapon.

Armed with the ownership papers that Teddy had given her, Summer had convinced the Oxfordshire police to release what was left of the motorbike into her care. No tests had been done on it. As far as the police were concerned, Michael De Vere's accident was just that: an accident, not a crime to be investigated. As such, the bike wasn't evidence, it was simply private property. His girlfriend was welcome to it.

In full investigative journalist mode, Summer chipped away at every possible angle, determined to uncover Michael's "secret" and what relation it might bear to his accident. With this in mind, she'd hired a van, dumped the bike's twisted hulk in the back with the help of a neighbor, and driven down to East London at the crack of dawn. According to the Internet reviews, St. Martin's Garage and Body Shop in Walthamstow was the top Ducati specialist in the country. Certainly the young man in front of Summer now seemed to know what he was talking about, earnestly informing her about belt drives and cylinder heads and twist-and-go transmissions as he ran his hands lovingly over the Panigale's scraped red chassis.

"It's not salvageable, I'm afraid. I mean, technically we could rebuild it. But it'd be more new parts than old and it'd cost a fortune."

"What if I needed you to look at individual parts for me?"

"Such as?"

"I don't know. The steering. The brakes. If there were a technical fault of some kind, would you be able to find it? Or is it too far gone for that?"

The mechanic looked up at the gorgeous girl in front of him. Not many of St. Martin's clients looked like Summer Meyer, with those endless legs and that glossy mane of hair, like polished wood, rippling down her back. But there was something else about the girl, a steely determination in her eyes and the jut of her jaw that he hadn't noticed when she walked in. It was seriously sexy.

"I won't know for sure till I take her apart," he said. "But if there was a fault with the bike, then yeah, I reckon I'd clock it." He hoped he was impressing her. "I know these bikes like the back of me 'and."

"And how long might that take? Roughly."

"Come back at six and I should have some answers for you. I gotta tell you, though, these bikes are beautifully made. I'd be surprised if you find anything wrong with her."

Summer left her car in the garage forecourt—it was impossible to park in central London, so she might as well keep it here—and took the tube to Sloane Square. If the bike wouldn't be ready till six, it made sense to stay the night in town and head back up to Oxford tomorrow.

Everywhere she went, people were talking about the attempt on Alexia De Vere's life. Pictures of Gilbert Drake, the man who'd shot her, were on the front page of every newspaper, and updates on the home secretary's condition remained the lead item on every radio station's news. Summer had watched the thing happen live on television. Sitting at Michael's bedside, she'd even seen the glint of Drake's gun before he fired the shot. She wanted to call Teddy immediately, then realized this might be seen as an intrusion. Besides, with her mother calling her every five minutes for updates on Alexia's condition, she barely had time.

Now that she was up in London, however, and a few days had passed, she probably should give Teddy a call. She checked into the Orange, a pretty pub-cum-hotel on Pimlico Road and had a long soak in the Victorian copper bath before lying down on the bed with her phone. Her first call was to the John Radcliffe to check on Michael. (No change.) Then, steeling her nerves, she dialed Teddy De Vere's number.

To her surprise, he answered immediately. "Summer! How lovely to hear from you, my dear."

His voice was full of genuine warmth.

"You've heard the news, of course?"

"Of course. How is she?"

"Believe it or not, she's in the pink," Teddy said cheerfully. "The doctors say she'll be able to come home in a day or so. Better yet, she and Roxie finally seem to have patched things up."

"They have?" Summer couldn't hide her surprise.

"I know. Wonderful, isn't it? I think the prospect of Alexia actually dying was what made things shift. Anyway, Rox showed up at the hospital and the pair of them have been thick as thieves ever since. I wouldn't have believed it myself if I hadn't seen it with my own eyes. That bastard Drake might have actually done us all a favor. But enough of our dramas. How are you?"

"I'm fine. I'm in London, actually, just for tonight."

"Are you? Marvelous. We must have lunch tomorrow."

"Oh, no no no," Summer said hastily. "I wouldn't want to intrude at a time like this. You should be with your family."

"Nonsense. You *are* family," Teddy said kindly. "Besides, Alexia and Roxie only have eyes for each other at the moment. They barely know I'm there."

"Honestly, Teddy, it's a sweet offer, but I couldn't."

"Nonsense. Lunch tomorrow, twelve-thirty sharp. I insist. I'll book somewhere decent and let you know."

TEDDY TOOK HER TO THE ARTS Club in Mayfair. Completely revamped a few years earlier, the Dover Street town house was now one of the smartest, most exclusive members' clubs in London. Unfortunately it no longer lived up to its name, its clientele being made up almost wholly of investment bankers and hedge fund types. Summer felt their lecherous stares on her back as she made her way to Teddy's table.

"What a pleasure!" He stood up to greet her, looking like a disheveled Rupert Bear in a loud tweed suit and waistcoat, a jaunty red silk cravat tied at his neck. "You look delightful, as ever."

"If I'd known it was so formal, I'd have dressed up," said Summer, feeling awkwardly low-key in her Hudson corduroy jeans and dark green Gap T-shirt. Although after the shocking news she'd received last night, the Arts Club's dress code had been the last thing on her mind this morning.

"I'd have been just as happy in McDonald's, you know," she told Teddy.

"McDonald's?" Teddy shuddered. "I should hope I know how to treat a young lady a bit better than that."

They ordered food—salt-encrusted sea bass for Summer and a steak and kidney pie for Teddy—and conversation turned to Alexia and the shooting.

"Isn't it funny how often good things seem to come out of bad?" Teddy observed philosophically. "Like phoenixes rising from the ashes. I'd almost given up hope that Alexia and Roxie would ever reconcile. It's a shame it took a bullet in the ribs to do it, but there you are. And that's not the only positive change. On doctors' orders, Alexia has finally agreed to take some time off work. She's talking about flying out to the States and spending some time with your mother, actually."

"That's nice," said Summer, more because it was expected of her than because it was what she really felt. Her mom's close friendship with Alexia still made her uncomfortable, but she could hardly say that to Teddy.

"It *is* nice," Teddy agreed, smiling. "Alexia's been through so much this past year. First, Michael and now this."

"Hmm." Summer chased her fish around the plate with her fork. Obviously she wouldn't wish an assassination attempt on anyone. But she didn't find it so easy to forgive and forget Alexia's neglect of Michael, or the callous way she'd behaved since his crash.

"The problem is she's so very bad at saying no, especially when it comes to her work," Teddy went on. "My wife has such a strong sense of duty, you see. Of public service. Not very fashionable these days, but there you have it. Alexia never thinks of herself."

Summer almost choked. "Uh-huh." *Is he really that deluded? Did the bullet ricochet off Alexia's rib cage and lodge itself in Teddy's brain?*

"Anyway, enough about my family. What about you?"

Teddy went on. "What brings you to London? Culture or shopping?"

"Neither, actually. I've been looking into something."

Summer told Teddy about Michael's motorbike and her mission to the Walthamstow garage. A cloud descended over Teddy's kindly features.

"Do you think that's wise, my dear? Tinkering around with the ghastly thing?"

"Why not?"

"Well, surely if the police thought there were anything untoward going on, they'd have examined the motorbike themselves?"

"This may come as a shock to you, Teddy, but the police aren't infallible. As it turns out, there *was* a fault with the bike."

Teddy set his wineglass down carefully on the table. "Was there?"

"Well," Summer backtracked, "they couldn't be a hundred percent sure. But the mechanic at St. Martin's said the markings on the brake cables and the way they'd frayed suggested that they may have been tampered with before the crash."

"Tampered with?" Teddy's mind raced.

"Yes. Someone may have wanted Michael to crash that day."

Teddy shook his head. "No. I don't believe it. That can't be true."

"Does Michael have any enemies, that you know of?"

"Enemies? The boy was an events organizer, not a spy."

He still is an events organizer, thought Summer, but she held her tongue.

"I daresay he may have pinched the odd fellow's girl-friend over the years," said Teddy, adding tactfully, "Before he met you, obviously, my dear. But I can't imagine anyone wanting to hurt him. Not seriously."

"Maybe it wasn't Michael they wanted to hurt," Summer suggested. "Maybe it was you. Or Alexia. Maybe Michael was just a means to an end."

Teddy pushed his plate to the side. "You said the chap that you showed the motorbike to wasn't sure."

"Not absolutely sure, no. The evidence might not hold up in court. Not on its own, anyway. But it's a start."

"A start of what?" Teddy reached across the table for her hand. "Don't take this the wrong way, Summer. But do you not think that, perhaps, you might be hearing what you want to hear?"

Summer bridled. "I'm not making this up, you know."

"I'm not suggesting for a moment that you are. But by your own admission, the evidence is inconclusive. The brake cables could have frayed when Michael saw the lorry hurtling toward him at God knows how many miles per hour. Could they not have?"

"Technically, yes, they could have," Summer said grudgingly.

"You want there to be a meaning to all this. A reason for your pain, and for Michael's suffering. But the truth is, there *is* no reason. Any more than there's a reason why that lunatic Drake took a shot at Alexia. Bad things just happen."

"You don't know there's no reason for what happened to Michael." Summer was surprised to find herself close to tears. Teddy really knew how to push her buttons. "Someone may have tampered with those brakes."

"You can torture yourself with 'may have' Summer, but it won't bring Michael back to us."

"No. But it may bring us the truth."

"But *why*, my dear?" Teddy sounded exasperated. "Why would anyone want to kill my son?"

"That's exactly what I'm trying to figure out."

312

"By ignoring the answer that's staring you in the face? The answer is: they wouldn't! Michael didn't *have* enemies. This wasn't some dastardly plot. This was an accident. Brake cables fray in accidents."

Summer tried a different tack. She'd hoped the news from Walthamstow might rouse Teddy's curiosity at least, but he seemed determined to dismiss it. Instead she asked him the same question she'd asked Roxie at Kingsmere weeks earlier.

"Did Michael talk to you about a secret in the weeks leading up to the summer party? Something troubling he'd discovered."

"No. He didn't."

"Are you sure?"

"Quite sure. Roxie already asked me about this, so I've given it some thought. She said you mentioned this 'secret' to her too. But I'm afraid neither of us has the faintest idea what you mean. Michael was fine before the party. Nothing was troubling him."

"But he told me—"

"Summer." Teddy interrupted her. "You're building quite a conspiracy theory here. Mysterious secrets, frayed brake cables. Can't you see it's all smoke and mirrors?"

A heavy silence fell across the table.

"If I really believed someone had harmed my son deliberately, don't you think I'd be calling the police right now? Don't you think I'd want to know the truth as much as you do?"

Summer nodded.

Cupping a hand under her chin, Teddy lifted her face so her eyes met his and said, gently but firmly, "It. Was. An. Accident. Now . . ." He smiled broadly, breaking the tension like a snapped twig. "Let's order some pudding, shall we? The Eton mess here has to be tasted to be believed."

*

IN HER ROOM AT THE ORANGE a few hours later, Summer threw her few paltry overnight things into a bag.

Why does nobody believe me?

Why does nobody take me seriously?

Tears of frustration welled in her eyes. She remembered what her boss at the *New York Post* had said to her when he turned down a story on gang intimidation Summer had been working on for months.

"Don't bring me conjecture, Miss Meyer. Bring me the facts. This is a newspaper. We don't print fairy tales."

Was her theory about Michael a fairy tale? Had his crash really just been an accident, like Teddy De Vere and the rest of the world seemed to think?

Rubbing her eyes, she felt dizzy with exhaustion.

I need about a year of sleep.

BACK IN THE MAYFAIR OFFICE of his hedge fund, Kingsmere Capital, Teddy De Vere closed the door, took off his suit jacket, and sank into his plush leather Herman Miller task chair. Closing his eyes, he took a deep, calming breath.

One mustn't panic.

It wouldn't do to panic. Terribly un-English.

He picked up the phone.

"Yes, it's me. Look, I'm sorry to call when you're resting. But I think we need to talk."

SERGEI MILESCU WAS FRIGHTENED.

He'd been sure Sir Edward Manning would get him what he needed—enough dirt on Alexia De Vere to force her out of office, so that his paymaster could replace her with a more suitable, amenable candidate as home secretary.

314

But having squeezed the old queen like a lemon for over a year, Edward's drips of information were running out. So was Sergei's paymaster's patience.

"I paid in advance, in good faith."

He wore a Savile Row suit and spoke in the measured, educated tones of a businessman. But he was not a businessman. He was a merciless killer. Brought up on the streets of Tbilisi with nothing but his wits to recommend him, he had lied and threatened and robbed and deceived and bludgeoned his way to the top of the heap in the new Russia. Now he owned oil wells and diamond mines and chemical plants and nuclear power stations. The J. P. Morgans and Goldman Sachses of this world all courted him. In London, he mixed in the highest society, dated aristocratic girls, and gave lots of money to charity and to "helpful" political parties. The Tories *had* been very helpful, until that jumped-up bitch Alexia De Vere had had the temerity to question his business dealings, closing tax and other legal loopholes that he and his fellow London-based oligarchs relied on. The home secretary had crossed him, a grave mistake. Beneath the veneer of sophistication, he remained a ruthless savage.

Sergei Milescu had witnessed his savagery firsthand. A Ukrainian prostitute who'd shortchanged him had had her eyes gouged out. Rumor was he'd let her off lightly because she was a woman.

Sergei felt the sweat soak through his shirt.

"I'll return the money."

"I have no interest in the money. I want what I paid for."

"You'll get it."

"When?"

"Soon."

Sergei's paymaster clapped his hands. Two armed heavies burst into the room. Sergei mewled like a terrified kitten.

"Please! You'll get it! Very soon," he begged.

"I'm sure I will, Mr. Milescu. My security will show you out."

CHAPTER THIRTY

MARJORIE PILCHER SLIPPED OFF HER QUILTED Husky jacket as she cleared the brow of the hill that led down onto the Kingsmere Manor estate. As so often on her afternoon walks, Marjorie reflected on the beauty of the West Oxfordshire countryside and how privileged she was to live here. As chairwoman of the Kingsmere and Cotterill Women's Initiative, Marjorie Pilcher liked to think of herself as a pivotal figure in the local community. It was Marjorie who had persuaded Teddy De Vere, the biggest local landowner, to allow "respectful" walkers through his land, even though there was no official right of way on the manor estate. Watching her springer spaniel, Freckles, lollop down the hillside now, with the De Veres' idyllic house on her right and the ancient woodlands stretching out in front of her like a Narnian forest, Marjorie Pilcher enjoyed a warm sensation of triumph. Even the vicar, Reverend Gray, had been impressed by the way Marjorie had talked Teddy De Vere around.

"I can't think how you managed to charm him, Mrs. Pilcher," Reverend Gray had told Marjorie over a large plate of buttered scones at the vicarage. "But thank heavens you did. Generations of villagers will be in your debt, dear lady."

Marjorie Pilcher liked the idea of generations of villagers being in her debt. And to think her late husband, Frank (the bastard), thought she'd never amount to anything.

Oh Lord. What is that ridiculous dog doing now?

"Freckles! Here, boy. Come away."

Teddy De Vere's one stipulation had been that walkers and their animals must stick to the path through the parkland and woods and not stray into the private Kingsmere gardens. And now here was Marjorie Pilcher's own unruly animal rolling under the fence in clear violation of this sacrosanct rule, worrying away at the ground that had been cemented over for the proposed new pagoda.

"Freckles!"

Ignoring his mistress utterly, the springer spaniel continued to dig, his brown-and-white-flecked tail wagging excitedly as he worked.

"Freckles! Come here at once!"

Gingerly, Marjorie Pilcher picked her way over the nettles and through the thorny briars that formed a natural boundary between the parkland and the formal landscaped grounds of the manor house. Like most local people, Marjorie had deplored the idea of a pagoda on the Kingsmere estate, considering it "flash" and vulgar. But she hadn't objected formally for fear of irritating Teddy De Vere and losing her hard-won walkers' rights. As it turned out, it was the right decision. The ghastly thing had yet to be built and probably never would be now, what with the De Veres' son having that dreadful motorcycle accident, and now Mrs. De Vere being shot by a deranged taxi driver. Awful business. All that remained of Teddy's grand plans was an ugly concrete-filled hole, but that would soon be grown over. Although not soon enough for the errant Freckles. Marjorie Pilcher watched despairingly as the dog scrabbled around the perimeter of the slab, digging with a desperation she'd never seen in him before.

"What *are* you doing, you stupid dog?" Ripping one of her favorite tweed skirts as she hiked first one leg, then the other, over the dilapidated barbed-wire fence, Marjorie eased herself down into the estate gardens. She'd never hear the end of it at the WI if one of the Kingsmere groundsmen caught her trespassing, albeit in a good cause.

Oh God. She sighed. *He's got something in his mouth*.

That was all Marjorie needed, some half-dead stoat or weasel that she'd have to finish off with a spade or the heel of her boot. Truth be told, there wasn't much that Marjorie missed about the dearly departed Frank Pilcher, her husband of almost fifty years. She mostly remembered Frank for his phlegmy cough that used to set her teeth on edge and his irritating habit of asking her questions in the middle of her favorite radio show, *Gardeners' Question Time*. Beneath the muted disguise of her mourning clothes, Marjorie Pilcher had embraced widowhood with all the enthusiasm of a young girl in the flush of her first affair. But Frank *had* been handy when it came to killing animals. It might be a kindness, but Marjorie could never get used to the idea of walloping a living creature over the head. It just didn't feel right, especially when their bones made that dreadful cracking, crunching sound . . .

The dog came bounding toward her, its "gift" clamped between its jaws.

"Ugh, Freckles." Marjorie's lip curled. "What disgusting offering have you brought me this time?"

Tail still wagging, the springer leaped up at his mistress.

Marjorie Pilcher's scream could be heard all the way back in the village.

319

Hanging grotesquely from the dog's drooling mouth was a decomposing human hand.

REPORTERS WERE SWARMING OVER THE DE Vere estate like vermin. The police, also at Kingsmere in force, seemed powerless to control them.

"This is ridiculous," Teddy grumbled as his Bentley swept through the gates, past the flashing cameras and thrust-out microphones. "Haven't they anything better to do?"

Alexia, straight-backed and rigid-jawed in the passenger seat, said nothing. Beneath her crisp white shirt, her entire left side was swathed in bandages. The doctors had prescribed Percocet for the pain, but the pills made her feel groggy, so she'd stopped taking them. As a result she winced every time the car turned a corner. The speed bumps were pure agony.

Worse than the physical pain was the anxiety she felt oozing back into her chest like water into a leaky ship.

That's what I am—a leaky ship.

A sinking ship.

After the shooting and her reconciliation with Roxanne, Alexia had finally capitulated and agreed to take an extended leave of absence. The prime minister was delighted, as was Kevin Lomax, Alexia's archrival over at Trade and Industry, whom Henry Whitman had named acting home secretary in her absence.

Henry's statement made it sound like a temporary arrangement, a break in which the home secretary would recover physically and mentally from the attempt on her life. But Alexia knew that the party would never take her back now, not with a dead body unearthed on her private grounds. Mrs. Marjorie Pilcher's gruesome discovery was one scandal too many, even for a fighter like Alexia De Vere. Politically, she was finished, and she knew it.

"Mum, Dad. Thank God."

Roxie's relief was palpable. She'd returned to Oxfordshire alone a couple of days earlier, after Alexia was discharged from hospital, and was the only family member actually at Kingsmere when the severed hand was found.

"The police keep asking me questions but I don't know anything. I'm sure they think I'm hiding something."

"If anyone's been pressuring or bullying you, I want their names," Alexia said forcefully. In the last week, all her protective, motherly instincts toward Roxie had come surging back. She was in full lioness mode now, defending her cub.

A short, fat plain-clothed policeman with closely cropped gray hair walked confidently up to Alexia and Teddy and extended a hand.

"Chief Inspector Gary Wilmott, Oxford CID. We've been asking Miss De Vere a few routine questions, that's all. No one's been bullying anyone."

"You've clearly frightened her." Teddy looked at the forensic teams and tracking dogs invading his home with distaste. "Is this circus really necessary?"

Chief Inspector Gary Wilmott stiffened. "A man's been found dead in your garden, Mr. De Vere. We tend to take murder fairly seriously."

"That's over-egging the pudding a bit, isn't it? How do you know he was murdered?"

"Well, he was a bloody clever suicide if he managed to shoot himself in the chest and then bury himself afterward."

One of the forensic team giggled, earning herself an icy glare from her boss.

The fat detective looked from Teddy to Alexia. "Where can we talk, privately?"

"In my study. This way." Turning to Roxie, Alexia added, "You go and get some rest, my darling. Daddy and I will help the chief inspector with his inquiries."

"Thanks, Mummy."

"Actually, I'm afraid I'll need all three of you."

"What the hell for?" Teddy bristled. "Roxie's told you what she knows."

Chief Inspector Gary Wilmott was beginning to lose his temper. *Bloody aristos. Think the rules don't apply to them. Don't they care that a young man's been shot and left to rot in their garden?*

"Because you all live here, Mr. De Vere. It isn't rocket science."

Once in the study, Alexia took charge.

"Naturally we'll help you in any way we can, Chief Inspector," she said, wincing and clutching her side as she sat down. "But I wonder if I might also ask a few questions of you. You say it was a man's body that was found?"

"That's right. We don't know much at this stage. As you can see, my men are still excavating the site. Not easy, what with all the newly poured concrete."

Roxie said defensively, "I already told you, Chief Inspector. Daddy was throwing a party. My brother, Michael, was in charge of constructing a pagoda, but he . . . he never got a chance to finish it."

"I'm sure you're aware of what happened, Chief Inspector," said Alexia. "My son was in a motorcycle accident."

"Yes, ma'am. I understand it's been a difficult time for your family. Can I get you anything? A glass of water perhaps?"

Alexia shook her head. "I'm fine. What my daughter says is correct. The concrete was supposed to form the base of a pagoda that we were building as part of the tricentenary

322

celebrations. Michael was managing the project. After his crash, it got forgotten about. None of us were in the mood to build follies."

"So it *was* your son who dug the hole out there?"

"My son and his workmen, yes."

"And your son who filled it with concrete?"

"Yes."

Teddy spluttered, "I hope you're not suggesting that Michael had anything to do with this body business?"

"I'm not suggesting anything, Mr. De Vere."

"Good. Because the boy's on a bloody life support machine. He can't defend himself from your insinuations, but I sure as hell will."

Alexia put a hand on Teddy's arm, but he shrugged it off. She'd never seen him like this. Teddy was always the calm one. She was the hothead in the marriage.

"Chief Inspector," she asked, "do you know how long ago this man was killed? Or how long he may have been buried on our land?"

"Not yet, no. Although judging by the degree of decomposition and the damage to the skeletal remains we've unearthed so far, animal bites and whatnot, I would guess we're talking several years."

"There you are, then." Teddy looked at him triumphantly. "It couldn't have been anything to do with Michael, or the stupid pagoda. I only thought of the thing six or seven months ago and we didn't start work on it till June, long after your chappie was bumped off."

He pronounced it "orf." *Pretentious bloody snob.* For a moment Chief Inspector Gary Wilmott's professional mask slipped and he stared at Teddy De Vere with naked loathing. Thankfully he was interrupted by one of his team before he said something he might have regretted.

"Sir? You'd better come out here a minute."

Chief Inspector Wilmott left the room. Alexia, Teddy, and Roxie all looked at one another, shell-shocked. Roxie broke the silence.

"Do you think Michael knew?"

"Knew what?" asked Teddy.

"About the body."

Both parents looked at her as if she were mad.

Alexia said, "Of course not. Why on earth would you think something like that?"

"For the same reason the police think it," said Roxie. "That Pilcher woman's dog found the hand right on the edge of the pagoda site. Michael could have seen something when they were excavating."

"He *could* have. But obviously he didn't."

"Why is that obvious?"

"Because if he'd seen anything, he'd have told the police, wouldn't he? Or us. If he'd unearthed a dead body, he'd hardly put it back and say nothing about it."

"Unless he had a reason for keeping it hidden," Roxie mused. "Summer Meyer was asking me a couple of weeks ago about a secret. What if this was it?"

Alexia's tone hardened. She badly wanted not to upset the applecart with Roxie. But she couldn't allow these unfounded suspicions of poor Michael to stand unchallenged. "Summer's a sweet enough girl, and I daresay she's well meaning. But she really ought to mind her own business and stop banging on about secrets and conspiracies. It's all nonsense."

"I agree," said Teddy. He'd told Alexia yesterday about Summer's latest investigations into Michael's Ducati and its frayed brake cables. Alexia was not amused. "If your brother had found a body, he would have told somebody."

But Roxie wouldn't be deflected. "Unless he was the one who buried it," she said defiantly.

Teddy's eyes widened. "You aren't serious? You think Michael killed a man?"

"I'm not saying he *did*. I'm just saying, it's possible. We all sometimes do things in anger, or self-defense, or accidentally, in the heat of the moment. I love Michael. But I mean, we're all capable of murder, aren't we? In the right circumstances."

"Are we?" said Teddy.

"Of course we are, darling." Alexia had been watching Roxie while she spoke, wondering if there was a deeper message beneath her words, something more that she was trying to tell them. "There but for the grace of God go all of us."

"Well, I'm sorry," said Teddy, "but I still don't believe that Michael—"

Chief Inspector Gary Willmot marched back in without knocking. He looked grim-faced. "The dogs found some clothes buried separately, about sixty yards from where the bones were scattered. This was with them." He threw an old Swatch sports watch down on Teddy's desk. "I suppose it's too much to hope that any of you might recognize it?"

Teddy snapped, "Of course we don't recognize it. Why would we? Other than being unfortunate enough to have had someone decide to bury a body on our land, my family and I have nothing whatsoever to do with this."

Teddy ranted on, but Chief Inspector Wilmott was no longer listening. Roxie De Vere had begun making a strange noise, a sort of high, keening howl, like an animal caught in a trap. It was getting louder.

"Miss De Vere?" Chief Inspector Wilmott looked at her quizzically.

"Roxie, darling." Teddy was all concern. "Are you all right?"

"Miss De Vere, do you recognize this watch? Do you know who it belongs to?"

With a wild shriek, Roxie swiveled her chair around. Teddy watched in horror as she used her forearms to propel herself out of the chair and onto Alexia, knocking her mother off her feet.

Now it was Alexia who screamed, as the pain shot through her chest like a lightning bolt. With Roxanne slumped on top of her, she couldn't move. Instead she squirmed in helpless agony as Roxie gripped her neck like a vise, choking her and crushing her windpipe. Instinctively, Alexia kicked out in panic. She felt the breath leave her body and was sure she was about to pass out. Why was nobody helping her?

"Roxanne!" Teddy shouted. "For God's sake."

"You killed him!" Roxie screamed, shaking Alexia like a terrier with a rat between its teeth. "All this time you let me believe he left me. But you killed him! Shot him in cold blood like an animal and buried him here. *Murderer!*"

Belatedly, Chief Inspector Wilmott pulled the girl off, scooping her up into his arms. She weighed next to nothing. After the exertion of the attack on her mother, Roxanne sobbed weakly against his chest, as limp and fragile as a rag doll.

Meanwhile Alexia De Vere lay on the floor, clutching her throat and gasping for breath like a newly landed fish.

Placing Roxie gently back into her wheelchair, Chief Inspector Wilmott knelt down so that his eyes were level with hers.

"You recognize the watch?"

Roxie's voice was a whisper. "It belonged to my fiancé. Andrew."

With that, Roxie De Vere's eyes rolled back in her head and a great spasm swept through her broken body. Soon she was foaming at the mouth, seizing wildly.

"Do something! Help her!" Teddy sounded panicked. Alexia merely stared, too stunned and in too much pain herself to do anything for her daughter. Roxie looked as though she were being electrocuted, dancing in anguish before her parents' eyes.

"Call an ambulance," Chief Inspector Wilmott told his sergeant. "NOW!"

CHAPTER THIRTY-ONE

"INTERVIEW WITH MRS. ALEXIA DE VERE, Sunday, November twenty-sixth, two forty-four P.M. Chief Inspector Gary Wilmott present. Mrs. De Vere, can you please describe your relationship with Andrew Beesley, your daughter's fiancé?"

Alexia twisted the gold wedding band on her finger. "Not until I see my daughter."

"Your daughter's been taken to hospital. You'll be given word on her condition in due course."

"That's not good enough. I want to know what's happening now."

"Andrew Beesley, Mrs. De Vere."

"Do you think I care about Andrew bloody Beesley?" Alexia snapped. "All I care about right now is Roxanne."

Chief Inspector Wilmott said, "Most people would probably care that a young man they knew well had been murdered and that his corpse was found buried in their garden."

"Would they? I doubt it. Not if they knew Andrew," Alexia said bitterly. *I should stop talking. I should ask for my lawyer.* But it felt so good to speak the truth, to vent her hatred at last, she found she couldn't stop herself.

"Andrew Beesley manipulated my daughter in the most cynical, vile way imaginable. I didn't know him well. But I knew him well enough to realize that. All he ever wanted was Roxie's money."

"And was that why you killed him?"

Alexia laughed mockingly, then wished she hadn't as the pain once again shot through her ribs where Gilbert Drake's bullet had hit her. "Don't be preposterous," she said through gritted teeth. "I didn't kill anybody."

"Your daughter doesn't seem to find that idea preposterous."

"My daughter's in shock. Where's my husband? I want to speak to my husband."

"You know you're not helping yourself, or your wife, by refusing to answer our questions."

A few doors down the corridor from Alexia, Teddy De Vere was also being interviewed. Inspector Henry Frobisher, one of the Oxford police's most talented officers, had been drafted in by Chief Inspector Wilmott on the grounds that Teddy might open up more to "another poshy."

No such luck. With his arms folded across his chest and his head turned resolutely away, Teddy repeated the mantra he'd been intoning ever since he left Kingsmere. "I want my lawyer."

"When did you last see Andrew Beesley alive?"

"I want my lawyer."

"Are there any grounds for your daughter's belief that your wife may have been responsible for Mr. Beesley's death?"

"I refuse to answer any questions without my lawyer."

"Mr. De Vere, were you aware that Mr. Beesley was in

fact dead, and had not returned to Australia as you told your daughter?"

"Lawyer."

Inspector Henry Frobisher switched off the tape. "Get his solicitor here," he barked at his sergeant. "Now. And make sure someone's with the daughter. We need a statement as soon as she wakes up."

ALEXIA DE VERE WAS BECOMING MORE strident.

"I demand to see my daughter."

"I'm not sure you're in a position to demand anything just now, Mrs. De Vere."

"Turn off that tape recorder."

Chief Inspector Wilmott considered the request for a moment, then did as he was asked. Breaks in a case often happened when witnesses, or suspects, agreed to talk off the record.

"Is there something you want to say to me, Mrs. De Vere?"

"Yes, there is."

Chief Inspector Wilmott felt his excitement building. *This is it. She's going to confess.*

"I want to remind you that I'm still the home secretary of this country. And that as such, your boss, and your boss's boss, report to me. I could have you suspended. Like *that*." She snapped her fingers imperiously.

If he hadn't felt so disappointed, Chief Inspector Wilmott would have laughed. Alexia De Vere might be the Iron Lady, but she didn't scare him, and neither did her powerful friends.

"On what grounds?" He squared his shoulders. "A young man was shot to death on your estate, Mrs. De Vere. You may not care about that fact. But I do. What's more"—he paused for effect—"I think you killed him."

Alexia's upper lip curled. "Based on what? Roxie's paranoia? An old watch?"

"As it happens, I found your daughter to be a very convincing witness. I've a feeling a jury may feel the same. I mean, let's face it, ordinary voters haven't exactly been warming to you recently, have they? And that's all juries are, Mrs. De Vere. Just twelve ordinary voters."

Alexia eyed the fat policeman contemplatively.

"Turn on the tape."

Chief Inspector Wilmott pressed a button.

"Interview resumed, three-fifteen P.M."

ROXIE DE VERE OPENED HER EYES.

Everything was white and bright and beautiful. For a moment she felt a rush of intense happiness. *I'm in heaven. I'm in heaven with Andrew. He never left me. He loved me, he loved me after all.*

Then she saw the uniformed policeman standing by the door and her dream crumbled to dust.

This wasn't heaven. And Andrew wasn't some luminous white angel.

He was a rotted corpse, with dogs chewing the putrid flesh still hanging from his bones.

Her screams echoed down the hospital halls.

CHIEF CONSTABLE REDMAYNE OF THE THAMES Valley police read the statement for a second time, carefully weighing each word, before handing it back to Chief Inspector Wilmott.

The chief constable was a vastly fat man with ruddy cheeks and a shock of white hair that gave him a jovial,

Father Christmas–like air. In fact, Cyril Redmayne had a razor-sharp mind and was driven by the sort of ruthless ambition normally associated with politicians or rock stars. He was not at all happy to hear that the home secretary had been dragged down to Oxford police station like a common criminal. One misstep in a case like this and Cyril Redmayne's brilliant career could be over in a blink.

On the other hand, a man had been murdered. And no one, not even the likes of Alexia De Vere, should be able to consider themselves above the law.

Chief Inspector Gary Wilmott asked, "What do you think, sir?"

"What do *you* think, Gary?"

"I think she's lying. Through her perfectly white teeth."

The chief constable considered this.

"Hmm. I've had a call from Downing Street, you know. The prime minister wants to know if we're going to charge her."

"I can't. Not yet. I'd like to keep her in for questioning, though."

"Absolutely not."

"For another day at least. The husband too."

"Out of the question."

"But, sir . . ."

"Gary, she's the home secretary."

"So? She's involved in this, sir, I know she is."

"Then prove it. Find this psychologist. See if she corroborates Mrs. De Vere's story."

Chief Inspector Wilmott looked uncomfortable. "We have."

"And?"

"And she does corroborate the story. But that means nothing. They could easily have cooked it up together. Made

332

a contingency plan, in case the body was ever found. I need more time with Mrs. De Vere."

"Well, you can't have it. Not without more evidence."

Chief Inspector Wilmott got up to leave. The chief constable called after him.

"She might be telling the truth, you know. Just because you don't like her. It *is* a possibility."

"Pigs might fly."

After Wilmott had gone, Cyril Redmayne read through Alexia De Vere's statement for a third time. If it were true, then a lot of people had misjudged the home secretary. Not least her own daughter.

Statement to police:

Andrew Beesley was an Australian tennis coach who came to work for my family eight years ago. Shortly afterward, he began a romantic relationship with my daughter, Roxanne, which quickly became serious. Too quickly, in my view, although it was my husband who most vehemently disapproved of the match. Teddy felt Andrew was a blatant gold digger, and that it was our duty to protect Roxie and stop her from marrying him.

We discussed the idea of offering Andrew money to leave. I was against it, mostly on the grounds that I thought it unlikely the boy would accept, and that he might well tell Roxie we'd approached him, which would only make things worse between our daughter and ourselves. We agreed that our son, Michael, would talk to Andrew privately instead and see if he could warn him off. Anyway, not long after that, Andrew disappeared. He failed to show up for work one day, and that was that. Initially I didn't question it. I was delighted he'd pushed off; we all were. But weeks went by, and Roxie was becoming increasingly distraught and unable to cope. She couldn't accept that Andrew had dumped her so suddenly. That's when Teddy told me that he had paid Andrew off, even though I thought we had agreed not to. The boy had bitten his hand off apparently, and was only too eager to hightail it back to Australia with Teddy's check in his pocket.

The problem was Roxie. She'd suffered from depression as a teenager, quite badly, and her mental health was fragile at the best of times. Teddy and I had a private meeting with Dr. Lizzie Hunt, Roxie's psychiatrist, to discuss how we should handle Andrew's departure. Lizzie felt that having been abandoned by one man she loved, Roxie would not be able to cope with a second betrayal from Teddy— that she would see her father's intervention as a betrayal. So we agreed, the three of us, that I would allow Roxanne to believe it was *me* who had bribed Andrew to leave. That way Roxie's relationship with Teddy would remain intact, and hopefully she would one day rebuild enough trust in men to start a new, more appropriate romantic attachment.

Of course, things didn't work out as we'd hoped. Instead of facing her demons head-on, my daughter attempted suicide. She was lucky to survive. She wouldn't have recovered had it not been for her close, intensely close relationship with her father. So in that regard, I don't regret deceiving her. But Roxanne spent the next eight years of her life, right up until a few weeks ago, hating me for what she believed I did. That's been difficult.

I know that Teddy was telling the truth about paying Andrew off. Partly because he's a very honorable man. But also because Andrew cashed the check Teddy gave him. I saw that money leave our account. As far as Teddy and I knew, Andrew Beesley was still living somewhere in Australia. I have no idea how or when he died, and no explanation to offer as to how he came to be buried at Kingsmere. However, I can state categorically that I had nothing whatsoever to do with his death or the disposal of his remains.

Signed: Alexia De Vere

Chief Constable Redmayne had read thousands of statements. He prided himself on his instincts, his ability to read between the lines of the half-truths that most people chose to tell. But this one was tricky.

On balance, Cyril Redmayne disagreed with Chief Inspector Gary Wilmott. He was inclined to believe the home secretary's version of events. But there were anomalies. Clearly it would take a supremely loving mother, and wife, to make the sacrifices that Mrs. De Vere claimed to have made and take the blame for her husband's actions. Yet throughout her public life, and especially recently, since Michael's accident, she had become famous for being a cold and distant parent.

Still, you couldn't hold people in police custody because you found them cold and distant. The psychiatrist backed up Alexia's story. No doubt her husband, once he started talking, would do the same. The only two people able to contradict this version of events were the De Veres' son, Michael, who'd been involved in the family discussions about Andrew Beesley and his sister all those years ago . . . and Beesley himself.

One of those people was in a persistent vegetative state. The other was dead.

Something in the back of Chief Constable Cyril Redmayne's mind stirred uncomfortably at the neatness of it all. But he quashed his misgivings. All that mattered at the end of the day were the facts.

The facts were that Gary Wilmott had nothing on Alexia De Vere. The sooner they released her, the better.

BY SIX P.M., REPORTERS WERE CAMPED excitedly outside the Oxford city center police station, occupying the streets like fanatical tennis fans before a Wimbledon final. The line of television camera crews, both British and international, stretched back almost as far as Christchurch Meadows.

To their disappointment, and Chief Constable Redmayne's relief, the outgoing home secretary left the building by a back door. In the backseat of a blacked-out Range Rover, Sir Edward Manning was waiting, as unruffled and professional as ever.

"To London, I assume, Home Secretary? I told Number Ten we'd call from the car. Understandably the prime minister is eager to talk to you in person. In the meantime I've taken the liberty of preparing a preliminary statement."

"Thank you, Edward. But I'm afraid all that will have to wait. I need to go to the hospital to see Roxie. Then I want to find out what's happening with Teddy. They're still questioning him. Can you believe it?"

"Well, Home Secretary, I—"

"I distinctly heard Angus Grey's voice in the corridor, so at least he had the good sense to ask for a lawyer. But I want him out of there, ASAP. That vile little man Wilmott's clearly engaged in some sort of tiresome class

336

warfare. He's been gunning for Teddy since the moment we got home."

"Be that as it may, Home Secretary—"

"When all this is over I want his head on a plate."

Sir Edward Manning gave up trying to reason with her. Alexia was quivering, whether from anger or from shock over the events of the last twelve hours, he couldn't tell. Soon, he prayed, he would be working for a new home secretary, and his inability to read Alexia's moods would no longer matter. Sir Edward Manning hadn't heard from Sergei Milescu in weeks. He'd dared to hope that the nightmare was over—that now that Alexia had immersed herself in so much public scandal, Sergei's mysterious masters no longer needed any additional, private information from him. But the lingering doubt still cast a shadow over his every waking moment, like a cancerous tumor that could return at any time.

The blacked-out car pulled out into the street, gliding past the assembled media like a shadow.

"Very good, Home Secretary. To the hospital it is. But we must call Henry Whitman on our way. The government will need to make some sort of official statement to the media before tomorrow morning."

Alexia gazed out of the window as they left the city. "Don't worry, Edward. By tomorrow morning it will all be over."

"Home Secretary?"

"My family needs me. I'm going to resign."

It was all Sir Edward Manning could do not to weep with relief.

THE DOCTOR WAS KIND AND SCRUPULOUSLY polite. But he was also firm.

"There's absolutely no way I can let you see her, Mrs. De Vere."

"But I'm her mother."

"I know that."

"She thinks I've done something terrible. That's what's caused all this. But she's wrong. She needs to know the truth."

"Roxanne is extremely unwell, Mrs. De Vere. She's experienced what we call a psychotic break. Above all else she needs rest and calm, and to avoid all stress triggers."

"And that's what I am, is it? That's what I've been reduced to. A 'stress trigger'?"

"I'm afraid so."

"And the truth be damned, is that it?"

She was angry, but not with the doctor. It was her own lies that had brought her and her family here, well intentioned or not.

Back in the car she turned her frustrations on Edward. "Any word on Teddy?"

"No, Home Secretary. Not yet."

"Then take me back to London."

"Of course, Home Secretary."

"And stop calling me that! I've already told you I'm going to resign. In fact, give me the phone. I'll do it right now."

Sir Edward Manning looked alarmed. "Are you sure that's wise?"

"Just do as I ask!"

"No disrespect, Home Sec . . . Alexia. But you're very emotional. Wouldn't it be better if you spoke to the prime minister in a calmer frame of mind?"

"I am *not* emotional," Alexia shouted. And without warning, she burst into tears.

*

For the next twenty-four hours, Sir Edward Manning took over everything. Rather than take her home to Cheyne Walk, where scores of reporters were bound to be waiting, he checked Alexia into Blakes Hotel in South Kensington and put her to bed with a strong sleeping pill. When she awoke, disorientated but deeply rested, it was almost noon.

"The prime minister was very understanding," Sir Edward told her over a late breakfast of croissants and strong black coffee. "He's expecting your call this afternoon. I've drawn up a formal resignation letter, whenever you're ready to take a look at it."

"Thank you." Alexia took the proffered sheet of paper gratefully. "I'm sorry if I was rude to you yesterday, Edward."

"Think nothing of it, Home Secretary. I quite understand."

"And Teddy? Is he back at Kingsmere? Does he know where I am?"

"Ah, yes. Unfortunately he's still being held by Thames Valley police."

Alexia's eyes widened. "They kept him overnight?"

"It appears so."

"On what grounds?"

"Further questioning, I assume. I've arranged a meeting for you with Angus Grey at two-thirty P.M. It's at his offices in Gray's Inn Road. I tried to do it here but Mr. Gray has court at four P.M., then drives straight back to Oxford to see Teddy, so it wasn't possible."

"That's wonderful, Edward, thank you so much." Alexia took all this in. She felt immensely relieved to be seeing Angus. Angus would know what to do. "And the hospital?" she asked Sir Edward Manning. "I don't suppose you had a chance . . ."

"I called both hospitals and inquired after both Roxanne and Michael."

Alexia looked at him hopefully.

"No change, I'm afraid."

Her face fell.

Sir Edward Manning thought: *She seems vulnerable this morning. Fragile. If only voters and colleagues could see this side to her. The side that cares more about her children and her husband than the fact that she's about to end her political career.*

Still, it was too late now. Alexia had lost her political career. And Sir Edward Manning was about to get his life back.

ANGUS GREY, QC'S OFFICE REEKED OF power and privilege the way a racehorse reeks of sweat. From the oak-paneled walls, to the Oxford University Boat Club photographs on the wall, to the signed pictures of Angus with various Tory Party grandees that littered the desk, it was a room that reflected its owner's elite, establishment background to a T.

Angus Grey himself was a fit, still-attractive man in his early sixties with gunmetal-gray hair, a light tan from a recent week's break on the Italian Riviera, and a pair of intense blue eyes, which he focused now wholly on Alexia.

"My dear girl. You look tired. How are the ribs?"

"Fine," Alexia said truthfully. With so much else going on, her brain seemed to have tuned out the pain from her bullet wound.

"Good. Well, you must keep up your strength. Joan, bring Mrs. De Vere some tea, would you? And a slice of Battenburg."

Alexia sank down into a leather chesterfield sofa and closed her eyes for a moment.

"Sir Edward Manning tells me you've resigned." Angus had known Alexia a long time. He could afford to be direct.

She nodded. "They'll announce it tomorrow morning. Although if you listen closely, you can probably hear the trade and industry secretary rubbing his hands together with glee as we speak."

Angus smiled.

"I can't go on. I'm finished politically. And even if I weren't, too much is happening at home."

"I quite understand."

"First Michael, now this. Andrew Beesley, dead. Just when I thought he couldn't cause my family any more heartache! Roxanne's in utter pieces, blaming me. What on earth's happening, Angus? The world's gone mad. My world anyway."

"Best to tackle these things one at a time," Angus Grey said sensibly. "Let's talk about Teddy."

"Yes. Why haven't they released him yet? No one will tell me anything."

"I don't think there's anything fundamental to worry about. I was with him until eleven last night, and again this morning for two hours of questions. He admitted to offering the boy money to go back to Australia all those years ago, so your stories dovetail completely."

"That's because they aren't stories," said Alexia. "Is he a suspect?"

"Yes," the QC said bluntly. "Have you heard from Roxanne?"

Alexia slumped down in her chair, defeated. "No. They won't let me see her. What am I going to do, Angus? I feel completely lost."

Angus Grey leaned across the desk. "Try not to panic. Look at this rationally. Roxanne's in a safe place, getting the help she needs. As for Teddy, this isn't pleasant, but it's par for the course. The boy was murdered, okay? And he was buried on your land. By your own admission, you and

341

Teddy wanted rid of him. It's only natural that the police would focus their suspicions on your family first."

"It may be natural, Angus. It just happens to be wrong."

"What about Michael?"

Alexia stiffened. "What about him?"

"He didn't approve of this boy Andrew either, did he? Is it possible the two of them met to discuss things and got into a fight? They might have been drinking. Things could have got out of hand."

"Andrew was killed with a gun, Angus. At least that's what the police told Teddy and me. Two bullets to the back of the head. That's not a 'fight that got out of hand.' That's an execution."

"Is it possible that Michael . . . ?"

"No." Alexia shook her head vehemently. "My son isn't capable of that."

Angus Grey raised an eyebrow but Alexia was unequivocal. "No."

"Think about it, Alexia. Michael's unconscious and likely to remain so. If he were to be convicted of this, he'd know nothing about it. Nothing would change."

"Except that he'd have been branded a murderer. Falsely branded."

"Okay. But if they pin this on Teddy, he'll go down for life."

Alexia laughed despairingly. "This is insanity! Neither of them killed Andrew Beesley."

"How do you know?"

"Because I know them, Angus. I know them!" With an effort, Alexia calmed herself down. "Look. I don't know who killed Beesley and I don't know why whoever it was buried him at Kingsmere. Maybe they hoped to frame me for the murder? There are plenty of crackpots out there."

"It's possible, of course."

"I daresay Roxanne wasn't the first girl Andrew had ever deceived or hurt. Who knows how many enemies the boy may have made."

"Yes, but to dispose of the body in *your* grounds? There must be a link, a connection to your family."

"Not necessarily. Maybe the killer was simply a local who thought the corpse was unlikely to be disturbed in an obscure part of the estate. They were right, in a way. It was the pagoda that brought the remains to the surface. If that had never been built . . . *or*, if it had been finished, and the concrete foundations poured like they were supposed to be . . . no one would ever have found him. He'd have had his own, private mausoleum. Which was more than he deserved, by the way. He was a thoroughly unpleasant young man."

She watched Angus Grey's brilliant mind ticking.

"You mentioned the possibility of somebody trying to frame you. Is there anyone in particular you were thinking of? Anyone with a vendetta against you or a reason to go to such drastic lengths?"

"No. The Patel people, I suppose. But I don't think they'd kill a man just to get back at me." Alexia thought about it. "There *were* a couple of incidents around the time I first took office. Teddy's dog was poisoned."

"Where? At Kingsmere?"

Alexia nodded. "It was horrible actually. Poor Teddy was terribly cut up at the time."

"I'll bet he was."

"Yes, but come on, Angus. It was a dog. Not quite the same thing as slaughtering a man in cold blood, is it?"

*

343

Sir Edward Manning looked at his watch as he hurried along the Strand.

Two forty-five. He couldn't be long. He must be available when the home secretary got out of her lawyer's meeting. But he needed to give Sergei the good news.

Alexia De Vere was about to resign.

Sergei's bosses, whoever they were, would get what they wanted.

In the back of his mind, Sir Edward Manning feared that this might not be the last he heard of Sergei Milescu. The bastard had those pictures, after all. He could still blackmail him, still use him for his own ends in the future, if he chose to. But for now, at least, the immediate danger was past. Sir Edward sensed that Sergei had become as scared as he was. He would want to know this. He would be grateful that Edward had told him personally, as soon as he was able.

Sergei's new flat was in a modern building on the Embankment. While not luxurious, it was certainly far more than he could afford on his salary as a House of Commons janitor. Running up the stairs to the second floor, Sir Edward Manning wondered briefly who was paying Sergei's rent. Then he put the thought out of his mind. By tomorrow morning, it wouldn't matter.

There was no bell, so he knocked firmly on the front door. To his surprise, it opened.

"Sergei?"

It wasn't like him to be so lax with security. Then again, the boy could drink, especially when he was agitated, as he had been recently. *He's probably passed out on the bed with a bottle of Stoli.*

But no. The bedroom was empty, a pile of neatly folded clothes the only sign that Sergei had been home at all. *Did he leave in a hurry and forget to close the front door behind him?*

Maybe. But again, there was nothing lying around to suggest such a rush. Everything was as it should be, ordered, organized, clean.

Sir Edward Manning pushed open the door to the bathroom. If Sergei had left town, he'd have taken his toiletries, his personal things. The boy's mind might be a depraved sewer, but his hygiene habits were irreproachable.

The bath was on a raised platform, a sort of marble pedestal. The first thing Sir Edward Manning noticed was that it was overflowing.

The second thing he noticed was that it wasn't overflowing with water.

It was overflowing with blood.

Sergei Milescu's corpse bobbed grotesquely in the water, sliced down the middle like a butchered pig. He'd been disemboweled.

Sir Edward Manning turned and ran.

EMERGING FROM THE QC'S OFFICE INTO the bright afternoon light, Alexia walked down Gray's Inn Road with no sense of where she was going or why. With Teddy by her side, she felt strong, capable, resilient. Without him, and without her political career to anchor her and give her focus, she was lost, drifting, as insubstantial and helpless as a feather in the wind.

I'm frightened.

The realization came as a shock. She stopped. Part of her wanted to run back to Angus Grey's office, to have Angus reassure her that Teddy was bound to be released tonight, that it would all be all right. The police could only hold him for forty-eight hours unless they charged him. But Angus would be on his way to court by now.

She could go to Oxford and wait for news, but where would she stay? The thought of another night in a hotel depressed her deeply. *I can't live my life on the run.* But she could hardly go home either, not with her resignation about to be announced tomorrow. Kingsmere was still a crime scene, and would be crawling with police and news reporters for the next few weeks at least. Cheyne Walk was her best bet, but that too would be surrounded by journalists awaiting news of her resignation like wolves slavering at the prospect of fresh meat. *I can't face them yet. Not alone. Not without Teddy.*

"Excuse me."

An unseen hand tapped her on the shoulder. She jumped.

"What? What do you want?"

The hand belonged to a woman. She looked at Alexia curiously.

"Your phone's ringing."

In a daze, Alexia pulled the cell out of her bag. "Hello?"

Lucy Meyer's voice was like a message from another planet. "Alexia. Thank Gaaad you picked up. What on earth's going on over there? We saw something on the news about a murder at Kingsmere, but Summer hasn't told us anything. Is it true?"

"It's true," Alexia said bleakly. "They found a body. It was Andrew, Roxie's ex."

Lucy gasped. "No way."

"I know. It's insanity, Luce. The police are still questioning Teddy."

"But surely they don't think Teddy—"

"I don't know what they think. I've resigned from the cabinet."

"Oh my God, Alexia, no! You can't."

"I had to. Roxanne's had a collapse. I really . . . I can't

346

begin to describe how bad things are." Her voice was breaking. Aware that people on the street were staring at her, Alexia ducked into an alleyway. "I don't know what to do. I don't know where to go."

"I do," Lucy said immediately. "Come here."

Alexia pictured Lucy in her kitchen at Martha's Vineyard, apron on, hands covered in flour. How she longed for that wholesomeness, that normality, that safe, stable predictable cocoon in which Lucy Meyer lived her life. A life without ambition, without risk, without tragedy.

"You're so sweet."

"I'm not sweet," said Lucy. "I'm serious. Come here. You need to recuperate anyway. It was only a couple of weeks ago that you got shot, for God's sake. You're not superwoman."

"So it would seem," Alexia said sadly.

"So do it. Get on the plane. Ride out the storm somewhere private and far away. Summer said you were thinking of coming anyway."

"I was. But that was before."

Why am I saying no? What's wrong with me? This is exactly what I want. What I need. I need to be far away. I need to be safe.

"I can't. Thanks for the offer, but Teddy's still in Oxford being questioned, and Roxie's in a terrible way." An insistent *beep beep* on the line told her someone else was trying to get through. "That might be the hospital," Alexia told Lucy. "Or Teddy. I've gotta go."

With infinite reluctance, she dropped Lucy Meyer's call. "Hello?"

"Are you still in the vicinity?" Angus Grey sounded shaken.

"Yes. I thought you were in court."

347

"I should be. I *will* be in five minutes. But I just received a call from Thames Valley police."

"Oh, thank God. They've let him go. Is he on his way to Kingsmere?"

"I'm afraid not, Alexia."

"Then what?"

"Teddy's been charged with murder."

For a moment Alexia slumped back against the wall of the alley, winded with shock. But she quickly pulled herself together.

"That's impossible. That's ridiculous. You said so yourself, they don't have any evidence."

Angus Grey said, "Unfortunately, they don't need any evidence. Not anymore. Teddy's made a full confession."

CHAPTER THIRTY-TWO

THE ROOM WAS MORE LIKE AN office than a prison cell. Teddy sat at a desk, his legs stretched out in front of him as if he were at home in front of the fire, while Alexia paced nervously back and forth.

Things had moved quickly. By the time Alexia and Angus Grey arrived in Oxford, Teddy had already been in front of a crown court judge and remanded in custody pending trial. In less than an hour he'd be transferred to a secure wing of Oxford Prison.

Alexia asked, "Is it true?"

"Is what true, my dear?"

"Did you really kill Andrew?"

She felt as if she were talking to a stranger. As if this were all some awful, bizarre dream and she would wake up at any moment.

"I did," Teddy said calmly. "Somebody had to. I hadn't planned to confess, but there was no other way. Not with that dreadful man Wilmott on the scent, like a dog with a bone. If I'd kept quiet any longer, it would only have dragged things out. I didn't want the family name sullied any more than it needs to be. Better to get the thing over with now."

Alexia clutched her head. *This can't be happening.*

Angus Grey said, "Can you tell us exactly what happened, Teddy?"

"Surely." Teddy smiled, as if recounting an amusing anecdote. "I went to meet Beesley at the Garrick, as Alexia knows. I offered him money to push off back to Australia."

Alexia nodded. "He took the money. I checked our accounts myself. That check was cashed."

"So it was, my dear."

"And he moved back to Australia."

"He did. But some vestige of conscience must have got the better of him, because about a month later, blow me down if the little shit didn't come back. I remember it vividly. I was at Paddington station about to catch the train when I felt a tap on my shoulder. I turned around and there he was, bold as brass. Beesley. Told me he'd had a change of heart, that he was in love with Roxie and he wanted to return the three hundred grand."

Angus Grey asked, "What happened then?"

"Well, I was shocked, obviously. Had to think on my feet. He was talking about marrying Roxie. Clearly I couldn't let that happen."

"But why not? He came back for her, Teddy!" Alexia had tears in her eyes.

Teddy's expression darkened. "Came back for more money, you mean. He knew we'd never cut her off. That if he married her, he'd be set for life. Besides, darling, be reasonable. The man was a tennis coach! Hardly an appropriate match for a De Vere."

Alexia couldn't believe what she was hearing. The man opposite her looked like Teddy. He sounded like Teddy. But the things he was implying—that he'd murdered a man out of nothing more than snobbery—that

350

wasn't the Teddy De Vere that she knew. Thought she knew.

Teddy went on. "I told him to come and see me the following day, at Kingsmere. We'd go shooting and talk about things."

"Did you intend to kill him?" Angus Grey asked bluntly.

"I did. I was worried I might not be able to go through with it. I didn't know for sure if I could . . ."

"If you could shoot him?" Alexia whispered.

"Yes. But it was easier than I thought. He was such an oaf, trying to play the big man, telling me he would marry Roxanne with or without my permission, that there was nothing I could do to stop him. You should have heard him, Alexia. If ever a fellow got what was coming to him, it was Andrew bloody Beesley."

Angus and Alexia exchanged horrified glances. Neither of them had ever seen this side of Teddy before. He told the story without a shred of remorse.

"What happened after you shot him?" Angus asked calmly. As Teddy's senior counsel, he needed to have a handle on all the facts, however damning.

"Nothing happened," said Teddy. "That was the beauty of it. I dug a hole, buried him, and that was that. I kept waiting for something to happen, for the police or his family to knock on the door. But there was nothing."

Alexia looked away. She remembered a time, long ago, when she too had waited for retribution, for justice that never came. Thinking about it now, she could still feel the prickle of anxiety on her skin, the gnawing fear churning in her stomach and tightening like a knot in her chest. *How did I not see that in Teddy? I was there. How did I miss the signs?*

351

"Then poor old Rox had her accident," said Teddy. "To be perfectly honest, I forgot about Beesley after that. Roxanne was all that mattered."

"You forgot?" asked Angus.

"I'm afraid so. The years passed. I had no reason to remember. Beesley was dead and buried and the secret was safe. I didn't think I'd left him so close to the pagoda site, but I suppose I must have. In any case, when I buried him it was far too deep for an animal to uncover. Michael must have found the body and moved it."

Alexia shook her head. She had to believe in Michael's innocence at least. "No. He would have said something."

Teddy said gently, "I suspect that he recognized the watch, just like his sister did, and put two and two together. Remember, as far as Michael knew, it was *you* who'd scared Beesley off, not me. That was the story we agreed on, you see," Teddy explained to Angus. "For Roxie's sake. Michael probably thought *you'd* done Andrew in. I imagine he was trying to protect you, Alexia."

Alexia began pacing again, walking faster and faster until she was almost running. Teddy's theory had a hideous ring of truth to it.

Michael crashed that bike believing that I'd done it. That I'd executed that boy in cold blood. That's why he was so distracted. He thinks I'm a murderer, and now I may never have a chance to tell him I'm not.

Angus Grey tried to be practical. "All right, Teddy. Well, you've been very honest. As far as sentencing goes, I think the key will be to acknowledge that honesty and to make it clear that you sincerely regret what you did."

Teddy looked confused. "Regret it? Why should I regret it, Angus? My duty, my purpose in life, is to protect my family and to preserve the good name of the De Veres.

Andrew Beesley got what was coming to him. He threatened the family and I neutralized that threat."

Alexia started to cry. *What happened to my Teddy, my gentle giant?*

"Angus, would you leave us for a moment?" said Teddy. As soon as he and Alexia were alone, he put his arms around her, hugging her tightly. "Why are you crying?"

"Because I don't know you!" she sobbed despairingly.

"Yes you do," said Teddy. "Everything I've ever done, I've done to protect our family. I killed Andrew to protect Roxanne. I've killed for you too, you know."

At first Alexia thought she'd misheard him. "What?"

"Oh, come now," said Teddy. "You don't mean to tell me that you never suspected."

Alexia's head was spinning. She felt as if she were drunk, or high, two feelings she hadn't experienced in forty years. "Suspected what, Teddy?"

Teddy looked her in the eye and said:

"That it was me who killed Billy Hamlin."

CHAPTER THIRTY-THREE

The blood drained from Alexia's face.

"*You* killed Billy?"

"I had to. I did it for you, darling, don't you see? He was going to bring you down, to dredge up your past and all the scandal you've spent your life trying to hide. I couldn't let that happen."

Alexia sank down onto a hard metal chair. Her knees would no longer support her.

"You know about my past?"

"Of course." Teddy smiled. "I've always known."

"What do you know, exactly?"

"Everything. I know everything. You don't think that I would marry a woman without knowing who she was? That I would put the De Vere family name at risk, without knowing what I was getting into? I know that you were born Antonia Gilletti."

Alexia gasped.

"I know that you're American by birth. That you dabbled in drugs in your youth. That you were involved in a murder trial after the death of a little boy named Handemeyer. That Billy Hamlin was your lover."

"Stop. Please stop."

Alexia was shaking. It felt so wrong, hearing Teddy say these things. All these years she'd been terrified about him finding out about her past. Terrified of losing the one good, decent thing in her life. But he knew! He'd known all along. The fear, the deceit, the loneliness. It had all been for nothing.

All these years, I felt guilty for having fooled him. But it was really Teddy who fooled me. He knows me inside out. And I don't know him at all.

"Don't look so sad," said Teddy, reading her thoughts. "I loved you from the first moment I saw you, you know, behind the bar at the Coach and Horses. I'd heard rumors about the beautiful girl temping for Clive Leinster, and I wanted to see what all the fuss was about. Of course, once I saw you, it was clear. You were utterly out of my league."

"That's not true," said Alexia on autopilot.

"Of course it's true. I knew from the beginning that you weren't in love with me," Teddy continued with a sweet, self-deprecating smile. "Why would you be, a boring old duffer like me? Or young duffer, as I suppose I was then. But I also knew I had to have you. Naturally my family disapproved. They hadn't envisaged a barmaid becoming the next Lady De Vere. But I didn't care. Nothing would have stopped me marrying you, Alexia. I want to be clear about that."

Teddy took her hand and kissed it. Alexia tried not to think about that same hand stabbing poor Billy Hamlin in the heart, or pulling the trigger that ended the life of young Andrew Beesley.

"But I am a De Vere," Teddy went on. "And I take that seriously. I needed to know what I was getting myself, and the family, into. I needed to know more about you. So I did some digging."

"How?" asked Alexia. All these years she'd been in the public eye, and not once had a single journalist come close to unearthing the truth about her past. How on earth had Teddy managed to learn the truth, and without her hearing a thing about it? Whom had he talked to?

"One has one's ways," he said cryptically. "It's hard to change your identity completely without leaving some form of a paper trail. You told me you'd studied at UCLA, so I started there. It didn't take me long to discover that you hadn't always been Alexia Parker. Once I unearthed Toni Gilletti, the rest emerged in dribs and drabs. I found the formal warnings you'd been given for drug offenses and shoplifting in your teens. Nothing so terrible there. Then I stumbled upon Camp Williams, and the Handemeyer murder trial. There were rumors that Billy Hamlin had covered for you about the little boy's death, that you'd somehow been involved in it."

"Why didn't you ask me? Confront me?"

Teddy shrugged. "Because you clearly didn't want me to know. Besides, I didn't care about any of that. It all happened long before I met you. What mattered to me was that Hamlin must have loved you very deeply. If the rumors were true, and he took the blame. That's quite a sacrifice."

"Yes," said Alexia. "It is. It was."

"I assumed that when Billy got out of prison, he might come looking for you. So I decided to keep an eye on him. Nothing sinister, mark you. I simply made sure I knew when he was due for parole, that sort of thing. I didn't want him spoiling things between us. I didn't know how you felt about him."

"Oh, Teddy! Why didn't you talk to me?"

"For the same reason you didn't talk to me, I imagine," Teddy said. "Fear. I was terrified of losing you, Alexia." Reaching out, he stroked her cheek tenderly. "Anyway, as it turned out I needn't have worried. Not then, anyway. After he was released, he sniffed around your old haunts for a while, trying to find you. But after a few dead ends, he gave up. Got married, started a business, had a child. He seemed to be happy and I believed, I hoped, that that would be that. Unfortunately, it wasn't. You were appointed home secretary, and everything changed. Barely a week later, Hamlin shows up at Kingsmere like a rotten penny."

Slowly it dawned on Alexia. "You thought he'd come back to blackmail me."

"Why else would he have come, after all this time?"

"I don't know," Alexia said sadly. "I never gave him a chance to tell me. But I didn't want him harmed. I didn't want him dead, for Christ's sake!"

"Keep your voice down, darling," said Teddy. "Remember where we are."

Alexia looked around the holding cell with its stark walls and functional office furniture. In a few minutes someone would come and take Teddy away, lock him up for another murder. It was all too much to take in.

"If Hamlin had stayed away, got on with his own life in New York, everything could have continued just as it had been. But like Andrew Beesley, your friend Mr. Hamlin had an eye for the main chance. It was obvious what he wanted, darling: to extort money and drag the De Vere family name through the mud. I wasn't about to let that happen. Not after all our hard work."

"But, *Teddy*!" Alexia pulled at her hair in desperation. "You don't *know* any of that. What if Andrew really did love Roxanne? What if Billy Hamlin wasn't trying to hurt me at all? Maybe there was something he needed to tell me. Maybe he wanted my help, have you thought of that? He never asked me for money."

"Only because he never got the chance."

"He was such a gentle man," Alexia said sadly. "You didn't have to kill him."

Now it was Teddy who became exasperated. "Don't defend him! Don't you dare! He never loved you like I do, Alexia. Never! I did it to protect you. I did it out of love. Do you think you'd have had the career you've had, the life you've had, if it weren't for my protection? If I hadn't been there keeping your secrets, covering your tracks? I *made* you who you are, Alexia. I *gave* you your life."

It was true. Alexia had often thought so herself. She owed Teddy so much. She just hadn't realized that the price for his love had been so high. Two innocent men had paid for it with their lives.

"What about Billy's daughter, Jenny?"

Teddy's eyes narrowed. "What about her?"

"I'm assuming you know she's dead? Murdered, like her father. Drowned, in fact. You seem to know everything else."

Teddy shook his head. "No. I didn't know that."

"So you're telling me you had nothing to do with what happened to that girl?"

"Of course not. I just told you, this is the first I've heard of it."

He could easily have been lying. But something deep inside told Alexia that Teddy's ignorance was genuine. She didn't know whether to feel relieved or disappointed. At this point it would almost be easier to believe that Teddy had murdered Jenny Hamlin. That his warped sense of justice and family pride had been behind all the bad things that had happened.

"I'm sorry, Alexia."

She looked down and saw that her hand was still in his. Not knowing what else to do, Alexia left it there. But the comfort that hand had once held for her was gone now, gone forever.

Like everything else. Like my children, my career, my marriage, my future.

Piece by piece, brick by brick, the fortress that Alexia De Vere had built around her life was being dismantled by some unseen hand, some cruel, relentless fate.

"You haven't told the police, have you? About Billy."

Teddy pulled his hand away. "No. And nor must you. They've no reason to connect either of us to that case, and we've no reason to give them one."

"Yes we do, Teddy. We should tell the truth."

"Nonsense, Alexia. What's truth compared to family honor? Compared to reputation? If the police knew about Billy, they'd have to know about your past life. Is that what you want? Is it?"

Before Alexia could answer, the door opened. Two court officers walked in, followed by Angus Grey.

"Time to go."

Angus wrapped a comforting arm around Alexia's shoulder as they left the building. "Is there anyone I can call? You shouldn't be alone tonight."

"Thanks," said Alexia, "but there really isn't."

It was true. Teddy had always been her rock, her protector. But in the harsh light of the truth, he'd melted away, like butter in the sun. And now he was behind bars, unreachable. Both Michael and Roxanne were lost to her. There were people who would give her a bed, of course, out of pity, or propriety, or some other British notion of doing "the done thing." Sir Edward Manning, other political colleagues with whom Alexia had forged alliances during her long years in the trenches. But no one she considered a true friend. Not here anyway.

"Should I take you home?" asked Angus.

Home, thought Alexia. *Where is home?*

In that instant, she knew where she should go.

"Can I get you anything, love? Cup of tea? Some toast?"

Summer Meyer smiled at the ICU nurse but shook her head. It amused her the way the British considered a "nice cup of tea" to be the panacea for all life's ills. Terminal cancer? I'll put the kettle on. Boyfriend in a coma? Have a cuppa. It was an attitude that reminded her of her mother and home, although with Lucy food was the great cure-all: muffins, cookies, cupcakes. Lucy Meyer was a big believer in the healing power of baked goods.

But not even Lucy Meyer's magic baking could have handled the latest twist in the De Vere family's falling fortunes. The discovery of Andrew Beesley's body in a shallow grave on the home secretary's estate was *the* story on all the British news channels. Alexia had resigned, and now Teddy—*Teddy!*—had been charged with Andrew's murder. A less likely killer than the soft, warmhearted Teddy De Vere would be hard to imagine. Although in some ways picturing Teddy as a killer was easier than recasting Alexia as a selfless, loving mother. Apparently she'd concocted the story about driving Andrew away, taking the blame for years solely to protect Roxie's bond with her father.

Summer stroked Michael's limp hand. "I love you," she whispered. "But your family is insane. You do know that, right?"

"Not all of us, surely?"

Alexia stood in the doorway. Thin and stooped, she wore baggy trousers and a white cardigan that hung off her bony frame like feathers on a dying bird. Her usually perfect hair was limp and tangled, and her eyes and cheeks bore the hollow look of acute suffering. If Summer had to pick one word to describe her, it would have been a word she had never associated with Michael's mother before: *frail*.

"You look terrible."

"Thank you, Summer."

"No! I mean . . . I'm sorry. That came out wrong." Summer blushed. "Please. Sit down."

"I'm not disturbing you?"

"Not at all." Summer released Michael's hand and Alexia took it, tracing slow spirals across her son's palm with her thumb. "Any change?"

Summer shook her head.

Both women sat in silence for a while. Then Summer said, "Mom said you might be flying out to the Vineyard. Laying low for a while."

Alexia nodded. "I can't stay here. The press won't give me a minute's rest." She gazed at her son's inert body. "Do you think he can hear us?"

"I don't know. They say not. Sometimes I feel as if he can but . . . I don't know." Summer took a deep breath. "I heard they charged Teddy."

"Uh-huh. It's like a soap opera, isn't it?" Alexia giggled inappropriately, high on exhaustion. "Except that the characters and the plotlines are all real. Andrew Beesley's really dead. Michael's really lying here, like this. Teddy's really in jail. He confessed, you know."

"I heard."

"I never liked Andrew. But I hadn't realized just how much Teddy hated him. To shoot a man in cold blood like that." She shook her head disbelievingly. "That's not the man I married. It makes no sense to me."

Summer said thoughtfully, "I think it makes sense. Just

not the sort of sense we want to acknowledge. I'm not defending it, obviously. But I understand. People do crazy things when they love someone."

Alexia smiled wanly. "You're a smart girl. I can see why Michael fell in love with you."

"I misjudged you, Alexia," Summer blurted out. "I didn't know, about Teddy and Andrew, and you taking the blame so that Roxie wouldn't hate her father."

"Of course you didn't," Alexia said kindly. "Nobody knew. That was the point."

"I don't think I could do something that unselfish."

"You're here every day, aren't you? I'd call that pretty unselfish. It's more than I've managed to do. And I'm his mother."

"You had a big job. You couldn't just leave it."

"I could have, and I should have. But what's done is done. The irony is that now that I've actually resigned, I don't care at all. Isn't it bizarre how it takes awful, horrendous things like this to make one see what's important in life?"

Summer nodded. Alexia didn't take her eyes off Michael.

"Teddy thinks he must have found Andrew's body and reburied it, when he was excavating the pagoda. He kept it quiet to protect me." She stifled a sob. "That was the 'secret' he was hinting at to you. My son crashed that bike believing that I'd murdered Andrew Beesley."

"We don't know that, Alexia."

"It was bad enough, Roxie thinking the worst of me for all those years. But at least I'll have a chance to put things right with her, eventually. Michael might never wake up. I might never be able to tell him the truth."

Summer put her arms around Alexia. She could feel every one of her ribs, like bars on a xylophone.

"He *will* wake up. I'm sure of it. I'll leave you for a while."

Alone with her son, Alexia began to talk. She thought she'd feel awkward and foolish, but now that she was here, she found the silence comforting. Michael's presence was enough.

"So many secrets, my darling. So many lies. And I started it all! I thought I could run from the past, from my mistakes. But there's no escape."

The machine at Michael's side inflated his lungs with air then emptied them again, its gentle, rhythmic whooshing filling the silence, like waves lapping against the shore.

"I'm so desperately, desperately sorry, Michael. Please forgive me."

Michael De Vere had no answer to give his mother.

He simply lay there, motionless as a corpse.

PART IV

CHAPTER THIRTY-FOUR

SPRING CAME SLOWLY ON THE CAPE. While the rest of Massachusetts burst forth in a riot of color and warmth and life the moment February turned to March, winter clung to the Cape and islands like a wizened old man clinging to life. Long after the last of the snow had melted, Martha's Vineyard was still being whipped by bitter Canadian winds. Any primrose or daffodil foolish enough to allow its head to peek above the soil was dashed into oblivion for its presumptuousness, and islanders continued wearing their gloves, scarves, and mufflers as they went about their errands in town. When the long-awaited warmer days finally arrived in early May, the mood among the locals was euphoric.

Alexia De Vere felt particularly privileged to witness the late changing of the season. Unlike her friend Lucy Meyer, Alexia hadn't minded the prolonged winter. Somehow the bitter weather and heavy blanket of snow had felt like an extra layer of protection from the cruel world that lay beyond the island's shores, the world Alexia was escaping from, hiding from like a prisoner on the run. At the same time, spring's new beginning seemed to echo the sense of renewal she felt inside.

Physically she'd made a remarkable recovery from Gilbert Drake's attempt on her life. Her ribs had healed completely. A small, half-inch scar where the bullet had pierced her side was the only reminder that the incident had ever happened. For a woman her age, she was very, very lucky. But it was the emotional shifts that affected her the most profoundly. Huge, important chapters in Alexia's life had come to an end. Her political career was over. So was her marriage, at least in the form she had always known it. Teddy was still in custody in Oxford, awaiting sentencing—cutbacks in the British courts meant there was a huge backlog of cases and *Crown v. De Vere* was unlikely to be heard before late summer.

Relations between Alexia and Teddy were cordial, even warm. They wrote letters to each other about the weather and the garden and Teddy's prison routines, never mentioning Andrew Beesley or Billy Hamlin or any other "difficult" subject. There was nothing to say anyway—nothing that would help. Reverting to their old way of being seemed the easiest and safest course of action. Alexia had long since decided that she was going to stand by Teddy. He had kept her secrets faithfully for forty-odd years. Now it was her turn to return the favor. Being away had helped her to detach emotionally, to push thoughts of Billy Hamlin and Andrew Beesley and everything that had happened out of her mind and to focus on the present. She tried not to think about the past or the future, although she knew that Teddy would go to prison for a long, long time and the thought scared her.

From now on, I'll have to be my own rock. Rebuild my own life. Start afresh. I've done it before, and I'll do it again.

The hardest part was the children. Michael had now been moved to a specialized critical care unit in London.

The doctors had been as kind as they could be to Alexia, but she knew what the move meant: Michael would never get better. There was no more hope. At some point she knew she would have to face reality and turn off the life support machines. But not now. Not yet. She wasn't ready. And there were also Summer Meyer's feelings to consider.

Meanwhile a shroud of mental health professionals had descended over Roxie's life, shutting Alexia out completely. Apparently Roxie was staying at an "assisted living" facility somewhere in the west of England. But Alexia was expressly forbidden to visit or even to know her exact whereabouts, on psychiatrist's orders.

I gave birth to her! Alexia wanted to scream. *I love her. Who the hell are you to tell me I can't see my own child?* But she knew that Roxie was not a child, and that Roxie herself was the one who'd insisted on banishing her. Perhaps a period of separation was best for Roxie's recovery. But it still hurt, a raw wound that bled and bled and that no amount of distance, or time, would ever fully heal.

Meanwhile the radio silence from the people in Alexia's old political life was deafening. She hadn't spoken to Henry Whitman since the day she resigned, and not one of her cabinet colleagues or former constituency staff had called to see how she was doing. Edward, dear Edward, had sent a couple of gossipy e-mails. But that was it. After twenty years of devotion to the Tory Party, such utter abandonment ought to have hurt desperately. But it didn't. On the contrary, it felt liberating. Walking the deserted, windswept beaches and cranberry bogs of Martha's Vineyard, sometimes alone, sometimes with Lucy, Alexia could smell her future in the crisp, wintery air.

Perhaps, despite what she'd said to Michael, she really

could leave the past behind this time. Reinvent herself and start again, far away.

This time around, the past seemed willing to let her go.

LUCY MEYER WATCHED ALEXIA AS SHE pored over her computer screen. It was only a few months ago that Lucy thought she'd lost her friend for good. That some crazy taxi driver's bullet was going to rob her of one of the most important people in her life. But Alexia had survived. She'd recovered and she'd come out here, where Lucy could keep an eye on her. "You're not going to tell me, are you?" Lucy mumbled through a mouthful of cake crumbs.

"Tell you what?" Alexia didn't look up.

Lucy had popped over, ostensibly to borrow a hoe for the garden, and ended up staying for coffee and cake. But from the minute she arrived, Alexia had been itching to get back to her MacBook.

"What you're working on? Beavering away over there, all secret squirrel."

Alexia grinned. "So what am I, a squirrel or a beaver?"

"You're a politician, honey: avoiding the question."

"Not anymore I'm not."

"So what are you working on? It's not Teddy's case, is it? Because I really think you need to put that out of your mind. There's nothing you can do from here."

"I have put it out of my mind." Alexia shut the computer and joined Lucy at the kitchen island. "And it's not Teddy's case."

Lucy had an uneasy feeling. "What then?"

"It's . . . something else I've been working on," Alexia said evasively. "It's not important."

Lucy raised an eyebrow and waited.

"Okay, okay." Alexia capitulated. "It's a cold case I'm looking into. You remember I told you about Billy Hamlin, the boy who—"

"I remember," Lucy cut her off.

"And you know he was killed?"

Lucy nodded.

"Well, so was his daughter. Jennifer. She was murdered last year, in truly horrific circumstances, and no one seems to have any idea why, or who did it, or anything."

Lucy frowned. "Okay. Well, that's sad. But what does it have to do with you?"

"When Billy came to England those times, when he tried to see me and I turned him away, he was trying to tell me something about his daughter. I think he was scared something bad was going to happen to her."

"And then something bad did happen to her."

"Yes."

"And you feel responsible?"

"Not responsible, exactly. But I feel I owe it to Billy to help now."

"Why?"

"Because I didn't help then," Alexia said simply. "I could have. I should have. But I turned my back on him. Maybe, if I'd listened, Jenny would still be alive today."

"That's crazy talk," Lucy said robustly. "This has nothing to do with you."

"I started looking into Jenny's murder last year, back when I was still in office. But there was so much going on then, at home and at Westminster. I didn't have time to focus on it. Now I have nothing but time."

Lucy pushed away her half-eaten cake. "I thought you came here to get away from the past. From all the stresses back home."

"I did," Alexia admitted. "And I have. Mostly."

"Then why reopen such an awful can of worms?"

"Because nobody else is going to, Luce. No one cares who killed Jenny Hamlin. The media moved on after a couple of weeks. The police have totally given up. Maybe, if I can uncover the truth, if I can find some justice for Billy's daughter, I can make amends."

"Amends to whom?"

"To Billy. To my own children. I don't know, Luce, I can't explain it. It just feels right to do something. To at least look into it."

Lucy shook her head. She knew Alexia well enough to realize that nothing she said was going to change her mind at this point.

"What does that mean, 'look into it'?" she asked. "If the police couldn't find anything, what makes you think you'll be able to, sitting at a computer on Martha's Vineyard?"

Alexia smiled. "I don't. That's why I'm going to New York."

"New York? When?"

"Soon. Tomorrow, if I can get a flight."

Lucy cleared away the coffee. "Okay, it's official. You've lost your mind. You're supposed to be relaxing, switching off, regaining your strength, remember? Not running around the city on some ludicrous wild-goose chase, all for the sake of a girl you never even met. A girl whose father, by the way, was probably trying to ruin you."

"I don't believe Billy meant me any harm," Alexia said. "And I've regained my strength. I need to do something, Lucy. I need a purpose. You do understand, don't you?"

"I guess. Just be careful, Alexia. There are doors that,

once opened, can't easily be closed again. Start digging around in this girl's life and who knows what you might find."

TOMMY LYON SAT AT THE AMERICAN Bar in London's Savoy Hotel, checking out the businesswomen and sleek yummy mummies as they wandered in. Most wore wedding rings, although the curvaceous brunette at the corner table had a promisingly bare left ring finger, despite sporting a plethora of diamonds everywhere else.

Late thirties? No, early forties with good, subtle Botox. Divorced. Rich. Probably a tigress in the sack.

Tommy prided himself on being a good judge of women, the same way that a betting man might pride himself on a good knowledge of horseflesh. Michael had been the master, of course. Michael De Vere could smell a woman's likes and dislikes, her desires and weaknesses, from a thousand paces. Tommy Lyon had never quite matched his friend as a ladies' man. Despite being tall, blond, and athletic, with a strong jaw and soulful brown eyes, every bit as handsome as Michael, somehow Tommy had always ended up playing second fiddle. He lacked the De Vere dazzle, that ineffable charisma that used to draw women to Michael like dust into a vacuum cleaner.

Tommy Lyon missed Michael De Vere dreadfully. But it was nice occasionally to be the guy that got the girl. The brunette caught Tommy's eye and smiled. He smiled back, and was about to send a glass of champagne over to her table, when a showstopping girl walked into the bar. She was wearing jeans, sneakers, and a pale green T-shirt from Gap, and had no makeup covering her lightly freckled face. In a bar full of overdone, stiletto-wearing cougars, she stood out like a fresh orchid amid a sea of cheap plastic flowers. Miraculously, the goddess seemed to be walking toward him.

"Tommy?"

"Summer?"

Tommy had never met Michael's girlfriend. She'd been away in America for most of their relationship, and when she was around, Michael had kept her under wraps. Now Tommy understood why. Michael always managed to land gorgeous girls, but this one was exceptionally attractive. Every man in the room was gazing at her, and glaring at Tommy. Suddenly he felt a rush of pride that it was he she'd come to meet.

"Thanks for seeing me." Summer kissed him on both cheeks, European-style. "I know you must be crazy busy."

"Not at all. It's a pleasure." Tommy patted the bar stool next to him. "What can I get you? Wine? Champagne?"

"Thanks, but I'm fine. It's a bit early for me."

"Nonsense. If Michael were here you'd be drinking. Come on. How about a nice glass of Cristal?"

Summer wrinkled her nose. *Cristal? Really. Michael would never have trotted out a cheesy line like that.* Not wanting to be rude, she said, "I'll take a beer. Budweiser, if they have it, in a bottle."

Tommy bought the beer, and they decamped to a quieter table, passing the disappointed brunette on their way. Watching Summer put the beer bottle to her lips, Tommy registered a familiar stirring of desire. He tried to remind himself that this was Michael's girlfriend. On the other hand, Michael was never going to wake up, a fact that Tommy Lyon had long ago come to terms with, even if Summer Meyer had not.

He made polite conversation. "So, you're at *Vanity Fair* now?"

"Not exactly. I'm freelance, but I'm working on a piece for them."

"What's it about?"

"Wealthy young Russians in London. The excesses of their lifestyle, that sort of thing."

Tommy warned, "Mind where you tread. Russian oligarchs don't tend to take kindly to exposés, of any sort. I'm sure you've read the stories of Western journalists in Moscow being found with a bullet to the back of the head."

"My piece is hardly Woodward and Bernstein stuff," said Summer. "It's more which shoes is Dasha Zhukova wearing this week? Boring and vacuous. Not that I'm complaining. It's a job and it means I can stay in London, close to Michael."

Tommy tried not to be distracted by the rise and fall of her breasts beneath the fitted cotton T-shirt. "You still go to the hospice every day?"

"Of course. And it's not a hospice," Summer said defensively. "It's a long-term care facility. He hasn't gone there to die."

Oh, yes he has, thought Tommy. But he didn't say anything.

"I've been meaning to talk to you for months," said Summer, "but what with Michael getting moved down to London, and me having to find a flat and a job and everything, it's been crazy. You know I've been researching his accident."

"I didn't know that." Tommy rubbed his chin thoughtfully. "Is there much to research? Wasn't it . . . well, an accident?"

"You'd be surprised."

Summer told him about her trip to the Ducati mechanic in East London, and her suspicions that Michael's bike might have been deliberately sabotaged.

Tommy asked the obvious question. "Why would anybody do that?"

"That's what I was hoping you might be able to tell me," said Summer. "You know about Teddy, of course?"

"The body in the garden, you mean? Sure," said Tommy. "He'll go down for life, I reckon. Still find it hard to believe, though. Teddy always seemed so . . . soft."

"I know," Summer agreed. "Anyway, it looks likely that Michael found the body when he was excavating the pagoda and reburied it."

"Christ." Tommy blew out air through his teeth. "Really?"

"Yeah. And I'm wondering, if Michael knew about Andrew Beesley's murder, perhaps there was some connection between that and what happened to him."

"Like what?"

"I don't know. I was hoping you might."

Tommy looked blank.

"Was there anything unusual, anything at all that happened in the days leading up to the party that struck you as strange? Did Michael meet anyone new?"

"No one sinister," said Tommy. "Suppliers, caterers, bar staff. It was a crazy time . . . we were run off our feet."

Ignoring Summer's protests, Tommy bought another round of drinks and ordered some bar snacks. Privately he thought her theories about foul play were nonsense, a fantasy she'd created to prevent her having to deal with the loss of Michael. But she was a stunning girl, so sexy and sensual with that silken mane of hair and those long, long legs. He didn't want her to leave.

She resumed her questioning while Tommy shelled pistachios.

"Did Michael ever talk to you about being threatened?"

"No. Never."

"And he never confided in you about the body?"

"No."

"You're sure?"

"I'm not likely to forget something like that."

"Did he have any enemies that you knew of?"

"You know Michael. Everybody loved him."

"Not everybody, it appears. Someone wanted him dead. Or at the very least silenced. And they got what they wanted."

"Look," said Tommy. "I think you're barking up the wrong tree, I really do. But if it's enemies you're looking for, you should focus on Michael's mother. Alexia had plenty of nutters out to get her. Like those Patel people. That was the nature of her job."

"Yes!" Summer brightened. "Michael kept a file on all of them in the flat. I want you to take a look at it, when you get a chance." After her second drink the room was spinning slightly. Summer realized she must have forgotten to eat lunch. "But you're right, Tommy," she went on excitedly. "Alexia could well be the key to this. Cutting *her* brake cables would be almost impossible. As home secretary, she'd have had a security detail, a driver, people watching her vehicles twenty-four/seven. Michael's bike would have been a far easier target. And what better way to hurt a parent than to injure her child, right?"

She was so adorably earnest, Tommy could stand it no longer. Leaning over, he slipped a hand around the back of Summer's neck and pressed his lips to hers.

For a second she was too surprised to do anything. But then she pulled away angrily. "What the hell are you doing? Have you lost your mind?"

A combination of embarrassment and sexual frustration,

fueled by one too many drinks, made Tommy react angrily. "What's your problem? It was a kiss. Why shouldn't I kiss you?"

"Why shouldn't you kiss me?" Summer repeated incredulously.

"I didn't realize you'd taken a vow of celibacy."

"I'm with Michael, you asshole. Your so-called friend." Summer stood up shakily.

"Hey . . ." Tommy put a hand on her arm. "Michael *was* my friend, okay? My best friend. There was no 'so-called' about it. But Michael is dead, Summer."

"He is not!"

"Yes, he is. Clinically and in every way that matters." Every customer in the bar turned to stare at the drama playing out at the corner table. Tommy's volume levels were rising. "Michael's in a coma and he is never going to wake up. Never."

"Fuck you!" Summer shouted.

"Is this what you think he would want?" Tommy shot back, tightening his grip on her arm. "For you to sacrifice your whole life for him, like some Hindu bride throwing her body onto her husband's funeral pyre? Because if you think that, you didn't know him at all."

With a wrench, Summer pulled herself free from Tommy's grip. Grabbing her purse, she ran out of the bar, tears of anger and humiliation clouding her vision as she stumbled toward the exit.

"He wasn't a saint, you know," Tommy called after her. "He wasn't even faithful to you."

Summer turned and glared at him. "Liar!"

"It's true. The week before you came to Oxford, Michael told me about an older woman he'd been seeing. He called her his 'sugar mummy.' She was the one who bought him that damn bike, if you really want to know."

Summer's stomach lurched.

She turned and ran.

THE LONDON TRAFFIC WAS SO BAD, it took her an hour to reach the facility where Michael was being cared for, a redbrick Victorian building close to Battersea Park.

"You look terrible," one of the nurses observed, not unkindly, when Summer walked in. Her hair was disheveled from having run her hands through it so many times and her cheeks were puffy and swollen from crying. "Are you okay?"

"Not really." Summer took up her usual place in the chair next to Michael's bed, but was too upset to take his hand. She knew that what Tommy Lyon had said was true. At first, when she left the Savoy, she tried to convince herself it was a lie, a cruel fabrication that Tommy had made up out of spite because she'd rejected his advances. But as her black cab crawled across the river, she accepted the truth. *I knew it myself, all along. That was why I came to Oxford, to confront him. I knew there was someone else.*

"How dare you lie there so peacefully, you son of a bitch!" she sobbed into the silence. "How could you do this to me?"

Scores of questions tormented her, like tiny needles pricking at her brain. Had this older woman been there that night, before Summer arrived? For all Summer knew, she could have shared Michael's bed only hours earlier. She wanted to know, needed to know. But Michael had denied her even that small shred of comfort, the comfort of closure.

"You owe me an answer. You *owe* me!" she shouted at Michael as he slept, willing him to hear her. And she cried because there was no answer.

There would never be an answer.

CHAPTER THIRTY-FIVE

POLICE CHIEF HARRY DUBLOWSKI OF THE NYPD smiled at the attractive woman sitting opposite him.

Harry knew when the woman called that he'd heard her name somewhere before. It was an exotic name. Aristocratic. International politics wasn't exactly a passion of Harry's, but when he googled "Alexia De Vere," it all came back to him. The new Iron Lady! England's answer to Hillary Clinton, complete with an errant husband. Except that where Bill's worst crime had been having some fat chick give him head in the Oval Office, Teddy De Vere was doing time for murder.

What Harry Dublowski hadn't expected was to discover that Mrs. De Vere was actually a great-looking broad. Most women Harry's age looked like hags. Either that or they had weird surgery faces that made them look embalmed. But Alexia De Vere was a genuine looker. Her Google pictures did not do her justice. According to her bio, she was in her sixties, but she could have passed for a decade younger. In a simple, flesh-colored shift dress and heels, with a caramel cashmere scarf draped across her shoulders, she could have used a bit more meat on her bones. But she was still elegant and, to Harry's rheumy old eyes, damned sexy. He'd always been a sucker for classy women. God knew he came into contact with precious few of them in this job.

Alexia sized up the overweight, middle-aged cop across the desk and reached a swift conclusion: *The man wants to be flattered*. In this case, she was going to catch more flies with honey than vinegar.

"Firstly, Chief Dublowski, let me say again how very grateful I am to you for making time to see me."

"Not at all." Harry Dublowski beamed. "Happy to help."

"As I mentioned on the phone, I'm here about the Jennifer Hamlin murder investigation. It's purely a personal interest."

"You knew the victim?"

Alexia said carefully, "She was a family friend."

Harry Dublowski stood up and waddled over to an old-fashioned filing cabinet in the corner of the office.

"Everything's computerized these days," he wheezed, "but I'm a sucker for hard copies. There's something about the physical feeling of paper in your hand that helps you to think, right? Or maybe that's just me."

"No, no," Alexia assured him. "I'm the same. I always insisted on paper briefing notes at the Home Office. I'm sure it drove the young staffers mad."

Dublowski handed her the file, allowing his stubby fingers to brush against hers as he passed it over. "I'm sure I don't need to tell you, Mrs. De Vere, but this is strictly off the record. We're not usually in the habit of showing information from murder investigations to the victims' friends and relatives. And nothing can leave this room."

"Of course not. As I said, I'm very grateful." Alexia was already reading. She remembered Sir Edward Manning handing her the FBI file on Billy Hamlin, after Billy first reappeared in her life. Had that really been two years ago? It felt like yesterday. And yet so much had happened since then. So many terrible things.

"You never arrested any suspects?" She looked up at Chief Dublowski, her eyes a piercing ice blue.

"No." His face darkened. "It was a frustrating case, to be perfectly honest with you."

"How so?"

"Well, as you know, the young lady was abducted and held for some period of time before her death. That usually opens up more avenues for investigation. So we were hopeful at first."

"What sort of avenues?"

"More time in which someone might have seen something—a car perhaps—or heard something. Maybe the girl screamed. Or maybe someone noticed something unusual about a certain residence or place of business. As a general rule of thumb, the more complicated a crime—if it occurs in more than one place, for example, or over a period of days—the more likely the perpetrator is to make a mistake. Clues are just mistakes by another name."

"But that didn't happen in this case?"

"No. This killer was careful. Careful and smart. And he didn't fit the normal profile either."

"Profile?"

"A homicide like this, where a young woman is targeted and killed so sadistically, we'd expect to see more crimes with the same MO. More girls washing up with similar injuries. More deaths by drowning. The start of a pattern. But it didn't happen. Thank God, in one way, right? But it left us kind of nowhere with the Hamlin investigation. Forensics drew a blank on the corpse."

"What about circumstantial evidence?"

Harry Dublowski shrugged. "The victim lived one hell of a quiet life."

Alexia nodded. She knew this was true from her own, limited research on Jennifer. The girl had led the most uneventful, inoffensive existence imaginable. She'd never even gotten a parking ticket.

"What about her father?"

Harry's eyes narrowed slightly. "What about him? You knew the dad?"

"A long time ago," Alexia said hastily. "Like I said, I'm an old family friend. The last time I saw Jennifer's father he expressed concern for her safety."

If it seemed odd to Chief Dublowski that a high-ranking British politician had been family friends with an ex-con from Queens and his murdered daughter, he didn't mention it. Instead he said matter-of-factly: "The father was an ex-con, a paranoid schizophrenic. No offense, but Jennifer's dog woulda made a more reliable witness than her old man. The guy heard voices, and yes, some of 'em were about his daughter. He wanted my men to come and check them out for him. It was sad, really."

"And did you? Check them out, I mean."

"Oh, sure. We have to take all reports of threats seriously, even if they come from crazies. But he had no evidence. Nothing whatsoever. It was all in his head. Besides, all of that was at least a year before Jenny Hamlin was killed, maybe longer. Trust me, there's no connection."

"I see. Well, thank you anyway." Pulling a silver Montblanc pen out of her Balenciaga purse, Alexia smiled sweetly. "I appreciate that the information is sensitive and I can't make copies. But I wonder, Chief Dublowski, would you mind terribly if I took a couple of notes?"

*

Chief Harry Dublowski hadn't been kidding when he said the police had had little to go on. The smattering of personal information they had on Jenny had almost all been gleaned from a single interview with her former roommate, a girl named Kelly Dupree.

Alexia paid Kelly a visit at work. Kelly's Nails was a hole-in-the-wall manicure place, squeezed into a sliver of a building between a convenience store and a pharmacy in a nondescript Brooklyn neighborhood. But its proprietress had made an effort to bring the place to life. There were stylish leather chairs, the gleaming white walls were newly painted, and an appetizing array of Essie nail colors was arranged in the shape of a rainbow along the back wall, giving the salon the look of an old-fashioned candy store.

"I'll be right with you!" the eponymous Kelly announced cheerfully. She lost some of her sparkle when Alexia explained that she wasn't a customer, that she was here about Jenny.

"Look, I'm working, okay? I don't have time. I already told the cops everything I know."

"I appreciate that. I'm just concerned that maybe the police gave up a little easily."

Kelly's eyes narrowed skeptically. "Uh-huh. You're concerned. Right."

"I'm not a reporter. I'm a friend of a friend."

"Listen, lady. If this is a scam and you misquote me in some salacious bullshit article, I swear to God . . ."

"It's not a scam. A few minutes of your time, that's all I need."

Kelly had to admit that the polished older lady with the British accent didn't look like a reporter.

"Okay," she said, against her better judgment. "I'll meet you in Starbucks when I'm done here. Right across the street. Say five o'clock?"

She was as good as her word. At five on the dot, Alexia ordered coffees and the two women sat down to talk.

Kelly Dupree was red-haired with pale Irish skin and a smattering of freckles across her nose that made her look younger than her twenty-eight years. She had the over-plucked eyebrows of a professional beautician, and she tapped her acrylic nails loudly and nervously on the table as she spoke.

"I'm sorry if I was a little abrupt before. It was awful what happened to Jen. But a lot of the newspapers and TV people treated her death like entertainment. As if it were some sort of sick reality show, you know? It's made me wary of talking about her."

"I don't blame you," Alexia said. "I used to be a politi-cian—I'm retired now—but I certainly understand how manipulative the media can be."

"So what *is* your interest in Jenny? No offense, but I'm having trouble believing you're a 'friend of a friend.' Jen didn't know too many people like you."

"I knew her father, many years ago. We lost touch. When I heard about Jennifer's death and what happened, I felt I owed it to Billy to try and find out the truth. Perhaps I'm wrong, but it seemed to me as if the police kind of let things slide."

Kelly Dupree laughed bitterly. "You're not wrong. The cops were as bad as the media. Worse in a way. For a few weeks Jen's murder was a hot story. Then everybody forgot about it and moved on to something new. They had no leads. Their so-called investigation was a joke. As soon as they realized it wasn't Luca, that was it. They gave up."

"Luca Minotti? Jenny's boyfriend?"

"Fiancé. Right. Sweetest guy on earth. Luca wouldn't step on a spider if he could help it. Lucky for him he was in Italy when she went missing, otherwise the NYPD would have pinned it on him for sure. They wanted it to be Luca so bad. That's all they asked me about."

Alexia sipped her Americano. "And what about you? Do you have any theories, any thoughts as to who might have killed her?"

Kelly shook her head. "Not really. Some psycho. I mean she wasn't robbed. She wasn't raped. There was no *reason* for it. It was so senseless."

"Was Jenny troubled at all before her death?"

"She was cut up about her dad. You knew he was murdered too, right? In London, the year before Jenny."

"Yes," Alexia said quietly, banishing an image of Teddy from her mind. "I knew that. Were they close?"

"Oh God, yes. Very. Billy was a little odd, you know, but Jen was his only child. He adored her. She worried about him a lot."

"About his mental health, you mean?"

Kelly nodded. "Yes, that. And his loneliness. But you know, there were other things. He'd been in jail a long time ago, before Jenny was born. I never quite knew the details, but Jenny seemed convinced he was innocent of whatever it was he got sent down for. It made him paranoid. Right before he died, I remember he called the apartment and told Jenny that the British government was out to get him. That they'd drugged him and put him on a plane or some nonsense. He was really frightened."

Alexia's hand tightened on her coffee mug. *Poor Billy! He came to me for help and I scared him out of his wits. And then to have nobody believe him, not even his own family.* The guilt was like a stone around her neck.

Kelly Dupree went on. "Things were amicable between Jenny's parents, but her dad never fully got over the divorce.

And then there was the business going down the tubes. And his best friend, his business partner, taking off and leaving Billy holding the bag."

Alexia cast her mind back to Edward Manning's file on Billy. She dimly remembered something about a business partner—was the name Bates? But she hadn't realized he and Billy had been close friends.

"Jen used to say it was like her dad was cursed. And we were all like 'no, no, that's crazy.' But it did sort of seem that way, you know?"

Alexia knew.

"The irony was, toward the end Billy became totally obsessed with Jenny's safety. Like, she was here, worrying about him, and Billy was on the other side of the world, obsessing about something happening to her. We all thought he was crazy, to be perfectly honest with you. But maybe he knew something we didn't."

"'We all'?"

"Me. Luca. Jenny's friends. Her mom."

"So Jenny's mother didn't believe her daughter was in any danger?"

"No. None of us did. Why would she be? We thought Billy was just rambling. Maybe he was. But it does seem kind of odd that Billy gets knifed to death in London and then a year later some psycho does this to Jenny, don't you think? Like, maybe someone out there really *really* doesn't like that family."

Family.

For some reason, the word struck a chord with Alexia. She and Teddy had been a family once. Back in the mists of time, when Michael and Roxie were children, untouched by tragedy, blissfully unaware of the misery the future held for all of them. It occurred to her that in some ways, her own experiences mirrored Billy's. The sense of being cursed, of having somehow brought calamity down on themselves and their families. Both she and Billy had lost their marriages, both lost their children. Billy's business had failed; Alexia's career had collapsed. When Kelly Dupree spoke about someone holding a grudge against the Hamlin family, Alexia thought, *That's how I feel. As if my family are all puppets, and some sadistic, malevolent puppeteer is up there pulling the strings, picking us off one by one.*

Of course, she knew it was nonsense. Teddy had killed Billy. And Teddy knew nothing about Jennifer's death. So there was no connection. Just like there was no connection between Roxie's suicide attempt and Michael's accident, or between Teddy's imprisonment and her own ruined political career. *It's human nature to try and tie these things together. To find a pattern, to believe there must be a purpose behind the misery. It's what Summer Meyer had been trying to do with Michael's accident. And now I'm doing the same, with Jenny Hamlin's murder. But the truth is there is no reason, no connection, no mysterious person pulling the strings.*

It was almost seven by the time Alexia left the Starbucks. Kelly Dupree had given her addresses for Jennifer Hamlin's fiancé, Luca, and for her mother, Sally, but it was too late to pay either of them a visit tonight. Alexia would eat, sleep, and see what more she could find out in the morning.

Back at her hotel, a town-house boutique in the East Village, Alexia collapsed onto her bed, suddenly exhausted. After the slow pace of life on the Vineyard, just being in New York tired her. The lights, the noise, the relentless energy of the city. *I'm too old for this. Maybe Lucy was right. I should have stayed at The Gables and let sleeping dogs lie.*

Nothing she'd heard today encouraged her to believe that she was going to succeed where Chief Harry Dublowski and his men had failed. She wasn't going to find Jennifer Hamlin's killer. Suddenly the whole enterprise seemed pointless. *What the hell am I doing, raking around in another family's grief? As if I don't have enough grief of my own.*

She checked her messages. Since their bonding session at Michael's bedside, Summer Meyer had taken to texting Alexia regularly from London, just to check in, or send pictures of a sleeping Michael. But today there was nothing. Summer's mother, Lucy, had called twice, but left no message. It was odd, Alexia reflected, the degree to which the Meyers had filled the void left by her own crumbling family. Lucy, Arnie, and Summer were all she had now. Alexia thanked God for them.

She considered calling Summer herself, just to make sure everything was okay. But before she could figure out what time it was in England, exhaustion overtook her. The phone slipped from her hand and she sank into a deep, dreamless sleep.

SALLY HAMLIN PATTED DOWN THE EARTH around the newly planted hydrangeas and surveyed her front yard with satisfaction. Spring had fully sprung in Tuckahoe, the quiet Westchester suburb Sally had retired to three years ago, and the scent of summer already hung tantalizingly in the air. Back in Queens, Sally had never had a yard and had always wanted one. Now she derived deep, intense pleasure from her little rectangular patch of grass and flower beds. The simple satisfaction of planting something, tending it, and watching it grow filled her with contentment and peace, and gave a much-needed sense of control and order to her world. After so much loss, so much horror, Sally had learned to take pleasure in the small, predictable joys of life.

Sally saw the woman approaching from a block away. Tall and elegantly dressed, with a purposeful walk and an erect, almost regal bearing, this was no local Tuckahoe housewife out for a Sunday-morning stroll. The woman slowed as she approached Sally's fence, obviously looking for something.

"Can I help you?"

"I'm looking for a Mrs. Sally Hamlin."

It was the British accent that gave it away. Sally knew at once who the glamorous stranger must be. Brushing the soil off her pants, she stood up and proffered her hand.

"You found her. I'm Sally Hamlin. You'd better come in, Mrs. De Vere."

THE HOUSE WAS AS NEAT AS a pin. Alexia took off her jacket and hung it carefully on the back of a kitchen chair while Sally made them coffee. Pictures of Jennifer were everywhere, on the refrigerator, the bookshelves, even perched on top of the television set in the living room. There were none of Billy.

Sally sat down, and Alexia immediately noticed the deep grooves etched around her eyes. She was an attractive woman, perhaps a decade younger than Alexia herself, with carefully dyed chestnut-brown hair and a trim, girlish figure. But grief had taken its toll on Sally Hamlin's face.

"You've come about Billy, I suppose," Sally said. "I heard he'd been bothering you and your family in England, before he died. I'm sorry about that."

"There's nothing to apologize for, believe me."

"He used to talk about you all the time. Alexia De Vere this, Alexia De Vere that. He was convinced he knew you. That the two of you were friends. I think he had you confused with an old girlfriend or something. But he was so ill."

Alexia thought, *So she doesn't know the truth. She doesn't know my past. Billy protected me right to the end. Protected both of us.*

"I did see your husband briefly," she said. "When he was in London."

"Ex-husband," Sally corrected her. "Billy and I divorced a long time ago."

"And that is why I'm here, in a way. He mentioned something to me then about your daughter. I got the sense that he felt she might have been in danger. That somebody might have been trying to hurt her."

At the mention of Jennifer, Sally Hamlin visibly shrank in her seat, her shoulders slumping. The pain was clearly still desperately raw.

"I'm afraid I didn't take it seriously at the time," said Alexia. "But after I heard about what happened to Jennifer, I . . . well, I wondered if I could have done more. It played on my mind."

Sally Hamlin looked surprised. "Don't take this the wrong way. I mean, it's very kind of you to care and all. But I don't understand why my family's troubles would seem important to you. You didn't even know Billy."

"No," Alexia lied, "I didn't. But my encounter with him stuck in my mind. I'm retired from politics now—I've had some family problems of my own—so I had time to follow it up."

Sally nodded. Her mind had already drifted away, to her daughter and the awful nightmare that had overtaken her.

"If it's not too painful," Alexia prodded gently, "perhaps you could tell me a bit more about Jennifer?"

"Of course."

Once Sally started talking, she couldn't stop. She told Alexia everything, from the story of Jennifer's birth to the divorce and how it had affected Jenny, to her daughter's happy relationship with Luca Minotti. She also spoke about the special bond that Jennifer had shared with her father. Despite the obvious problems posed by Billy's schizophrenia, it struck Alexia that his ex-wife still spoke of him with sincere warmth and affection.

Thank God he married someone kind and selfless like Sally, and not someone selfish and ambitious like me. I hope they were happy, for a while at least. Billy deserved that.

When she finally ran out of words, Sally went upstairs and returned with a box file of Billy's old papers and photographs. "For what it's worth. It's mostly business stuff, and I highly doubt it has any bearing on Jennifer's murder. But it's all I have."

Alexia took the file. "Thank you."

"I think Billy's real psychotic break happened when Milo took off," said Sally. "Milo Bates was his best friend. His only real friend, other than me. The divorce wasn't easy on Billy, but Milo leaving the way he did, abandoning Billy to deal with the debts and the business collapsing on his own? That crushed him. That was when the voices started, and the paranoia. He developed these awful morbid fantasies."

"What sort of fantasies?"

Sally shook her head. "Oh, it was crazy. At first he talked about Milo being 'taken.' Abducted, you know. He couldn't accept the fact that Milo had left deliberately. Then it was that Milo had been killed. Eventually Billy started saying that *he'd* been abducted, that he'd actually witnessed Milo being murdered. The fantasy kept getting bigger and more elaborate. It was awful."

392

"Did he ever say who he thought had taken Milo?"

Sally smiled. "Oh yes. 'The voice.'"

"I'm sorry?"

"The voice. The voice was to blame for everything. We all knew it was in his head, of course, but to Billy it was totally real, as real as you or me. The minute he came off his antipsychotic drugs, boom: the voice was back. It started right around the time that Milo left town and it pretty much never stopped. He'd call the cops to tell them the voice was on the phone. He complained constantly about threatening calls."

"But he never saw this person. Only heard them?"

"That's right. Auditory hallucinations are very common with schizophrenics."

"Did he tell you what it sounded like?"

Sally looked Alexia in the eye. "Like a robot. Like a machine. Synthesized."

The hairs on Alexia's forearms stood on end, like a thousand tiny soldiers called to attention. Her mind jumped back to another phone call. One she'd received herself two years ago, back home in Cheyne Walk. She remembered the call as if it were yesterday. The sinister, synthesized voice:

"The day is coming. The day when the Lord's anger will be poured out. Because you have sinned against the Lord, I will make you as helpless as a blind man searching for a path."

Her throat felt dry. "Did he ever say anything about the voice using religious language? Fire and brimstone, that sort of thing?"

Sally's eyes widened. "Yes! That's amazing. How did you know that?"

*

ALEXIA WASN'T SURE HOW SHE MADE it back to her rental car. Climbing into the driver's seat, she sat motionless, staring straight ahead.

The voice wasn't in Billy's head.

It was real.

It called me too.

What else had been real? Milo Bates's murder? Had Billy really been forced to watch his friend die, like he told the police? And what about the threats to his daughter?

"Was that what you were you trying to tell me, Billy?" Alexia said aloud, her cracking voice echoing round the empty car. "Why didn't I listen?"

She must find out who "the voice" really was. Not just for Billy and Jennifer Hamlin's sake, but for her own.

Because whoever it is, they're not done yet.

They're coming after me too.

CHAPTER THIRTY-SIX

ROXIE DE VERE LOOKED OUT OF the French doors that led from her room onto the gardens and took a deep, calming breath. There were few places more beautiful than Somerset in springtime. The gardens at Fairmont House, the stately-home-turned-exclusive-rehab where Roxie was currently living, were some of the most exquisite in the county. One couldn't help but be uplifted by the blossom-laden buddleia bushes, smothered in butterflies, or the peaceful rose garden with its formal box hedges and gently winding gravel paths. There was a lake with a man-made island and folly in the middle, across which "guests" (Fairmont House wasn't crass enough to have patients) could row for picnics or meditation or sunrise yoga sessions. All in all it was a bit like living in an illustration from a Jane Austen novel: tranquil, idyllic, and utterly unreal.

Opening the doors, Roxie allowed the warm air to flood her room and turned the radio to Classic FM. Today for the first time, she would permit a tiny slice of the outside world to intrude upon her safe cocoon. Summer Meyer was coming to visit her, the first friend Roxie had agreed to see in almost six months. The prospect was both exciting and nerve-racking.

"I feel like an Indian bride about to meet my arranged-marriage husband for the first time," Roxie told her therapist, Dr. Woods, a gentle, professorial Canadian in his sixties who'd inevitably become something of a father figure. "The stakes seem so high."

"They're only as high as you let them be," Dr. Woods reassured her. "Don't put too much pressure on yourself. It's tea with a friend, that's all. You can do that, Roxanne."

Roxie had thought she could do it. But now that Summer was actually coming, would be here any moment in fact, she felt all her old nervousness returning.

Roxie had been so ill when she first got to Fairmont, haunted by terrible dreams about Andrew and gripped by daily panic attacks. *I mustn't allow Summer's visit to set me back*. It had taken weeks for her to accept that it was Teddy, her beloved father, who had shot and killed the man she loved. But knowing the truth and changing all one's emotions to fit it were two very different things. Why couldn't it have been Alexia? Hating her mother was easy. It had become a habit, like slipping on a familiar overcoat. For the better part of a decade, Roxie had defined herself as a victim of Alexia's cruelty and selfishness. That had become her identity, her self. But now, in the midst of her shock and grief over Andrew, she was supposed to do a complete about-face. To accept that Alexia had been loving and *un*selfish all along. Acknowledging that fact meant negating her whole adult life. As Dr. Woods said, it was like another death. Like *her* death. No wonder it was frightening.

In the course of a few months, Roxie had lost her brother, her father, and Andrew, all over again. Everything she'd believed for the last ten years of her life had been a lie. Nothing was what it seemed. The world outside of Fairmont House had become a frightening place. And now Summer

Meyer was arriving to bring her news of it. To remind her that it was still there . . . that one day she would have to go back.

"Wow, Rox. You look so *well*."

Summer had walked into the room unannounced. Before Roxie had time to think about it, she found herself enveloped in a hug. Instinctively she hugged her friend back.

Roxie felt relieved. The real Summer was nothing like the frightening visitor of her imagination. Having her here felt right. She smiled.

"It's a gorgeous day out there. Shall we go for a walk?"

SUMMER STRETCHED AND SWUNG HER ARMS as she strolled down toward the lake, with Roxie wheeling her chair beside her. At Fairmont House, everything was all about helping oneself, becoming independent physically and emotionally. Roxanne's days of being wheeled around by other people were over.

It had been a long, hot drive down from London. Summer's joints ached from being cramped up in her tiny Fiat Punto, so the fresh air and space felt like a luxury. European cars all seemed to have been designed for either Munchkins or children.

"This place is stunning." She sighed. "No wonder you don't want to leave."

"I'm not on vacation, you know," Roxie said defensively. "It's a hospital. I'm here because I need to be."

"I know that," said Summer. "I only meant that it's a beautiful setting. Peaceful. I didn't mean to imply anything."

"Sorry. I guess I'm a little tense. It *is* peaceful. And you're right in a way. I *am* lucky to be here."

"Is it very expensive?"

Roxie shrugged. "Probably. Dad's health insurance pays for it, so I haven't seen a bill."

The mention of Teddy was unexpected. Part of the reason for Summer's visit was that it was Teddy's sentencing next week. Alexia was due to fly to London for the hearing and had asked Summer to sound Roxie out in advance, to see if she might be willing to meet her mother face-to-face.

As Roxie had brought him up first, Summer asked cautiously, "Have you had any contact with Teddy? Since . . . you know."

Roxie looked away. "No. Absolutely not."

They walked on in silence for a while. Then Roxie said, "I've tried to forgive him. I want to forgive him. It would be easier for me if I could. But I don't think I can."

Summer nodded. "I understand."

"I doubt you do understand," said Roxie, although she wasn't angry. "All those years of him comforting me, supporting me, pretending to care."

Summer played devil's advocate. "Do you think he was pretending? I'm sure he loved you, Roxie."

"Maybe. But love's not enough. He knew what he'd done. He let me believe the worst of Mummy, and of poor Andrew, just to save his own skin. How selfish is that? I thought I knew him as well as I knew myself." She gave a short, empty laugh, "Then again, knowing myself hasn't exactly been my biggest forte."

"You need to cut yourself some slack," said Summer. "You've been through hell, more pain than most people suffer in a lifetime. You're doing okay."

Roxie smiled. "Thank you. Anyway, enough about me. What's been happening in your life? Are you writing again?"

They talked about Summer's work for a while, until inevitably conversation turned to Michael. Summer still couldn't bring herself to discuss with anyone what Tommy Lyon had told her about Michael's mistress. It wouldn't be fair to burden poor Roxie, or to sully her memories of her brother. But she chatted about his new care facility, the nurses, the encouraging articles she'd read on long-term coma patients making miraculous recoveries.

Eventually, with some trepidation, Summer brought up the subject of Alexia, and how the two of them had become close in recent months.

"She's flying over for your father's sentencing next week. She'd like to see you."

Roxie's shoulders tensed. "I don't think that's a good idea."

"She misses you," said Summer. "Your mother has a hard shell, but underneath it all she's a good person. A compassionate person."

"You never used to think so."

"I misjudged her. I didn't know the facts. Look, Roxie, I know she's made mistakes."

"That's a bit of an understatement, don't you think?" Roxie spluttered.

"Okay, *big* mistakes. But she wants to put things right. Won't you meet her, just for a few minutes?"

Roxie shook her head vigorously. "I can't."

"She never meant to hurt you."

"I know that." Roxie looked up at Summer with tears in her eyes. "But she did. She did hurt me. Okay, so she didn't drive Andrew away like I thought. But she's not blameless, Summer. She still lied. She lied, and lied, and I built my life on those lies! You can't imagine what it's like, realizing that everything you thought you knew about yourself and your family was just smoke and mirrors!"

Summer thought, *I understand more than you think.*

399

Everything I thought I knew about me and Michael was a lie. But here I am still living that lie, too pathetically in love with him to move on.

"Your family's so wholesome, so normal," Roxie went on. "You have no idea how lucky you are to have Lucy for a mother. To have two happy, functional parents."

"I know," said Summer.

They walked back up to the house, and the staff served them tea and homemade walnut cake in Roxie's room. Before Summer left she promised to send Roxie pictures of Michael and to keep in closer touch.

Folding her long legs back into the minuscule car, Summer said, "Think about what I said. Your mother gets here next Friday. She's desperate to see you. At the end of the day, Rox, whatever her faults, she's the only mother you've got."

Speeding back down the tree-lined drive, Summer thought about Roxanne. Their lives had taken such different paths. But certain things bound them together.

We've both been fools for love. Me for Michael. Roxanne for Andrew Beesley. Even Alexia, standing by Teddy after everything that had happened, was living proof that love was blind.

Roxie was right. Her mother had lied to her.

But aren't we all liars when it comes to love? Liars to others and liars to ourselves?

She drove on.

THE DRIVE BACK TO TOWN WAS a nightmare, with the single-lane A303 winding endlessly into the distance like the Yellow Brick Road of Oz.

NO SERVICES FOR 35 MILES read the sign. Summer hadn't

been hungry before, but the unexpected announcement that no food would be available for at least an hour suddenly started her stomach rumbling. Reaching across to the passenger side of the car, she began rummaging in the glove box for candy, accidentally sending papers fluttering all around. Picking one up, she saw it was the registration document for Michael's Ducati, the one she'd taken from Kingsmere almost a year ago now, the night she had dinner with Teddy.

It listed the name of the dealership that had delivered the bike: Drake Motors. There was an address too, in Surrey, just off the A3. She was going to drive right by it.

Since the evening at the Savoy when she met Tommy Lyon, Summer had abandoned her investigation into Michael's accident. Her feelings were still so conflicted, and in any case the whole thing had begun to feel like a monumental waste of time. She wasn't ready to leave England, to turn her back on Michael completely. But in other respects she'd decided to take her mother's advice and focus on her own life, her own future. Michael had behaved selfishly, after all. Why should she sacrifice her every waking moment trying to get justice for him?

Tommy Lyon had hurt her deeply, but he had also forced her to accept some home truths. Michael hadn't been perfect. More importantly, even if Summer succeeded in finding out the whole truth about his accident, it wasn't going to bring Michael back to her.

But now, stuck as she was in traffic, bored, and with the document in her hand, her interest was piqued. It would be stubborn and foolish, surely, to drive right past Drake Motors without even stopping in. Who knew when she'd be out this way again.

*

401

Sir Edward Manning was astonished to hear Alexia De Vere's voice.

In the months since Mrs. De Vere had left office, Edward had almost forgotten the nightmare his life had been back then. Sergei Milescu's sadistic threats, the cloud of terror hovering constantly over him, the knot of anxiety coiled permanently in his chest, like a cobra ready to strike. As for the horrifying image of Sergei in the bathtub, his entrails floating around his bloated head like a string of pork sausages . . . that still sometimes came back to him in dreams. But he reassured himself that what it actually meant, for him personally, was that the horror was over. Alexia's resignation had come too late for Sergei to avert his paymasters' displeasure. But it had saved Sir Edward Manning's life.

The police who found Sergei's body had been to the House of Commons to interview the other members of the janitorial staff. Apparently the method of Milescu's execution was the one preferred by the Russian Mafia. But nobody knew what links the Romanian custodian might have to any Russians. And nobody linked him with Sir Edward Manning.

Kevin Lomax had his strengths and weaknesses, both as a boss and as a home secretary. It did not escape Sir Edward's notice that the very first thing Lomax did in office was to withdraw the tax legislation that had threatened London's wealthy Russian elite. But Sir Edward made no comment. Lomax's arrival at the Home Office had ushered in a period of peace and safety for Sir Edward Manning.

Alexia's voice on the telephone shattered that peace in an instant.

"I'm sorry to disturb you on a weekend, Edward. But I wondered if I might ask you a favor."

"Of course," Sir Edward Manning blustered. "Although I don't quite see—"

"I need some information."

A telling few seconds of silence.

"It's sensitive information. I'll understand if you say no."

"Go on."

"I want to know everything you've got about a man named Milo Bates."

Nothing to do with Russia. Or Lomax. Or Milescu's murder. Sir Edward exhaled.

"Milo Bates." The name was familiar. It took a few moments for him to place it. "Ah yes, I remember. William Hamlin's partner. Is that who you mean? The one who disappeared."

Alexia was impressed, though not surprised. Edward had a memory bank bigger than the British Library.

"Exactly. I'd also like a list of all unidentified bodies found in the New York region in the year that Milo went missing."

The silence was longer this time. Alexia held her breath, but at last Sir Edward Manning said, "I'll see what I can do. Where can I reach you?"

DRAKE MOTORS WAS AN ALTOGETHER MORE sophisticated establishment than St. Martin's garage in Walthamstow. The front showroom, complete with marble floors, fountain, and snooty receptionist in head-to-toe Victoria Beckham, was crammed with top-of-the-line sports cars, from the latest Bugatti in trendy matte silver to gleaming vintage Jags and Bentleys in wine red or sporting green. Summer felt instantly out of place in her sweaty T-shirt, jeans, and sneakers. Nor was she sure that she was even in the right place. She couldn't see a single motorbike on display. Perhaps there was another Drake Motors on the A3?

"May I help you?"

The man was middle-aged and handsome, with a cut-glass accent and an expensive suit.

The manager, thought Summer. Unlike his receptionist, he seemed welcoming and not remotely fazed by Summer's distinctly casual attire. *He's been in the luxury car business too long to judge a book by its cover, or a potential customer's net worth by the scruffiness of her jeans.*

"I hope so. A friend of mine was given a motorbike as a gift about a year and a half ago. It came from your garage. It was a Ducati Panigale."

A blush crept up Summer's neck and into her cheeks. It was ridiculous to hate inanimate objects, but ever since Tommy Lyon told her Michael's bike had been a gift from his lover, she had loathed the thing as vehemently as if it had been a person.

"Well," the manager said smoothly, "we don't sell very many bikes, to be frank with you. I'd probably remember the sale, if you told me the name of the purchaser."

"That's the thing. I know my friend's name, obviously. I have his certificate of ownership here. But I don't know who actually paid for the bike."

She handed the registration document to the manager. It took a few moments for Michael's name to register.

"De Vere. Not *the* De Vere? The home secretary's boy?"

"That's right."

Summer waited for the sympathetic platitudes. Instead she was met by a hostile glare.

"How did you get this?" All the manager's former friendliness was gone. "Are you a journalist? Because if you're sniffing around for a scandal, you won't find it here. All our merchandise is checked and double-checked, understand?"

"As a matter of fact, I *am* a journalist," Summer said angrily. She resented the way people in Britain put journalists on a par with pedophiles and murderers. As if they didn't all buy newspapers or watch television. "But as it happens, I'm not here in a professional capacity. I'm Michael De Vere's girlfriend. And I'm not looking for scandal, just information. There may have been a fault with the Panigale."

"Not when it left here there wasn't."

"Would you have a record of who paid for the bike?" Summer asked wearily. "That's all I want to know."

The manager relented a little. If she really was the De Vere boy's girlfriend, she'd been through a tough time. "I don't know. We might have. Follow me."

Summer accompanied him through the marble atrium into a poky office at the side of the building. Here a much less glamorous secretary in a Next polyester suit tapped away at a computer.

"What was the date of the purchase?" the manager asked.

Summer told him, "It would have been some time between July first and July twentieth of last year."

He turned to his secretary. "Karen, would you check those dates for me? Looking for a Panigale Ducati motorcycle."

After some more tapping and a few seconds' wait, the secretary said brightly, "Yup. Here we are. July twelfth. Paid for in full, by wire transfer."

Summer asked hopefully, "Is there a name?"

More tapping. "Nope. 'Fraid not. No name. Just an account number, and a SWIFT code. Citibank Zurich."

The disappointment felt like a punch to the stomach.

"Thank you for your help anyway."

The manager handed Michael's documents back to Summer, looking a little sheepish. "Sorry about before," he mumbled. "I got the wrong end of the stick."

"That's all right."

Summer left the office and had almost reached her car when the secretary came running out after her.

"Miss. Miss!" she panted. "Was it red, the bike? A 'boy racer' sort of thing?"

Summer nodded. "That's right."

"I remember it," the secretary said triumphantly. "I remember the buyer 'n all. It was a woman. She came to collect it herself."

"Can you describe her?"

The secretary thought about it. "She was American. Dark hair. Quite pretty."

Summer's heart pounded. "How old would you say she was?"

The secretary shrugged. "Middle-aged, I suppose. Not old, not young."

"But she never gave a name?"

"No. She did say the bike was a present. I *think* she said it was for her son. But that can't be right, can it? Not if this was Alexia De Vere's lad."

Summer's head was spinning. "Can I borrow a pen?" she asked. "And a piece of paper?" She wrote down her cellphone number and e-mail address and handed it to the woman. "If you remember anything else, anything at all, would you give me a call?"

"Of course." The secretary looked at Summer curiously. "You're going to think I'm mad. But do I know you from somewhere? Your face looks awfully familiar."

"I don't think so," said Summer.

"You're not on the telly, are you? An actress?"

"I'm afraid not."

"Oh well." The woman smiled cheerily. "Good luck anyway." She bustled back inside.

Summer suddenly felt extremely tired.

It was time to go home.

CHAPTER THIRTY-SEVEN

Alexia sat in a Starbucks, reading. Edward Manning's report was dishearteningly short.

Milo James Bates, born in Bronxville, New York. Married Elizabeth (Betsy), three children. Reported missing by business partner and later by his family. Left considerable debts.

So, Alexia thought, *Billy wasn't the only one who was worried about Milo. His family also reported him missing. I wonder why Chief Dublowski never mentioned that.*

Hamlin claimed Mr. Bates had been abducted by person(s) unknown, and that he (Hamlin) had also been abducted and forced to watch a home movie of Bates being tortured. Agents Yeoman and Riley (FBI) investigated, found no substantiating evidence. Bates divorced in absentia by his wife, January 1996, on grounds of abandonment. No further contact with family.

Alexia read between the few, simple lines. A man who by all accounts had been happily married and a devoted father suddenly disappears without a trace. Did Milo Bates panic over his debts? Was that reason enough to walk away from an entire life? Not just his wife and business partner, but his children too? Or had something more sinister happened to him?

The second page of Edward's report was even briefer.

> . . . 4,587 unidentified human remains were discovered in the United States in the year that Milo Bates went missing. Of these, 986 were still unidentified a year later. 192 of these still-unclaimed corpses were from the New York region. 111 were adult males.

Alexia paused to absorb this depressing information. In one year alone, in one city, over a hundred men had died or been killed that nobody cared about. All of them had been someone's son. Just like Michael. She forced herself to read on.

> . . . 17 corpses bore evidence of torture. All but 3 of them were of Caribbean descent.

Gangs. Drug wars. Alexia felt the beginnings of excitement. Ever thorough, Edward had listed the causes of death for the three white males.

Shooting.

Shooting.

And the third, the very last word of Edward Manning's report, lurking at the bottom of the page as quiet and deadly as a cancerous mole:

Drowning.

Alexia heard Chief Harry Dublowski's voice in her head. *"We'd expect to see more cases with the same MO. More girls washing up with similar injuries. More deaths by drowning."* This body wasn't a girl's. But was that lone white male Milo Bates? Had he been tortured, just like Billy said? And tossed into the Hudson alive, drowned, like poor Jennifer? After all, there was no reason Jennifer's killer should have targeted only women. Jenny hadn't been sexually abused. Perhaps her sex was irrelevant. Perhaps it was her connection to Billy that had sealed her fate, just as it had sealed Milo Bates's. Billy, the poor, confused, schizophrenic ex-con. Billy, whom nobody had believed, nobody had listened to. Not even Alexia herself.

"Are you done?"

A sullen barista removed Alexia's empty coffee mug. Alexia looked at her watch, pushing her wild speculations about Milo Bates to one side for now. *Because that's all they are*, she reminded herself firmly. *Speculations. That body could have been anybody's. Milo could be alive and well and living in Miami, for all you know.*

Today was her last full day in New York, and she had to make it count. Tomorrow night she'd be in a plane to London, to attend Teddy's sentencing. She only had twenty-four hours to get through the last four names on her list.

Sally Hamlin had given her a bunch of papers relating to the time when Billy's business had gone into free fall. Not only was this when Milo Bates had disappeared, but it was also the time when "the voice" had first made itself heard in Billy's life. This was the crucial period, the start of it all. Searching through the files, Alexia had carefully pulled out the names of all the creditors, clients, and suppliers who'd had dealings with Hamlin Motors during

410

that time. It was a long shot. But there was a chance one of them might remember something significant.

JEFF WILKES RAN A HAULING COMPANY in Queens that had been one of Billy's biggest and most consistent customers until things started to go wrong. A hugely fat man in his midfifties who smelled of garlic and body odor and had sweat patches the size of dinner plates under each arm, Jeff Wilkes seemed neither pleased nor impressed to be meeting Britain's former home secretary.

"Look, lady, I don't care who you are," he informed Alexia rudely, scratching his balls under the Formica desk of his filthy office above his truck garage. "I don't discuss my business dealings with nobody except my accountant and my bank manager. And then only if I can't help it."

"Billy Hamlin was a friend of yours," Alexia said frostily. "Both he and his daughter were found murdered. If you had information that could help solve those crimes, wouldn't you want to share it?"

"With the cops, maybe. Not with some woman I've never seen before in my life. I don't know you."

"I've told you who I am."

Jeff Wilkes shrugged. "So? I don't have information, okay? I don't know shit about no murders. And Billy Hamlin was a business contact, an acquaintance. We weren't friends."

Clearly appealing to Wilkes's better nature was going to get her nowhere. Alexia reverted to a trick she'd learned in politics—repeating the question again and again and again until the other person broke down and answered despite themselves.

"Why did you terminate your contract with Hamlin's?"

"Look, I told you—"

"Why did you cut Billy off?"

"Are you deaf?"

"Was the quality of his work unsatisfactory?"

"No. It had nothing to do with that."

"Did the two of you have a falling-out?"

"No! I told you already. We weren't friends. You know, I got a business to run here."

"Why did you terminate your contract with Hamlin's?"

Within a minute, Jeff Wilkes had caved. Alexia thought: *He wouldn't last a day in the House of Commons.*

"I got squeezed, okay?" Jeff blurted out. "In my business, it happens. The Mafia, the protection rackets. You don't mess with that if you're a hauling company in New York City."

"Someone pressured you to stop doing business with Billy? Is that what you're saying?"

"I'm not saying anything."

"Were you threatened?"

"I'm not naming names, I'm not making accusations, okay? I'm just a small businessman doing the best I can."

"But your relationship with Billy Hamlin became a problem?"

"It came to my attention," the fat man said, "that it would be better for *my* business if Hamlin's business didn't work on my trucks no more. Okay? I didn't owe the guy anything. I paid him in full and on time for all the work he did. But"—he opened his arms wide—"we went our separate ways. That's it. End of story."

It wasn't the end of the story, of course. But it was as much as Alexia was going to get out of the odious Jeff Wilkes today.

HER NEXT STOP WAS AN AUTOMOTIVE-PARTS distributor, also in Queens. To her surprise, this time the boss was a woman.

412

"Yeah, I remember Billy Hamlin. Sure. Kind of a quirky guy. But I liked him."

The woman hadn't heard about Billy's murder, or his daughter's, and was shocked when Alexia told her the details. "My God. I did read something about that body being washed up. But I didn't put two and two together with the name. To be honest with you, I never knew Billy had a daughter. That's terrible."

Her reasons for ceasing to do business with Hamlin's were more prosaic than Jeff Wilkes's. "Those were tough times in the automotive sector generally. A lot of firms were going under. Truth is, we were lucky enough to get a huge contract with one of the big boys, De Sallis. We dropped ninety percent of our smaller clients after that. We were stretched to the limit. I do remember hearing rumors about Hamlin's, though, now that you mention it."

"Oh?" Alexia's ears pricked up.

"Some people were saying Billy and Milo'd been black-listed. I don't know whether they had trouble with one of the gangs, or it was something else. But everything those guys touched seemed to turn to shit, if you'll pardon my French."

Alexia knew the feeling. Her last year in politics had felt the same.

"Do you know who took over supplying Hamlin's, after you quit?"

The woman scrawled down a name. "You think any of this has a bearing on him and his kid getting killed?"

"Probably not," said Alexia. "I'll see myself out."

ALEXIA MADE FOUR MORE STOPS THAT day, three to former clients and one to another supplier. The stories were the same everywhere. It was either, W*e were threatened. We got calls warning us off.* Or, *We got a better offer.* Hamlin's was undercut by rival mechanic shops. Billy's two closest local competitors, Queens Cars and MacAdams Auto Services, both received large injections of cash from white knight buyers that enabled them to slash their prices—bizarrely, given that the auto business generally was in a severe recession at the time.

Alexia got back to the hotel at five, took a power nap and a shower, and was about to go out and grab an early bite to eat when her phone rang.

"Where are you?" Lucy Meyer's voice was as warm and conspiratorial as ever.

Alexia grinned. "You know where I am. I'm in New York, the city that never sleeps."

"Still?"

"Still. I fly to England tomorrow."

"I see. So, have you solved the case yet, Sherlock Holmes?"

"No, not yet. I've been chasing my tail, as usual. What's going on with you?"

"Look out of your window."

Alexia did a double take. "Look out of my window? Now?"

"No, in two weeks' time. Yes, now!"

"But why?"

"Just do it!"

Alexia walked over to the window and jimmied it open. Below her, on the street, stood Lucy, grinning like the cat that swallowed the canary. She had her cell phone in one hand and a cluster of Barneys shopping bags in the other.

"I thought I'd come and check on you!" she shouted up. "So where are you taking me for dinner?"

*

414

They ate at Elaine's, at Lucy's insistence.

"I only get to New York once in a blue moon, so I may as well treat myself."

"I thought I was getting dinner?"

"That's *right*, you are. Even better. Think I'll go for the caviar, the lobster ravioli, and a nice bottle of vintage Chablis. And you can explain what on earth you've been doing here all this time, not to mention when you decided to go to London. I thought you said you weren't planning to go to the sentencing."

"I wasn't. But I changed my mind."

"Because . . . ?"

Alexia took a sip of her white wine. "Teddy's done a lot of terrible things. But then so have I, in the past. He's still my husband."

"And that makes it all okay, does it?"

There was a bitterness to Lucy's tone that Alexia hadn't expected, a hard edge she didn't remember hearing before.

"No, of course not. Nothing can make it okay. But it means I should at least try to forgive."

"I don't see why." Lucy hid her face behind the menu, so Alexia couldn't gauge her emotions. "Do you still love him?"

Alexia paused. "Yes," she said at last. "I suppose I do. I daresay it sounds ridiculous, but meeting Billy Hamlin's ex-wife this week really got me thinking."

"Meeting Billy Hamlin's . . ." Lucy shook her head despairingly. "Now you really have lost me. What on earth does she have to do with you and Teddy?"

"Sally and Billy had been divorced for well over a decade before Billy was killed. But when I met her, she still had so much compassion for him, so much love. It was really touching. Like they were two parts of the same body."

"Please." Lucy gave a dramatic eye roll, drained her glass, and poured herself another.

"I'm serious," said Alexia. "And it struck me, that's what it's like with Teddy and me. After all these years together, he's as much a part of me as my arm or my leg. I can't just cut him off. You must feel the same with Arnie, don't you?"

"I don't know if I do or not," Lucy said matter-of-factly. "Arnie's never killed a man, buried him in our backyard, and lied about it."

"True. But if he had? Don't you think you'd forgive him?"

"No." Lucy was so certain, so brutally final about it.

"Even if he did it to protect Summer?"

"No. Never."

"Really? But how can you know that, Lucy? You've never been in that situation."

Lucy shrugged. "In my book, some things are beyond forgiveness. It's as simple as that. Let's eat."

They ordered food, and the mood instantly lightened. Alexia filled Lucy in on the progress of her search. Her meetings with Chief Harry Dublowski, with Jennifer Hamlin's friends and family, with the various business associates who had abandoned Billy and driven him bankrupt back in the nineties. Finally, she told Lucy about the information on Milo Bates that Sir Edward Manning had unearthed for her.

"Billy always claimed his partner had been abducted and killed, but everyone dismissed it as a morbid fantasy. The police, his wife, everyone."

"But you think differently?" Lucy sipped her ice-cold Chablis and speared a deliciously buttery sliver of lobster ravioli with her fork.

"There was a body, just one body, of a white male, washed up in the Hudson the year that Milo Bates took off."

Lucy laughed. "But that could be anyone! A homeless man or a kid on the run. Do you have any idea how many people go missing in this city? How many wind up dead?"

"Yes, I do," Alexia said excitedly. "Close to a thousand. But only half are men, and only a handful show signs of torture, which is what Billy said happened to Milo. This one white guy had been tortured and thrown into the river alive, to drown. That's exactly what happened to Jennifer Hamlin. Exactly!"

Lucy took this in. "Where's the body now? Can you test it? For DNA or . . . something. Whatever it is they do on *CSI*."

"Unfortunately not. Unclaimed John Does are cremated after two years. But I'm certain it was Milo Bates, that he was killed by the same psychopath who murdered Jennifer Hamlin. Billy's voices weren't all in his head. One of them was real."

"So you keep saying. But how do you know?"

"Because the same person called me, in my early days as home secretary. Right after Billy showed up in London. They called Cheyne Walk spouting biblical mumbo jumbo, making threats. And they used a voice distorter, just like the one Billy described. I hardly think that's a coincidence, do you?"

Lucy frowned. "You never mentioned any weird phone calls to me at the time."

"Didn't I?"

"No. And you told me everything else. Your whole past life, Billy, what happened in Maine that summer. How come you never brought this up?"

"I guess I didn't think it was that important." Alexia waved a hand dismissively. "If I'd let every crackpot out there bother me, I'd never have succeeded in politics for as long as I did."

"So the calls didn't scare you?"

"Not really. Maybe a little. But I never took them too seriously. Till now, that is. When Sally Hamlin described the voice Billy was so afraid of, I knew at once. It was the same bastard who called me. I'd bet good money that the voice is our killer. And he's still out there."

"You think he killed Milo Bates?"

"Yes."

"And Jennifer Hamlin?"

"Yes."

"What about Billy? He doesn't exactly fit the pattern, does he?" said Lucy.

"No." Alexia looked away. "I don't know what happened to Billy."

Part of her wanted to tell Lucy the truth: that it was Teddy who had ambushed Billy at his London flat and stabbed him to death. She'd told her everything else, after all. What difference would one more gruesome secret make? But something in Lucy's tone made Alexia hold back. She couldn't bear the thought of alienating Lucy, her one remaining rock and only support. Besides, she had promised Teddy she would keep his secret about Billy, and Alexia De Vere honored her promises. This wasn't her confession to make.

Lucy scraped the last of the creamy lobster sauce off her plate with a small sigh of satisfaction. "I take it you've gone to the police with this new information?"

Alexia's silence spoke volumes.

Lucy dropped her fork with a clatter. "You haven't, have you?"

"It's not that simple."

"Alexia! You just said yourself you might be in danger from this 'voice' person. He's still out there. Why wouldn't you report what you know?"

"Because I have no proof. No recordings, no phone records. Nothing. And because the police already decided they don't believe Billy's testimony. And because I fly to London tomorrow. I don't have time for statements and interviews, especially when I know they won't be followed up anyway. It's not as if I'm still in office. Nobody cares what happens to me."

"I care," Lucy said angrily. "I don't like this at all."

They ordered dessert—sticky toffee pudding for Lucy and a simple sorbet selection for Alexia. *No wonder she looks so thin*, thought Lucy. *She eats like a bird*. And after a few minutes, they fell back into their usual friendly banter. Alexia paid the bill and the two women walked outside together to hail separate cabs.

"Is it strange," Lucy asked, "being back in New York after so long in England?"

The city lights twinkled around them like the lights of a giant Christmas tree. Manhattan felt alive tonight. Both women sensed its pulse in the warm summer air, the throbbing heartbeat of a living, breathing city.

"You know the strangest part?" said Alexia. "And you're the only person in the world I can say this to. But for the first time in forty years, I feel connected to Toni Gilletti. To the girl I used to be."

Lucy said, "Is that right?"

"I've spent most of my life telling myself Toni was dead and buried. But she's *here*." Alexia touched her chest. "She always has been. Teddy knew that, and he forgave her. More than that, he loved her, despite everything. Maybe that's why I can forgive him now. I'm not condoning what he did. But I'm trying to hate the sin, and not the sinner. If that makes any sense."

A single yellow cab pulled over.

"You take it," said Lucy. She seemed distant all of a sudden, as if tiredness had finally caught up with her.

"Are you sure?" Alexia asked. "You have further to go than I do."

"Positive. You have an early flight in the morning. Go. I'll get another one in a minute."

The two women kissed on the cheek and went their separate ways.

BACK AT HER HOTEL, ALEXIA FOUND herself too wired to sleep. Her theories about Milo Bates, running around talking to Billy's old contacts, her surprise dinner with Lucy, and reflecting so much on her own past had all set her mind racing. Then there was Teddy's sentencing to think about. Returning to England after so long, and in such difficult circumstances, was nerve-racking. Alexia still didn't know whether Roxanne would agree to see her, or whether she could face visiting Michael. Just the thought of the media frenzy that would accompany Teddy's hearing was enough to send her adrenaline levels into overdrive.

More in an attempt to distract herself than anything else, she switched on her computer and began cataloging the information she'd gathered from today's interviews. There was something soothing about the logic of data, the way facts stacked up, one on top of the other, eventually revealing a conclusion—a truth. Human truth was so elusive and illusory. There was a comfort in the solid, predictable world of facts and figures. Alexia felt the edge coming off her nerves and her brain starting to clear as she typed away.

It was almost one in the morning when she saw it.

At first she thought she'd made a mistake, and went back to cross-reference the information. But no. She was right the first time. In the small print of all the company records, one name came up over and over again—*HM Capital Inc.*

Woolley Trucking, Jeff Wilkes's business, was a wholly owned subsidiary of HM Capital. Trammel Logistics, another of Billy and Milo's big clients, had been part owned by HM Capital in the year that Hamlin's went under, although the firm had sold its stake soon afterward. Queens Auto Parts, the supplier Alexia had visited this afternoon, had no obvious connection. But when Alexia typed "De Sallis" into Google, the name of the white knight client who had rescued Queens Auto in the nineties and squeezed Hamlin's out, there it was again: *HM Capital.* According to the company's annual report, HM Capital was a 25 percent shareholder. All in all it added up to a pronounced interest in the Queens and Brooklyn car business, for a private equity group whose other investments were exclusively in the financial sector. Up until 1996, the only businesses in HM Capital's portfolio were small-cap emerging-market institutions. HM had taken over savings and loan companies in Mogadishu and bought out insurers across the former Soviet Union. All of which begged the obvious question:

What the hell were they doing dabbling around with Hamlin Motors' clients?

Another forty minutes of searching online failed to provide an answer. Alexia rubbed her eyes wearily. She had to get up and head to the airport in less than five hours and still hadn't slept a wink. Just as she was about to switch her laptop off and try again to sleep, a thought occurred to her.

Clicking on Advanced Search, she typed in: "HM

Capital Directors, Executives." A list of around twenty names popped up on the screen. About halfway down the list, Alexia did a double take. There was a name she recognized.

It was the last name on earth she'd expected to see.

CHAPTER THIRTY-EIGHT

TEDDY DE VERE'S HEARING WAS BEING held at London's famous High Court on the Strand. Part of the Royal Courts of Justice, a late-Victorian Gothic edifice complete with turrets, ornately carved arches, and an orgy of statuary, from biblical figures to famous lawyers of the day, the High Court provided the stage on which so many of England's great legal dramas had been played out. In recent years the court had become synonymous with celebrity. The inquest into Princess Diana's death was held here, along with the privacy trials of various Fleet Street newspapers, with actions brought by Michael Douglas and Catherine Zeta-Jones, Naomi Campbell, and a host of other A-list names.

Teddy De Vere might not be quite in this category. But together, he and his wife remained one of the best-known, and most controversial couples in British politics. The fact that Alexia De Vere had exited public office stage left at the height of her family's scandals last year, turning her back on Britain and its media, only served to make her appearance at her husband's sentencing more newsworthy. The big question was not "How long would Teddy De Vere get?" but "What would Alexia De Vere be wearing?" Had she aged? Had stress made her lose weight or gain it? Did her poor crippled daughter, the erstwhile fiancée of the murdered man, Andrew Beesley, still despise her famous mother, Britain's second "Iron Lady"? Or would a touching family reconciliation be glimpsed on the High Court's famous stone steps this morning? These were the burning questions to which the *Daily Mail*'s readers demanded answers. They might not be in the public interest, as such. But they certainly interested the public. Hundreds of ordinary people had gathered on the Strand to catch a glimpse of Alexia De Vere arriving at court. Between the spectators, the news crews, and the paparazzi, the scene outside the High Court was, as Alexia had rightly predicted, a madhouse.

Happily, she had Angus Grey to guide her through it.

"Just hold my arm, my dear, and keep your eyes fixed straight ahead."

Angus was looking even more dashing than usual in his barrister's wig and gown. If Alexia hadn't known him better, she'd have suspected that a touch of the dermatologist's needle had softened the lines around his eyes and mouth, although Angus swore a three-week holiday in Mauritius was behind his more youthful look.

"Remember not to look down," he told Alexia. "It makes you look guilty."

"For heaven's sake, Angus. I'm not the one on trial."

"You are by that lot." The QC nodded toward the crowd as their car pulled up. As usual, he was right. The moment Angus and Alexia stepped out of the vehicle, the barrage of questions and catcalls was deafening.

"How does it feel to be back?"

"What do you expect today, Mrs. De Vere?"

"Will you stand by your husband?"

"Will your daughter be attending? Mrs. De Vere!"

Alexia's heart began to race in something akin to panic. *To think I used to enjoy this attention. Thrive on it, even. All I want now is to see Teddy and get this over with.*

With Angus Grey leading her, she made it inside the building. A seat had been reserved for her beside Angus at the front of the court, so she didn't have to face the gawkers in the spectators' gallery. Even so, walking into the court-room, she could feel their stares burning through the back of her cream bouclé Chanel jacket.

"Is it just me, or is it warm in here?" she joked to Angus.

"Try to tune them out. Teddy will be here in a minute. He'll be the last to arrive before the judge and he'll come through there." Angus pointed to a carved oak door that looked as if it belonged in a church. "The proceedings shouldn't take too long. The crown prosecution get to make a brief statement. Victims' families can also come before the bench at that time, but there's no one in this case."

"Really? No one came to speak for Andrew? How sad."

"It's a good thing for us," Angus Grey assured her. "Sobbing mothers and sisters are the last thing Teddy needs. Although the truth is, the judge will already have studied the case in detail. Chances are he made up his mind days ago as to the sentence. All this . . ." He waved around the courtroom. "All this is just for show. Anyway, after the crown's finished, I say a few words in mitigation, and then it's straight to the judge's address. Some of them waffle on for about ten minutes. Usually it's a minute of moralizing at most. Then they pass sentence, and Teddy will be led down to the cells."

"Right," Alexia said grimly. She knew all of this, but hearing Angus spell it out in black and white was still painful.

"You should be able to see him then if you want to. Let me know if you do and I'll submit the request to the court now."

Alexia's mind flashed back to that earlier trial, a lifetime ago and a world away, when Billy Hamlin had been taken down to the holding cell. Her father and Billy's father had almost come to blows, and she'd slipped in to see Billy, and it was all just awful, terrible, and he'd proposed and she'd accepted—*what else could I do?*—and when she left she knew she would never see him again. But she *had* seen him again, and since that day everything, her whole world, had come crashing spectacularly down.

"Alexia?" Angus Grey was looking at her curiously. "Are you all right?"

"I'm fine."

"Would you like to see Teddy after sentencing?"

Alexia nodded. "Yes. Definitely."

Just then a commotion broke out at the back of the courtroom. There were gasps and shouts. Something important was happening, but it was going on behind her, so Alexia couldn't make out what it was.

"What's going on?" she asked Angus. But before he could say anything, her answer came down the central aisle toward her. Dignified and beautiful in a simple black shift dress and Teddy's mother's pearls, Roxanne wheeled herself to her mother's side.

"You came," Alexia whispered.

"Yes."

"For Daddy? Or for Andrew?"

"Neither. For myself. And maybe a little bit for you."

Without thinking, Alexia bent down and put her arms around Roxie. The whirring and clicking of cameras from the press gallery was deafening.

Angus Gray thought, *That's tomorrow's front page.*

There was another flashing of cameras as Teddy came into the dock. Alexia and Roxie squeezed each other's hands.

426

"He looks so thin," Roxie whispered.

"I know."

Teddy's Turnbull & Asser suit, always one of his favorites, hung off him ridiculously now, making him look like a little boy dressing up in his father's clothes. His perennially chubby cheeks looked gaunt and sunken. He was altogether shrunken, smaller, diminished. Catching sight of Alexia and Roxie sitting together beside his barrister, he flashed them a surprised smile.

"Don't encourage that. Look away," Angus hissed in Alexia's ear. "He's being sentenced for murder. He's supposed to look contrite."

He's supposed to be *contrite*, Alexia thought. *The problem is, he doesn't believe he's done anything wrong.*

"All rise. Lord Justice Caernarvon presiding. All rise."

Alexia felt dizzy as she got to her feet. *This is it.*

THE CROWN'S CASE WAS SIMPLE AND dispassionate: By his own admission, Teddy De Vere had shot Andrew Beesley dead in an entirely premeditated act of violence. He had successfully concealed the crime for nine years, and on being exposed had shown no remorse for his actions whatsoever. This apparent lack of understanding of, or concern for, the gravity of his actions rendered Teddy De Vere a danger to society. For this reason, and in the interests of justice, the crown were appealing for a full life sentence to be imposed.

Roxie listened to the prosecution's address in rapt silence. She'd decided to come to her father's sentencing in hopes it might bring her some closure. It was Summer Meyer's visit to Fairmont House that had first got her thinking about it. Not just about the court hearing, but about seeing her mother again, taking the first small step toward forgiveness. Dr. Woods, her therapist, defined resentment to Roxie in one of their sessions in a way that had touched a nerve. "It's like drinking poison, and then wondering why the other person doesn't die." Roxie realized: *I've spent most of my adult life drinking poison and wondering why mother didn't die. I mustn't make the same mistake with Daddy.* Coming to the High Court was an ordeal, a real trial by fire. But if she got through it, Roxie hoped, she'd emerge stronger, and with at least some of her demons purged.

In a sense, it had already worked. Seeing Teddy in the dock, a frail old man, she realized that he was still her father, still the man she'd spent a lifetime loving and trying to please. She could not forgive him. But she knew now with searing clarity that she could not stop loving him either.

As for Andrew Beesley, he was no longer real for her. His face, his touch, his voice . . . all had been lost so long ago. Roxanne couldn't associate today's proceedings with that person. Andrew was as much dream as memory, as much something she'd hoped for as something she'd ever actually had. It was all so very sad. But it was the past. Gone. Over. As the prosecution closed their address and Angus Grey stood up to speak, Roxie felt the future beckon, unknown and unknowable, but *there*, real, within her reach in a way that it hadn't been for a very, very long time.

Angus's speech was even briefer than the prosecution's. Teddy had pleaded guilty, sparing the crown and all parties the necessity of a costly trial. He took responsibility and was ready to face his punishment. As wrong as his actions were, he had been motivated by a sense of responsibility toward his daughter. He had always been of good character.

Lord Justice Caernarvon cleared his throat. He was extremely old and thin and had revolting flaps of loose skin on his neck, like a turkey ripe for slaughter. His was not a merciful face.

Sitting beside her daughter, Alexia braced herself for the worst.

"Heinous crime . . . vulnerable young man, lured to his death."

The judge's words washed over her.

"No sense of remorse."

Alexia glanced up at Teddy. For a moment his eyes met hers with a look of gratitude and love. He seemed so composed. If he was afraid, he didn't show it.

"Even allowing for good character, in the interests of justice . . ."

Did I ever really know him? thought Alexia. *Did we ever really know each other?*

"I sentence you to life in prison, with a recommendation that you serve a minimum of twenty years."

Boom. There it was. Twenty years. The same sentence as Billy Hamlin got, all those years ago. The sense of déjà vu, of being trapped in some terrible, inescapable cycle, was overwhelming.

He'll die in prison. I'll never share a bed with him again. Never hold him in my arms.

Teddy was being led away. Angus Grey was talking. Alexia watched the lawyer's lips moving but she couldn't make out the words. His voice sounded as if he were underwater. Once again, the waves were rising, pulling her under.

"Mummy." It was Roxie's voice that pulled her back. "Mummy, can you hear me? Are you all right?"

Alexia nodded mutely.

"If you want to see Daddy, you have to go now." Roxie prodded her mother gently. "Go on. Angus will take you."

SUMMER MEYER ANSWERED THE PHONE.

"Hello?"

"Oh, hi there. It's Karen."

"Karen?"

"Karen Davies. From Drake Motors? You came in a week or so ago about a Ducati."

The rude garage manager's secretary. Summer had completely forgotten she'd given the woman her number. "Of course. Karen. I remember."

"You said to call if I thought of anything, about the lady who picked up the bike. Well, I thought of something."

"You did?" Summer held her breath.

"Can't think why I never thought about it before, or why David didn't. He's my manager. He's a bit of a prat, to be honest. Anyway—what I remembered: we have CCTV in the showroom!"

Summer tried to contain her elation. "That's wonderful. And you think you might have caught this woman on camera?"

"I don't think. I know," Karen Davies said triumphantly. "I've got the tape here. D'you want to come by and pick it up?"

IF THE COURT PROCEEDINGS HAD FELT surreal, seeing Teddy face-to-face was even more so.

"Alexia. Dearest." He kissed her on both cheeks. "How *are* you? You must be simply shattered after your journey. Good of you to come."

He was behaving like a dinner party host welcoming an old friend. Not like a man about to begin a life sentence for murder.

"Sit down, sit down. Please." He looked past Alexia hopefully. "Is Roxie not with you?"

"No. She's outside with Angus. It was a huge step for her to come here at all. I think this"—Alexia gestured around the dreary room with its peeling paint and furniture screwed to the floor—"would be too much."

"Yes, well . . ." Teddy nodded sadly. "I suppose so."

"You don't look well, Teddy. You're terribly thin."

"I'm fine, darling. I had some sort of god-awful tummy bug, but I'm fit as a fiddle now."

"Have you seen a doctor?"

"A doctor? Heavens no. No need for all that fuss and nonsense. Believe me, I'm fine."

Alexia tried to believe him. "Will you cope, Teddy?" she asked anxiously. "I feel so helpless."

"Of course I'll *cope*." Teddy laughed. "What a question. I survived prep school. Prison'll be a doddle after that."

Alexia thought, *He means it*. She didn't know whether to laugh or cry.

Teddy said, "Let's not talk about that now. We probably only have a few minutes. How are *you*, my darling? How was the Vineyard?"

"The Vineyard was the same as it always is. Lovely. Peaceful."

"And New York?"

Alexia looked up sharply. "How did you know I was in New York?"

"I think Angus mentioned something," Teddy said nonchalantly. "I was surprised. You never mentioned it in your letters. I always thought you loathed the city."

"I needed a change of scene," lied Alexia. The last thing she wanted to discuss with Teddy was her research into Jennifer Hamlin's murder. Since his confession about Billy, they hadn't touched on the subject again. They couldn't, not if the marriage was going to survive. But there was one question she needed to ask. Now, while she had the chance.

"Have you ever heard of a company called HM Capital?"

Teddy looked bemused. "What on earth makes you ask that?"

"It's a long story," bluffed Alexia. "Nothing important. I just wondered if the name rang any bells."

"All right. Well, yes, it does, as a matter of fact. It's one of Arnie Meyer's shell companies. An investment vehicle. Based out of Cayman, if memory serves."

Alexia felt a tingle of something—excitement, or maybe apprehension—hearing Teddy confirm what her own research suggested. When she first saw Arnie Meyer's name on the list of company directors, she thought she must have made a mistake. But it soon emerged that Arnie was not only a director, but the founder and primary investor in HM Capital. The other names on the directors' list were all professional trustees, lawyers, and accountants who provided the business with tax advice. HM Capital *was* Arnie Meyer. And it had systematically set out to destroy Billy Hamlin's business.

"What does it invest in?"

"Emerging markets," Teddy said confidently. "Former Soviet republics primarily. Oil and gas."

"Nothing else?"

"Not that I know of."

"They don't invest in automotives, for example? In the U.S."

"No." Teddy frowned. "What's all this about, darling?"

"Honestly, it's nothing." Alexia smiled reassuringly. "I was thinking of making an investment, that's all. I wanted to get your thoughts."

"I'll give you my thoughts." Teddy suddenly sounded furious. "Tell Arnie if he wants to try and get money out of this family, he can damn well come to me. How *dare* he prey on you like that, at such a vulnerable time? I knew he was having some liquidity problems, but I never realized things had got that bad."

"Please calm down, darling. No one's been pressuring me, least of all Arnie. I shouldn't have brought it up."

To Alexia's relief, two prison guards came in at that moment and, very politely, asked her to leave. Taking her in his arms, Teddy forgot about Arnie Meyer.

"Thank you for coming to see me."

"I'll come as often as I can. Just as soon as they tell me where you are." Alexia kissed him tenderly on the cheek.

"Look after Roxie," Teddy called over his shoulder as he was led away.

"I'll do my best."

Alexia watched as the man who'd shared her life for forty years was led along the corridor, out of sight. A wave of emotion surged up within her, but she pushed it back down. There was nothing she could do for Teddy now. But she could still help bring Jennifer Hamlin's killer to justice.

Arnie Meyer had a connection to Billy Hamlin. As bizarre as that sounded, it was true. Teddy had confirmed it. Arnie Meyer, Alexia's neighbor and friend, had used his shell company, HM Capital, to deliberately wreck Billy's business. According to Billy's ex-wife, that more than anything was what had driven poor Billy over the edge.

Teddy clearly knew nothing about it. His bafflement

earlier had been genuine and he'd bought Alexia's investment excuse hook, line, and sinker.

But somebody must know.

I have to talk to Lucy.

SUMMER MEYER STARED AT KAREN DAVIES'S computer monitor. She was so disappointed she could have wept.

"This is it? This is all you have?"

"That's it," said Karen. "She was in and out very quickly. No one you know, then?"

Summer *might* have known the woman on the screen. But it was utterly impossible to tell from this footage. Grainy, low resolution, and in black and white, it showed her only from behind and above. As she approached the front desk there was a split second when the camera captured a partial profile. But other than that, her face was hidden the entire time. For a moment Summer had thought there was something familiar about her—the way she walked, perhaps, or her body language as she leaned forward over the desk. But she quickly realized she was clutching at straws.

I want to see something so badly I'm making it up.

"Would it be all right if I took a copy of the footage home with me?"

She didn't expect to glean much more from the images, but at least if she had them on her home PC, she could study them more closely.

The secretary glanced warily around her before ejecting the disc and pressing it into Summer's hand.

"I don't have a copy, only the original. Take it and bring it back to me when you're finished with it. But for God's sake, don't lose it. David would have my guts for garters if he knew. He didn't even want me to call you, you know. He was well ruffled after you came in the first time."

"Was he?" said Summer, pocketing the disc. She wondered what Drake Motors' manager felt he had to hide. "Well, thank you, Karen. And I promise to take care of it."

"My pleasure." The older woman winked. Summer Meyer's little "investigation" was the most interesting thing that had happened to Karen Davies in a long time. "We girls have got to stick together, 'aven't we?"

LATER THAT NIGHT, SUMMER LAY SPRAWLED out on the couch in her rented flat in Bayswater, watching Karen Davies's CCTV footage for the umpteenth time. The more she watched the slender gray figure move across Drake Motors' shop floor, the more her feeling of familiarity grew. But there was nothing to connect it to. The woman's clothes, a knee-length skirt and sweater, were dull and unremarkable. She wore a head scarf—no one Summer knew wore head scarves—but perhaps she'd been conscious of the cameras, and done this to help conceal her face? Certainly she could hardly have done a better job of making herself anonymous, short of a balaclava.

Putting the computer aside, Summer turned on the television, flipping the channels to BBC news. Teddy De Vere had been sentenced today. His twenty-year-term was the evening's top story. Even now, after so many months, Summer found it hard to believe that soft, kindly, cuddly Uncle Teddy could have killed a man, shot him in cold blood. She was amazed to see that Roxie had turned up at court—two weeks ago she'd been adamant about wanting nothing to do with either of her parents. The news footage

435

showed her looking pretty and relaxed in a fitted black dress, leaving the High Court in her wheelchair at her mother's side.

Summer smiled. If Alexia and Roxie reconciled, at least some good would come out of this sorry mess. She noticed that Alexia was wearing the cream Chanel jacket that Lucy had given her last year on her birthday. Summer remembered the day well. How resentful and furious she'd felt back then, watching her mom walk across the room with the Chanel shopping bag in her hand, yet another expensive present for a woman Summer had perceived then as coldhearted and self-centered in the extreme. That was before she knew the truth, of course. She remembered Alexia stretching out her arms to receive the bag, and how greedy and graceless Summer had thought her: a spoiled queen accepting a tribute from one of her groveling courtiers.

And then it hit her. So hard, she gasped out loud.
Oh my God, I know.
I know who it is.

Heart hammering, she picked up her laptop again, cursing the seconds it took the disc to reload. At last the grainy figure reappeared. There could be no mistaking it now. There she was.

Michael's lover.

The woman who had bought him the bike.

The woman who had destroyed his life, and Summer's.

For a split second Summer felt a rush of satisfaction. She'd solved the puzzle. She'd won. She *knew*. But the truth was so unspeakable, so unnatural, so *wrong*, her feeling of achievement soon turned to revulsion. Dropping her head into her hands, Summer Meyer started to sob.

Once she started, she couldn't stop.

*

ALEXIA FLEW BACK TO AMERICA TWO days after Teddy's hearing. The flight was in the early morning, and there were no photographers at Heathrow to see her go, only her daughter, Roxie.

"I'll be back soon, darling," Alexia promised. "There are a couple of things I need to talk through with Lucy. But it won't take long. Then you and I can work out a plan for the future."

On the plane, in the comfort of her first-class seat, Alexia finally allowed herself to relax.

Tomorrow she would see Lucy. Lucy would know the truth about Arnie. Lucy would tell Alexia. Lucy trusted Alexia.

They trusted each other.

Alexia De Vere smiled as she soared up into the blue.

CHAPTER THIRTY-NINE

"THE TOAST IS BURNING."

Arnie Meyer looked up briefly from the *Wall Street Journal*. He was in the kitchen of his home on Martha's Vineyard, sipping the finest Colombian coffee and enjoying the view across his gardens to the harbor, when the unexpected, acrid smell of smoke disturbed him. Unexpected because Lucy never burned anything. Ever. Her meals were always things of beauty, delivered perfect and piping hot on pretty bone-china plates, timed to perfection like miniature military campaigns. It was a precision and attention to detail that Arnie Meyer both appreciated and expected. He was a man used to getting his own way.

"Hmm?" Lucy looked at Arnie, then at the toaster. "Oh my God! Why didn't you *say* something?"

"I did."

Lucy wasn't listening. Pressing cancel, she ejected the two charred squares, opened the kitchen door, and carried them outside, still smoking.

"Careful, honey," Arnie called after her. "You'll burn your fingers. Do you want me to put on some more?"

Outside in the cool morning air, Lucy Meyer took a

deep, calming breath. "No, no," she said cheerfully, the competent housewife once more. "I'll do it."

From behind the shield of his newspaper, Arnie watched his wife as she bustled around the room, slicing bread from the fresh baker's loaf and whisking up the eggs for his smoked-salmon scramble. *She's still beautiful to me*, he thought affectionately. He loved Lucy's slender waist—slim, but not too thin, like her friend Alexia. Mrs. De Vere was looking gaunt these days, in Arnie Meyer's humble opinion. A woman should have a little meat on her bones. In a cornflower-blue shirtwaist dress, with a floral apron tied over the top, Lucy had an old-fashioned, 1950s look about her this morning that conjured up the wholesome happiness of earlier, simpler times. She reminded Arnie of his mother as a young woman: feminine, nurturing, a soft, welcoming respite from the slings and arrows of the world.

"I love you."

Lucy turned around, a curious smile on her face. Arnie wasn't usually big on verbal displays of affection. "Well, that's good." She laughed. "Because at this point you're pretty much stuck with me."

Arnie finally put down his paper. "Is something the matter, Luce? You seem kind of jumpy this morning."

"Why, because I burned the toast?" Lucy laughed again, but he sensed there was an edge to it.

"I don't know. Maybe. You never burn the toast. You never burn anything."

"Nothing's the matter, Arnie." Putting the pan of eggs on a low heat, she came over to the table and kissed him. "If anything, I'm a little excited. I haven't seen Summer in so long. It'll be a treat having her here."

"Oh, shit." Arnie Meyer put his head in his hands. "It's today, isn't it? I totally forgot she was flying in."

"Arnie!"

"I know. I'm sorry. I arranged to go fishing with Jake McIntyre."

"Well, you'd better un-arrange it," said Lucy, returning to the stove, wooden spoon in hand. "You agreed to pick Summer up at the airport. She's expecting you."

"Can't you do it? I promised Jake—"

"No, I cannot do it," Lucy said, annoyed. "I'm hiking with Alexia, remember? She called from England especially to ask if we could have some time alone today."

"But you can see Alexia anytime."

"For God's sake, Arnie, Teddy's just been sent to jail! You can see Jake McIntyre anytime. Alexia needs me right now."

Arnie Meyer held his hands up like a soccer player admitting a foul. After three decades of marriage, he knew when he was fighting a losing battle.

"Okay, okay, I'll go get Summer. What time's her flight land anyway?"

SUMMER PRESSED HER FACE TO THE window of the little, single-engine plane, watching the contours of Martha's Vineyard take shape below. An almost perfect triangle, with the Atlantic Ocean at its base and the Nantucket and Vineyard Sounds along the other two sides, it looked so peaceful and unchanging. As the plane began its descent, she could make out the familiar white clapboard homes, dotted like dollhouses around the island. Swimming pools glinted blue, like tiny square-cut sapphires in the emerald-green yards. Everything was ordered and manicured and unthreatening, mocking the turmoil that Summer felt inside.

As a child, she used to relish these short plane rides

from Boston. The first glimpse of the island was always magical and exciting, marking the beginning of a summer of adventures. Summer had been cripplingly shy in those days: overweight, tongue-tied, socially awkward. But her mom had made sure that her childhood was idyllic, despite those disadvantages. Always there to defend her, to hold her hand, comfort her, boost her confidence, Lucy Meyer was the mother that every other kid wanted.

For the hundredth time on her long journey from London, Summer's eyes welled with tears.

How could she? How could *she?*

When Summer first realized that the woman on Drake Motors' CCTV footage was her own mother, her natural response was disbelief. Yes, the walk was Lucy's, and the body language and the way she moved her arms. (It was that, more than anything, that had triggered Summer's memory. Picturing her mother handing that birthday present to Alexia, the Chanel jacket.) But the idea that her own mother had had an affair with Michael? That simply didn't compute. It was like being told the world was square, or the sky green. However many pictures someone showed you, you wouldn't believe it. Lucy being Michael De Vere's "sugar mommy" defied all laws of nature, of probability, of reality as Summer knew it.

Unable to trust her own judgment, or even believe her own eyes, Summer had done what every good journalist would do. She'd looked for corroborating evidence. Karen Davies at Drake Motors had given her the details of the anonymous offshore bank account used to pay for Michael's Ducati. At the time they'd meant nothing to Summer. They were just a string of random numbers: IBAN and SWIFT and routing codes. But when she checked them against the spreadsheet Arnie had made for her years ago, detailing all the Meyer family's bank holdings, they were a perfect match.

Lucy bought the bike.

Lucy was Michael's mistress.

Had Lucy tried to kill him too? Had she tampered with the Panigale deliberately?

A sharp bump dragged Summer back to the present. *We've landed.*

Unfastening her seat belt, she wiped away her tears and tried to focus on her anger, wrapping it around her like a protective cloak. How had her mother dared do this to her? How had Michael! What had they been thinking? Michael's betrayal hurt Summer deeply, but her mother's was worse. Didn't Lucy realize that Summer had now lost everything? Not just Michael, and her hopes for a new family, but her old family as well. All her memories, her childhood happiness, all of it had been tainted, poisoned, destroyed. It would have been less painful if Lucy had cut off her arms or thrown acid in her face. And all the while she'd made herself out to be this perfect mother! That was the worst of it.

Summer thought back to what Roxie had said to her at Fairmont House.

"You have no idea how lucky you are to have Lucy for a mother.

"You can't imagine what it's like, realizing that everything you thought you knew about yourself and your family was just smoke and mirrors!"

Summer could imagine it now.

She'd already decided what she was going to do. First, she would tell her father. She would show Arnie the footage, show him the bank transfer, let him know that his wife, the saintly Lucy Meyer, was a liar and an adulteress and a fraud and . . . a killer?

442

It was at this point that everything started to unravel. Even now, knowing what she knew, Summer couldn't bring herself to believe that Lucy would have tried to kill Michael by deliberately sabotaging his bike. For one thing, she had no reason to want to hurt him. Apart from everything else, he was her best friend's son. Lucy had known Michael since boyhood. Besides, the mechanics at the St. Martin's garage weren't *certain* that anyone had tampered with the Ducati's brakes. It could have been an accident. Summer didn't know what to believe anymore. The only person who knew the truth was her mother, but did Summer have the strength to confront her? What did one say in these circumstances? She'd had the last twelve hours to think about it, but still had no idea how to begin.

Mom, I know you were fucking my boyfriend.

Mom, did you try to murder Michael?

It was all too surreal.

Summer walked across the tarmac in a daze, retrieving her luggage and bracing herself for the arrivals terminal. She did her best to compose herself before the electric double doors whooshed open and she found herself standing in a sea of smiling faces. Everyone was wearing the Vineyard uniform of khaki shorts and button-down shirts, waiting for their friends and relatives to arrive as if this were a normal day, as if the world hadn't stopped spinning. Summer scanned the crowd. She couldn't see her dad. Annoyance mixed with relief—at least she wouldn't have to break the news to him yet. But as she walked out to the taxi stand, there was Arnie, panting as he ran toward the terminal. Catching sight of Summer, he slowed down, walking up to her and pulling her into a bear hug.

"Sorry, baby."

He smelled of aftershave and coffee and cigars—*the dad*

443

smell. Despite her best efforts, Summer started tearing up again.

"So good to have you back," said Arnie, mopping the sweat from his brow. "Do me a favor. Promise not to tell your mother I was late."

And in that instant Summer realized: *I can't tell him. At least not until I've talked to Mom. Not until I know the truth for sure. It'll totally destroy him.*

"Hi, Dad. It's good to see you too." She tried to hold them back but it was impossible. There, in her father's arms, the tears began to flow uncontrollably.

Arnie looked horrified. "Sweetheart, what's wrong?"

Everything.

"Nothing. I guess I've just really missed you, that's all."

"Oh, honey. Mom and I have missed you too. But you're here now. Don't cry. Come on." Arnie picked up Summer's suitcase in one hand and took her arm with the other. "The Jeep's just outside. Let's get you home."

ALEXIA LOOKED AT LUCY'S BULGING RUCKSACK with alarm.

"What on earth have you got there? You look like you've packed for the North Pole."

"It's only a picnic," said Lucy.

"For who? An invading army?"

"I may have brought along a few other essentials. One should always come prepared."

Alexia felt anything but prepared. She'd arrived on the island the previous night. Jet lag was still dulling her reactions, making her feel foggy. It had all seemed so straightforward back in England. She would fly back to the Vineyard, tell Lucy what she'd discovered in New York—that Arnie's company, HM Capital, had deliberately driven Billy Hamlin out of business—and ask her what she knew. Simple.

Only it wasn't simple. Now that she was here, actually *with* Lucy, Alexia realized the full implications of what she was about to ask. This was Arnie they were talking about. Lucy's husband. The man she loved. Alexia was about to suggest that he was implicated, not just in threats and extortion, but in murder too. Lucy would have every right to tell Alexia to stick her theories where the sun didn't shine.

And really, why should she believe me? At this point I'm not sure if I believe myself.

Alexia had known Arnie Meyer for as long as she'd known his wife. She could imagine him being tough in business, even underhanded if the situation demanded it. But she couldn't picture him as some sort of psychopath, making threatening phone calls using a voice distorter, pursuing some unknown vendetta, kidnapping and murdering innocent people. Then again, after everything she'd learned about her own husband in the last year, Alexia no longer fully trusted her own judgment.

I won't accuse him of anything. I'll put the facts to Lucy. Calmly. Rationally. Dispassionately.

She watched as Lucy laced up her hiking boots, applied sunscreen and insect spray and checked their water bottles. One look at Lucy Meyer's open, round, makeup-free face reminded Alexia forcefully that her friend's world was very different from her own. Alexia had become so used to drama and tragedy in the last two years nothing shocked her anymore. But Lucy's world was still as it had always been: simple and safe and normal and predictable. The very idea that Arnie might have known Billy Hamlin would sound preposterous to her, never mind the thought of him setting out to do Billy and his family harm.

Because it is *preposterous. None of this makes sense.*

Lucy smiled. "Ready?"

No. Not remotely.

"Ready. Where are we going, by the way?"

Lucy looked at Alexia cryptically. "It's a surprise. You'll see."

THEY TURNED LEFT OFF OF PILGRIM Road, toward the center of the island. Here salt marshes and cranberry bogs were intersected by an apparently limitless maze of sandy tracks, none of them signposted. Occasionally other hikers would appear on one of the paths, or four-wheel-drive vehicles would bounce past, their tires partially deflated so they could drive on the dunes. But mostly the whole area was deserted, save for the deer and rabbits that were to be found everywhere on the island.

Lucy walked in front, occasionally consulting her map or stopping to sip from her water bottle. She looked over her shoulder every now and then, smiling at Alexia, checking she was okay. But she made no attempt at conversation. Alexia was the one who had proposed this hike, who had said repeatedly that she needed to talk. Lucy assumed she would do so when she was ready.

An hour passed, then two. It was past noon now and the sun, pleasantly warm earlier in the morning, now blazed above the two women with a punishing heat. Alexia had never been to this part of the island before. She could hear the ocean, the waves crashing wildly against the cliffs, and realized they must be approaching the north shore. Currents were stronger on this side of the island, and the tides were unpredictable. As always, the sounds of the sea frightened her, calling her back to another time, another beach that would always be with her.

"Do you think we could rest for a moment?" she shouted ahead to Lucy. "It's so hot."

"Sure," Lucy called back. "Let's just get through the moor here to the top of the cliffs. There's a bench there where we can sit."

The "bench" turned out to be a roughly hewn log, plunked unceremoniously down about fifteen feet from the cliff's edge. It wasn't a sheer drop in front of them. A steep, rocky path that looked like it had been made by deer rather than humans wound down from the clearing to a hidden cove below. But they were elevated enough to have spectacular views across the sound toward Nantucket. Thick gorse and heather moorland stretched behind them as far as the eye could see, just as the blue water rolled out endlessly in front. It made Alexia feel as if she were perched on the edge of the world.

Sinking down gratefully onto the log, Alexia took a long, deep drink of water. Lucy did the same. Suddenly, here in this peaceful, isolated place, Alexia felt ready to talk.

"There's something I need to ask you about."

"I figured. The call from London, when you said you really needed to talk to me and to arrange some time alone? That kind of tipped me off."

Alexia tried to smile but she couldn't. "It's . . . not easy."

"I figured that too."

"I wouldn't want you to take this the wrong way."

Lucy frowned. "Alexia. After all the things you've told me over the years, you really think I'm going to freak out on you now? Come on. You know you can tell me anything."

"It's about Arnie."

Lucy couldn't hide her surprise. "Arnie?"

"Yes. When I was in New York, I met with Jennifer Hamlin's mother. Billy's ex-wife."

447

"I know. You said. Sally. She was the one who made you decide to forgive Teddy."

Wow. She must really have been listening at Elaine's.

"That's right. She was the one who told me about the threatening phone calls Billy had complained about. She also gave me a bunch of information, contacts and stuff, from when Billy's mechanics business was still going."

"Okaaay." Lucy looked confused.

"The calls from the crazy Bible basher began during the period that Hamlin's went bankrupt," Alexia explained, "so she thought there might be a link. Well, it turns out there was."

Lucy waited.

"The link was a company called HM Capital. Do you know it?"

"Sure. That's one of Arnie's businesses."

"Exactly. I saw his name on the directors' list. Later I asked Teddy about it, and he told me that Arnie was the founder-owner."

"That's right," said Lucy.

She didn't seem angry or ruffled so far. Encouraged, Alexia went on.

"Okay. So over a period of two years, HM Capital systematically set about poaching Billy Hamlin's clients and buying out his suppliers. There are too many connections for it to be a coincidence, especially given that the company had zero involvement in the automotive sector either before or after that time. As crazy as it sounds, Arnie wanted to ruin Billy Hamlin. And he succeeded."

Lucy was quiet, apparently taking this information in.

"So my question is, why? Can you think of any connection, any connection at all, that Arnie might have had with the Hamlin family? However tenuous?"

Lucy shook her head. "No. I really can't."

"Please try," Alexia pleaded. "There must be something. This is serious, Luce. Billy's daughter and his business partner, Milo Bates, were both murdered."

"I know that," Lucy said calmly.

"When I told you about Billy Hamlin coming to find me in London, the last time we walked out to this side of the island . . . when I told you about my past . . . had you ever heard his name before?"

Lucy was smiling, but it was a strange smile. There was something off about it, something unfamiliar and not quite right.

"Maybe Arnie mentioned him?"

"Arnie never mentioned him."

Lucy stood up and began pacing slowly back and forth, between the cliff edge and the bench.

Alexia wondered if Lucy was angry. If she'd somehow gone too far in mentioning Arnie. She tried to backtrack.

"I'm not accusing Arnie of anything. It may be he had nothing to do with the phone calls, or the murders. I don't know."

"You're not accusing him," Lucy repeated robotically.

Something was definitely wrong. Had Lucy gotten too much sun?

"But Arnie's company's name popping up like that, not just once but multiple times, everywhere. It *can't* just be a coincidence. There must be some form of link."

"Of course there must!"

Lucy laughed loudly, but there was no joy in the sound. It was more of a cackle, bordering on the hysterical. She was squatting on her haunches now, rummaging in her backpack. Alexia thought. *Good. She clearly needs some water. And some food. The shock must have been too much for her. Either that or we're both getting too old for midday hikes through . . .*

Her thoughts trailed off.

Lucy Meyer had pulled out a gun. Pointing it right between Alexia's eyes, she had stopped laughing. Hatred blazed out of her like light from the sun.

"It's you, Alexia, don't you see? *You're* the link. Although I must start calling you by your real name. *Toni.* Antonia Louise Gilletti, sly, scheming, hateful bitch that you are ! Everything that happened, all the death, all the pain—it was all because of you."

CHAPTER FORTY

Summer Meyer threw her bag down on her bed, then lay down wearily beside it. She felt desperately tired, but not the kind of tired that would ever lead to sleep. Instead her body twitched with the restless exhaustion of the emotionally shattered. Staring at the ceiling, which was still half covered in glow stars from her childhood, she felt as wired and tearful as a junkie in withdrawal.

I have to talk to Mom.

Arnie had told her in the car that Lucy had left on a hike this morning and wasn't expected back till late afternoon. "She's with Alexia."

This brought Summer up short. "What do you mean? Alexia's in England."

"Nope. She's with your mother."

"Dad, she's been all over the news in the UK. This business with Teddy. I saw her on TV."

"Yes, well, all I can tell you is she telephoned your mother and said she had something important to discuss with her. So important it couldn't be dealt with over the phone, apparently. She flew in last night."

This threw a major wrench in the works. When Summer

confronted her mother, it had to be alone. She would tell Alexia, of course. Alexia had the right to know the truth about her son's relationship with her so-called best friend. But there was no way Summer could say what she had to say in front of an audience.

On the other hand, the idea of waiting until nightfall was unbearable. She already felt stretched to a breaking point. Six more hours and she'd be foaming at the mouth.

Not sure what else to do, she took a shower, brushed her teeth, and changed into cooler, more comfortable clothes: a pair of cutoff jeans and a thin cotton shirt from James Perse.

"You look cute, honey." Arnie smiled warmly as she came downstairs. "Shall I get Lydia to make us a late lunch?"

"No thanks, Dad. I couldn't eat."

"What do you mean you couldn't eat. You have to *eat*, Summer. Are you sure nothing's the matter?"

"I'm fine, Dad. A bit nauseous, that's all."

"You're not pregnant, are you?"

"Pregnant? Jeez, Dad, no! How could I possibly be pregnant?"

"Well, go sit outside, then, and Lydia will bring you out some cheese and fruit. You can manage that much at least."

Protest was clearly useless. Summer walked toward the kitchen door.

"Oh, by the way, your mom left this for you." Arnie handed her an envelope on her way out. "She asked me to give it to you as soon as you landed, but I forgot. Don't tell her, okay?"

"What is it?"

"Beats me. I usually find, with envelopes, the mystery becomes clearer when you open 'em."

In normal circumstances, Summer would have laughed

at that. Now she took the envelope in silence and walked away.

Arnie Meyer thought, *There's something wrong with that girl. What the hell's gotten into the women in my family today?*

"GET UP."

Lucy Meyer held the gun steady. Her voice was normal again, the same soft singsong that Alexia knew so well. All traces of her earlier hysteria were gone, replaced by a chilling calm. *She means business.*

Alexia stood up.

"You know, for someone so smart, someone who made it to the top of their game, you can be damned stupid sometimes."

"That's probably true. I—"

"Stop talking!" Lucy commanded. "*I'm* talking. Over there." She jerked the pistol in the direction of the cliff edge. Slowly, Alexia walked to where she was directed until she heard Lucy say, "Stop."

"I think the funniest part of all of this has to be you pointing the finger at Arnie. *'I'm not accusing him of anything.'*" Lucy mimicked Alexia's accent perfectly. "That's just flat-out hilarious. As if you, YOU, who killed an innocent child, are in a position to accuse anyone of anything! You smug, entitled, self-righteous bitch."

"You who killed an innocent child." Alexia's mind raced.

"This is about Nicholas Handemeyer."

"That's right," Lucy said simply. "Nicholas Handemeyer. The little boy you left to drown. He was my brother."

SUMMER RAN INTO THE HOUSE, LUCY's letter still in her hand.

"Where did they go, Dad?"

Arnie was slicing bread at the kitchen counter. "Where did who go?"

"Mom!" Summer practically screamed. "Mom and Alexia! Where are they? We need to find them, now! Right now."

"Calm down, honey." Arnie rested a hand on her shoulder. "I don't know where they are exactly. Somewhere on the north of the island. What's the panic about?"

Summer handed him Lucy's letter. After a few seconds she watched the blood drain from his face.

"Jesus Christ," he whispered. "Call the police."

Summer was already dialing.

"BUT . . . YOUR MAIDEN NAME WASN'T HANDEMEYER." Alexia spoke without thinking. As frightened as she was, her need to understand, to know the truth, was overpowering. "It was Miller."

"That's right. Very good," said Lucy. Finishing her bottle of drinking water, she dropped it on the ground. "Bobby Miller was my high school sweetheart. We married at eighteen. It only lasted six months, but I kept the name. Handemeyer held too many sad memories by then. Terrible memories." She lifted the gun again, shaking the barrel at Alexia like an angry fist. "Do you have any idea, *any* idea, what you did to my family? You and Billy Hamlin?"

Alexia said nothing. Her eyes were fixed on the gun.

"Nicko was the sweetest kid in the universe, so trusting, so darling. It broke us all when he died, but my mom . . ." Tears filled Lucy's eyes. "My mom was shattered. She never recovered. She killed herself two years later, on the anniversary of Nicko's death. Did you know that? Hung herself in our barn with Nick's old jump rope."

454

Alexia shook her head in mute horror. She remembered Mrs. Handemeyer from Billy's trial. *Ruth*. How dignified and gracious she'd been in the courtroom. How pretty she was, with her butterscotch hair and brown eyes, so like her dead son's. She tried to remember Lucy back then, but drew a total blank. There *had* been a sister at the trial, a girl clasping the mother's hand. But Alexia hadn't focused on her at all. She couldn't bring her face to mind now.

"Dad died less than a year after. His heart just cracked. You took everything from me. And you thought I was just gonna sit back and let you disappear, dance off into the sunset and live happily ever after, without paying for what you'd done? Of course, for decades, the longest time, I didn't know it was you. Like everyone else, I thought Billy Hamlin murdered my brother. He was the one I needed to punish."

"But Billy *was* punished," said Alexia. "He went to jail."

"Fifteen years? In a comfortable, safe cell with three decent meals a day? Are you kidding me? That wasn't *punishment*. That was a joke." There was no mistaking the loathing in Lucy's eyes. "I thought about shooting him in the head as soon as he got out of prison." Her tone was totally deadpan. "But that was way too swift and painless. Do you know how long it takes a person to drown?"

Alexia shook her head.

"No? On average. Have a guess."

"I don't know."

"Twenty-two minutes. That's twenty-two minutes of blind terror poor little Nicko went through, praying, pleading for someone to rescue him. No way was his killer gonna get a clean death. He had to suffer, the way my family suffered, the way *I* suffered. He had to know what it felt like to lose everyone he loved, to lose a child. So . . ." She shrugged.

"I had to wait. I waited for Billy Hamlin to get married, to have a child, to build a business. The bastard had to get a life before I could start to destroy it, the way he destroyed mine."

Except he didn't destroy yours! Alexia thought desperately. *I did. Poor Billy never hurt you, or your family. He never hurt anyone. It was all me!*

Lucy went on. "I watched him for years and years before anything happened. And life went on in the meantime. Arnie and I married. I had Summer. We bought the estate here. But I never lost sight of Billy Hamlin. Not for a day, not for an hour. Anyway, the Lord must have been looking out for me and helping me. Because around the time Billy was released, I discovered that I wasn't the only one spying on Billy Hamlin. An Englishman by the name of Teddy De Vere was sniffing around him too. The PI I was using at the time was the one who first alerted me. If it hadn't been for that"—she smiled—"I'd never have found you. I'd never have gotten to the truth. *'And you will know the truth and the truth will make you free.'* John, Chapter Eight. "

Alexia gasped. "The voice. The threatening phone calls. It was you!"

Lucy bowed theatrically. "You got there at last. Now, where was I? Oh, yes. Teddy. When I learned Teddy was in the private equity business, I found a way to set up a meeting between him and Arnie. I thought a business connection might help me figure out what this guy's interest was in Nicko's killer. But of course, it didn't. I had no idea, and in the end I gave up trying to figure it out. The rest you pretty much know. Arnie and Teddy became friends. Teddy bought the house on Pilgrim. And you and I met. You could say it was fate."

Alexia's skin tingled with adrenaline. It was an odd

sensation, a combination of physical fear—Lucy's gun was still directed at her head—and intellectual excitement. Every word Lucy told her was like a puzzle piece slotting into place. A sick puzzle. A terrifying puzzle. But the satisfaction of solving it remained.

From her position on the cliff edge, Alexia could see the rocky path down to the cove more clearly. It was steeper than she'd first thought, and more treacherous. The only possible escape would be to return the way they'd come, through the moorland brush. But that would involve getting past Lucy and somehow disarming her before she had a chance to shoot. There was no way.

I'm trapped.

Bizarrely, this realization made Alexia relax. The certainty that she was going to die here, in this spot, emboldened her. She needed to know the truth, the whole truth, before she left this world.

"So it was you who drove Billy out of business?"

"Of course. That was just the start."

"And Arnie knew nothing about it?"

"Not a thing. I'm the primary shareholder in HM Capital, not Arnie. HM is short for 'Handemeyer,' by the way. I guess your little foray into Internet research didn't get you that far."

No. It didn't.

Somewhere behind them, in the moorland, a twig cracked. Both women froze. Alexia contemplated screaming for help, but she knew if she did that, Lucy might shoot. It wasn't death itself that frightened her, as much as dying before she knew the truth, before Lucy had finished her story.

"Down!" Lucy whispered, pointing at the shingle path with her gun.

"It's too dangerous," Alexia whispered back. "We'll fall."

Lucy released the safety catch on her gun with a faint but audible *click*. "Down," she repeated.

Alexia crawled toward the cliff.

OFFICER BRIAN SULLIVAN READ THE LETTER. He'd seen suicide notes before. But nothing quite like this. If any piece of Lucy Meyer's confession was true, any one piece of it, the Martha's Vineyard Police Department was way out of its depth.

He told Arnie Meyer, "We'll need help. Helicopters. Dogs. I'm gonna have to call Boston. You've no idea where they are, you say?"

Arnie shook his head helplessly. He was clearly still in shock.

"But it was somewhere to the north of the island?"

"Yes. Lucy knows those paths like the back of her hand, but it's a maze out there. Summer's already gone out to look for them, but I haven't heard from her."

Officer Brian Sullivan looked alarmed. "Your daughter went after them alone?"

"I couldn't stop her." Arnie Meyer started to cry.

ALEXIA LOST HER FOOTING, GASPING AS the scree and talus crumbled beneath her. Instinctively she clutched at the rock face to her left. Behind her, Lucy Meyer did the same.

"Keep going!"

It was unnecessary advice. The "path" above them, such as it was, had already flaked away to almost nothing. Even if Alexia somehow overpowered Lucy, she'd have no way to get back up the cliff now. Once the tides rose, the cove would be flooded. The only way out would be to swim, but the currents on this side of the island were lethal.

Alexia tried not to think about it as she scrambled down the bank, falling the last ten feet onto the sand and twisting her ankle painfully. She let out a sharp cry.

"Be quiet!" hissed Lucy. Sliding down after Alexia, she landed comfortably on her feet, her pistol still clasped firmly in her hand. They were completely hidden from view now, tucked beneath the overhang of the cliffs. While Alexia shuffled backward, dragging her legs painfully across the sand, Lucy resumed her earlier monologue.

"By the time I was ready to act against Billy Hamlin, he was already getting divorced. He'd destroyed his marriage on his own. So the next thing to destroy was the business."

Alexia had her back against the cliff now, pressed to the smooth stone. Her ankle throbbed, but if she kept it still, the pain was bearable. She focused on what Lucy was saying.

"I figured I'd start small, then move on to the things and people Billy really cared about."

"Like Milo Bates?"

"Like Milo Bates."

"So you did kill Milo?"

"Not personally." Lucy smiled. "I weigh a hundred pounds. Milo Bates was a big man, bigger than Arnie. But I arranged his death, yes."

It was like listening to Teddy talking about Andrew Beesley's murder. Lucy seemed to have no remorse at all.

"But Milo Bates was completely innocent," said Alexia. "He had a family of his own. A wife and three children."

"DON'T YOU DARE PREACH TO ME!" Lucy roared. "No friend of Billy Hamlin was innocent. Bates knew about Billy's conviction. He knew what that bastard had done. But he still went into business with him." She took a few deep breaths, eventually regaining her composure. "Milo Bates's death was strike one. It was actually very easy. Even kidnapping Billy afterward, showing him the tape of what we did to his friend . . . Hamlin was so paranoid by then. A few phone calls, a little pressure on his business, that was really all it took. By the time he told the cops what we did to Milo, no one believed a word he said."

She said it with pride.

Alexia thought, *You're insane. Completely insane.*

"What about Jennifer Hamlin? I'm assuming you killed her too?"

"I'm getting to that," said Lucy. "You really must learn to be patient, Toni."

Alexia recoiled. Even now, she hated being called by that name.

"So, Hamlin had lost his wife. He'd lost his business. And he'd lost his only real friend. But there had to be something more. I'd looked into his birth family years earlier, but they were all dead. His father passed away shortly after the trial, and he had no mother or siblings. There was *his* child, of course, Jennifer. But I wanted losing his daughter to be the grand finale, the last thing the son of a bitch suffered before his own death. It wasn't her time yet. I needed someone else."

Slowly it dawned on Alexia where this was going.

"I'd heard rumors about a woman," said Lucy. "Someone Billy had loved in his youth and apparently still carried a torch for. He was drinking quite heavily by then, and he used to talk about her—about you, Toni—in bars and at pool halls, to anyone who'd listen. I dimly remembered the name from the trial. *Gilletti*. But it wasn't until I finally saw an old picture that I was able to put two and two together. Well, you can imagine my shock. My horror. *You*, my neighbor, probably my closest friend in the world. *You* and Hamlin had been lovers! You were there when Nicko died! Now I finally knew why Teddy had been tracking Billy all these years, just like I was. It was because of you. I was torn at that point, I'll admit it. Billy had gone to England to try and find you. I guess he wanted to warn you. Maybe he sensed you were next in line, I don't know. But the truth is, I hadn't decided."

"Decided what?" Alexia asked.

"Whether to kill you or not. Oh, I scared you a little. With the phone calls, although those worked a lot better on Billy . . . and getting someone to do away with that awful little rat of a dog that used to follow Teddy everywhere. What was his name?"

"Danny." Alexia felt sick.

"But I honestly didn't know if I had the heart to go through with killing you. The problem was, I liked you. Loved you even. Our kids grew up together. You were like a sister to me. It was hard."

Is she asking for my sympathy?

"But once again the Lord opened my eyes. He brought you to me, here, on this island, and you told me, told me to my *face,* that it was you all along. *You* were the one who let my brother drown! Billy Hamlin, the man I'd devoted my entire adult life to destroying—he was merely your accomplice. An afterthought." Lucy shook her head in disgust. "Can you *imagine* what that felt like, Toni? Can you even imagine? I'd shared dinners with you. Laughed with you. Cried with you."

"Terrorized me," said Alexia angrily. "Butchered my dog." Lucy's cloying self-pity was too much to bear, like being drowned in a vat of cream. "Your brother's death was an accident. An *accident*."

461

"No! It was murder. The court said so."

"The court? The court that convicted the wrong man, you mean?" Alexia scoffed. "What the hell did that court know about the truth? They wanted a scapegoat and Billy Hamlin provided one. I was there when Nicholas died, Lucy. I don't need to guess what happened. I know. It was an accident and that's a fact."

"Be quiet!" Lucy commanded. Walking over to Alexia, she kicked her hard in the ankle, her heavy hiking boot zeroing in on the pain like a drone missile. Alexia screamed in agony. "You do not speak, do you hear me? You do NOT speak. You listen. You're not in Parliament now. No one's hanging on your every word. There's no one left who even cares if you live or die. *I'm* talking now."

The pain in her leg was so excruciating, Alexia didn't even have the strength to nod. Instead, whimpering quietly, she allowed Lucy's insane ramblings to wash over her.

"After that, I knew I had to kill you. Of course, in the end that taxi driver, Drake, almost beat me to it! Can you imagine if he'd succeeded? But the Lord didn't let that happen. He spared you such a clean, painless death. He was saving you for me. He knew I had to make you suffer first, just like Billy had suffered. And that wasn't easy, what with your *position* and all." She spat the word out tauntingly. "For a while I wondered if I'd done the wrong thing by persecuting Billy Hamlin for all those years. But then I figured, no. Billy Hamlin lied for you. He protected you. He knew you were responsible for Nicko's death and he did everything he could to help you evade justice. So now you both had to suffer equally. Billy had to know what it felt like to lose a child. And so did you."

"Michael." Alexia breathed the word softly.

"Oh, yes, well, Michael." Lucy waved a dismissive hand.

"Michael survived, unfortunately. Although I try to comfort myself with the knowledge that he's as good as dead. Perhaps, in a way, that's *more* painful," she mused.

Alexia felt a rush of hatred so strong she could have choked on it.

"My biggest disappointment wasn't that your worthless son survived," Lucy continued. "It was that Billy Hamlin never got to see *his* child die. After decades spent patiently watching and waiting, biding my time, I was robbed of the chance to make Billy suffer the ultimate loss. Some junkie in London stuck a knife in his heart and gave him a clean, easy death."

Lucy shook her head bitterly. The evil spewing out of her mouth was breathtaking.

"That was hard to take."

"I'll bet," said Alexia, through gritted teeth. The pain in her ankle was unbearable. "But you had Jennifer Hamlin murdered anyway. Just for the hell of it. A wholly innocent young woman."

"Aren't you listening to me?" Lucy screeched. "That bastard never got to see his daughter's death, her suffering, the way that my mother had to with Nicko. He'd already evaded so much justice. You both had. I had to put things right. An eye for an eye . . . it was what God wanted. One child's death deserves another."

There was no point trying to reason with Lucy. Alexia could see that now. Years of grief had been carefully nurtured till they morphed into hatred, then rage, and ultimately psychosis. Yet she couldn't allow Lucy to end *her* life without striking back, without making Lucy suffer in some small way for what she'd done to Michael, and all the other victims.

"You talk about truth," Alexia said. "But you still don't know the truth. After all those years of watching and waiting, you missed so much! It's pathetic."

Lucy's eyes narrowed. "What do you mean?"

"Billy Hamlin wasn't killed by 'some junkie.'"

"Yes, he was. The police report said so. He was stabbed by an addict looking for cash."

"Rubbish," Alexia taunted. "The police didn't have a clue who did it. They still don't. But I do. It was Teddy!"

A look of profound confusion passed across Lucy Meyer's face.

"No. That's not possible."

"Of course it's possible. It's a fact." Alexia relished twisting the knife. "He confessed to me privately, after he was charged with killing Andrew Beesley. He did it to protect me, to protect our family. Teddy thought Billy was trying to blackmail me, you see. He knew the truth all along and he forgave me. So after all those years of waiting, Teddy beat you to the punch!"

"Shut up!" Lucy shouted. "I don't believe you."

Alexia smiled. "Yes, you do."

"It doesn't matter anyway. Who cares? Hamlin's dead, his daughter's dead. And soon you're going to join them." Reaching into her backpack, Lucy pulled out a set of handcuffs. "Get on your knees."

Alexia shook her head.

"DO IT!" Lucy pressed the barrel of the gun to Alexia's temple.

Alexia said calmly, "I can't do it, Lucy. My ankle. I can't move."

"Fine," Lucy snapped. Lifting up her own left foot, she stamped down hard on Alexia's ankle. The last thing Alexia heard was her own screams as her bones shattered. Then everything went black.

*

SUMMER STOPPED AND LISTENED, AS STILL and alert as a deer in the forest.

Was that a seagull shrieking? Or a human scream?

She froze, hoping, praying to hear it again. But there was nothing.

She'd walked these paths before with her mother, but not since her teens. They were more of a maze than she remembered them, and the heat, combined with her own exhaustion and panic, made it hard to concentrate.

She tried not to think about her mother's letter. Part suicide note, part confession, it was the rambling product of a truly addled, broken mind. The tone shifted wildly throughout. There was the matter-of-factness with which she wrote about Michael—*I know it'll hurt you darling, but I'm afraid it had to be done*—the eerie biblical references woven through the text that showed how wholly deranged and psychotic Lucy had become. *She's ill*, Summer thought. *She needs help.* But nothing could excuse or conceal the bald facts of what her mother had done, and what she intended to do.

I have to find her. I have to.

If she sees the police, she'll panic.

Summer was close to the ocean now, could hear the rhythmic crashing of the waves against the cliffs. A crunch beneath her feet made her stop. She stooped down and picked up an empty plastic water bottle. It was Nantucket Springs, the brand her mother bought.

"Mom!" she shouted into the wind.

Nothing.

"Mom, it's me, Summer. Can you hear me?"

But her words were swallowed, not by the wind or the tide, but by another noise.

A noise coming from above.

*

Lucy Meyer looked up.

Helicopter. That's all I need.

It was probably just the coast guard on a routine flight. Then again, Summer would have read her letter by now. She couldn't take any chances.

Alexia was still unconscious. Pulling her hands behind her back and locking the cuffs into place, Lucy dragged her back under the brow of the cliff. She was so frail and malnourished it was like pulling a rag doll. No chopper would see them here. But they couldn't hide out forever. Already the tides were rising. Within an hour, the cove would be completely submerged.

"Wake up, damn you." Lucy shook Alexia by the shoulders. A faint movement of the lips, little more than a flutter, but it was enough. Lucy felt relief flood through her.

She's coming back.

Arnie Meyer spoke into his mouthpiece.

"See anything?"

The police reconnaissance officer shook his head. "Not yet."

"Can you ask the pilot to go lower?"

"Not really. We have to be careful. Winds can be very changeable out here and these cliffs are no joke."

"Yes, but my daughter . . ."

The policeman reached across and put a hand on Arnie's shoulder. "If she's out here, sir, we'll find her. Doug, take her down a little, would you?"

They swooped lower over the waves.

466

CHAPTER FORTY-ONE

ALEXIA WOKE UP TO FIND HER legs submerged in water. She felt a moment's blind panic—*where am I?* Then the pain in her ankle reasserted itself, shooting through her like a lightning bolt, and it all came back.

Lucy.

The cove.

The gun.

"I want you to cast your mind back to that day."

Lucy's voice came from behind her. She must still be under the lee of the cliff. Alexia had been dragged forward into the surf and positioned on her knees, like a prisoner about to be executed.

"It was a hot summer in Maine. You were there on the beach—you, Billy, and the children. It was right after lunch."

Horror stole slowly into Alexia's heart as it dawned on her what was happening.

She's re-creating her brother's death.

She's not going to shoot me.

She's going to drown me.

She tried to move, to roll over, anything, but she was

stuck fast. Lucy had clipped some sort of weights to her handcuffs, anchoring her to the spot.

"Think about the children now," Lucy was saying. "Try to picture their faces. Can you see my brother? Can you remember him?"

Remember him? His face has haunted me all my life. Every day. Every night. I tried to kid myself that I'd moved on, that I'd outrun my past. But Nicholas was always there. Always.

"What's he doing?"

"He's playing." Tears rolled down Alexia's cheeks.

"Playing what?"

"I don't know."

"TELL ME!"

"Tag, I think. I'm not sure. He was running around on the sand. He was happy."

"Good! Very good," Lucy encouraged. "Go on. What happened then?"

"I don't know," Alexia sobbed. The water was rising. It was up to her waist now and as cold as the grave.

"Of course you know! Don't lie to me. I'll shoot off your fucking fingers one by one, just like I did with Jenny Hamlin. What happened?"

Alexia closed her eyes. "I lost sight of him. Billy was playing the fool, diving for pearls. He went under and he didn't come up again and I thought—"

"I don't care about Billy Hamlin!" Lucy screamed. "Tell me about Nicko. What happened to my brother?"

"I don't know what happened!" Alexia shouted back. "He was in the water, in the shallows, playing. He was with the others. When I looked back he was gone."

"NO! That's not good enough. You must have seen something."

"Jesus, Lucy, if I'd seen, don't you think I'd have done something? Don't you think I'd have tried to save him?"

Alexia was frightened by the desperation in her own voice. She wasn't afraid of death. But drowning had always been her worst nightmare. To sit helplessly as the water rose around her, sucking her in, to gasp for breath as it filled her lungs, choking her, slowly starving her brain of oxygen . . . She'd lived the terror so many times in her dreams, Alexia thought she had understood Nicholas Handemeyer's suffering. That she'd atoned for it somehow. But she realized now she knew nothing. The reality, here in the waves, pinned down like a trapped animal, was far, far worse than even her most fevered imaginings.

"You? Try to save him?" Lucy laughed. "All you cared about was yourself. You didn't have an unselfish bone in your body. Not then, when you were plain old Toni Gilletti. And not now, as Mrs. High-and-Mighty De Vere. You, you and Hamlin, you let Nicko die!"

The water was almost at Alexia's shoulders now.

"That isn't true. You weren't there, Lucy. You don't know what happened. I loved your brother. He was a lovely little boy."

Lucy let out a howl, more animal than human. She put her hands over her ears. "Don't you dare! Don't you dare say you loved him."

"It's the truth!" Alexia spluttered. "He was always my favorite. He used to make me little cards."

Before she could say any more, Lucy ran at her with a roar of purest rage. Grabbing her from behind, she forced Alexia's head down under the waves.

After a moment's sharp terror, Alexia stopped struggling. This was it. This was the end.

Beneath the surface, all was dark and silent and peaceful.

469

There was no Lucy here, no shouting, no madness, no pain. Alexia's earlier calm returned. She allowed herself to go limp, each of her muscles submitting to the cold embrace of death.

There's nothing to fear.

Everything slowed down. She was aware of nothing but the faint drumbeat of her own pulse. One by one, the people she loved came to her.

Michael, healthy again, smiling and laughing, bursting with life and youth and promise.

Roxie, walking toward her, her arms open with love and forgiveness.

Teddy, as he was when they met. Funny, kind, self-deprecating, adoring.

Billy Hamlin, young and strong and smiling on a Maine beach.

Alexia started to pray. *Let Michael be at peace. Let Roxie forgive her father.* But for herself she had nothing to ask.

How arrogant she'd been to think she had any control. To think she could escape her fate.

Lucy was right about one thing: Nicholas Handemeyer's death *did* deserve a sacrifice. But that sacrifice had to be Alexia's. All her life the ocean had called to her, pulling her back, demanding she return and pay what she owed: a life for a life, a soul for a soul. Now, at last, the circle was closing.

It was time.

"WHAT'S THAT?"

The pilot pointed through the glass.

Arnie Meyer and the surveillance officer both followed his finger.

"What?" said Arnie. "I don't see anything."

"Under the rock face," said the pilot. "We've passed it now. I'll circle back. I thought I saw . . ."

"Figures." The surveillance officer lowered his telescopic binoculars. "Definitely, at the water's edge. It has to be them."

"I don't see anything," said Arnie desperately as the chopper banked sharply to the right, swooping low over the ocean like a bird scanning for fish. "Where? Was Summer with them? What did you see?"

The surveillance officer ignored him. "Coast guard!" He barked coordinates into his radio. "We need urgent assistance. Two females. Uh-huh. No, we can't go in from here."

"What do you mean you can't go in from here?" Arnie Meyer felt the panic creep through his veins like snake venom. "The tide's coming in. They'll drown!"

The surveillance officer looked him straight in the eye. "We can't go any closer without hitting the cliff."

"But we have to do something!"

"We'll crash, Mr. Meyer. We cannot reach them. I'm sorry."

I'M SORRY.

Alexia De Vere was still praying.

Please forgive me. For Nicholas. For Billy. For all the suffering I've caused.

Lucy Meyer had released her a few minutes ago, scrambling up onto a small ledge on the cliff face so she could watch her die more slowly. As Alexia gasped for air, wincing with pain as the oxygen surged back into her lungs, it occurred to her for the first time that Lucy was also going to die. The waves would claim her too, just minutes after Alexia's own life had ebbed away.

471

She must have known that when she brought me here. She doesn't care about dying any more than I do. She wants it. The peace. Just as long as she sees me punished first. All she wants is closure. We're so alike, in the end, Lucy and I.

A noise distracted her. At first she thought she was imagining the low, droning sound, like the buzz of a bee. But then it got louder and louder, overpowering even the cymbal-like crashing of the waves. Alexia tipped her head back and looked up.

A helicopter! Rescue!

She hadn't felt afraid before. When she thought death was inevitable, she'd been able to accept it, to make her peace. But now that there was a chance of life, of salvation, adrenaline and desperation coursed through Alexia's body once more.

I want to live!

Only her face was above the waterline now. Instinctively she tried to wave her arms for help, but they were cuffed and weighted beneath the waves. She began to cry.

"I'm here!" she shouted futilely at the sky. "I'm here! Please, help me!"

The helicopter hovered directly above for a few seconds, so close and yet so tantalizingly out of reach. Alexia strained her eyes against the brightness, searching for a ladder or a rope. Instead, without warning, the chopper turned and sped off into the blue.

"NO!" Alexia screamed. There was no mistaking her terror now. "No, please! Don't leave me!"

From her ledge-top vantage point, Lucy Meyer smiled.

This is for you, Nicko, my darling.

Soon they would be together again.

*

Summer dug her fingernails into the crumbling rock as she descended the path.

They're here. They have to be here.

The way down to the cove was steeper than she remembered it, and the tides were so high she couldn't see any beach at all from the top of the cliff. But the water bottle had confirmed it. This deep into the moor, there was only one place her mother could be going.

Then suddenly, like two figures in a dream, there they were. Rounding the bend where the path doubled back on itself, Summer saw her mother, crouching on a ledge above a sliver of sandy shore. She wouldn't have seen Alexia at all had she not followed Lucy's gaze to a point about twenty feet in front of her. Out in the water, a lone human head bobbed like a buoy.

"Mom!"

Lucy spun around. "Get out of here!" she screamed at Summer. *How on earth did she find us so quickly?* "Get back up the cliff. It's too dangerous."

"Not without you."

"I said go back!" Lucy raised her gun.

Summer's eyes widened with shock. *She wouldn't shoot, would she? Not her own daughter.*

"Go back!" Lucy shouted again.

Summer hesitated. As she did so, the sandy rock crumbled beneath her.

Arnie Meyer was the first out of the helicopter.

Ripping off his headphones, ignoring the shouts of the two policemen, he ran out onto the moor, half stooping, perilously close to the still-whirring propeller blades.

"Stop, you idiot!" the surveillance officer yelled after

him. But Arnie kept running, blindly, toward the edge of the cliff.

He heard a woman's scream, then another.

Dear God! Don't let me be too late.

Lucy watched, horrified, as her daughter fell, screaming, her arms and legs flailing wildly like a puppet with its strings cut. Summer landed on an open ledge about halfway down the cliff face. Her head hit the ground with a sickening thud. The screams stopped.

Lucy looked out to sea. Alexia was almost completely submerged now. She turned back to her daughter, lying prone and lifeless on the ledge.

This isn't right! It's not supposed to happen like this.

She wanted to watch Nicko's killer drown. She'd waited so long for this moment. All her life. But what if Summer were still alive? What if her baby needed help, desperately, and she stood by and did nothing? Irrationally, Lucy felt a rush of anger. *Why did Summer have to come here? Why did she have to ruin it all?*

"Police!"

Lucy looked up. Three men were at the top of the path. One had his gun drawn and trained on her. A second was scrambling along the ledge toward Summer. Lucy looked closer. *Oh my God, is that Arnie?*

"Drop your weapon and put your hands above your head."

Lucy ignored these instructions, turning her attention instead to the third man. Rappelling down the cliff face, a life ring tied to his waist, he was clearly headed toward Alexia.

"Ma'am. I said drop your weapon!"

Lucy closed her eyes and tightened her grip on her gun. It was so hard to concentrate.

The man at the top of the cliff was still shouting. "Drop it now or I'll shoot!"

Why won't he be quiet? I can't think with all this noise.

To her left, Lucy saw that Summer was sitting up. Arnie had managed to reach her. He was holding her now, talking to her.

That's good. They have each other.

Below her, the rappelling cop had reached the ground and was unclipping himself from his safety rope. Lucy watched him dive into the water. Only the top of Alexia's head was visible now, but it could take so long to drown. She was probably still alive. If he got her to the beach and resuscitated her fast enough . . .

It was then that Lucy knew what she had to do.

Taking careful aim, she fired a single shot directly at Alexia's skull.

Arnie Meyer screamed.

"Lucy. No!"

Too late. It's done.

Turning to face Arnie, Lucy blew him and their daughter a kiss. Then, before the cop at the top of the cliff had time to react, she slipped the barrel of the gun into her own mouth and pulled the trigger.

Down on the shore, the softly lapping waves kept up their peaceful, timeless rhythm.

Only now they were red with blood.

CHAPTER FORTY-TWO

ENGLAND. ONE YEAR LATER.

Roxie De Vere gazed out of the train window in a reflective mood.

It was a beautiful line, the slow train into London from West Sussex, taking its passengers through woods blanketed with bluebells, past pretty flint cottages and impressive stone manors, across rivers and deep into valleys lined with lush green pastureland, some of the richest and most fertile in England. Signs of spring were everywhere, in the blossoming apple and cherry trees, in the plaintive bleating of the newborn lambs searching out their mothers, in the crisp, cool breezes gusting in across the Channel from France.

Roxie De Vere thought, *It's the kind of day that makes one feel lucky to be alive.* And Roxie *did* feel lucky, albeit a luck that was tinged with sadness, and with regret for all that was lost. She only had one parent now. One person left living in this world with whom she could share her childhood memories. Reminisce over happier days. Cry over the sad ones.

Shared happiness, shared pain, shared regret. It wasn't the easiest of foundations on which to rebuild a relationship. But it was all that Roxie De Vere had. That and a couple of days a month of visiting time. Contrary to popular belief, Her Majesty's prisons were no bed of roses. Life there wasn't all open-ended visiting hours and strolls through the grounds. A stark room, smelling of disinfectant and despair, full of tables with inmates on one side and visitors on the other. That was to be the setting for all their meetings from now until . . .

No. I mustn't think about that.

Roxie forced herself not to think about the future.

If the past few years had taught her one thing, it was that anything could happen. *Live for today. Love for today. Forgive for today.*

She repeated the mantra softly to herself as the train rattled on.

THE WORST THING ABOUT PRISON LIFE was the boredom. The monotony of each day, broken only by bells and meals, and divided into chunks of time—work, leisure, exercise, sleep—that seemed to bear no relation to reality, to the rhythms of the world outside.

The only way to make it bearable was to detach from your former life completely. To forget who you had been on the outside, and accept this new world fully and without question.

Inmate 5067 had become adept at such detachment. Of course, having a famous name made things harder. Other prisoners were less willing to put aside the past, to forget who Inmate 5067 really was—who the prisoner had been. They remembered why Inmate 5067 was here, despite the aristocratic name and political connections, rubbing shoulders with drug dealers and killers and stooping to manual labor just like the rest of them.

There was no violence. No intimidation. At least, there hadn't been yet. But Inmate 5067 would never be accepted into mainstream prison society. Life was lonely. Then again, that was part of the punishment, wasn't it? *Part of what I deserve.* Roxie's visits were a lifeline in some ways, but they were also painful, a sharp reminder of all that prison had taken away.

Waiting in the visitors' room as the prisoners' families and friends filed in, Inmate 5067 felt breathless with anticipation. *What if she hadn't made it? What if something happened and she changed her mind?* But no, there she was! Roxie, smiling as she maneuvered her wheelchair through the tables, the proverbial ray of sunshine.

My daughter. My darling daughter. God bless her for finding it in her heart to forgive.

Roxie opened her arms, full of love.

"Hello, Mother." She was beaming. "It's so good to see you."

CHAPTER FORTY-THREE

WHEN THE FULL STORY OF ALEXIA De Vere's past life and secrets emerged in the British press, it caused the biggest political scandal since the Profumo Affair back in the 1960s. Politics didn't get dirtier, or more salacious than this. Shoot-outs on an American beach, murder, perjury, a secret identity and a string of corpses as long as your arm. The whole affair was a Fleet Street editor's wet dream.

Of course, for those actually involved, the reality was both more tragic and more prosaic. Alexia De Vere herself felt lucky. Lucky to be alive—Lucy Meyer's shot on the beach had merely scratched her shoulder, and the police rescue team had pulled her out of the water and given her mouth-to-mouth before any permanent brain or other damage was done. Minutes later, *seconds* later, and it could all have been over. Alexia tried not to think about that.

She was lucky in other ways too. Lucky to have had a chance to reconcile fully with Roxie, and with her darling Teddy before he died. (Teddy De Vere suffered a massive heart attack in his prison cell, the same week as Alexia's extradition hearing in America.) She even felt lucky to be here, in a British jail rather than an American one, atoning at last for the sins of her past. Maybe now, finally, her dues to the gods would be paid. When she finally walked out of Holloway Women's Prison, she would be a free woman, in more ways than one.

That terrifying day on the beach at Martha's Vineyard had changed everything for Alexia. Whether it was God who saved her, or fate, or blind luck didn't matter. What mattered was that she *had* been saved. She was convinced that she was alive for a reason. And the reason, at last, was clear.

She had to tell the truth. To bear witness.

There could be no more secrets.

From her hospital bed in Boston, Alexia told the police everything. She admitted being negligent in Nicholas Handemeyer's death, from all those years ago, and allowing Billy Hamlin to go to jail in her stead. Double-jeopardy rules meant it was too late for her to be tried for involuntary manslaughter. In the end she was given a six-year sentence for perjury and perverting the course of justice.

She also told the authorities that Teddy had been responsible for Billy Hamlin's murder. She'd kept his secret thus far, but the whole truth had to come out now. Teddy was serving a life sentence anyway, and Alexia owed poor Billy that much at least.

Teddy had been good about it, writing Alexia a typically kind and amusing letter from his own jail cell. *The worst part about it is that I shall have to go back to court and face all those ghastly reporters again. I'd happily sign up for a year in solitary if it meant never setting eyes on another white-sock-wearing pleb from the* Sun *ever again.*

He still had no remorse about what he'd done. It was as if there were a gene missing. He seemed incapable of guilt. But by the same token, he shared none of Lucy Meyer's hatred for his victims, none of Lucy's blind, psychotic thirst for violence and for vengeance. In Teddy's mind, he had merely done his duty—protected his family. The fact that two innocent men lost their lives as a result was dismissed as collateral damage, an unfortunate side effect that couldn't be helped. Teddy died in his sleep a week before he was due in court for Billy Hamlin's murder. Perhaps it was more than he deserved, after all he'd done. But Alexia took comfort in the fact that he had died peacefully. She loved him to the last.

As for herself, she'd already applied for permission to serve her sentence in England. Thanks to her full and frank confession, the fact that she had two "disabled" children in the UK, and her political and personal links with the country, the U.S. courts agreed. Alexia had arrived at Holloway three months ago and had seen Roxie on three occasions since.

"Has anyone else been to see you since I last visited?" Roxie asked.

"No, my darling. But you mustn't worry. There's no one else I want to see."

Roxie found this hard to believe. She thought back to her childhood and how social her mother had been. Both her parents, in fact. Politics was a social profession if ever there was one. It had been Alexia's drug for well over half her life.

"Really? No one from the old days? What about Henry Whitman?"

"Henry?" Alexia laughed loudly. "You must be joking. Do you know, the entire time I was in the Home Office, he thought I was about to expose him for having an affair? Can you believe it? He only appointed me because he thought it would keep me quiet. Keep your friends close and your enemies closer."

"Why would he think that?"

Alexia shrugged. "Rumors. Westminster gossip. Who

481

knows? I certainly never had the slightest intention of shopping him."

"So he never made contact, not even after Daddy died?"

"I never expected him to, darling. Word is he's angling to become the next UN secretary-general. With friends like me he won't need enemies."

Her mother seemed sanguine about it, but Roxie was aggrieved on her behalf. "Surely there must be someone from Westminster who keeps in touch? All those years . . ."

"I did get a sweet letter from Sir Edward Manning," Alexia said wistfully.

"What did he say?"

"Oh, this and that. Political gossip mostly. He offered to visit, but it wouldn't have felt right. He did send me a copy of Jeffrey Archer's prison diaries, though. Have you read them? They're terrific."

"I haven't."

An awkward silence fell across the table. Both women longed to reconnect with each other. But after so many years of estrangement, conversation didn't flow easily. They had so little in common. Roxie was artistic and creative, Alexia pragmatic and ambitious. The one thing they shared was their family bond. But after everything that had happened, family was the one topic they both struggled to avoid.

"How's Summer?" Alexia asked eventually. "Do you two see much of each other these days?"

Roxie brightened. "We do. We try to. She still visits Michael every day, you know."

Both women marveled at Summer Meyer's loyalty. Lucy's affair with Michael was public knowledge now. The letter that Lucy had written to Summer, before she and Alexia set out to the beach that fateful day, was made public at her trial. Lucy Meyer had been posthumously convicted of the killings of Milo Bates and Jennifer Hamlin, as well as the attempted murder of Michael De Vere. She was buried in the family plot in Martha's Vineyard, where Arnie apparently visited her daily. Still in love, still grieving, still unable to process the revelations that had surrounded his wife's death. *Poor man.*

Lucy's letter made it clear that she had always intended to kill herself once she'd "disposed" of Alexia. Like Alexia, Lucy had wanted justice, closure, and for the truth to be known. The only difference was that Lucy Meyer's view of justice, of right and wrong, had been so skewed and poisoned by decades of hatred that it bore no relation to Alexia's, or to any thinking person's. There was no hint of apology in her note to her daughter, not for what she'd done to Michael or for anything else.

Summer and Arnie had both witnessed Lucy's gruesome death. The police told Alexia afterward that Summer had been just feet away when Lucy blew her brains out. You never got over something like that. Arnie coped by denial, but Summer was too rational for such a strategy. Instead she'd fled to England and to Michael, burying her feelings as best she could. It was a wonder she wasn't a total basket case.

"Give her my love when you see her," said Alexia.

"I will."

"And your brother, of course."

"Of course," Roxie mumbled guiltily. The truth was, Roxie no longer visited Michael. There was no point. His body might be there in the bed, but *he* was gone. But it would only upset her mother to tell her that. Better to focus on the future, on happy things.

"By the way, it's not a big deal or anything. But I'm seeing someone." She blushed endearingly.

Alexia's face lit up.

"That's wonderful, darling! Who?"

"His name's William. William Carruthers."

Alexia dimly recognized the name.

"He's an estate agent," Roxie went on. "Actually, he's the chap who sold Kingsmere for us after Daddy died."

Alexia frowned. She was about to say, *So he knows exactly how much money you're worth and he's moved in for the main chance.* But with an effort she bit her tongue. It wasn't her place to try to manage Roxie's life, romantic or otherwise. At some point she had to trust her daughter's judgment. After all, how much worse could it be than her own?

"It's early days," said Roxie. "But I'm very happy."

"Then so am I." Alexia squeezed her hand. "I'd like to meet him sometime."

"Sometime." Roxie blushed again. "Let's see how it goes."

The two women talked for a few more minutes. Then the inevitable buzzer sounded to indicate that visiting time was over. Around the room, prisoners embraced family and friends. Some stoically, others in a flood of emotion, particularly the mothers with young children. Alexia felt for them. Those precious childhood years, once gone, could never be recaptured. *Roxie and Michael had happy childhoods, I think. Teddy and I gave them that much at least.*

She watched her daughter push her wheelchair through the double doors and out of sight, and she tried to feel hopeful for her future. Would this William Carruthers really love her, and care for her? Or would he break her heart, like all the prior men in Roxie's life? Just the thought made Alexia feel sick with anxiety as she walked back to her cell.

You can't protect her, she told herself firmly. *And you shouldn't try. To love is to take a risk. And life without love is no life at all.*

The future belonged to Roxie now.

What she made of it would be up to her.

EPILOGUE

S UMMER MEYER STARED OUT OF THE window in Michael's hospital room, lost in thought.

It was a stunning day. Outside, the modest London garden burst with life like a miniature Eden. The scent of cut grass and sweet honeysuckle hung in the air like a summer mist, and the long, trailing branches of a willow tree tapped gently against the glass of Michael's window, as if inviting him outside to enjoy it all.

Or perhaps it's me the tree's beckoning? thought Summer. *Perhaps I'm the one who needs to be rescued?*

Her father certainly thought so. Arnie called Summer daily, begging her to come home, to "move on with life" and not "chain herself" to Michael and to the past. *Darling Dad.* Summer loved him so much it was painful. But Arnie couldn't see that staying on the Vineyard and spending hours by Lucy's grave every day was chaining *himself* to the past and in the worst, most painful way imaginable.

The truth was Summer had no idea what the future held for her. Right now it was all she could do to survive the present, to breathe in and out. But she did know she would

485

never set foot on Martha's Vineyard again. Never, ever, for as long as she lived.

She still dreamed about Lucy's death almost nightly. The cove, the crack of the gunshot, the red water staining the sand like cranberry juice spilled in sugar. Phrases from the letter too came back to haunt her, in Lucy's distinctive, gentle, maternal voice.

He had to die, darling. It was the only way.

The affair was simply a means of getting close to him.

I do so hope you understand. . .

Understand? Summer thought.

She looked at Michael, then out of the window again. What her mother had done was beyond understanding. Beyond forgiveness. The best Summer could do was accept that Lucy had been mentally ill. That something had snapped in her at an early age, with her beloved brother's death. And that the break, instead of being treated and healed, had been hidden from view, left to get deeper and more fractured until Lucy's entire personality had split in two.

One side was the mother and wife that Summer had known and loved all her life. That was the side she grieved for. The other side . . . she tried not to think about the other side.

Picking up Michael's limp fingers, Summer stroked them tenderly, as she had so many thousands of times before. She couldn't go back to her old life in America. But she couldn't go on like this either.

I'm hiding. Hiding from life, from the future. And I'm using Michael as an excuse. I'm being a coward.

And then she felt it. The tiniest twitch, so small that at first she thought she was imagining it.

"Michael?"

A few seconds of nothing. Then there it was again, harder the second time. A finger, a single finger, moving against her palm.

"Nurse!" Summer's screams could be heard all the way down the corridor. "Nurse!"

Tomorrow was once again another day.

ACKNOWLEDGMENTS

M Y THANKS ARE DUE TO THE Sheldon family, especially Alexandra and Mary, for their ongoing trust in me and their support and encouragement. Also thanks to my editors, May Chen in New York and Sarah Ritherdon and Kimberley Young in London, and to all at HarperCollins who have worked so hard on this book. To Luke and Mort Janklow, my incredible and tireless agents. And to my family, especially my husband, Robin, who provided a lot of inspiration and advice as I grappled with this story.

The Tides of Memory is dedicated to my sister-in-law, Heather Hartz, a strong woman and great mother who has turned her life around and amazed us all. I hope you like the book, Heath.

Read more Sydney Sheldon novels
y the internationally bestselling author
Tilly Bagshawe

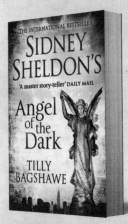

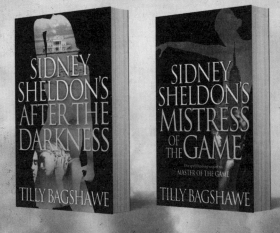

Discover where it all began –
the original novels by

SIDNEY SHELDON

the master of the unexpected…